T0277429

OTHER BOOKS AND AUDIOBOOKS
BY TIFFANY ODEKIRK

CONTEMPORARY

Love On Pointe

Love Unscripted

Love Sidelined

HISTORICAL

Summerhaven

COLLECTOR'S EDITION

SUMMERHAVEN

INCLUDES

THE *Making* OF AN *Earl*
A SUMMERHAVEN NOVELLA

TIFFANY ODEKIRK

A REGENCY ROMANCE

SUMMERHAVEN

TIFFANY ODEKIRK

PROPER ROMANCE

SHADOW
MOUNTAIN
PUBLISHING

For Kevin,
Thank you for encouraging me to follow my dreams.
I love you.

First published in paperbound 2022 by Covenant Communications, Inc.
First published in hardbound collector's edition 2024 by Shadow Mountain Publishing

This is a work of fiction. Characters and events in this book are products of the author's imagination or are represented fictitiously.

Visit us at shadowmountain.com

Library of Congress Cataloging-in-Publication Data
Names: Odekirk, Tiffany, 1985– author.
Title: Summerhaven : a Regency romance / Tiffany Odekirk.
Description: Hardback collector's edition. | [Salt Lake City] : Shadow Mountain, 2024. | "First published in paperbound 2022 by Covenant Communications, Inc."—Title page verso. | Summary: "Hannah Kent and Oliver Jennings promised their childhood hearts to each other. Years later, Hannah receives an invitation to Oliver's family estate. But upon arriving at Summerhaven, her expectations shatter. Oliver appears indifferent until his nuisance brother, Damon, unveils a surprising proposal. As pretense blurs between Hannah and Damon, Hannah faces a challenging journey to discern between love and illusion"—Provided by publisher.
Identifiers: LCCN 2024017831 (print) | LCCN 2024017832 (ebook) | ISBN 9781639933655 (hardback) | ISBN 9781649333360 (ebook)
Subjects: LCSH: Friendship in children—Fiction. | Man-woman relationships—Fiction. | Brothers—Fiction. | Great Britain, setting. | BISAC: FICTION / Romance / Historical / Regency | FICTION / Romance / Clean & Wholesome | LCGFT: Historical fiction. | Romance fiction.
Classification: LCC PS3615.D435 S86 2024 (print) | LCC PS3615.D435 (ebook) | DDC 813/.6—dc23/eng/20240531
LC record available at https://lccn.loc.gov/2024017831
LC ebook record available at https://lccn.loc.gov/2024017832

Printed in China
RR Donnelley, Dongguan, China

10 9 8 7 6 5 4 3 2 1

CHAPTER ONE

London, July 1817

THE FIRST NOTES OF MAMA'S melody flowed from my fingers and filled the parlor of our London townhome. Although I did not play the square pianoforte with as much passion or pleasure as Mama had, the memory of her song wrapping around me like a warm blanket on a cool night would forever pull me back to the bench.

I nearly reached the crescendo when a *tap, tap, tap* sounded at the door, and I hit a wrong note. *Drat!* I'd been so close this time to playing the song without making any errors.

Papa stirred in his armchair, and his newspaper fell to the uneven wood-plank floor.

Knowing Mrs. Potter would answer the door, I quickly returned my hands to the keys, hoping to lull Papa back to sleep. But only a few lines in—and with just as many mistakes—I could do nothing but sigh. If only I'd put forth greater effort to practice while she'd been alive, I might now have her music to comfort me.

Another knock came at the door, the staccato sound more urgent than the first, and Papa snorted awake.

Where was Mrs. Potter? I would have answered the door myself, but the last time I'd done so, she had given me such a displeased look that I did not dare do it again. It was probably just an impatient messenger anyway—we rarely had callers anymore.

I rose and replaced the bench, then retrieved Papa's newspaper from the floor.

"What would I do without you, Hannah?" he said.

"I daresay not read the newspaper." I kissed the top of his head and handed it to him, minus one sheet, which I reserved for myself, of course.

I sat on the sofa situated under the window and parted the curtains. As I'd supposed, a postboy stood on the top step.

Finally, Mrs. Potter emerged from the kitchen downstairs. Wiping her flour-dusted hands on her apron, she muttered the entire length of the corridor. She was perhaps not the most amiable of servants, but she and her daughter, Nora—our maid of all work—were the only help we had, and I was grateful for their service.

The front door creaked open, and a gust of wind carried a pungent odor into the parlor: horse dung and raw sewage—parting gifts from the *ton* as they vacated the city for their family seats in the country.

Though the view was nothing special, only a long row of terrace homes lining the cobbled stone street, the light was perfect for reading. I smoothed the broadsheet in my lap and skimmed an article about how the last year and a half of unprecedented rainfall was causing crops to fail all over England.

"A letter, Miss Hannah."

I looked up from the newspaper and found Mrs. Potter holding out a tray. On it, a single missive. "For me?"

"You are Miss Hannah, are you not?"

I pressed my lips together to hide my amusement. Mrs. Potter had grown increasingly irritable these past several months. In truth, we all had; despite it being summer, the weather was so dreary. I set aside the newspaper and retrieved the letter from the proffered tray. "Thank you."

With a huff, she shuffled back to the kitchen.

"Is it from Henry?" Papa asked hopefully.

"Hmm." I examined the letter; on the front, only my name was written, and on the reverse was an intricate red wax seal. Though the stationery was certainly fine enough to suit my brother's elegant wife, Georgiana, she and Henry had left London only two days earlier at the close of the Season. "Sorry, Papa. I don't believe they would have had opportunity to write us yet."

"No, of course not." Papa smiled, but there was a heaviness to his brow that hinted of sadness. Papa had asked Henry to extend their stay by at least another week, but Georgiana had insisted they return home to Bath. I couldn't blame her for wanting to leave—even without the unseasonably cool weather, London was still a dreadful, odiferous city this time of year.

I rubbed the smooth paper between my fingers. Although I was anxious to open the letter and discover its sender and contents, Papa needed a diversion to lift his spirits even more—and he loved guessing games. "Would you like to guess again?"

Papa lowered his newspaper. "Perhaps it is from one of your friends from Bath?"

"Perhaps," I agreed, though I knew it was not. We'd only lived in Bath for a few years in an effort to improve Mama's health, and the young ladies I'd become acquainted with there had long since ceased writing. Although I'd considered them some of my close friends at the time, it only took so many unanswered letters after we'd parted before I'd realized they didn't feel the same camaraderie for me.

"Might it be from your former governess then?"

"Possibly," I said, though it was unlikely to be her or anyone else. I had been so focused on Mama these past years that I'd become rather unsociable. I didn't regret how I'd spent my time, but I could think of no one who would write to me—especially not someone who had use of such exquisite paper.

Well, there was *one* person, but I scarcely dared to let myself hope.

I studied the crest pressed into the red wax seal more carefully. It was the image of a checkered shield lying in a bed of ivy. And around the circumference it read: *Conservabo ad Mortem*. Though I couldn't translate the words—Latin was not among the subjects of my education—they *were* familiar. I'd read them every summer of my childhood as I'd entered the doors of Summerhaven.

My heart leapt.

Could it really be him? After all these years of waiting, had the time finally arrived for us to reunite? A nervous sort of excitement filled my chest and warmed my cheeks. I could no longer resist the temptation and slid my finger under the seal and unfolded the paper. My gaze darted to the bottom of the page. It was signed, *Lady Elizabeth Winfield.*

Though the letter had not been penned by Oliver Jennings as I'd hoped, but rather his mother, there was not a doubt in my mind the correspondence had been made at his behest.

> *My dearest Hannah,*
>
> *It has been far too long since I have written to you. Please forgive my neglect and know you have been ever present in my mind. I have missed you and your mother these past several years. How I yearn for summers long past. Which brings me to the purpose of this letter. It is my deepest desire that you will accept my invitation to visit Summerhaven. I should like for you to stay through summer, if it be agreeable to you and your father.*
>
> *With Love,*
> *Lady Elizabeth Winfield*

My heart soared! To leave London. To see Ollie again. To ride the hills on horseback where Mama and I had once ridden. I could think of nothing in this world I wanted more.

"The color in your cheeks makes me think I must challenge someone to a duel." Papa chuckled.

I protectively pressed the letter to my chest. "You will challenge him to no such thing."

"Aha!" Papa said. "Your missive *is* from a gentleman. You are discovered, my dear."

"Actually, the letter is not from a gentleman, but rather a gentleman's *mother.*"

"Whose name is . . . ?"

I bit my lower lip. Revealing the name of the sender—Mama's dearest friend—would cause Papa undue pain. Though our official mourning period had long since passed, reminders that she was gone still hurt him. I searched my mind for a way to avoid answering, some means of sparing his feelings, but there was nothing for it.

"Elizabeth Winfield," I said quietly.

Papa's gaze drifted to Mama's vacant bench at the pianoforte. "What has she written?"

"She has invited me to visit Summerhaven until the autumn."

"Nearly six weeks," Papa said softly. "Such a long time."

My elation sank like a skipped rock slipping beneath a river's surface. I could not go. With Mama's passing and Henry's marriage, I was all Papa had left. No matter how much I disliked London or longed to be with Ollie, I could not abandon Papa. Not now.

"It was a kind invitation." I folded the missive and set it aside. "But I think I will refuse."

Papa's bushy brow rose over the rim of his round spectacles. "Why would you do a thing like that?"

"As you said, six weeks is a long time."

Papa's gaze turned thoughtful. "Do you not want to go? Does the place hold too many sour memories?"

I reflexively touched the front of my hair, thinking of Ollie's highbrow older brother Damon. As the oldest son of an earl, he'd seemed to delight in playing cruel pranks on me as a girl. Still, my happy memories at Summerhaven outweighed the *un*happy ones.

"No," I said. "It is not that. Summerhaven is just so far. And with Henry gone . . ."

"You do not want to leave me alone," Papa surmised, his mouth turning downward.

"Perhaps next summer when we have had a little more time to adjust." To being back in London, to Henry being married, to living life without Mama.

"My dear girl. You will never know how grateful I have been for your care of me, but I have been a poor companion."

"Nonsense. You are the best part of my day."

"And you are mine. But you must ache for a friend, for female companionship."

I ached for Mama. "I could not hope for better companions to share my evenings with than you, Sir Walter Scott, and Lord Byron."

"Yes, well. So long as Lord Byron is confined to the pages of a book, I have no objections."

Even if Lord Byron had not been exiled from London, the notorious beau was no threat to me. "I only enjoy his beautiful words, Papa."

"Very good. But you must admit," Papa continued, "that you would enjoy having another lady in the house during the morning hours when I'm attending to the needs of the church."

As a clergyman, Papa spent his mornings studying the gospels and preparing sermons. I joined him at the small chapel down the road where he preached when appropriate, but not often. Papa did not relish leaving me to myself, but it could not be helped.

I shook my head. "*The Morning Post* is a most diverting breakfast companion." I'd picked up the habit of reading the newspaper when Mama had taken to her sickbed. However unladylike the habit, I was loath to give it up now. Knowing what was happening in the world gave me some sense of my place within it.

Papa shifted in his seat. "And what of your afternoons?"

"My charity work with the poor occupies much of my time."

"You know I am proud of the service you have done for the church—you've helped so many—but you cannot spend all your days giving charity. Surely you wish for a friend to accompany you to places like the milliner or the modiste?"

"After the experience I had there with Georgiana this summer, I am not inclined to go anywhere with anyone—save my favorite authors Miss Radcliffe and Miss Edgeworth." Just as the newspaper helped me understand the world, books helped me understand myself.

"I fear I have raised something of a bluestocking in you." Papa sighed. "I do believe your mother would have my head for not establishing you more properly in Society."

Since Mama's passing two years earlier, trivial diversions like balls and operas and luncheons had become something of a chore. The one time I'd allowed Henry and Georgiana to drag me to a ball this Season, I'd danced only one set, and Georgiana had not hidden her displeasure. Little did that matter now though; those pastimes were meant for securing a husband, and I'd already met my match in Ollie. And a good thing too, as I did not have any other suitors. What a dreadful state it would be indeed to end up as spinster, entirely dependent on Father and one day on my brother.

But thankfully, I had Ollie.

He'd written to me regularly after my last visit to Summerhaven, and his letters—coming first from Summerhaven and then from Eton—had brought me comfort while Mama was sick. He'd become too involved with his studies to write me while he was studying at Cambridge, but I did not fault him. In fact, I was glad he'd taken his education so seriously. It showed his steadiness and strength of character.

And even though his letters had ceased, my faith in him had never wavered. We had only been twelve years old when we'd huddled together under the old oak tree and Ollie vowed to marry me, but from the moment he sealed his vow with a kiss upon my hand and then my cheek, I'd always known he'd one day return to keep his promise. It had been eight years since that summer, and I was twenty now, but our hearts were forever bound.

I could already envision our life together. We would marry on a midsummer's day in Papa's chapel, then we would travel north to Winterset Grange—the small estate Ollie would inherit from his mother—and once there, we would establish our home. Ollie's allowance, which he would retain from his father's estate, would provide us a blessed life, and we would use those blessings to care for our tenants. And in time, we would have children, then, God willing, grandchildren. Our life together would be simple and happy.

But as much as I wanted that life to begin right away, I couldn't bring myself to leave Papa alone.

"If you truly desire to stay home," Papa said, interrupting my thoughts, "then I will respect your decision. But I wonder, how you will explain your refusal to visit to Mr. Oliver Jennings?"

I sucked in a surprised breath and heat crept up my neck.

"You didn't think I knew about your attachment to him, did you?"

I shook my head.

Papa relaxed further into his armchair. "I remember one particular summer you and Mama arrived home from the country one full day later than I had expected. I'd been so worried that when you walked through our front door, I cried with relief. Your mama could not stop smiling though. She explained that when she told you it was time to return home—"

"I convinced Ollie to hide in the garden with me so I would not have to leave." I remembered the day well. Ollie and I had been chasing each other in the garden, dashing down the hedgerows and darting around flowerbeds. His blond curls had bounced and shone in the sunlight. I could almost hear his laughter now.

"She could scarcely stop talking about your little games with the young master. She told me about how she spent her last day there, sitting in the library window seat with Lady Winfield, watching you and Oliver play in the garden and planning your future nuptials."

"Truly?" I asked.

Papa nodded. "I believe seeing you happily settled with Oliver Jennings was her last wish."

My heart swelled like a rain cloud ready to burst. Perhaps this revelation shouldn't have surprised me; I'd taken little care to disguise my tender feelings for Ollie, so of course Mama had known of my affection, but I had no idea she'd wanted the same dreams for me as I did.

"After all we have lost, I thought I had done right in holding you close. But I see now that it was selfish of me to deprive you of so much." Papa removed his spectacles and laid them on the side table. "Mama would've wanted you to go to Summerhaven, Hannah."

I twisted the emerald mourning ring Papa had fashioned for me from Mama's wedding band around my finger. The thought of visiting the country without her was more painful than a summer without sun. But Papa was right; Mama knew best. She *would* have wanted me to go. To keep making memories. To be happy. And Ollie most decidedly made me happy.

With a deep breath, I nodded. "Then I will write to Lady Winfield and accept her invitation."

CHAPTER TWO

THE CARRIAGE LURCHED FORWARD AND, with it, my stomach. Oh no. Not again. I quickly parted the curtain and let down the side glass. Fresh country air rushed into the interior, and I breathed deeply. Nausea or no, I was relieved to be free of London's constant olfactory assaults.

"Almost there, miss." Nora patted my arm.

"Only a few miles more," Papa added reassuringly.

I forced a smile and returned my gaze outside. I was glad Papa had insisted on escorting me to the country. Though he would only stay a few short days before returning to London to attend to his parishioners, his presence was comforting.

Every year of my childhood, when Lord Winfield sat in parliament, Mama and I traveled to the country to spend our days at Summerhaven. But when Mama became sick and took to her sickbed, my visits to the country had ended. I was now relieved to not have to travel to Summerhaven alone.

I shifted in my seat, trying to get comfortable. Lady Winfield had insisted we use her private carriage, and I was grateful for her kindness; the conveyance was well-sprung and far nicer than any we could have hired. But after two tumultuous days of traveling, my stomach was in knots, and my body ached. I was more than ready for our journey to end.

But try as I might to wish away the miles, the carriage only continued clattering down the lane. I closed my eyes and tried to distract myself with happy memories of Ollie. Running through the garden hedgerows. Skipping rocks on the river. Him kissing my cheek and hand under the old oak tree. We had so many magical memories together, and I could not wait to make more.

I could hardly wait to see the man he'd become. Yes. All this bumping about would be worth it when at last I saw his smiling face.

But I hoped his hateful older brother would not be in residence.

Damon had been so cruel the last time I'd visited—placing frogs in my drinking glass, locking me in a traveling trunk, and worst of all, cutting my hair in the dead of night—that his father, Lord Winfield, had banished him to Eton. Damon was distraught at having to go away. Ollie tried to console him, but Damon was so angry that he punched Ollie's nose.

Although many years had passed since that summer, Ollie's letters made it obvious the brothers had not reconciled.

The horse's hooves suddenly beat a bright *clip clop, clip clop, clip clop* as they came into contact with the stone bridge—a sure sign that our journey was almost at an end.

And then in the distance, beyond a sloping green hill, was Summerhaven.

With twisted chimneys, ornamental parapets, and mullioned windows, the estate was even more beautiful than I'd remembered. Ivy grew in thick veins up the symmetrical stone wings, and white roses decorated the base of the central volume. Somehow, the grand house appeared even larger than when I was a child. Though Summerhaven was not my home and never would be—Damon was the eldest son and heir, not Ollie—it still felt as if I were coming home.

Gravel crunched beneath the wheels as we traveled down the aspen-lined drive. And when at last we came to the circular fountain, the carriage slowed, then swayed, and finally stopped in front of the stairs.

A long row of servants dressed in green livery stood stiffly as if ready to greet the prince regent himself. Though servants were not generally called upon to leave their work and greet guests—especially guests of our station—this formal demonstration of respect for Papa pleased me.

As a clergyman, Papa was in the business of making saints out of scoundrels, gentlemen out of men. And although he often dealt with the peerage, and he was even considered a gentleman himself, Papa often felt like a visitor to the group, not a member.

The butler parted the doors and stepped aside to allow Lord and Lady Winfield to exit, and together, they descended the stairs. Behind them, a man with broad shoulders, dark hair, and a handsome face emerged from the manor.

At first, I supposed him to be their solicitor or a steward because of the way he trailed behind them. But no. The cut of his coat was far too fine, his breeches too exquisitely tailored, and the polish of his Hessian boots—well, I'd never seen such a shine.

Yet it was his bearing, the confidence with which he held himself, that gave him away; only a man with an overdeveloped sense of his own worth could achieve that level of grace and poise and arrogance.

Damon.

His stormy blue eyes lifted to the carriage and caught my gaze. Instead of giving me a polite nod or a gentlemanly bow, he stood straight and still, mouth quirked in a devilish grin.

Purposefully ignoring him, I craned my neck to see around him and view the open, and noticeably *empty*, doorway.

Where was Ollie? We hadn't corresponded in some time—several months, sadly—but he had to be aware of my arrival today.

A footman opened the carriage door. The conveyance bounced as Papa alighted, the jolt renewing my nausea. I moaned.

"Are you all right, miss?" Nora asked.

"I will be now that the carriage has stopped." I smoothed my skirts, hoping the small effort would make me look better than I felt.

Papa handed me down from the carriage, and securing my hand in the crook of his arm, we walked toward the family.

"Welcome," Lord Winfield bellowed as we neared. His deep baritone had frightened me as a young girl. I'd often hid behind Mama when he entered a room, and I found the inclination had not changed.

"The pleasure is all ours." Papa bowed respectfully.

Lord Winfield gave a slight tip of his head to Papa. "I trust your journey was uneventful?" His words came out gravelly and rough, and he cleared his throat with a cough.

"Indeed," Papa said, and I was grateful he didn't mention how unwell I'd been.

The two men continued their conversation, something about the condition of the roads.

Lady Winfield moved forward to greet me. The skin around her eyes had softened into permanent lines—a testament to her good nature—and her hair now held more gray than blonde. I'd always liked Lady Winfield. Her warmth and elegance reminded me of my own mother.

"Hannah." Lady Winfield stood in front of me for a long moment, observing me.

I couldn't tell whether she approved of me or was appalled, but I must have looked a fright. I relaxed my shoulders and attempted a small smile, wanting to appear a lady in composure if not in truth, wanting to be a credit to Mama. "I'm afraid the journey was rather long, my lady."

Lady Winfield blinked. "Oh no, my dear. I was only amazed at what a beautiful young woman you've become. You look so much like your mother." Lady Winfield wrapped her arms around me in an embrace, and it was as if my own mother's arms were around me once more. Like Mama, Lady Winfield smelled of lavender and love. Too soon we parted, and once again, I felt the loss of Mama.

Damon stepped forward, and his watch key and seal—visible reminders of his status and self-importance—clanked together. He bowed. "Miss Kent."

"My lord," I returned with a shallow curtsy.

The corners of his mouth curled into a smile. "I see someone has managed to make a lady out of the wild girl I once knew," Damon said, and before stepping back in line with his mother, he met my eye and added, "A pity."

My eyebrows pulled together in surprise.

"Do try not to scowl, Miss Kent. It will crease your lovely brow."

"Damon Jennings," Lady Winfield scolded. "You have been taught better manners."

"My apologies, Mother. Teasing a beautiful woman is one of few things that has yet to be lectured out of me."

I gaped. Never in all my life had a man spoken so casually to me. Damon may have grown into a man, but he was *not* a gentleman.

Lady Winfield let out a weary breath. "I promise I did *try* to teach him proper decorum, Hannah."

"You must not blame yourself, Mother. I'm certain it was not the teacher, but rather the pupil, who is to blame."

"Quite right." Lady Winfield frowned at her son, and then turning to me, she said, "You have no idea how he tortured me as a boy."

"Oh, but I do." I raised my gaze to Damon, expecting to see a sheepish look on his face, but instead, he seemed . . . amused?

Odious man!

"Oh dear." Lady Winfield grimaced. "How could I have forgotten how mercilessly he teased you?"

Remorse filled me. I'd not even stepped foot inside the manor, and already I'd managed to insult Lady Winfield, her parenting, and her son. Mama would haunt my dreams tonight to give me a scolding.

"Forgive me, Lady Winfield. I'm rather out of countenance from the journey." I touched a hand to my middle, hoping to still my stomach. "Carriage rides do not agree with me."

"Oh, you poor thing. Let's get you settled into your room. Damon, please escort Hannah inside so I can speak to Cook about preparing a tray."

He gave his mother the barest of nods, and she quickly ascended to the top of the stairs where Papa and Lord Winfield waited. The three of them walked into the entry hall, leaving Damon and me alone.

"Allow me to escort you indoors." Damon offered me his arm.

I glanced at it. Although my head was spinning and my stomach still turning, it seemed to me that avoiding interaction with Damon was the wisest course. "No, thank you." I moved to step away from him toward the stairs.

Damon blocked my way. "No, thank you?" He raised an eyebrow.

"I am quite able to manage on my own, my lord."

He frowned. "Are you to *my lord* me all summer?"

"Are you going to *be here* all summer?" Surely, he had someplace more important to be. London, perhaps.

"You could at least attempt to hide your displeasure." He laughed lightly.

"I can call you by another name if that is your desire. Although I do believe you will find *my lord* to be the most agreeable."

His lips twitched. "It seems I have some work to do in repairing my reputation."

"Please don't waste your effort." I stepped around him and began ascending the stairs, but my legs were heavy and my muscles weak.

Damon swiftly caught up.

I sighed. If only Ollie were here. I looked down the drive, hoping to glimpse him, but the road was empty; the carriage had been removed, and the servants had scattered. Where was he? He would never have missed my arrival without a reason. "I rather thought Ollie would be here to greet Papa and me." I glanced at Damon, hoping he'd offer some explanation, but he said nothing. "Do you know where he is?" I tried again, forsaking subtlety for plainness.

"I am not my brother's keeper, Miss Kent."

Anger coursed through me. Damon knew full well where Ollie was, and he refused to tell me. My stomach roiled, and my chest and throat burned. I clenched my teeth. I needed to sit. Immediately. I pushed past Damon.

"But perhaps his absence is for the best," he called after me. "My brother is much changed."

My steps slowed. How dare he speak ill of his brother? Ollie was all that was good in this world. I pressed my lips together to keep unpleasantries from escaping, but there was nothing for it; my need to defend Ollie was greater than my need to sit. I spun around to face Damon. Now standing higher than he, I looked down where he stood a few stairs below. "Even changed, Ollie is twice the gentleman you could ever hope to be, *my lord*."

I turned swiftly to retreat, the quick motion causing the world to spin, and my nausea returned full force. I swayed.

Damon was at my side in a flash, grasping my arm. "Are you all right?"

"I'm fine." I pulled my arm from his grip. But in truth, my body was too hot, my face too cold, and my bonnet . . . Why had I tied it so tightly? I yanked at the ribbons, untying the bow.

"You are ill, Miss Kent. Take my arm, I insist."

"No, thank you. I am fine." No sooner than I'd said the words, my stomach spasmed and then emptied on Damon's boots.

Mortified, I looked up at Damon.

He silently pulled a handkerchief from his coat's breast pocket and handed it to me.

Hand trembling, I took the fresh linen square and pressed it to my mouth.

"Will you now allow me to escort you inside?"

Though my pride begged me to refuse, my body demanded otherwise. "Yes. Thank you."

With a slight nod, he removed his soiled boots, taking care only to touch the clean portion at the very top, then extended his arm to me.

I threaded my arm through his, and together, we ascended the stairs.

CHAPTER THREE

FROM MY BEDCHAMBER WINDOW, I watched the lavender stalks dance in the breeze. The night before traveling to Summerhaven, I had worried at the possibility that the plants would not survive all this rain, but the bushes were as big and beautiful as ever. Perhaps even more so this year because everything else in the world seemed to be gray.

"It's time to dress for dinner, miss."

I startled at the sound of Nora's voice and let the curtain fall back into place. "I must have lost track of time." I'd been resting in this window seat, watching and waiting for Ollie to come home ever since the housekeeper had shown me to my room earlier this afternoon—right after the unfortunate incident with Damon's boots.

I rose, my legs stiff and my back sore. I glanced around the room. Nora had emptied my traveling trunk, and candles now lit the room. My nausea had vanished, and hunger had taken its place.

"Will this do?" Nora laid a green silk evening dress on the bed.

"It's just what I would have selected myself." I gently ran my fingers over the neckline, touching the delicate lace. Although the dress was a few Seasons old, it would always be one of my favorites, as Mama had selected it for my coming-out.

Nora helped me change, and then I sat at the vanity table so she could style my hair.

I grimaced at my reflection. My freckled skin was sallow, my curls limp, and my indecisive hazel eyes—which were neither brown nor green, but an ever-changing combination of the two—looked tired. I lifted my gaze to Nora. "Help."

"Not to worry." Nora patted my shoulder, then picked up my hairbrush. "I know just the thing."

"You always do."

Nora worked for the better part of an hour, styling my hair into an intricate coiffure. "There," she said, passing me a hand mirror so I could see the back.

"You're a miracle worker, Nora. Thank you."

"You are kind to say so, miss, but your natural curls do all the work. I only arrange them." Nora adjusted a pin in my hair. "But I think Mr. Jennings will be pleased."

"We shall see. That is *if* he ever makes an appearance." I sighed.

Nora's brow furrowed. "We are speaking of Mr. *Oliver* Jennings, are we not?"

"Yes."

Nora smiled. "Then you'll be pleased to know he came home earlier this afternoon, just after we arrived. I thought you knew."

"No." Why had he not come to me when he'd gotten home? Did he think I was too fatigued from the long journey? Or perhaps Damon had told him about the incident with his boots and he thought me ill.

"Well, you should not keep him waiting. I'm sure he's eager to see you."

Standing at the entrance to the drawing room, my eyes immediately found Ollie. He stood by the window, his handsome face lit by the glow of the moon. Like Damon, Ollie had grown into a man. He'd been gifted with golden curls that once framed his soft face, but his hair was shorter now and styled elegantly, revealing his profile. Straight nose, square jaw, full lips. He was devastatingly handsome.

"If you don't close your mouth, you will catch flies like a frog."

I snapped it shut and turned to face Damon. "It is rude to sneak up on a person, sir."

"Sir." He smiled. "An improvement from *my lord*, I think."

"Do not flatter yourself."

"Never," he said, stepping around me. "And I didn't sneak." He said this only loud enough for me to hear. "I was only walking down the corridor to enter the drawing room. I think it was *you* doing the sneaking. Or should I say *admiring*?"

I narrowed my eyes at him and stepped fully into the drawing room.

Ollie looked up, and when our eyes met, he smiled. "Hannah." He set his drinking glass on the mantel shelf and crossed the room to meet me.

I started to curtsy—expecting him to behave as formally as Damon had earlier—but Ollie stopped me.

"Must we be so formal?" he asked.

Relief washed over me. He may have grown, but he hadn't changed. "No," I said, and I peeked over my shoulder to be sure no one would overhear my next words. Damon moved toward the sofa with a thick green book, well out of earshot, but our parents stood nearer to us in the center of the room, so I lowered my voice. "You were not here to greet me when I arrived."

"Punctuality is not one of my virtues." He hung his head, making a show of his penitence. "Are you very vexed with me?"

"Tell me where you were, and all is forgiven."

"*Tell* you, you say." Ollie clucked his tongue. "Now where is the fun in that? Why don't you guess where I was, and I will tell you if you are correct."

"A guessing game?" I glanced at Papa.

Ollie followed my gaze. "Do you disapprove?"

"On the contrary. I was only thinking of how much Papa enjoys guessing games."

The center of Ollie's chin dimpled the same way it had when he was a boy. "Well. What is your guess then?"

"Let me think. You were out for a ride and lost track of time?"

He shook his head. "Guess again."

"Perhaps you were perusing the haberdashers and you were unable to decide between a beaver hat and a silk topper, and that is why you were late to greet me."

"I already have half a dozen shelves full of hats."

I rolled my eyes. Ollie had always been prone to exaggeration.

"I daresay you don't know me at all, Miss Kent."

"Nonsense." I nudged his shoulder. "I know everything about you. You prefer dogs to cats, salmon to pheasant, and you always loosen your cravat when you think nobody is watching."

"Yes." He chuckled. "That is all true. And yet you can't guess my whereabouts this afternoon."

I scowled playfully at him.

"Come now." He laughed. "Let me lead you to the fire where you will be warm."

What a fine gentleman he'd become. Mama would certainly still approve of him.

At the hearth, Ollie picked up his glass and swirled the amber liquid before taking a drink. "How have you been?" he asked, and his eyes skimmed over my form. "You *look* very well."

My cheeks heated. "That is kind of you to say."

"Not at all. The country air suits you."

"I'm not sure Damon's boots would agree with you," I mumbled, "but I admit, I'm glad to be free of London."

"As am I," Ollie said. "With Byron exiled and Brummell on the run, London is not what it used to be."

What it used to be? I blinked, confused. Ollie had been living in London? For how long? Well before April, I assumed, if he'd been friends with Byron. Why had Ollie not called on me? He'd not even written. Stunned by the revelation, I could only bring myself to ask, "What did London use to be?"

"Great fun." Ollie smiled to himself as if remembering some distant time I was not a part of, and he took another sip of his drink.

"You enjoy London then?"

"Excessively. Don't you?"

"I *suppose* the city has much to offer."

"Much to offer?" He laughed. "There is not a more diverting city in the world. Where else can you take a peek at Tattersall's in the morning, promenade Hyde Park in the afternoon, and enjoy the theater, opera, or supper at the Royal Salon by night?" Ollie grew animated as he spoke. "There is no other place better in all the world, I tell you. London is the height of fashion and pleasure."

Ollie had always loved the country, but now it seemed he was enamored with the pleasures of city life. Was *this* what Damon had meant when he'd said Ollie had changed? I glanced over my shoulder at Damon, but his book had captured his attention.

I squinted at the gold-embossed title, but the dim lit made it impossible to read from this distance.

"Hannah?" Ollie said, reclaiming my attention.

I quickly averted my gaze, not wanting him to think me a bluestocking for inspecting the book. "Yes?"

"Something I said bothered you. What was it?"

"Nothing."

Ollie leaned against the hearth and rested one arm on the mantel. "As you said, we have known each other nearly our entire lives. You can't hide your feelings from me. Tell me, Hanny. What is wrong?"

I gave a small shake of my head, embarrassed to admit the truth. "I thought you were still attending school at Cambridge. But you were living in London, same as me, and you didn't call on me."

"Is that all?" Ollie's face softened into a smile. "I thought you were still living in Bath. You see? A simple misunderstanding. Had I known you were living in London again, you would have had to chase me off your front porch with a stick."

Our townhouse did not exactly have a proper porch, only a top step—something he would have known had he bothered to call on me, but that was beside the point. Ollie had made an error. Simple as that. An easy enough thing to do, really . . . Although, hadn't I written about the ordeal of moving again and sent express directions to write me at our London address? Perhaps my grief had been too profound for me to remember things correctly.

Ollie bent slightly, and catching my gaze, he smiled. "Forgive me?"

Devil take that dimple! I could never be cross with him when he smiled at me that way. "Always. I'm just glad we are together now."

"Me too."

At the drawing room door, the butler announced dinner. Lord and Lady Winfield led the procession into the dining hall. Damon set down his book and fell into line behind them, engaging Papa in polite conversation.

The formality took me by surprise. On my previous visits, we hadn't entered the dining room by rank. But then again, Lord Winfield had rarely been in residence when I'd visited before. Perhaps things were different when he was home, or perhaps I'd merely forgotten.

Ollie offered me his arm. "May I escort you into the dining room?"

I took it eagerly. Too eagerly, judging by the reproving look Damon gave me, and Ollie led me into the corridor.

I frowned at the back of Damon's head. "Is Damon always so . . . superior?" I asked Ollie.

"Always." Ollie sighed theatrically. "My brother is a great lord, you know. Superiority, it seems, comes with the title."

This earned another censuring look from Damon, which in turn resulted in laughter from Ollie and me.

We were all grown, but in this moment, it felt as if we were all children again. Being here with Ollie—and even Damon—my world swung back into balance.

A rainbow of tapestries decorated the wood-paneled walls of the dining hall, and the savory aroma of rosemary and garlic and butter floated in the air.

The seating arrangement at dinner was most agreeable—save for Damon sitting directly across from me. I'd need to be careful that he didn't put any creeping things in my soup.

"I hear the weather has all but ruined the Season," Lord Winfield said to Papa. "Tell me how this affects your dealings with the church, Kent."

Papa dabbed his mouth and chin. "We have seen a slight decrease in the size of the congregation on Sundays," he admitted.

Lord Winfield nodded. "I daresay God sent the rain to ruin us all."

"Or perhaps he intends for us to reflect, not bring us to ruin, my lord."

"Spoken like a true man of God." Lord Winfield gave a derisive laugh. A laugh that shortly gave way to a deep cough.

"My lord?" Lady Winfield said. "Are you all right?"

"I have no need of a nursemaid, Elizabeth," he said, and he chased away his cough with drink.

"Of course not. I was only going to suggest we turn the conversation to a topic that all present can take interest in." She nodded toward me.

"You are quite right, my dear. What shall we discuss?" He chewed a bite of food. "Ah. I know just the thing: the Rumford Ball tomorrow night."

"Yes." Lady Winfield brightened. "Just this afternoon, Ollie requested the invitation be extended to our guests."

I glanced at Ollie and whispered, "Is that where you were when I arrived?"

He flashed me a smile. "Finally, you have guessed correctly."

I smiled too. I *knew* he'd had a reason to be absent. Why had I doubted?

"Mr. Kent," Lady Winfield said, "if it is agreeable to you, I would love to serve as Hannah's chaperone tomorrow night so you and Lord Winfield can enjoy the card room."

"I don't partake in playing cards," Papa said. "I've seen far too many of my parishioners lose their fortunes at the tables. But I should be happy to enjoy Lord Winfield's company, and I am certain Hannah will enjoy the ball far more with you as her chaperone."

"Wonderful," Lady Winfield said to Papa. "Hannah, seeing as I am now in your employ, Oliver will be glad to dance the supper set with you."

Ollie looked up mid-bite at his mother and held her gaze for a long moment, some unspoken bit of communication passing between them.

Uncomfortable, I smoothed the napkin in my lap. Perhaps he didn't like Lady Winfield meddling in his affairs.

Finally, he looked at me, an easy smile on his face. "What say you, Miss Kent? Would you—"

"I would."

Despite his reticence, I had no hesitation. I'd come to Summerhaven to begin my life with Ollie, and that was precisely what I intended to do.

"Very good," Lady Winfield said. "Damon, who will you dance the dinner set with?"

"No one," Damon said, without so much as glancing up from his plate.

"Not dance?" Lord Winfield snorted a laugh from the head of the table. "How absurd."

Lady Winfield placed her hand on her eldest son's arm. "There is always a shortage of eligible men. There must be someone who could entice you into dancing at least one set."

"No," Damon said between bites of food.

"No?" Lord Winfield repeated. "You will dance tomorrow night and fulfill your obligations. I will not pass my title to a dead line, Damon. If you refuse your duty to this family, you also refuse the benefits thereof. Do I make myself clear?"

Damon gave his father a scathing glare. "Often and rather forcefully."

"Good." Lord Winfield nodded. "You'll dance the first set with Lord Rumford's daughter."

Damon said nothing to this, but Lord Winfield resumed his meal as if satisfied. The scene felt well-rehearsed. How often did father and son act out some version of this same performance?

I felt unsettled the remainder of dinner.

When at last Lady Winfield announced it was time for us women to retire to the drawing room so the men could resume their talk of business and politics over a glass of port, I quickly rose and followed her out of the dining hall.

"Tell me about your coming-out," Lady Winfield said as we walked down the corridor toward the drawing room. "I regret to have missed it."

We'd just begun making preparations for my coming-out when Mama had fallen ill. Although Mama had wanted to invite Lady Winfield to attend the special event, Mama had insisted my coming-out happen sooner rather than later, which I was now glad for. Had we procrastinated, Mama would not have been well enough to attend.

I told Lady Winfield about all the wonderful things—the opulence of the queen's rooms and the delectable desserts.

"And your first Season? How was it?"

"I have not yet had a proper Season," I admitted. "Directly after my coming-out, Mama's health worsened, and we removed to Bath in hope of a cure."

"Oh, my dear." Lady Winfield hugged my shoulders.

I closed my eyes, welcoming her touch. Papa was affectionate, but not in the same way Mama was, and we rarely embraced. I missed this comfort.

"Well, I cannot give you a proper Season, but I can spoil you while you are here." She smiled softly, and it was obvious that she'd been born to be a countess. So kind and graceful.

We talked for a little time more about London. Her ears perked up when I spoke of my charity work with the church for the less fortunate. And I explained how after Mama had passed away, service had given my days meaning and purpose.

A little while later, Lord Winfield and Papa entered the drawing room. I glanced at the door for Ollie and Damon, but they did not come right away. So I excused myself to look at the art around the room. I had always been fond of fine art but did not have much talent for it.

Standing in front of an oil painting of the river that went through the Winfields' lands, I heard the low timbre of voices approaching in the corridor.

"You shouldn't dance with Hannah, Ollie," Damon said, and although he spoke quietly, his voice carried from the corridor into the drawing room where I stood.

"Whyever not?" Ollie replied.

"You *know* why not."

Anger stirred within me. Just because Damon didn't want to dance did not mean he needed to poison Ollie against me.

I hastily stepped into the corridor where the brothers stood. Ollie's back was to me, but Damon's eyebrows shot up. "Hannah," he sputtered. "I thought you were otherwise occupied in the drawing room."

"I am certain that is true," I said, and I angled my body so I faced only Ollie, hoping Damon would take the snub for what it was. "Shall we take a stroll in the garden tomorrow morning? From my window, I can see that the lavender is in full bloom. I would love a bouquet to scent my room."

Ollie looked at his brother and then at me. "I would enjoy that very much."

I nodded, satisfied that even though Damon disapproved of me, Ollie did not.

CHAPTER FOUR

OLLIE HAD ALWAYS BEEN AN early riser, often beating the roosters out of bed to watch the sunrise. He'd once written in a letter that there wasn't a more magical, hopeful time of day; like a filled teacup, the newness of the day brimmed with possibility. I'd thought the sentiment romantic at the time, but this morning, it was decidedly less so.

I had risen early for our walk and readied myself with anticipation, but when I'd come downstairs to meet him, I discovered him already out of residence. And worse yet, no one seemed to know when he would return.

I tried not to be cross as I walked back upstairs to my bedchamber, but it was exceedingly difficult. Had he forgotten about our walk? Or perhaps he'd grown tired of waiting for me? I had not taken so long to get ready, but I was a *little* late.

With a sigh, I perched myself on the window seat to wait for him. The sun was still creeping up into the sky. And although clouds obscured most of the light, a few rays escaped, making for a stunning sight.

Sunrises in the city were not nearly as extraordinary as in the country; buildings blocked my view, and as the sun rose, so did the stench. In truth, unlike Ollie, I'd always preferred sunset. Of reflecting on a hard day's work, listening to Mama play the pianoforte after dinner, and reading the *Evening Post* by the fire with Papa. Sunset brought the feeling of peace, if not possibility.

But our differences were what made Ollie and me such good friends and what would one day make us good spouses.

Together, we were whole.

Which is why I waited all afternoon for Ollie. But he did not return until it was time to dress for the ball.

As Nora helped me dress and styled my hair, I took a steadying breath, trying to calm my emotions. The Rumfords' ball tonight was supposed to mark the beginning of the rest of my life, and I did not want to go into the event, much less my future, vexed. Whatever reason Ollie had for not being present for our walk, it must have been important.

Once ready, I walked down the corridor toward the grand staircase to join the rest of the company downstairs in the entrance hall. As I neared the staircase, voices blended in conversation. I paused at the top of the stairs. Lord and Lady Winfield stood near the door with Papa, and Ollie conversed with Damon. Ollie stood stiff and straight in his dark tailored suit, looking every bit the gentleman. Damon, on the other hand, leaned against the wood-paneled wall, tugging at his cravat like a bored schoolboy.

Damon noticed me first. He took in my appearance, his eyebrows creeping up his forehead in unchecked approval, and then as if remembering himself, he nudged Ollie and motioned with his head to where I stood on the stairs.

Ollie glanced over his shoulder, and I hoped for the same unguarded appreciation Damon had given me. But the only indication he approved of my appearance was a slight smile.

I smoothed my hands over the empire waist of my white crepe dress. Though this dress was not the *latest* fashion, Nora had worked tediously to make several improvements to the bodice and trim. And she'd painstakingly secured my hair into the most elegant chignon, taking care to frame my face with ringlets and weave tiny white flowers into my hair.

I touched the top of my white gloves, ensuring one last time they were in place, then descended the stairs.

"My dear," Papa said, walking over to meet me at the base of the staircase. "You look as beautiful as your mother did on the night we met."

The night they fell in love.

My heart soared like a bird caught in a sudden gale. All my life, I'd dreamed of marrying for love like my parents had. I could hardly believe my own story was about to grow wings and take flight this very eve.

"The picture of beauty and grace," Lady Winfield agreed.

My face warmed with their compliments. "Thank you, Papa. Lady Winfield."

Papa rejoined Lord and Lady Winfield at the door, and I dared another glance at Ollie.

He stepped forward and bowed. "You look well this evening, Miss Kent."

Well, but not lovely. Hmm. "My maid will be pleased you think so," I said in a hushed voice so only he could hear my displeasure.

"And are you?" he asked.

I lifted one shoulder. "I would have preferred greater flattery than for you to comment after my health."

Ollie's head tilted to one side, a small smile playing on his lips. "You are cross with me."

"You promised we would gather lavender this morning."

"Ah, yes. I had business to attend to."

"Business?" I frowned. What *business* could possibly have arisen since last night to this morning?

He nodded. "I apologize for not being able to walk with you, but I did bring this for you." Ollie pulled out a sprig of lavender from his suit coat pocket and handed it to me.

I took the bloom and lifted it to my nose. I breathed in the rich scent, and some of my anger faded. Whatever business he'd had, at least he'd thought of me. I tucked the lavender into my hair. "Thank you."

"You are most welcome." He offered me his arm, and together we walked to where our parents stood by the door.

"Look at the pair of you," Lady Winfield smiled. "All grown up. Quite a lovely couple, aren't they, dear?"

"Quite," Lord Winfield agreed, though he did not look up from his pocket watch. "Shall we?" He motioned outside to where two carriages waited in the drive.

Damon pushed himself off the wall and trailed behind us. He appeared to have about as much enthusiasm to go to this ball as a prisoner being escorted to the gallows.

I'd not given much thought to the seating arrangements for the drive to the Rumfords' ball, but when Ollie did not join Papa and me in our carriage, disappointment took the seat beside me instead. No matter. We would have the supper set and all of supper.

The carriage ride to the Rumfords' was not an unbearable distance, and when we arrived, servants clamored to open our carriage door. I could not stop myself from staring at the remarkable home as I alighted. While Summerhaven was a warm and welcoming manor house, the Rumfords' home was a cold and cavernous castle.

Lord and Lady Winfield were announced at the ballroom door, followed by Damon and Ollie.

Several young ladies turned, smiling coyly. I worried one of them had their sights set on Ollie, but I was pacified when I saw that their attention was not on Ollie, but rather on Damon.

As he made his way to the card room, the hopeful women tried to gain his attention: a simpering smile, a well-timed step into his path, a fallen handkerchief, each girl cleverer than the last. But either Damon didn't notice the girls or he thought them *beneath* his notice, because he didn't stop to take their bait.

Papa and I were announced next, and as soon as we stepped into the ballroom, Lord Winfield led Papa into the card room. Only Ollie, ever the gentleman, remained with Lady Winfield and me—although another gentleman quickly pulled him into conversation.

Lady Winfield led me toward a group of women. My heart raced. I'd been so focused on Ollie that I'd neglected to consider the other long hours of the night. I was not an especially talented conversationalist. I could carry on a conversation with Papa or Henry or even Georgiana, but when dropped into a social situation with people I didn't know, I either tended not to speak at all or to speak too much. Luckily, Lady Winfield served as my chaperone, and she could likely carry on a proper conversation in her sleep.

"Lady Rumford," Lady Winfield said.

An elegant woman turned. "Lady Winfield." She smiled. "I am so glad you have arrived."

"The pleasure is all mine. Lady Rumford, please allow me to introduce Miss Kent."

"Ah, Miss Kent," she said, studying me. "Lady Winfield has spoken of nothing but you for weeks. I can't seem to recall though, where is your family seat?"

"My family has no seat, my lady. But we reside in London."

"Mayfair?" she asked.

I shook my head. "Cheapside, my lady."

"Oh. How lovely." To Lady Rumford's credit, her face remained a perfectly polite mask, though she must have wondered how I—a girl without so much as a family seat—had the fortune of being connected to such a high-ranking and genteel family as the Jennings. Cheapside was a perfectly respectable area of London, though not as fashionable as Mayfair.

"London is my favorite place to visit during the Season," Lady Rumford said.

"And Summerhaven is my favorite place to visit always."

"I'm sure Lady Winfield would not mind at all if our little piece of country became your more permanent residence." Lady Rumford shared a private smile with Lady Winfield.

"I would love to return to visit Summerhaven," I said, "but I hope to make my home in the north."

Lady Rumford raised a knowing eyebrow. "Winterset Grange, perhaps?"

My eyes widened in embarrassment. In stating my preference to make my home in the north, I'd inadvertently revealed my desire to marry Ollie and make his future home my own. Oh dear. How impertinent I must sound.

Lady Winfield must have sensed my embarrassment, for she kindly interceded. "I must thank you for extending the invitation to attend your ball to our dear Hannah. We would like to repay the favor. Would you and your daughter do us the honor of joining us for tea in two days' time?"

"I would like that very much. Speaking of my daughter . . ." Lady Rumford turned and pulled a young woman away from her conversation and into our circle. "Miss Kent, my daughter Miss Amelia Atherton."

Miss Atherton had fiery red ringlets, fair freckled skin, and a discerning gaze.

As we curtsied in greeting, the matrons turned to greet a nearby friend, leaving Miss Atherton and me to converse in private.

"How do you find the country, Miss Kent?"

"Most agreeable. Thank you."

"Do you miss London?"

"Not at all. The country air is most refreshing."

"I entirely agree." She nodded. "I'm sure your host has been most genial."

"Indeed. Lord and Lady Winfield have been very kind."

"And Lord Jennings?" Miss Atherton used Damon's courtesy title to not so subtly ask after my interest in him.

"I confess, I am fonder of the *younger* of the brothers."

Miss Atherton looked at me curiously, her eyes narrowing ever so slightly.

I'd made another social blunder. I grimaced. Mama always said feelings were like the rain, better outside than in. I believed in the sentiment, but it proved easier to live by in London—where speaking more openly was acceptable—than here in the country. I needed to watch my tongue; my tendency to be outspoken would reflect poorly not only on me but upon the Jennings family. And even more important, I wanted to be a credit to Mama in every way.

"Mr. *Oliver* Jennings?" Miss Atherton asked, and her head tilted to one side, her curls resting on her shoulder.

I nodded. "We've been friends since childhood."

"Well then." She righted her head with a genuine smile. "We must be friends then." She then quietly added, "We may be family one day, you know."

Miss Atherton and *Damon*? Did they have an understanding? It couldn't be. Damon hadn't even wanted to dance with anyone tonight. If they had an understanding, even a private one, he would have been eager to stand up with her for a set.

"Miss Atherton—" I began at the same time as the first set was announced.

"Excuse me," she said. "I must stand apart so Lord Jennings can more easily claim his dance." She took a step forward and locked her gaze on the card room door where Damon no doubt hoped to hide all night. Poor Miss Atherton. She had no idea how much he did not want to attend this ball much less dance tonight.

I searched my mind for possible topics of conversation to distract her from Damon's absence; no woman should be snubbed at a ball, let alone a ball held in her own home, but I hardly knew what would interest her.

Couples began gathering in the center of the room. My anxiety grew. Perhaps I could pretend to feel faint or suggest we take air on the balcony?

Finally, at the last possible moment, Damon appeared at the card room door. Lord Winfield stood close behind him as if ready to catch him by the collar should he decide to run.

Damon's lips pressed into a thin line as he surveyed the crush.

I glanced at Miss Atherton to see if she noticed how miserable he looked, but no, she only smiled as Damon made his way toward us.

It must be true then. Hopefully she had a high tolerance for toads.

"Miss Atherton." Damon bowed. "If you are ready?"

She took Damon's arm, and he escorted her to the dance floor.

Lady Winfield appeared at my side a moment later. "Come, my dear," she said and led me toward the edge of the room. There hadn't been time for any other young men in attendance to be properly introduced to me, so I would not be dancing this set.

Ollie, however, *would*.

Standing across the line from him stood a beautiful young woman. With ringlets the color of spun honey, bright-blue eyes, and a creamy complexion, she was stunning. The complete opposite of me, with my light-brown hair, hazel eyes, and unfashionably freckled skin.

"Who is that with Ollie?" I asked Lady Winfield, trying for casual but achieving concerned.

"No one you need trouble yourself with, dear," she said, but judging from the worry lines on her forehead, she obviously meant I *should* be troubled.

The music began, and a tightness formed in my chest as Ollie engaged his lovely dance partner in conversation. The dance seemed to stretch on forever. What were they discussing? She was undoubtedly better at the art of conversation than I.

The set finally ended, and as expected, Ollie escorted her to the refreshment table. However, they lingered there for an eternity, which was not expected. When they parted, the knot in my chest relaxed.

Between sets, Lady Winfield made my acquaintance with several ladies and their fine sons, who asked me to dance later in the evening. Though I had no interest in any of these men, knowing I would not have to decorate the wall *all* night made it easier to sit out now.

Each man was a polite and proficient partner, but my gaze kept wandering in search of Ollie. It felt like ages before the supper set was announced. Standing by Lady Winfield, I waited for Ollie. I hadn't seen where he'd gone after the last set. Minutes ticked by, and couples took their places in line.

Had Ollie forgotten our dance?

No. It wasn't possible. Maybe he'd gone to the card room and not heard the set announced? I glanced at the card room door and felt reproved. Had I not earlier felt sorry for Miss Atherton for doing the same thing?

Damon stood near the door, observing the ballroom. And even though there were not enough men to serve as dance partners, just as his mother had said would be the case, he only watched the crush with indifference.

I looked around the room, slowly and with a smile, trying not to appear desperate. There. Walking inside from the balcony terrace that overlooked the garden strode Ollie.

He'd not forgotten me! He'd only been seeking respite from the stuffy ballroom—for which I could hardly blame him.

Our eyes met, and he crossed the ballroom, moving swiftly between people to reach me. "Hanny," he said, ushering me back toward a more private corner of the hall. "You'll not believe my good luck."

"Oh?" I said with a smile. "What is it?"

"Miss Digby has agreed to dance a second set with me. The supper set."

My eyebrows tightened together. "The supper set? But that was to be—"

"Our dance. I know." He winced. "But I have waited such a long time for an opportunity like this; she's the daughter of a well-respected and wealthy merchant marine, Hanny. Do you know what her favor could do for me?"

Her favor? I blinked, confused. What was he even talking about? He was the son of an earl. Why would he care whether the daughter of a merchant marine favored him? Unless . . .

"I hate to ask this of you," he continued, "but she's perhaps the most beautiful woman I have ever laid eyes on." His gaze drifted to the woman I'd seen him dancing with earlier. "Would you mind terribly if I dance the supper set with her instead?"

My throat constricted, holding my words for ransom. All at once, I understood.

Ollie did not love me.

I could only shake my head.

"You really don't mind?" Ollie said, sounding relieved. "I was so worried you would be cross with me. You're a good friend. I promise to make this up to you." Ollie hurried away to his Miss Digby without a backward glance.

The young ladies standing nearest me watched and whispered. My face flamed with embarrassment. My knees felt weak and wobbly. The room spun, and I glanced around, desperate for something to anchor me. My gaze settled on Damon.

He gave me a look of sympathy. No, of pity.

The whispers seemed to grow louder.

Air. I needed air.

I forced my way through the thick crush of people to the balcony. The cool night air hit my face, and tears stung my eyes. My hands shook as I grabbed the balustrade, and I tilted my head toward the sky.

I would *not* cry.

The only thing that could make this night worse would be to have red, puffy eyes at dinner. A dinner that I'd planned to enjoy at Ollie's side but would now have to watch instead.

I tore the lavender sprig from my hair and dropped it to the ground. Tonight was supposed to be the beginning of everything but instead—

"There you are, Miss Kent."

Damon. His eyes sunk to the sprig of lavender at my feet.

I groaned inwardly. He was perhaps the only person who could make this night worse. Had he sought me out to gloat? To tease me?

Behind him, a cluster of young women craned their necks to see who the future earl was speaking to.

An audience. Delightful.

"Miss Kent," he said again, and more loudly than necessary. "I have come to claim my set."

His set? "I beg your pardon but—"

"Are you feeling faint?" Damon interrupted my sentence without apology. He stepped close and said quietly, "The only way to silence the whispers that have already begun to circulate is if we give them something more interesting to talk about. Now take my arm and do try not to frown as I lead you to the dance floor."

I nodded in understanding, and then said, loudly enough so others could overhear, "I *was* feeling a little flushed, but I am recovered now."

"I am glad to hear it. I have been waiting all evening to dance with you." Damon led me inside.

Earlier I may have imagined a dozen pairs of eyes on me, but as Damon— the most eligible young man in attendance—led me to the dance floor, I knew they were on me for certain. I guessed from his open disdain that Damon didn't dance at balls often. After all, he'd been compelled to dance the first set with Miss Atherton.

Miss Atherton!

She would think I had lied to her about not having any interest in Damon. I would have to explain to her exactly what had happened—embarrassing as it would be. She had been kind to me, and I did not want to hurt her or, worse, make an enemy.

Damon did not stop moving until we stood at the front of the ballroom.

Other couples quickly joined us, each person studying me—the woman who had lured Damon out of the card room for a dance. They took formation around us, not in a line but rather a square.

A quadrille, I realized with horror. And worse, *I* was the lead lady charged with beginning the dance—a dance I did not know.

Oh, why could it not have been a simple country dance? I could not even fake my way through the quadrille. Not with so many eyes on me. Not without embarrassing myself and my hosts. Not without being a discredit to Mama.

While we waited for the other squares to assemble, I searched for some means of escape. But onlooking chaperones blocked the ballroom door, and the balcony was not even visible through all the unpartnered bystanders.

"Looking for Ollie undermines the purpose of our dancing together," Damon said quietly.

"I wasn't looking for Ollie."

He raised an eyebrow in disbelief.

"I was searching for an escape."

"Am I really so loathsome?" Damon said.

"Yes. I mean no." I clenched my jaw, frustrated my words would not come out correctly. "Damon, I cannot do this. I can't dance the quadrille."

"You can, and you will. Your reputation and mine depend on it."

"You don't understand," I said quietly, even as the musicians poised their instruments to play. "I don't know the steps. Mama fell sick during my lessons, and I never had the opportunity to properly learn the quadrille, much less perfect it."

Understanding lit his eyes.

The music began, and I honored Damon with a curtsy.

He bowed close, locking his icy blue eyes on mine. "Do exactly as I say," he whispered. "Long balance to partners *à droite*, *à gauche*, then right-hand turn with the man opposite you."

I did as Damon said, stepping first to the right, then to the left, and finally, turning in the center with the man across the square from me.

Before I had time to even wonder what forms came next, Damon grabbed my left hand and, pulling me near, he said, "Promenade through the middle, then round the outside."

Again, I followed his instructions. Damon was an able lead. Without him, I would have been lost.

He didn't take his eyes off me. To some, it may have looked as if he was enamored with me—at least I hoped that's what they saw as it was preferable to the truth.

Back in our original positions, Damon talked me through the remaining steps of the first round. And when the second lady took the lead, I very nearly deflated in relief.

"You did well," Damon said as we watched the other couples in our square dance.

"Thank you for assisting me, Damon. Truly."

"I had little choice, Miss Kent. You were looking quite green, and my boots can only handle so much abuse." His eyes shone with mirth in the candlelight.

How ungentlemanly of him to bring *that* up. I glared at him.

He smiled slightly and resumed observing the other dancers.

Damon proved to be an accomplished and graceful dancer, but I was glad when our set ended. Glad until I remembered that I was stuck with Damon for the whole of supper.

CHAPTER FIVE

DAMON HAD SAVED MY REPUTATION, but he'd also brought upon me the wrath of every young woman and chaperone in attendance; their glares were sharp talons digging into my back. I gripped Damon's arm as we rounded the corridor into the dining hall.

The table was beautifully set with fine china, and an army of footmen dressed in gold livery stood around the perimeter, ready to serve.

Damon and I were seated near the head of the table, but Ollie sat closer to the middle of the long table. Part of me felt bad for him—having to sit apart from one's family could not have been easy—but selfishly, after how he had treated me, I was relieved I would not have to endure his presence. Sitting across from Miss Atherton would be stressful enough.

Though I tried not to, I glanced in Ollie's direction and found him staring at me, his expression inscrutable.

"Miss Kent," Damon said, commanding my attention, "you appear to be searching for a particular dish. The *grenouilles*, perhaps?"

Not for the first time, I wished I'd paid more attention during the French lessons Mama had insisted upon. "Yes. The *grenouilles*. Thank you."

Damon stood to serve me.

"I didn't know you were fond of frog legs, Hannah," Lady Winfield said.

My gaze snapped to Damon, and he gave me a crooked grin. There was no food on earth I detested more than frog legs, and he knew it. Ever since he'd put a frog in my drinking glass as a girl, I'd detested the blob-shaped creatures. With their slimy skin, bulging eyes, and spindly legs, they were disgusting.

When I turned back to address Lady Winfield, Miss Atherton scowled at me from across the table. I couldn't blame her. The fact that Damon had *supposedly* remembered my culinary preferences did little to aid my friendship with her. Another thing I would have to explain.

"I am also fond of frog legs," Lord Rumford said. "Miss . . . ?"

"Kent," Lord Winfield quickly supplied to our host.

"Kent," Lord Rumford repeated thoughtfully. "Any relation to the Duke of Kent?"

Lord Winfield eyed me. "Perhaps distantly," he said, though we both knew there was no relation, distant or otherwise. Was he trying to ingratiate me to Lord Rumford or himself?

"Well, relation or no," Lord Rumford said, "I am glad to find a young woman with such a refined palate seated at my table. Please tell me how you like them, Miss Kent."

I was trapped. I couldn't refuse to eat the frog legs. To do so would be to call Damon a liar *and* insult my host. There was nothing for it. I would have to not only eat the frog legs but also pretend to enjoy them.

"May I?" Damon gestured to the platter.

I glared privately at Damon, then said sweetly for all to hear, "You are *too* kind, my lord."

Damon served me a large pair of frog legs.

"Please don't be shy, Lord Jennings," Lord Rumford said. "I'm sure Miss Kent would prefer a more generous portion."

Oh please no.

Damon pressed his lips together as if trying to hide his amusement.

"Only one more please," I said to Damon. "And you must not forget to serve yourself. I should hate for you to be left out of our enjoyment."

"Unfortunately, my palate is not as refined as yours or Lord Rumford's."

Lord Rumford grinned. "The lady is your superior, Jennings."

"To be sure," I said only loudly enough for Damon to hear.

He gave me a small grin. "One need only look at her to confirm that fact."

"Hear! Hear!" Lord Rumford held up his glass in Damon's direction, and both men drank in my honor.

Heat pooled in my cheeks. Being the center of attention was foreign to me, and I did not like it.

"It seems it is only you and me then, Miss Kent, who are lucky enough to enjoy such pleasures," Lord Rumford said. "Please. Ladies first."

With a nod, I used my fork to peel away some meat from the bone, and juices flowed onto my plate. My stomach squeezed.

Damon watched me closely.

If he thought I would back down, he thought wrong. I'd survived both Ollie's rejection and dancing the quadrille. I could eat a few bites of meat.

I quickly placed the bite in my mouth. The flavor was not so off-putting, but the slimy texture was too much to overcome; I swallowed the bite whole.

"Well, Miss Kent, how do you find them?" Lord Rumford asked.

"Fresh and well-prepared. My compliments to the chef. And I thank you, my Lord Rumford, for your generosity."

He beamed with the compliment. "The pleasure is all mine."

When Lord Rumford turned away, Damon chuckled. I kicked his shin under the table, and he sucked in a sharp breath, choking on his drink. He coughed into his arm, drawing attention.

"Are you all right?" I feigned worry.

"Yes." Damon cleared his throat. "Thank you for your concern. It was most heartily felt."

"I am *so* glad."

Shaking his head, Damon smiled down at his plate. And despite all that had happened tonight, I smiled too.

After supper, Damon escorted me back to the ballroom. No sooner had we entered the room than he released his hold and turned toward the card room.

I stared at his back in disbelief. "Are you really not going to dance?" Asking young ladies to dance was a gentleman's duty, especially since—as his mother had predicted—there were not enough men by half.

"I know that you yearn for my company, but you really should not be so forthright with your feelings. People will think we have formed an attachment." He winked.

I frowned. He knew I wasn't asking him to stay for myself, so why tease me?

"Now that you have had a set with a future earl, I should think you will have more than enough willing partners to keep you occupied. Enjoy the rest of your ball, Miss Kent." And then, with a smirk, he retreated into the card room.

Annoying, arrogant, insufferable man! Did he really have so much money to burn that he could spend hours upon hours gambling it away?

I thought of all the people I'd served back home in London; they were destitute, so poor they had to rely on the generosity of the church for their daily bread. And yet, young lords like Damon, who had never worked a day in their life, were free to idle away their time, their talents, their capital, and not want for anything.

This world was so unfair.

When dancing resumed, I indeed had more interested partners than lines on my card. If my suitors only knew my true identity—a daughter of a clergyman without title or rank or fortune—perhaps they would not have been so eager.

After one particularly rousing set, I found myself at the refreshment table at the same time as Ollie.

"You appear to be having an enjoyable evening," he said. "What would it take to get you to dance with me?" Ollie asked, but despite his playful tone, his wish to dance had little to do with me and everything to do with my sudden rise in desirability.

"Well, I suppose you would need to turn back time in order for that to happen." I moved to step away.

"Hanny." He caught my elbow. "Will you truly not dance with me?"

Was he honestly confused by my refusal? For a man as educated as Ollie, he could be quite dense sometimes. "I'm sorry, but I have already promised the remainder of my sets to other gentlemen."

"Can you not forget one name?" He flashed me his dimpled-chin smile.

I tried desperately not to be charmed, but I'd spent my whole life loving that dimple and could not help it. Still, I had more pride than that and certainly more integrity. "I'm sorry, Mr. Jennings. I would never cast off one dance partner for another. It isn't right or kind. Please excuse me."

I tried to enjoy myself the rest of the evening, but my feet hurt from dancing, and no matter how hard I tried not to, my thoughts—and gaze—kept returning to Ollie. Although he, too, had no shortage of willing and beautiful partners, he looked as miserable as I felt.

When the time came to leave, my feet were sore and my heart heavy. I'd come to this ball hoping to leave with Ollie by my side, but Papa escorted me to the carriage instead.

"Did you enjoy the ball, my dear?" Papa asked as the horses' hooves beat the ground back to Summerhaven.

"It was tiring," I said. "I don't know how people do this every night during the Season." I didn't know why they would want to. Nothing could be more exhausting, both physically *and* emotionally, than large social gatherings.

I rested my head on Papa's shoulder. I would never make sense of this night. But one thing was certain; without Ollie, there was nothing left for me at Summerhaven but memories.

CHAPTER SIX

THE MORNING AFTER THE BALL, I didn't join the family for breakfast. There wasn't time. Papa was journeying home today, and I intended to join him. After last night, six weeks would be impossible to bear.

I held up two bonnets, trying to decide which to wear and which to pack.

"Wear the blue," a deep voice said. Damon stood in the corridor outside my bedchamber. His gaze dropped to my open trunk. "What are you doing?"

"Packing," I replied and handed Nora the blue bonnet to place inside the trunk.

He laughed a little. "Yes, I can see that. Why?"

"Because that is what one does when one intends to travel."

"You're leaving."

"How observant of you, my lord."

He leaned against the doorframe. "You're not the first person to pay me that compliment."

"And yet it took you several questions before you came to a conclusion."

He smiled bemusedly. "Yes, well. A man can never be too certain of a lady's mind."

"Seeing as you are now informed, you had best leave me to pack. If Papa and I are to reach the inn by nightfall, I must make haste." I turned my back to him and gazed at the contents in my trunk. My riding habit sat atop the pile. "It is a shame this will go unused," I said to Nora. "I was so looking forward to riding the hills."

On my previous visits, Ollie and I had been too young to do anything more than trot in the open pastures, but now that we were all grown, I'd dreamed of riding the hills together at a gallop.

"Perhaps you should stay then."

I glanced up and found Damon still at my door. "No," I said. "Now if you will excuse me?"

"I think not." Damon crossed his arms.

Had he nothing better to do than goad me? "What is it you want, Damon?"

"Originally, to inquire as to why you didn't join us in the breakfast room this morning. But seeing as that question has been answered, I'm now here to stop you from leaving."

"My mind is made up."

"We shall see." Damon turned to Nora. "Is Miss Kent looking a little . . . fatigued to you?"

Nora glanced at me. "No, my lord."

Damon tapped the toe of his boot against the doorframe. "I must disagree with you. I do believe your mistress is about to faint. You must trust me in this matter; I have experience with swooning women."

Nora smiled. I shot her a look of disapproval, and she quickly sobered.

Damon stood tall then, filling the doorframe with his form. "Will you be ever so kind—I'm sorry, what is your name, miss?"

"Nora, my lord."

"A lovely name."

She blushed, and I frowned at Damon.

"Nora, won't you please bring a tray for your mistress?" he asked.

Nora's gaze moved from Damon to me. She looked unsure, but I couldn't tell if she was questioning the propriety of the situation—leaving Damon and me alone was not strictly proper—or trying to decide whether her loyalty should lie with her mistress or with Damon, future lord and master of this estate.

Hating to see her in such a position, I said, "Lord Jennings is correct. I'm suddenly quite fatigued from this conversation and require refreshment if I am to endure."

"Yes, miss." Nora bobbed a curtsy and quit the room.

I turned back to my open trunk, knowing Damon could—and likely would—carry on the conversation without any effort on my part.

"I had hoped after last night we'd made some progress repairing our relationship," Damon said.

"Asking me to dance was the act of a gentleman, and I thank you for that."

"But . . . ?"

"You made me eat frog legs, and I should never forgive you for that."

His lips lifted at the corners. "Which is precisely why I can't let you leave. I must make amends. My reputation cannot endure the least bit of tarnish."

"I have never known you to care one whit for your reputation."

"True enough," he said and stepped inside my room.

My eyes widened. "You can't be in here. What if someone sees you?" What they might think!

"The door is full open, and we are not standing anywhere near each other." Damon walked to the vanity table and perched on the edge. "Besides, we grew up sleeping in the same nursery, Hannah."

I clenched my teeth. The last time we'd shared a room, he'd cut my hair while I slept. I trusted him about as much as I trusted a highwayman. "We are not children anymore."

"No, we are not," he said. "May I speak candidly?"

"I would prefer it." The sooner he got on with it, the sooner he would leave and I could resume packing.

Damon looked about to say something when a light pelting sound came from the window.

No! I hurried over and pushed back the curtain. Rain. If it continued for long, the roads would become soaked and our journey home would be delayed. I said a quick prayer that the rain would stop, and then I let the curtain fall closed and turned back to my unwanted visitor.

"Something occurred to me last night during dinner," Damon said.

"What is that?"

Damon rubbed his jaw. "I will tell you, but first, answer me this: why did you come to Summerhaven?"

He knew exactly why I'd come. How ungentlemanly of him to ask me to voice it. "Because your mother invited me."

"Yes, I know, but why did *you* accept her invitation?"

"I wanted to be away from the chaos of city life. London can be quite stifling."

He gave me a knowing look. "That is not why you came. You are here because you wish to marry Ollie."

I gasped at his audacity. He well knew that fact to be true, but to say it out loud was beyond the pale. Heat crept up my neck and settled in my cheeks. "My feelings are much changed after last night."

"Would that were true, but alas, your feelings for my addled brother are *not* changed. It is only your pride that has been wounded."

The heat in my cheeks became a roaring fire. "I'd thank you to leave my room now."

"Don't be cross. I did *try* to warn you."

Perhaps he had, though he could have tried a little more intently. "What is it you want?" I asked again.

"Your help."

Doubtful that we could help each other do anything other than go mad, I raised an eyebrow. "How exactly do you want me to help you?"

"I want you to allow *me* to court you."

A most unladylike snort escaped my nose. If I had been sipping tea, I would have spewed it all over his cravat. "You cannot be serious."

"I assure you, I am in earnest."

He was mad.

"You have as much interest in courting me as you do the stable boy," I said.

"My plan *is* still brilliant."

"Except that I have about as much interest in being courted by you as I do in a horse."

"That would make you an exception to the rule."

I rolled my eyes. "Humility is not a virtue you possess, my lord."

"Lords have little use for humility." He shrugged. "Now please allow me to explain the brilliance of my plan before your maid returns."

I glanced at the door, remembering once again that we were alone. Should anyone happen to pass by and overhear our conversation . . . Well, that would be very bad indeed. For my reputation. For Damon's. Oh dear. Where *was* Nora?

"Go on then." I urged him to hurry.

"My father is intent that I marry by the year's end. He's seen fit to parade every eligible young woman in this part of the country in front of me in hopes I'll choose a wife. But if I pretend you have caught my eye, that I intend to court you, then I would not have to court another, you see."

"Oh yes. I *do* see." Only two nights earlier, Lord Winfield made clear his expectation that Damon not only dance with eligible young women but eventually marry one—a grim eventuality for a man content in his bachelorhood. "But I will only be here a short time. When I leave, you will be no better off than you are now. Your father will still demand you court and marry another young woman, will he not?"

Damon shrugged, and I tried not to notice how his broad shoulders strained against the seams of his coat. "Much can change in a short period of time."

"Perhaps," I said, though I thought it rather unlikely. "But I still don't see how our pretending to court would help *me*."

"You wound me." Damon held one hand to his chest. "But to answer your question, Ollie has always wanted what's mine," Damon said simply. "If he thought *you* were mine—"

I held up my hand, stopping him. "Ollie is not so juvenile."

Damon laughed a little. "Unless I'm mistaken, Ollie only came around to you *after* we'd danced at the Rumfords' ball."

I bit my lip. It was true that Ollie had come to ask me to dance after Damon and I had danced the supper set, but wasn't that because he'd felt bad for casting me aside earlier that evening?

"My hypothesis," Damon persisted, "is that when Ollie sees us spending time together, he will become green with envy, just like at the ball, and he will rush in to steal you away from me."

"There is only one problem with your plan."

"Only one?" He laughed, his voice deep and rich. "Pray tell me."

"We don't *like* each other."

"I like you just fine, Miss Kent. That said, many couples don't like each other."

"That may be, but such courtships are generally based on mutual benefit." I returned to the window and pulled back the curtain. The rain fell in sheets now. Water flooded the gardens and walking paths. Even if the rain stopped this moment—which it seemed it would not—the roads would be too wet to travel today. Defeated, I sat on the window seat and crossed my arms in frustration.

"I see you're not convinced," he said.

"It is good to know your eyesight is working properly."

Damon stood from the vanity and walked to the window seat. "My plan *would* work, Hannah."

"It would not." I stood from the window seat and pushed past him. "Don't be absurd."

"Absurd?" He followed me to my trunk. "To say that your affections could have moved on to Ollie's titled and obviously more handsome older brother? Yes. That *would* be absurd."

I shook my head. "Nobody would believe our courtship."

"The Rumfords' ball was a good demonstration of my preference for you, was it not?"

Had he been planning this scheme all along? I stopped packing and met his gaze. "Is that why you asked me to dance?"

"No," he said flatly. "But that doesn't mean it can't work in our favor."

"Must I spell it out for you? No one would believe that *you*—a titled gentleman—would be interested in *me*—a woman of no consequence. Perhaps if I stood to inherit a substantial fortune, but I do not."

"Not all marriages are based upon mutual financial benefit. What if what people saw was a love match?"

"I'm no great beauty." I looked at my slippers.

"If you believe that, perhaps you should have *your* eyesight checked."

I heaved a sigh, increasingly tired of his fictive flirtations. I felt bad for all the women he'd ever pretended to be interested in. He no doubt had a string of broken hearts from here to London.

I frowned at the thought. Even *I* would have believed him sincere in his attentions.

What if Damon's plan could work? What if Damon pretending to court me could turn Ollie's head? I bit my lip. But if his plan didn't work, then I'd be stuck here all summer, forced to watch Ollie fall in love with another woman— the most *beautiful* woman he'd ever seen. I could think of nothing worse.

"You look as if you're about to reject your breakfast," Damon said.

"I suppose it's fortunate for your boots that I did not make it down to the breakfast room this morning."

"Quite," Damon said, then he waited silently for my answer.

Part of me wanted to stay, but . . . I didn't wish to have to *fight* for Ollie's affection. I wanted him to love me simply because he loved me. I wanted what my parents had, the type of love that just exists.

I couldn't do it. I couldn't pretend to be interested in Damon in hopes of winning Ollie. I'd barely made it through last night's ball. There was no way I would be able to endure an entire summer of the same. It was impossible.

"I'm sorry, but I'm going to go home with Papa as soon as the weather permits."

Damon nodded curtly and walked toward the door. At the threshold, he paused. "I didn't think you had it in you to give up so easily."

His words stung, but they did not change my mind.

"I don't believe your plan will work," I explained.

"Let me show you that it will." He glanced down the corridor, then stepped back into the room. "We will stage an experiment. Tonight, after dinner. I'll demonstrate my preference for you, and you will respond to my advances. I will prove to you that a pretend attachment between us will open Ollie's eyes to you. If my plan works, you stay. If it doesn't—"

"I leave." I pondered his proposal. I didn't want to stay here another night, but I didn't have a choice. "Forgive me if I'm wary of your experiments." I smoothed the ringlets framing my face behind my ears.

"I saved you at Rumfords' ball. You owe me this much."

I narrowed my gaze at him. "I owe you nothing. One measly set does not make up for an entire childhood of torture."

"Torture?"

I glanced purposefully at my trunk, then trained my gaze on him. "I could hardly call it otherwise."

A muscle in Damon's jaw ticked. "Call it what you will. The fact remains that until the rain stops and the roads have dried, you are stuck here."

He was right. And I had to admit, curiosity tugged at my mind. If his experiment failed, I lost nothing. But if it succeeded, I stood to gain everything. Slowly, I nodded. "You have one night."

CHAPTER SEVEN

LATER THAT AFTERNOON, MY TRUNK was packed, and I paced the length of my bedchamber, my mind alternating between replaying events from the ball with Ollie and my conversation with Damon. No matter how hard I tried, I couldn't make sense of anything that had transpired. Not Ollie's denying me our dance and certainly not the ridiculous charade Damon had suggested.

"You're going to wear a hole in your slippers, miss." Nora warily eyed my feet from her seat at the vanity.

"If I come to a resolution, it will have been worth it."

Nora sighed and returned to her mending.

I resumed my pacing. My thoughts were in such a knot that I didn't think I'd ever untangle them. Ollie had barely glanced in my direction all through the night before, and when he had, it had been without affection. If only I could make him see me, he would realize that I was as worthy a marriage prospect as any other young lady, better even because we had a solid foundation, an entire lifetime of shared memories.

Though I hated to admit it, Damon was correct; I didn't have it in me to give up on Ollie so easily.

I stopped in the center of the room.

Nora looked at me hopefully.

"I'm going for a walk." And with any luck, I'd find Ollie, and we would sort out this misunderstanding.

"An excellent idea, miss." She sounded more than a little relieved to be free of me, and I tried not to take it to heart.

I stepped into the corridor and shut the door gently behind me. Now, where would Ollie be at this hour? It was late enough that he would have already taken his morning ride, so I didn't think he was outdoors, but my search of the library, drawing room, and conservatory also proved in vain. The only place I didn't search was Ollie's bedchamber because despite what Damon thought, that would have been highly improper.

In the entry hall, I stopped a housemaid. "Excuse me," I said. "Do you know where Mr. Oliver Jennings might be?"

"He is away, miss. Has been since early this morn."

"Do you know when he will return?" I asked.

"I couldn't say, miss." She bobbed a curtsy before continuing on her way.

Dejected, I returned to my room, much to Nora's chagrin, and passed the remainder of the afternoon with a book.

My hands shook at my sides as I stepped into the drawing room. Perhaps I should not have agreed to Damon's experiment. If only I could blend into the brocade walls. Alas, I could only search for a safe place to stand.

Ollie sat with his mother on the sofa, and they were speaking in hushed conversation—I hoped she was giving him a scolding for his atrocious behavior last night.

I thought to take comfort with Papa, but he and Lord Winfield appeared to be deep in discussion. I glanced at Damon, worried that the moment he saw me, his little experiment would begin, but he sat in an armchair, engrossed in the thickly bound evergreen book again. There appeared to be no ready companion for me, and for the first time in my life, I didn't feel as if I had a place at Summerhaven.

I walked farther into the room, and a floorboard squeaked beneath my foot.

Lady Winfield looked up and smiled at me in greeting, then gave Ollie a stern look.

With a nod, he squared his shoulders and made his way over to me like a petulant child. He bowed formally, and I begrudged him a curtsy. Ollie straightened, looking as uncomfortable as I felt. Before either of us could speak, a servant appeared at the door and announced dinner.

"May I escort you to dinner?" He held out his arm to me.

I wanted to refuse him but didn't want Lady Winfield to think poorly of me, so I lightly rested my hand over his, and we took our place at the rear of the procession.

"I trust you had a nice day," Ollie said as we walked.

Was he in earnest? If he thought I was content to brush all that had transpired at the ball between us under the rug, he was mistaken.

"No," I said. "I did not have a good day."

Ollie looked at me with surprise.

We had relative privacy at the back of the group, but I still kept my voice low when I said, "Surely you understand why."

He swallowed hard. Ollie had never liked confrontation, always preferring lighthearted jokes and smiles to serious talk and frowns. And today was no different.

"*Do* you understand the implications of your actions on me?" I asked again.

He tugged at his collar. "I was not thinking last night."

"Had Damon not been there—" I shook my head. "I should hate to even think about what gossip would now be circulating about me."

"I did not mean to hurt you."

"But you *did* hurt me."

"I am sorry." Ollie's remorse caused me to soften, and more than anything, I wanted to forgive him. But before I could move on, I needed to understand why he'd acted the way he had. I tugged his arm, slowing us to a stop in the corridor.

"Have you no explanation?" I pressed.

Ollie watched the others file into the dining hall, nodded for the butler to hold the door, and when we were alone, he faced me. "I . . . suppose I didn't appreciate Mother forcing us to dance."

"You felt *forced* to dance with me?"

"No," he said quickly. "It's not that I didn't *want* to dance with you, I did, but I must make every effort to secure the best future for myself."

Though I wanted to argue that *I* was the best future for him, I'd asked him for clarity, and he'd given it to me plainly. He didn't see me as his best option for the future. There was nothing more to say. I pulled my arm from his and turned toward the dining room.

"Hannah," Ollie called after me, but I didn't turn back. It was too painful. He stood so close but was so far out of reach. Why had he even invited me to come to Summerhaven? Perhaps he hadn't. Perhaps Lady Winfield had acted of her own accord and invited me without his knowledge or permission.

No. I pushed away the thought. Ollie, whatever his faults, had wanted me to come to Summerhaven, even if only as a friend.

Dinner passed in an unending blur of conversation. I kept my head down as I ate so I wouldn't be called upon to participate. I just wanted this night to be over. If only Mama were here to comfort and guide me.

When at last the meal was finished, Lady Winfield and I withdrew to the drawing room. "You were quiet this evening, my dear."

"I apologize for not being better company. I confess I am still exhausted from last night's ball."

Lady Winfield nodded kindly. "Is there anything I can do to make you more comfortable?"

I shook my head. She looked as if she wanted to say more, but I was grateful she made no further attempt to pull me into conversation. I would have been unable to set aside my emotions long enough to string more than a few words together.

Not long after we sat, the men joined us in the drawing room. Ollie continued past me, taking up residence by the hearth, and Damon lingered somewhere behind. How long did I need to stay before excusing myself?

"Dinner was delicious," Papa said to Lord Winfield as they sat in armchairs opposite the sofa.

Lord Winfield beamed with obvious pride. "Our chef is from France. I believe he even studied under the same master as the prince regent's chef. Isn't that right, my dear?"

"I hardly remember," Lady Winfield said modestly. "Shall we have some music on the pianoforte this evening?"

I glanced at the grand pianoforte on the opposite side of the room and tensed, worried she would ask me to play.

"Splendid idea," Lord Winfield agreed a bit too heartily, and he coughed. "I would be delighted to hear you play, my dear."

My shoulders relaxed in relief.

"You have never heard her superior, Kent."

Papa's face fell. Mama had been as talented at the piano as she was lovely. How I missed her melodies.

"What song will you delight us with tonight?" Lord Winfield asked his wife.

"We shall see what speaks to me." Lady Winfield sifted through some music sheets and selected a lively sonata. Mozart. One of Mama's favorites. I wondered if Lady Winfield knew.

Papa and Lord Winfield listened for a short while, then resumed their speaking.

Unguarded, my gaze wandered to Ollie, his handsome profile highlighted by the firelight.

"Miss Kent?" Damon stepped in front of me, blocking my view, and he raised an eyebrow.

"I'm sorry. What did you say?"

"I asked if you would care to join me in a game of chess." He gestured to a small table where a chessboard was set. Damon's gaze flickered to Ollie and then back to me.

Ah yes. The experiment. I had momentarily forgotten.

After the clarity Ollie had provided me in the corridor before dinner, I hardly felt up to it. I opened my mouth to tell him as much, but Ollie spoke first. "She doesn't want to play with you, Damon."

Mother's temper flared within me. "On the contrary," I said. "A game of chess sounds delightful."

Ollie's nose crinkled. "But you hate games of chance."

"Chess is not a game of chance. It's one of strategy, one I very much enjoy given the right opponent." I didn't actually consider Damon the right opponent for me, but Ollie had no right to speak for me, and he needed to know it.

Ollie resumed his place at the hearth, and Damon led me to the table and assisted me with my chair.

"What manners," I said. "Thank you."

"I know this may be surprising to you, but some women find me charming." Damon walked around the table and settled into his seat.

"You are correct," I said.

"That I'm charming?"

"No." I laughed. "That I find it surprising."

With a frown, Damon pointed at my side of the board. "White goes first."

"As I'm well aware. You have no need to explain the rules." I'd gotten enough practice playing the game while Mama had lain in her sickbed.

Damon held up his hands in surrender, relaxing back into his seat.

I studied the ebony and ivory squares, considering my first move. The chessmen laid before me were made of ivory; intricately turned and carved, they were lovely to distraction. The king and queen were adorned with reticulated crowns and surmounted by fleur-de-lis finials. The rooks, bishops, and pawns, though simply designed with rounded bases and simple collars, were equally becoming. But the detailed knight and its windswept mane captivated my attention.

"Do you know the history of this game?" Damon asked.

"No." I moved one of my pawns two spaces forward. "But I expect you're about to tell me." Damon, always having his nose stuck in a book, had a wealth of random bits of useless knowledge. I'd forgotten that about him.

"Indeed." He perused the board. "There was once a tyrannical king of India. A wise man wanted to show the king that each person in his kingdom had value: pawns, rooks, bishops, knights, kings, and so he invented this game."

"A revolutionary concept."

"That each person has value?" he asked. "Is it?"

"I daresay only *half* the population is assigned to any legal value, and then only the noble and great ones have a voice."

"I suppose you're correct." Damon moved his knight. "But it should not be so."

My forehead tightened. Did he really think that all people, regardless of their sex or station, should have a say in their government? I believed it to be so, but for a future peer of the realm to think so, well, that *would* be revolutionary. I searched his face for answers, but his expression was as stony as the cobblestone streets in London. I must have misunderstood him; such a belief would not serve a man in his position. I returned my gaze to the board.

"Don't look now," Damon said, "but it seems our experiment is working. Ollie is beside himself with jealousy."

"Truly?" I started to turn.

"I said *don't* look," Damon snapped. He stole another glance, then nodded to me when it was safe.

I peeked over my shoulder. Ollie glared at the fire, his mouth turned down and brow creased. He looked miserable. As miserable as me. With a heavy heart, I turned back to the game and made a mindless move.

Damon *tsked*, then unrepentantly captured one of my bishops. He placed the intricately carved knight on the square where my bishop had been.

We continued alternating moves. I'd capture one of Damon's pawns, and then he'd claim two of mine. He was infuriatingly good at this game. I needed to be more focused.

I studied the board for a long moment, but there was nothing for it. Until I set my mind at ease, I could do little more than offer up sacrifices to Damon. "Do you really think Ollie will marry Miss Digby?"

"Her or someone like her," Damon said absently. "If you leave now, he will have no reason not to."

Though I'd tried to convince myself otherwise, Damon spoke the truth. Ollie was nothing if not single-minded, and it seemed he had a mind to pursue and marry Miss Digby. Unless I did something to prevent it—like drive him mad with jealousy and make him realize his feelings for me.

Perhaps Damon's scheme wasn't so ridiculous after all.

I didn't wish to make Ollie feel bad, but I hated the thought of my best friend falling in love with another woman even more. We were perfect for each other in every way; he'd only forgotten because of the time and distance we'd been parted. If it took a little jealousy to make him see reason, to see *me*, then perhaps scheming was worth the discomfort.

Could I trust Damon though? As a child I'd trusted him, and I had been devastated. But what choice did I have? If I left, Ollie would marry another. If I stayed, I gave us a chance.

I had no choice.

"Does your offer still stand?" I asked Damon.

"Yes." He didn't even hesitate.

"You must desperately wish to avoid marriage. Is the institution so bad that you'd truly welcome this arrangement?"

"You have no idea the lengths I'd go to subvert my father."

I did not understand, but I supposed I didn't need to. Damon had his reasons for entering into this ruse, and I had mine. So long as we both played our parts well, that was all that mattered.

"Then perhaps we should discuss the terms," I said.

Damon's gaze snapped up to mine. "You needn't worry over trifles. I shall be the most doting beau."

"Until you are not," I said. "I do believe the siren song of the card tables may prove too strong a temptation for you to keep your promises."

Damon's gaze narrowed. "You think so little of me?"

I lifted one shoulder. "Half a dozen ladies at Lord Rumford's ball tried to catch your eye, yet you did not dance with a single one."

"I danced with you, did I not?"

"You *rescued* me. It is different."

"Hmm." Damon refocused his attention on our game.

I shifted in my seat. I hardly thought Damon would care about such a label. Though it hadn't been my intention to insult him, to insinuate a gentleman was a scoundrel *was* offensive.

"You are a man," I explained. "And I've learned of late that a man's heart is as changeable as the weather in England."

Damon sat back in his seat. "Ollie's heart had little to do with his decision, I'm afraid."

"Yes, well. Forgive me if I don't want to be slighted by both Jennings men in one summer." My reputation, let alone my heart, couldn't bear it.

"I would never. But to ease your mind, we should promise to only have eyes for one another. I will not entertain advances from other women, and you won't fawn over Ollie."

"I do not *fawn*." I scowled at Damon over the chessboard and made another move.

"You do," he said, "but you must not if this is to work. You and I must appear to be interested only in each other."

I frowned. "If we only have eyes for each other, then how will I encourage Ollie to propose?"

"You won't have to encourage him," Damon said. "In having eyes only for me, you will drive Ollie so mad with jealousy that it would be impossible for him to not recognize the depth of his feelings for you. I expect he will be so besotted with you by the end of summer that you will receive the engagement you desire."

"And what happens to you when our charade is over? If you were to pretend to court me, and then I refuse you for your younger brother, people would talk. No mother in her right mind would allow her daughter within a hundred paces of you."

"That is the point," he said.

"And what would *your* mother think?" I pressed.

"You have no need to worry. All's well that ends well."

He quoted Shakespeare, in hopes of putting me at ease. But I'd read enough of his plays to know that the course of true love never did run smooth. This was an ill-advised plan . . . but what other option remained?

"You must promise me, Damon. You can't reject me when this arrangement of ours no longer suits you. Being courted and then rejected by an earl—"

"I am not an earl," Damon interrupted.

"Not yet, but you will be. And should you show interest in me and then snub me, that would be enough to ruin my reputation."

Damon sobered. "I'd sooner marry you. You have my word as a gentleman; the responsibility of ending our ruse will be left to you alone to execute."

"Then I agree to your terms."

"I promise you won't regret this," he said.

I could only hope that proved true. It felt dangerous and wrong to enter into this agreement but also thrilling.

Damon looked deep into my eyes, and warmth washed over me. "Check."

My gaze flashed to the board. He had me cornered. I searched for a way to extricate myself and save the game, but there was nothing for it. I made my final move.

"Never underestimate a dark knight, Miss Kent," Damon said, and he claimed my king.

"Ollie would have let me win." I frowned.

"I am not Ollie."

"As I'm well aware."

He looked directly at me. "Winning is worth very little when not earned. You should always strive to play the game with a worthy opponent or you will have wasted your time."

I only stared at him.

"I see you're at a loss for words. Perhaps your mouth is too dry from gaping at Ollie all night to form words. As a gentleman, allow me to fetch you a drink." Damon stood, and I tried not to scowl at his back as he walked to the sideboard.

"I'm sorry you had to endure him for so long."

I flinched in my seat. I hadn't even heard Ollie approach. "Don't be," I said, trying to compose myself. "Your brother is quite good at chess."

"Yes, well. He cheats." Ollie sat in the seat Damon had vacated.

"I don't doubt it."

Our conversation fell silent. And as glad as I was that he'd finally sought me out, I didn't know *why* he'd sought me out. "Is there something you wanted?"

Ollie straightened his cravat. "I don't like what's passed between us. Can we set it aside and be friends again?"

Friends. The word brought fresh pain to my already festering wound. I reset the pieces on the chessboard for no other reason than to occupy my hands and my mind.

Not a moment too soon, Damon returned with my drink. I took the cup and checked for frogs or other creeping things before taking a sip.

Damon grinned.

"Thank you."

"You are most welcome. Now if I may be so bold, this morning you mentioned you'd like to ride the hills. Seeing as the rain has stopped, I would be honored if you would allow me to accompany you tomorrow afternoon."

I listened for the faint sound of rain, but heard nothing. How long ago it had stopped, I hadn't the faintest clue. "If the ground is dry enough, I would like that very much."

Ollie leaned forward, resting his elbows on the chessboard. "I had hoped we could walk in the gardens."

My emotions tugged at my heartstrings. I wanted desperately to stroll in the garden with him, but even more, I wanted to walk down an aisle to him one day.

I glanced at Damon. He had proved the thesis of his experiment true. With Damon's attention on me, Ollie was green with envy. But if I agreed to this charade, from this point forward, there would be no going back. I would be saddled with Damon for six excruciating weeks. But it was the only chance Ollie and I had.

"I'm sorry, Ollie, but I prefer to ride with Damon tomorrow."

"Perhaps I will join you then."

"I'm not sure that is wise," I forced myself to say. "I want to ride as long as the weather permits, and I know you have been quite consumed with your *business* affairs in town. I would not wish to waylay you should another business concern suddenly arise again."

Ollie clenched his jaw. "Of course." He stood abruptly, his chair scraping across the floor, drawing the attention of our parents across the room, and then with a quick bow, he quit the room.

"I think that went rather well, don't you?" Damon said once Ollie was out of earshot.

"I hardly know," I said, but I had the distinct impression that I was about to find out.

CHAPTER EIGHT

THE NEXT MORNING, THE ROADS were dry enough for Papa to travel home. Though I wished he could delay his journey, he needed to return to London and care for his parishioners. Still, as he climbed into the carriage, my heart clenched. This was the first time in my life that I would be without either of my parents to guide me.

I watched Papa's carriage disappear down the lane, then joined the family in the breakfast room.

"Lady Rumford and her daughter are coming to tea today," Lady Winfield said.

"Oh . . . how nice," I said, but in truth, I'd been so consumed with thoughts of Ollie, and with my plan with Damon, that I'd forgotten Lady Winfield's invitation to Lady Rumford and her daughter. Though I wanted things right with Miss Atherton, I fretted over what was bound to be an uncomfortable afternoon.

What she must think of me. I'd told her that I had no interest in Damon, but the events of that night certainly didn't convey as much. And things would likely only grow worse between us once she learned of my and Damon's courtship. Perhaps I could delay the conversation until I'd had adequate time to consider what to say to her.

"Lady Winfield," I said, "I must confess, I'd forgotten about Lady Rumford and her daughter coming to tea."

"Not to worry. There will be plenty of time to ready yourself before they arrive."

"Yes, of course. It is only . . ." I glanced at Damon across the table, hoping he would tell his mother about our plans to ride on horseback, but he was too busy with his breakfast to even notice my predicament. What good was my partner in crime if he refused to come to my aid? "Damon invited me to ride the hills on horseback this morning."

"Oh," Lady Winfield said, sounding surprised, and her gaze moved between Damon and me.

Lord Winfield lowered *The Morning Post*, the crisp paper crinkling in his hands, and he looked from me to his eldest son. "I am afraid *Damon* is unavailable, Miss Kent."

My cheeks heated. Lord Winfield prided himself on formality, and I'd called his son, his *heir*, by his Christian name.

I bit my lip, embarrassed to have made such a blunder, and Damon smiled so wide it was a wonder his teeth didn't fall out. I shot him a censuring glare, and he turned to his father. "I don't recall being previously engaged, Father. You must excuse me from the meeting as I have urgent business of my own this morning."

"More important than seeing to matters of your future estate?" Lord Winfield coughed into his napkin. "No. You will reschedule your business and attend my morning meeting with Mr. Bancroft."

"I'd rather not," Damon said.

"Must I compel you in *all* matters?"

Damon's grip tightened around his fork. "No."

"Quite right," Lord Winfield said, then he stabbed a piece of breakfast meat and chewed, effectively ending their conversation.

Lady Winfield gave her son a sorrowful look, then turned to me. "You should probably stay in residence anyway, my dear. You caused quite a stir at the ball, and I shouldn't be surprised if you have a caller or two of your own today."

Ollie choked on a biscuit. "Sorry, Mother." He grabbed a cup of juice and swallowed a gulp. "I bit off more than I could chew."

"We've all noticed," Lady Winfield said, her voice full of displeasure.

Breakfast continued without further incident, although no one was in a particularly pleasant mood, except for Lady Winfield, who was excited about Lady Rumford and Miss Atherton coming to tea.

As soon as our meal was finished, I retired to my room to change into something more appropriate for entertaining company.

Nora selected a pale-green dress with tiny white rosebuds embroidered on the bodice.

As she pinned up my hair, I worried about what to say to Miss Atherton. She'd been so kind to me at the ball, and I'd hoped we could be friends. All my life, I'd wanted a friend to confide in the way Mama had with Lady Winfield. I'd always longed for a close friendship like they'd shared, never realizing how unique their friendship was until I'd grown.

"You're quiet this morning," Nora said, setting a hairpin into my curls.

"This visit has not gone entirely to plan. I have much to think on."

"Mr. Jennings?"

"He's at the center of my troubles, yes." Although it was my ruse with Damon that was currently causing me problems.

"He seems like a good man, but even good men have lapses in judgment. He will come 'round. You'll see."

"I hope you are right."

When Nora was done with my hair, I thanked her, then made my way downstairs to the drawing room, where Lady Winfield waited.

Lady Rumford and Miss Atherton arrived at a quarter to three. The butler led them promptly into the drawing room.

Once we were all seated, Lady Winfield asked the housekeeper to bring in the tea service. As she poured, the matrons spoke about the upcoming social events and other trivial matters. Not once did Miss Atherton look at me.

I twisted mother's emerald ring on my finger. I needed to come up with an excuse to pull Miss Atherton away so we could talk, and I needed to do it quickly, for I did not know when another opportunity to speak in private would present itself.

As we continued to sip our tea and converse, I glanced about the room. My gaze landed on a painting of a landscape. It was not unique enough as to require further inspection, but it would have to do.

"Miss Atherton, there is a lovely painting on the other side of the room that I would love to show you. Will you join me?"

"Of course," she said politely, but she took her time setting her teacup on the saucer.

"You've said very little today," I said as we crossed the room.

"Yes, well, you have taught me a valuable lesson on the virtues of keeping to myself. I must compliment you, Miss Kent. You are a talented actress."

"I promise I'm not. Though I *am* striving to be."

"I don't understand."

We stopped and stood in front of a painting of a landscape. "It is true what I told you at the ball; Ollie is my dearest friend and the man I hope to marry."

"I don't believe you." She frowned. "I saw how you and Lord Jennings danced the supper set. You stood so close to one another, and he spoke to you every chance he had."

"I understand how it looked, but you are mistaken. Damon came to my rescue. He was only being a gentleman."

"What happened at the ball that you would need rescuing?"

It would hurt to speak of it, but it was the only way to make her understand the truth. "Ollie refused his set with me in favor of another woman, Miss Digby. Damon saw the slight and asked me to dance."

Miss Atherton's face fell. "I'm sorry. I didn't know. I haven't heard a whisper of gossip."

"I am not surprised. Anything Damon does has a way of overshadowing Ollie's actions."

"I must admit, it's odd to hear you call Lord Jennings by his Christian name."

I grimaced. "I probably should not call him by his Christian name, but it is a habit not easily broken, I'm afraid. He and I have been friends—*er*, adversaries since we were children."

"I'm relieved to hear that. Not that I wish you to be *adversaries*, but—" She shook her head. "I am sorry for what you endured at the ball. I likely did not make your night any easier."

"Thank you," I said, and as tempted as I was to leave my confession at that, if Miss Atherton and I were ever to become true friends, then she needed to know the whole of it. Confiding in her involved some risk, but wasn't it vulnerability that made Mama's and Lady Winfield's friendship so special?

"There's more," I said, taking a step closer and lowering my voice. "Before I tell you though, I must know that I can trust you to keep my secret."

"You can trust me," Miss Atherton said.

With a nod, I took a steadying breath and said, "Damon isn't ready to enter into marriage."

Her face softened, and she laughed lightly. "That is hardly a secret."

"Perhaps not, but in the coming weeks, it may *appear* as though he's ready to marry."

"Oh?"

"Damon's asked my permission to court me."

Her eyes widened.

"It is only a charade," I added quickly, "to appease his father so he won't have to court another young lady and marry before he is ready."

"But what of your feelings for his brother?" she asked.

I quickly explained how Damon's plan aided my desire to catch Ollie's eye. "That is—"

"Ill-advised, I know. Do you hate me?" I asked.

Her delayed response did little to comfort me. If she didn't approve of my and Damon's plan, would she tell others?

"I don't hate you. In fact, it's rather refreshing to have an honest friend. Not many exist, you know."

"I *do* know, which is why, after the kindness you showed me at the ball, I couldn't bear you thinking poorly of me. I want us to be friends."

"As do I. You can't know how difficult it was to sit through supper across from you and Lord Jennings. The way he looked at you—"

"He was teasing me. There's nothing I can't palate more than frog legs."

"And he made you eat them." A hand flew to her mouth, to hide her amusement. "I'm sorry," she said through a giggle. "I'm only so relieved. I thought I had been betrayed all over again."

"Again?"

The humor drained from Miss Atherton's eyes, and she glanced over her shoulder at the sofa, where her mother and Lady Winfield sipped tea. "It is all rather embarrassing." She moved closer. "During my first Season, my dearest friend, Rose, fancied herself something of a matchmaker. All Season, she conspired to pull me and a Mr. Wheaton together; she dragged me to every ball, tea, and opera."

"Did you fancy him?" I asked.

"Not in the beginning, but Rose convinced me that Mr. Wheaton was half in love with me, and with each clandestine meeting, I fell in love with him. By the end of the Season, I fully expected him to declare his suit. Instead, he confessed he'd fallen in love with Rose and that she loved him as well. They were married last fall."

"Oh, Miss Atherton." I touched her arm. "I'm so sorry."

"No need for pity." She smiled. "I gave my heart to a man who didn't deserve it, but I've recovered, and I won't make the same mistake twice."

"I believe you won't," I said. Miss Atherton had such an air of strength and determination about her.

She raised her chin. "That is why I have set my sights on Lord Jennings. He has no interest in love, so my heart will be in no danger of breaking."

She spoke the right words, but to lose the man she loved to her closest friend? I couldn't imagine anything worse. "Why does it have to be this way between women? Always a competition."

She lifted one shoulder, then let it fall heavily back in place. "Friendship seems to be a luxury only *married* women can afford."

"Until they have daughters of their own," I said. "Then the race for the most eligible son-in-law begins."

"I had not thought of that. I suppose we'd better pray for sons. Then we shall have all the friends in the world—friends with daughters, that is."

"Oh, Miss Atherton." I giggled.

She shook her head. "We are friends now, so you must call me Amelia."

"I would like nothing more, so long as *you* call *me* Hannah."

"It is settled. Now then, I can't say I agree with your plan," Miss Atherton—or rather, Amelia—said. "But if you love Mr. Jennings as much as you claim to, then I can't fault you for trying to win him back by any means available. Lord Jennings's ruse included." She paused and tucked my hand into the crook of her elbow. "As your friend, I'll do all I can to help you."

"Truly?"

Amelia nodded. "We women need to stick together. And I should also like to be around when your ruse with Lord Jennings comes to an end." She winked.

I smiled. Amelia had set her mind to a loveless marriage, but one of mutual benefit. I wondered, though, was this what she really wanted? There had to be a man out there somewhere who could make her believe in love again. A gentleman she could love as much as I loved Ollie.

"Amelia," Lady Rumford called. "What are you and Miss Kent chattering on about? Your tea is getting cold, and you've not even touched your cake. Come sit."

"Yes, Mama."

Amelia and I walked back to the sofa and sat.

Lady Rumford nodded, pleased. "I was just telling Lady Winfield about our trip to the modiste."

"Mama's enamored with the new shipment of muslin," Amelia said. "She is set on ordering a blue print, but I am in love with the yellow."

Lady Rumford sighed over her teacup. "Yellow is a lovely color, dear, but the particular shade you've set your heart on is more fitting for a child than a woman trying to attract a husband."

"You see the predicament," Amelia said to me.

"Perhaps Lady Winfield and Miss Kent will join us at the modiste's tomorrow so we can finally settle this debate and purchase the blue," Lady Rumford said.

"A splendid idea," Lady Winfield said. "I should like to spoil Hannah."

"As would I, Mother," a deep voice said behind us.

I quickly turned in my seat, and my gaze flashed to the threshold of the drawing room. Damon leaned against the doorframe, his gaze intent upon me. A flush crept up my neck.

"Please excuse my son, Lady Rumford. He seems to have lost his manners."

"It is true." Damon walked into the room, riding crop in hand. "They have been misplaced for quite some time. However, I'm doing my best to locate them. In fact, that's why I've come. I'm hoping Miss Kent is available now to join me for our ride and search them out."

Lady Rumford laughed lightly.

But Lady Winfield did not look amused. Her brows pulled together, forming a delicate V on her forehead. "I believe your father wished for you to be present for his meeting with Mr. Bancroft."

"It is already finished."

"Well, as you can see, we still have company."

"Oh no," Amelia said. "Don't let us keep you. Mother and I wanted to explore the garden before the weather turns again."

"We did?" Lady Rumford asked her daughter.

"Yes, Mama. Don't you remember? We spoke this morning about how lovely the blooms are this time of year."

"Oh, yes." Lady Rumford chuckled uncomfortably. "How could I have forgotten?"

Damon's eyes narrowed on me.

I'd hoped not to have to tell him that I had let Amelia in on our secret, but now it was inevitable.

"I suppose a ride would be fine," Lady Winfield agreed.

"Well then. It's settled." Damon tucked the crop under one arm and held out the other to beckon me. "Miss Kent?"

I rose from my seat to join him, and as we left the drawing room, he leaned close. "I believe you have some explaining to do, Miss Kent."

CHAPTER NINE

I DID NOT HURRY TO change into my riding habit. The longer I took to get ready, the more I delayed explaining to Damon why I'd told Amelia about our charade.

When I finally emerged, Damon already waited at the bottom of the grand staircase. "Ah, Miss Kent. There you are." He wore shades of gray and brown that might have looked plain on another man, but not on Damon; the earth-toned clothes complimented his dark, thick hair and highlighted the unusual warmth of his blue eyes. "I was beginning to think you'd changed your mind about joining me for a ride."

"Not at all, my lord. A woman just needs time to prepare."

"Napoleon could have prepared an entire regiment for war in the time it took you to get ready."

"Napoleon." I gaped at Damon's vile comparison. "You don't truly mean to compare me to such an abhorrent man as *Napoleon*, do you?"

Damon's mouth quirked into an amused grin. "The analogy felt appropriate." He gave me an unrepentant shrug.

With a frown, I turned on my heel to walk back up the stairs. We'd agreed to help one another, but that didn't mean I had to tolerate his poor manners.

"You don't want to do that," Damon said.

I slowed my step but didn't stop. "Don't I?" I tossed the words over my shoulder.

"No. I've had a stallion prepared for your particular use."

Excitement bubbled within me, but it wasn't enough to overcome my pride. He'd compared me to Napoleon, for pity's sake!

Damon cleared his throat. "And if that's not enough to tempt you into joining me for a ride, I have it on good authority that Ollie's had a groom prepare his horse."

"Oh?" I stopped.

Damon nodded. "I expect my brother should be in the stables this very moment." He held out his arm. "Shall we?"

It would take all my forbearance to endure this day in Damon's company, but for a chance to see Ollie, I would endure. With a nod, I descended the stairs and begrudgingly took Damon's arm. And as he held open the door for me to exit, his muscles flexed beneath my hand.

His strength surprised me. As a boy, Damon had not been athletic. He'd never even shown interest in sport, preferring to read books instead. It had been Ollie who climbed trees, swam in the river, and wrestled in the grass. But now, Damon's strength was obvious; his breeches clung to his well-defined calf muscles, and his finely tailored coat fit snugly across his broad shoulders.

"Are your baskets full?" Damon's voice startled me as we passed through the rose garden.

"Pardon?"

"You were woolgathering," he said. "What has commanded your attention so completely?"

"It is nothing." I set my gaze straightforward on the vast expanse of lawn before me, hoping he'd take no notice of my embarrassment, but my cheeks heated as if I had forgotten my bonnet on a midsummer's day.

"You are a terrible liar." He brushed his gloved fingers across my cheek.

I swatted at his hand, pushing him away.

Damon only laughed.

"If you must know, I was only admiring the fine cut of your coat."

Damon glanced at the lapels of his coat and smiled. "Truly terrible." He shook his head. "You should not even try."

I set my gaze on the stable ahead. It had never seemed so far away. Wanting to change the subject, I blurted, "I told Amelia of our arrangement."

"I gathered as much," Damon said. "Though I cannot guess at your strategy. May I ask *why* you told her?"

"She was kind to me at the ball, and we became fast friends," I explained. "It did not feel right keeping this information from her, not after she confided in me."

"What did she confide in you?"

"You must know she has set her cap for you."

"If *that* is your criteria for deciding who should know of our plan, then I fear you will have to tell every young lady in England of our scheme."

I rolled my eyes, and I did not even care that it was unladylike. "You are the most arrogant man with whom I have ever conversed."

Damon said nothing in response. I couldn't guess at his feelings. After some time had passed in silence, I grew uncomfortable.

I cleared my throat. "Are you angry with me for telling Amelia?"

"Anger is a rather unbecoming emotion," Damon said.

"You did not answer my question."

"I am not angry, but I do hope Miss Atherton is a better liar than you have proved."

As did I.

When we finally reached the stable, Damon stopped before we turned the corner to the entrance. He studied my face and frowned.

"What is it?" I touched one hand to my cheek.

"That expression will not do. You must at least *pretend* you are enjoying my company. Perhaps you could smile."

"Perhaps *you* could say something worth smiling about."

He laughed lightly. "I am no Wordsworth, but I could allow you to admire the cut of my coat again. Would that tempt a smile from you?"

My face warmed, and I pressed my lips firmly together.

"Not *quite* the expression I hoped for, but the rosy color in your cheeks should serve our purposes well enough." Damon tucked my hand into the crook of his arm and led me inside the stable house.

Just as Damon predicted, Ollie stood in the long corridor. He didn't look up when we entered. He must not have heard us over his conversation with the groom.

"Brother," Damon called.

Ollie turned. His gaze landed first on Damon, then shifted to me. "I forgot you were riding together today."

Damon's gaze slid to the horses saddled and waiting for us. "I'm surprised our readied horses didn't serve as a reminder."

I wasn't surprised in the least; Ollie had never been very observant. He was always in much too great a hurry to execute whatever mission he was on to give regard to the things around him.

"Yes, well." Ollie cleared his throat. "Seeing as there are two *stallions* saddled, and no gentle mare, I could hardly have been expected to remember."

The groom took a step back, as if worried he had made an error.

"I see no issue," Damon said.

Ollie frowned. "Are you daft? Hannah cannot ride a stallion."

"Whyever not?" I asked.

"Because you are a woman. It is not safe, much less proper."

I gritted my teeth.

"It is plenty safe," Damon said.

"But not proper," Ollie said.

Damon turned to me. "What is your preference? The stallion or the mare?"

"I . . ." My sentence hung in the air. I appreciated that Ollie cared for my safety, but I was also flattered Damon thought me capable of riding such a fine horse. But as flattered as I was, Ollie knew me and my abilities best. With neither the means to invest in riding lessons, nor the time to devote to such a luxury, I'd quite fallen out of the practice since Mama's passing.

"Though I appreciate your faith in me, Damon, Ollie is correct. I'm not so accomplished on horseback. I should be glad to ride the mare."

"A wise and proper choice." Ollie rewarded me with a smile that made my stomach flutter.

"I quite disagree," Damon said, "but if that is what you desire—"

"It is," I said quickly, wanting to put the argument to rest.

"Then I will tell the groom to ready a different mount." Damon released my arm and went to speak with the groom, leaving Ollie and me alone.

For the first time in my life, I didn't know what to say to him. Things between us had never been so uncomfortable, so strained. It was as if I were standing with a stranger. A stranger, that is, who knew all my deepest secrets— save for the secret I kept with his brother.

"I must admit," Ollie said, toeing a pile of hay with his freshly shined boot, "I didn't expect this from you."

"Expect *what* exactly?"

"Your sudden interest in spending time with Damon."

"We have always spent time together. Why would it surprise you now?"

Ollie laughed under his breath. "Because you do not like my brother."

There was that. I'd even told Damon as much. "Perhaps that used to be true, but ever since we danced the supper set at the Rumfords' ball, I've found him to be much more agreeable."

A guilty expression stole over Ollie's face. "How long are you going to be cross with me? I have apologized for not dancing with you."

"One apology does not make everything right between us."

"Neither does avoiding me."

No, but avoiding him was easier than conversing with him at the moment. Not wanting to argue, I moved to step past him and rejoin Damon.

Ollie caught my arm, keeping me at his side. "Of all men," he said, his breath warm against my ear, "why Damon?"

Hurt and confusion saturated his voice, but I could not be moved. I raised my chin and met his gaze, bringing our faces much too near. The truth clawed at my throat, demanding to be set free, but I swallowed against it. It was better he hurt for this small moment than for us both to hurt for the rest of our lives.

"What aren't you telling me, Hanny?" Ollie persisted. "Do you feel obligated to him in some way? Because he danced with you? You must know his intentions aren't honorable."

"I have no reason to believe that. Damon has done nothing untoward."

"I would not say *nothing* untoward."

I jumped at the sound of Damon's voice behind me.

"We should go before the rain begins," Damon said.

I tugged my elbow from Ollie's grasp and followed Damon down the long row of stalls toward the door. Ollie's gaze was hot on my back, but I didn't dare look at him. If I did, I would lose my resolve.

"Why do you do that?" Damon asked after we were out of earshot. "Make yourself small for my brother?"

"I do no such thing."

"You do. When Ollie is near, you talk more softly, you smile more, and forgive me for saying this so bluntly, but it is as if you forget you have an opinion."

"You are wrong," I said, but as he led me to the stableyard, I considered his accusation. When Ollie was around, I *did* have a tendency to be demure, but only because I wanted him to view me as a proper lady. A lady who was soft and kind and gentle. Like Lady Winfield. Like Mama.

Outside in the stableyard, the groom waited with our horses. In one hand, he held the reins of Damon's impressive black stallion—Ares. The animal's sloped, powerful-looking shoulders and muscular body indicated its power, and its thick, glossy mane and low-set tail denoted its elegance.

In the groom's other hand, he held the reins of a chestnut mare—Andromeda. Though a beautiful animal in her own right, she was shorter and smaller, and she did not appear nearly as agile, nor as elegant as Damon's stallion.

With a frown, I walked to the mounting block, and the groom assisted me into the saddle. I looped my legs around the U-shaped horn, then I smoothed my skirt over the horse's back. The groom handed me a crop, and I held it in my hand opposite my legs.

Next to me, Damon slid one foot into the foothold, then swung one leg over the horse's back. The motion was swift, strong, and steady.

I tried to focus my attention on the horse instead of its rider, but it was all but impossible. I looked in the opposite direction and accidentally caught Ollie's gaze.

Behind us, Ollie sat rigidly atop his own horse. He watched Damon and me with a hard stare, then kicked his horse's flanks, riding out of the stableyard.

"Now, where were we?" Damon maneuvered his horse in front of me, blocking my view of Ollie. "Ah yes. I remember. We were discussing your infatuation with my brother."

"*Shh!* " I hissed. Even though Ollie had ridden a considerable distance away, there was a possibility of the wind carrying our words, and I didn't want him to overhear anything.

"I only broach the subject," Damon said undeterred, leading us out of the stableyard, "because the better I understand your feelings for Ollie, the better I can hold up my end of our scheme."

"'Tis *your* scheme, not mine. But to answer your question, there are many things I admire about Ollie."

"Such as?"

"He is . . . thoughtful." It was not the most eloquent of answers, but it *was* true. When Ollie missed our walk the other morning, he'd taken care to bring me back a sprig of lavender—my favorite flower.

Damon nodded. "That particular virtue of his was on full display at the Rumfords' ball."

"*That* was an exception to the rule." I frowned.

"Was it?"

"Yes," I very nearly shouted.

Damon held up his hands in surrender and peered down at me from his high horse. Fitting, I thought.

"Perhaps we should improve the ride with silence." I clicked my tongue, encouraging my horse to put some distance between myself and my unwelcome companion.

"I would rather we speak," Damon said, closing the space between us without noticeable effort. "Can you not think of any other traits you admire in Ollie?"

"Of course I can, but conversing was not part of our deal."

"True enough. Shall we wager for it?"

"Can you not leave gambling to the tables?"

"I can," Damon said, "but for reasons you needn't concern yourself with, I choose not to."

"Then we are at an impasse. I do not wager."

He nodded thoughtfully. "A friendly race then. To the crest." He pointed to the top of a grassy knoll in the distance. "Whoever reaches it first will decide the topic of conversation—or lack thereof—for the rest of our ride."

I glanced at the crest. Normally, a gentle horse such as mine could not compete with a thoroughbred like Damon's. But the crest wasn't far, and I was already a few lengths ahead of him. I tightened my legs around the horn of my saddle.

"I accept." I kicked Andromeda's flank on one side and used my crop on the other to spur her forward.

"Yah!" Damon shouted behind me.

I flicked my wrists, snapping my horse's reins, but her response was half-hearted, her steps slow.

Damon pulled even with me, spared me a grin, then raced ahead.

I leaned forward. "Come on, girl. Faster."

Andromeda increased her speed, but her effort was too little, too late. My mare was no match for a stallion, and Damon crossed our finish line first.

Dash it all!

"Conversation it is," he said smugly as we pulled our horses to a slow walk. "When did you first know you were in love with my brother?"

I had no desire to answer his question, but I wouldn't go back on my word. Besides, the quicker I answered, the sooner we could move on to less-embarrassing questions. "It was the end of my twelfth summer," I said, still a bit winded from our race. "We were standing under the old oak tree saying goodbye; he kissed my hand and then my cheek, and . . . I just knew."

Damon smiled as if amused. "Is that all it takes for you to fall in love with a man? A kiss on your hand?"

"And my cheek."

"Had I known it was so easy." He chuckled under his breath.

"You mock me." I frowned. "You have no doubt given and received many kisses. I probably seem foolish or naive to someone like you."

"Someone like me?" His eyes narrowed.

"An heir to an earldom must have an endless supply of willing women to kiss."

"Ah yes. The title is quite attractive to your sex. Though to be fair, many women find my estate more alluring." Damon laughed lightly, like the fact that women wanted his title more than they wanted him didn't bother him in the least. But the overly cool way in which he spoke made me wonder if somewhere, hidden in the deepest recesses of his heart, he had a desire to be loved not for *what* he was, but for *who* he was.

"Do you deny it?" I asked softly, wanting to know the truth.

"Most emphatically. I am not the libertine you imagine me to be."

"Perhaps not, but Ollie would have let me win the race to the crest."

"Had you ridden the stallion instead of the mare, you would not have needed me to let you win. You could have won on your own merit." Damon kicked the horse's flanks, demanding his mount forward.

Every time I thought I'd gained the upper hand in our conversation, he found some way to outwit me. I glared at the back of his head for a long moment, then guided my horse in the same direction.

Damon made no attempt to continue our discussion, and I let my gaze wander over the breathtaking view. Lord Winfield owned the land as far as the eye could see. The hills and the river that passed through it. Every rock, blade of grass, and animal that dwelled within my sight would one day belong to Damon.

"What are you thinking?" Damon said, breaking the silence.

"I was wondering what it would be like to live every day in such a paradise."

"Purgatory."

I frowned. I couldn't imagine anyone disliking Summerhaven, much less its future lord and master. "Do you hate Summerhaven?"

"Hate, like anger, is futile," Damon said, "but I will confess to disliking what she requires me to be."

"What does she require you to be?"

"My father's son and heir."

My brow pulled together in surprise. "Why would you hate that?"

"You would not understand."

My hands fisted around the reins, making my gloves unbearably constricting. I tugged them off and set them in my lap. "Because I'm a woman?"

"No." Damon gave me a reproving look. "Because you have a father who *adores* you."

"As do you."

He let out a humorless laugh. "As I said before, you would not understand."

He was right. I *didn't* understand his relationship with his father. But I *did* know Lord Winfield only wanted the best for his son. Why else would he want Damon to marry well or have him attend business meetings to learn the running of the estate?

"Explain it to me then."

Damon worked his jaw as if chewing his words, but he said nothing.

It didn't surprise me that he and Lord Winfield were at odds with one another; fathers and sons often were. Even Papa and Henry didn't always see things eye to eye all the time. I imagined having more possessions would only serve to produce more disagreements.

"If your father is strict, it is only because he wants you to be the best lord you can be."

"You should not speak about things you know nothing about."

His censure was as swift as his stallion.

I frowned. Lord Winfield could be demanding, but to not want to be his heir, his *son*? Damon didn't know how lucky he was. I would do *anything* to have even one more conversation with Mama.

"Was that your mother's ring?" Damon nodded toward my hand.

I followed his gaze to the ring, which I'd been unconsciously twisting on my finger. "It was," I said, and though I didn't wish to abandon the subject of his father, Damon's eyes pled with me to do exactly that. Perhaps if I was candid with him now, he would later be candid with me.

"Papa gave the gold band to her on their wedding day, and this emerald was taken from her favorite necklace."

"It's beautiful," he said.

"It is," I agreed. "She wore the ring every day of her life, until her condition worsened and her finger became too thin."

Damon nodded, listening.

"She wanted me to wear it for safekeeping, but it didn't feel right—wearing it when she couldn't—so I left it on her nightstand where it would at least be near her; so she could wear it when she finally recovered her health."

"But she didn't recover," Damon said quietly. "I remember how close you were. I am sorry for your loss."

"Thank you," I said. "After she passed, I went to retrieve the ring, but it was missing. I searched everywhere, but it was gone. I thought it was lost forever."

"Where did you find it?" Damon asked.

"I didn't. Papa had taken both the ring and the necklace from the bed table to have them fashioned into a mourning ring for me. He gave it to me the day of her funeral, and I've not taken it off since."

My eyes filled with tears, but I blinked them away. I'd not cried since Mama's passing, and I would not start now, not here, not in front of Damon.

I tightened my grip on the reins and coaxed Andromeda into a trot. The cool breeze brought a little relief from the sudden swell of emotion, but it wasn't enough. I nudged her flanks with my heel, urging her into a canter. A few wisps of hair escaped my bonnet, tickling my cheeks.

I kicked her flanks to prod her into a gallop, but she stubbornly remained at a canter.

Damon rode even with me now, and though he easily could have passed me, he made no move to take the lead. "Give your horse her head," he shouted against the wind.

I relaxed my grip on the reins, and my mare sprung forward. The hills flew past me in a blur, and the wind whipped against my face.

We continued at the feverish speed for a long while, my horse setting the pace and Damon riding steadily beside me. Sitting straight in his saddle, with his heels down and his chin up, he was a strong and confident rider. He seemed almost one with the animal, like beast and man shared some unspoken bond, connection, and purpose.

Finally, we slowed. "You are a skilled rider," I said.

"Flattery will not soften me into letting you win our next race."

"Not flattery, an observation. You really are talented."

Damon shifted uncomfortably in his saddle. "My skill, if I possess any at all, is merely a product of my education."

I shook my head. "No one can ride the way you do without some degree of passion."

"You wish to speak of passion, do you?" A rakish grin pulled at his mouth.

He did this often—tried to transfer his discomfort to me by uttering some quip. Only, now that I knew *he* was uncomfortable, *I* wasn't. "You love horses. It is as plain as day. Why deny it?"

He shrugged. "Horses can only ever be a pastime, not a passion."

"Well, he is beautiful. What breed is he?"

"A Friesian." Damon affectionately rubbed the horse's neck. "I won him at the tables and decided to keep him for myself."

"As opposed to . . . ?"

Damon glanced at me in question. "Pardon?"

"You said you decided to keep him for yourself, as opposed to what?"

"Oh." He shook his head. "Nothing."

He was avoiding the topic, but I could not figure out why. Perhaps he was embarrassed of his gambling. Rightfully so. It was a ghastly habit.

We continued on, and a few moments later, he huffed a laugh.

"Something funny?" I asked.

"I was only remembering something. When I was a boy, I once planned to run away and ride across all of Europe. Rome, Spain, Greece . . ."

"What stopped you?"

"You mean, besides England's confinement to an island and being forever at war?"

"Yes." I rolled my eyes. "Besides that."

His smile dimmed, and he looked into the distance. "*Conservabo ad mortem,*" he said almost to himself.

I recognized the words from the Jennings family crest. Conserve? Death? I could guess at the direct translation of the individual words, but I was far from fluent in Latin and didn't understand their collective meaning.

"Perhaps you're right," he said before I could ask. "Perhaps I do enjoy horseflesh. Let us give our mounts their heads again."

Damon didn't wait for me to agree before he spurred Ares into a gallop.

I followed at a distance this time, content to lag behind.

Damon was magnificent on his mount. He ran his horse fast and hard and ably. I got the distinct impression he was trying to outrun something. But what?

As we came to the end of the meadow, the woods loomed before us. I reluctantly pulled back on Andromeda's reins, slowing her to trot beside Ares. The smile on my face, however, I could not rein in.

"Never in all my life have I felt so wild. So *free.*"

"Freedom." Damon smiled. "Incredible feeling, isn't it?"

"Yes," I agreed. But what if Ollie had seen? What would he think of my behavior? What would *Mama* think?

I pulled back harder on the reins and did not let up until my horse had slowed to a safe and proper walk. "We should return our horses to the stables," I said.

Damon looked up. Clouds covered the sky, but they did not appear to be heavy with rain. In fact, they were rather light in color, like cream-whipped potatoes. He lifted a brow in question.

"There is no one near to witness our charade," I explained, "so we need not endure any more time in each other's company."

"Is that what we were doing?" Damon straightened in his saddle. And with a curt nod, he abruptly turned Ares, and we started back the way we'd come.

CHAPTER TEN

RAIN PELTED THE LIBRARY WINDOW. The Winfields had a diverse and large book collection. They even had a copy of *Guy Mannering*—the sequel to *Waverley*—which I'd enjoyed the previous year. I sat on the cushioned window seat and opened the book in my lap.

As I read the first page, I relished the feeling of escaping into Henry Bertram's world. Only, I couldn't fully focus on the story. Was it true that I made myself small for Ollie as Damon claimed? I didn't think so, but I had to admit that I'd been excited to ride the stallion until Ollie said it wasn't proper. But he had been correct—a stallion surpassed my skill level—so my choosing not to ride the animal hardly proved anything.

Satisfied, I smoothed open my book and reread the first sentence.

But something still tugged at me. I didn't like that Damon thought poorly of me. Even if I'd ridden the stallion, I would not have been the victor of our little race. I was unfamiliar with the horse, the terrain, and—Why did I even care what Damon thought?

Perhaps I wasn't bothered because of Damon's accusations, but rather because I cared about Ollie. The hurt in his eyes when he left the stable would haunt my dreams for a long while.

Though I didn't relish his pain, I admired the way he wore his heart on his sleeve. Why hadn't I been able to voice that quality to Damon earlier? Perhaps because there were so many things I loved about Ollie. Not only was he handsome, but he had a terrific sense of humor. No one else could make me laugh the way he did. He was intelligent, thoughtful, and kind; honest, articulate, and charming. The next time Damon asked what I saw in Ollie, I would be ready to recite him a long list of his fine qualities.

I set *Guy Mannering* aside and looked out the window. The garden outside was only barely visible in the fading light, but I could make out the outline of the hedgerows. A memory brushed across my mind of Ollie and me running through the garden. I circled Mama's emerald ring on my finger, thinking about what Papa had told me about Mama. How she and Lady Winfield had sat in this very window seat, watching Ollie and me running through the hedgerows and dreaming about us one day marrying.

I let the curtain fall back into place and turned away from the window. But nothing could banish the memory. It was like Mama had risen from the grave to tell me not to give up on Ollie.

Today had been toilsome, but this memory of Mama brought with it a renewed sense of purpose. My happy marriage to Ollie was her heart's desire. No matter how difficult things may become, I would not, *could not*, let Mama down.

I set my book on a side table so that I could return to read it tomorrow and slipped from the library into the corridor. I quietly made my way to my bedchamber, not wanting to run into anyone and have to explain myself. When I stepped inside, Nora stood at the base of my bed, readying my dinner clothes.

"The country air has done your complexion well, miss. Shall I help you dress for dinner?"

"No." I shook my head. "I wish to take a tray in my room tonight."

She frowned.

"I have a headache," I explained.

"I'd say more like heartache, but I'll tell a footman to request a tray all the same."

"Thank you, Nora."

She bobbed a quick curtsy and quit the room.

While I waited for her, I removed my slippers and stockings, then set to work pulling the pins from my hair. I had just pulled out the final one when she returned.

As Nora assisted me into my night rail, she asked, "How was your ride with Lord Jennings?"

Onerous, I almost said, but I somehow resisted borrowing Damon's word. "The country air is so refreshing."

"And the company?"

"It was fine."

"Oh dear. That does not sound good."

"The ride was enjoyable. That is all that matters. Now tell me, how are *you* settling in?"

Nora smiled. "Wonderfully. Everyone here is so kind. I don't think I ever want to leave."

"Nor I."

Just as I slipped into bed, a knock came at the door.

Nora hurried to the door to accept my dinner tray, then carefully closed the door with her foot, and carried it to my bedside table.

My eyes widened at the spread. In addition to a fine meal, the tray also held a copy of *Guy Mannering* and a small bouquet of lavender.

I hesitated to hope that this gift could be from Ollie, but it certainly wasn't from Damon. He didn't know of my love for the Waverley books, and he didn't know I preferred lavender to other flowers. But Ollie did. I'd written to him about my love for the first Waverley book last year, and I'd mentioned to him that I wanted lavender to scent my room the night before the Rumfords' ball. With a smile, I picked up the flowers and sniffed their sweetness.

"Shall I fetch a vase of water?" Nora asked.

"No, I wish to hang them from my bedpost to dry." Now that I was convinced this gift came from Ollie, I did not want to forget this moment. Ever. "But there is something I'm hoping you can quietly help me with."

"What is it?"

"I need dancing cards to learn the quadrille." I'd considered asking Lady Winfield for help learning the different forms, but I didn't want her to think less of Mama for not being able to train me.

"I'm sure one of the maids could attain a set for you. I'll say it's for myself, and no one will be any wiser."

"Thank you, Nora."

"Good night, miss," she said and left the room.

After a delicious supper, I set my tray aside, and snuggling into my bed, I opened my book.

No matter what Damon thought of his future estate, I could not think of any place more heavenly. I could avoid socializing and listen to the rain while reading a book from my favorite author, all while in the comfort of my bed. Yes, Summerhaven was nothing short of heaven.

CHAPTER ELEVEN

SITTING IN THE FORMAL GARDEN the next morning, I closed my eyes and tipped my head back, wishing the sun would peek through the endless clouds and warm my face. Yesterday had been such a trying day, but today I'd awoken refreshed. As soon as Lady Winfield was ready, we would travel by carriage into town to meet Amelia and Lady Rumford at the modiste.

"I have been looking for you."

I blinked out of my reverie and found Ollie standing before me. I quickly righted my bonnet and made sure the bow beneath my chin was nicely tied. "You were looking for me?"

"I was." He stepped forward, and gravel crunched beneath his boots. "I tried the library first."

The library had always been my favorite place to spend my mornings at Summerhaven. "Am I really so predictable?" I teased.

"Not lately," Ollie said on a sigh, and then he gestured to the bench where I sat. "May I?"

"I would like nothing better." I moved over to make room for him.

"How was your ride with Damon yesterday?" he asked.

"Delightful. Damon is an *impressive* horseman."

I didn't miss how Ollie gripped the edge of the bench, so I wasn't surprised when he said, "I do not like how we left things yesterday."

"Nor I."

"I want for us to be friends," he said. "As we once were."

"I do too," I said.

"But you are still cross with me because I didn't dance with you."

I shook my head. It was so much more than that. I had been cross with him, but it had been replaced with something much more difficult to quell. "I'm hurt," I admitted.

"I should not have danced with Miss Digby at the ball." He looked at his boots. "I understand now that I should have danced with you like I promised."

Promised. My heart sank at the word. He'd promised me so much but had delivered so little. Ollie thought he understood, but he didn't. I wasn't hurt because he danced with Miss Digby at the ball; I was hurt because he *wanted* to dance with her. Because it was she who occupied his thoughts and not me.

"Please don't be angry with me. I cannot stand it. What can I do to earn your forgiveness?"

When I didn't answer, he sighed heavily and glanced around. "Do you remember the last time we were together in this garden?"

"Of course I do."

He smiled. "You used to chase me through the hedgerows," he said. "I'd run through the winding pathways until I lost you, and then I'd hide until you were near—"

"And then you would jump out and startle me to the sky."

We both smiled.

"I miss those times, Hanny."

"Me too. Things were much simpler when we were children."

"Things are not so difficult now," Ollie said. "We are older, it is true, but that doesn't mean we can't have fun." He stood and held out his hand. His eyes held a familiar twinkle.

"I am not going to chase you, Ollie."

"No." He laughed. "I am asking you to dance with me. To make up for the one I missed."

The only dance meant for two people was a waltz, and that was practically indecent even in a ballroom.

"We should not," I said, though I wanted to be in his arms more than he knew. "What if someone sees us? It could ruin both our reputations."

"You never cared about things like that before."

"There are a great many things I did not care about before. But again, we are grown and must act like it."

"You are even beginning to *sound* like Damon."

"If that is true, then your brother is wiser than I have given him credit for." I patted the bench beside me.

Ollie begrudgingly sat like a scolded child. "Damon is a great many things, but he is not *wise*."

"Don't say that. Your brother has been kind to me."

"My brother is opportunistic. Do not mistake that for kindness."

Perhaps that was true, but he didn't understand the whole equation. Damon *had* used my situation to his advantage, but what Ollie didn't know was that it was to *my* advantage as well.

Feeling guilty, I looked away and focused my attention on the lavender stalks blowing in the breeze. I closed my eyes and breathed deeply, inhaling the perfumed scent.

"I should not have said that." He dragged a hand through his hair, mussing it. "I didn't seek you out to quarrel."

"Why *did* you seek me out?"

"To offer an olive branch." He leaned forward and rested his elbow on his leg, bringing his gaze even with mine. "What would you say to a picnic?"

Time alone with Ollie? It was precisely what I'd longed for. "I would say that I like the idea."

"Good. Because I have already proposed the idea to Miss Digby, and she's looking forward to meeting my dearest childhood friend."

I couldn't decide which word I disliked more: *Miss Digby* or *friend*? "Oh."

"Hannah?"

"Sorry. It's just, three people would make for an uneven set."

"I had not thought of that." Ollie was quiet for a moment. "Shall we include Miss Atherton then? I believe you got on well with her at the ball. We will also invite her brother, Mr. Atherton. You will like him."

"That is good, but our numbers would again be unequal." My perfect picnic with Ollie was slipping through my fingers the larger our party grew. I needed to turn this picnic in my favor. "We must invite one other gentleman."

"Yes." He nodded. "But who? Lord Graham is still in London, and Lord Chilcott—"

"Damon," I said. "We must invite Damon."

Ollie frowned. "The last time we picnicked with Damon, the day did not end so well."

"Not well at all," I agreed. "But that was ages ago, and I highly doubt he will have the time or the inclination to catch any frogs."

"I wouldn't be so sure." Ollie glowered.

"Damon is the obvious choice. It would be unkind to exclude him."

Ollie slid his tongue across his teeth, jutting out his lips. "Very well," he said. "I will extend the invitation, but I do not think he will accept. He rarely condescends for social events these days."

"Then let me ask him. I'm sure he'll agree to come."

Ollie's eyes narrowed.

Before he could investigate the subject, I stood. "I should be going. I don't want to keep your mother waiting; we are going into town today."

"Yes, I know. To the modiste with Lady Rumford and Miss Atherton. It's all mother can talk about." He smiled. "Prepare yourself; I believe she means to spoil you."

"She's said as much, but I don't mind." It had been so long since I had been doted on by a motherly figure, and I couldn't wait.

"You *hate* shopping. Truly, you may want to consider faking an illness."

I frowned. "I *used* to dislike shopping, but now I find it rather enjoyable."

"Oh," Ollie said with a shake of his head. "My apologies. Enjoy your trip into town then."

"Thank you."

We said goodbye, and I excused myself. I was glad Ollie still cared about me, that he wanted my good opinion and my friendship, but it wasn't enough.

Before today, I'd thought the problem was that he didn't see me, but that wasn't the problem. The problem was that he still saw me as a little girl he could be friends with and not as a woman he could love.

Did he love Miss Digby?

She was beautiful to be sure, but real love was built upon more than just a pretty face. True love, like Mama and Papa had, was built upon a solid foundation of friendship and memories and sacrifice.

Ollie and I had that in spades. I only needed to remind him.

But how?

Lady Winfield was standing by the carriage when I rounded the corner. "Ah! There you are, my dear."

"Please forgive my lateness, Lady Winfield. I was enjoying your garden and was about to come to the carriage when Ollie found me. I lost track of time."

Lady Winfield smiled. "Think nothing of it."

A footman handed Lady Winfield into the carriage and then me. No sooner had the door closed when it opened again.

"Mother. Hannah," Damon said with a cool smile, but his eyes had a flash of mischief. "Might I accompany you ladies into town? I must see to some business."

"We would be delighted." Lady Winfield shifted her legs to make room for her son to enter, but Damon didn't immediately climb into the carriage.

"Do you think you can *endure* my company, Miss Kent?"

I frowned. I hadn't meant to injure his pride when I'd used that word to end our ride yesterday, but it appeared I had. And I knew I should smile and make room for Damon in the carriage, so he could have his choice of seats, but I'd been looking forward to spending the day in the company of women.

But as much as I wished to exclude Damon, to do so would be not only unkind, but rude, as I'd told Ollie in the garden. I did not want Lady Winfield to think badly of me, so I smiled tightly at Damon. "I can endure it, my lord. I have a strong constitution."

Damon's mouth twitched, and he climbed into the carriage, taking the rear-facing seat across from Lady Winfield and me.

Damon situated himself in the carriage. "You look lovely this morning, Hannah," Damon said. "I trust you slept well?"

"I did." My answer came out more curtly than I'd intended.

Lady Winfield gently touched my arm. "You had us all a little worried last night when you missed dinner."

Oh. I softened both my expression and my tone. "I'm sorry for causing any worry. The ride yesterday left me with a slight headache."

"Not from the company, I hope." Damon's knee bumped mine, and it was *not* an accident.

I adjusted my position away and straightened my skirts.

Damon laughed under his breath.

"Speaking of your ride." Lady Winfield looked pointedly at Damon. "I must insist that should you choose to ride together again, you employ a chaperone."

My face flamed with embarrassment. Taking a chaperone on our ride yesterday had not even crossed my mind. Damon was *Damon*, but Lady Winfield was correct in her reproach. It was improper of us to ride without a chaperone.

"Yes, Mother. My apologies, Miss Kent. Please forgive my oversight." It was impossible to tell whether or not Damon was earnest in his apology, but Lady Winfield seemed satisfied, so I nodded for her benefit.

The carriage swayed, and my stomach caught. Oh, not again. Hopefully the ride into town was a short one. If not, I would be in grave danger of losing my breakfast. I glanced at Damon's boots. They appeared freshly shined.

The carriage jolted as if hitting a rock or a dip in the road, and I braced myself against the wall.

"Perhaps I misspoke earlier," Damon said. "Hannah, your pallor is . . . dare I say, green?"

"Damon," Lady Winfield scolded. "That is no way to speak to a woman."

"He is correct. How much farther to town?"

"Only a short distance more."

I nodded. The rest of the ride into town, I made sure to look out the side glass. Seeing the direction of the road somehow helped me feel better. Damon and his mother chatted idly, but I paid them no attention.

When the carriage finally came to a halt, I exhaled with relief.

Damon alighted first and held out his hand to help me down. Still upset with him for inserting himself into my day, I wished I could decline his assistance. But the last time I had felt unwell and refused his help, it had ended poorly for both of us. So I took his hand, stepped down, then quickly let go.

He smiled to himself, then reached out to help his mother.

I took a few deep breaths and relished the cool country air on my face. Thankfully, my nausea began to wane.

The town was exactly how I remembered it: a long row of shops stretched out on either side of the lane, and flowers spilled from window boxes in a cascade of pink and purple and white. The air even smelled sweetly of confections, just as it used to.

Lady Winfield joined me at my side. "Do you feel well enough to shop?" she asked.

"Oh yes. I'm excited for the adventure."

Lady Winfield smiled at me, then turned to her son. "And what of you, Damon? Are you to join us at the modiste?"

"As thrilling as that sounds, I must attend to business."

Business. I frowned. The use of the word seemed to be a man's way of excluding female companions from conversation.

"Very good. Your father will be pleased," Lady Winfield said, then stepped a few paces away, looking for Lady Rumford and Amelia.

Damon turned to me. "Do try not to frown, Miss Kent. I will be back at your side before you're done selecting your fabric."

"That is not—"

"For our charade to be effective," he said, interrupting my protest, "we must be seen together."

"We rode together yesterday."

"Privately," he said. "And while that may work for your purposes, we must be seen together publicly for our bargain to work to *my* advantage."

Pretending to be interested in Damon in front of Ollie was one thing, but in front of Amelia? Lady Winfield? Society? *That* was another matter entirely.

"Until later, Miss Hannah." He touched the brim of his hat, and smiling, he walked away.

CHAPTER TWELVE

A BELL ANNOUNCED OUR ARRIVAL as we stepped inside the modiste's shop. Both Lady Rumford and Amelia glanced up from a bolt of fabric.

Amelia clapped her hands. "I'm so glad you're here. You must tell me your thoughts on Mother's beloved blue fabric."

Lady Winfield and I walked to where they stood over two large bolts of fabric, one a lovely shade of yellow and the other the most depressing dark blue.

"You see the problem?" Amelia said.

I hesitated to nod for fear of offending Lady Rumford, but Amelia was correct; the blue print was more appropriate for mourning than attracting a mate.

Lady Rumford watched and waited as I considered my words.

"Both would look lovely on Amelia," I said, "but the yellow fabric is my favorite."

"You see, Mama?" Amelia said. "I *must* have the yellow for a new gown."

Lady Rumford sniffed. "You are correct, Miss Kent. They would *both* favor my daughter." And then to the modiste, she said, "We will take them both."

"*Oui*, madam. An excellent choice." The modiste's French accent curled around each word like a puff of smoke.

Lady Rumford specified how much she required.

"Hannah," Lady Winfield said. "Take a turn about the shop and select a fabric for your own dress. I promised to spoil you, after all."

I opened my mouth to protest, but Lady Winfield spoke first. "I have been blessed with two sons but no daughters. Please allow me this pleasure."

"Thank you, Lady Winfield. You are so kind. I don't even know where to start." Mama had always selected the fabric for my dresses before she'd taken ill, and now, Nora had taken the task upon herself.

"Allow me to help?" Amelia asked.

I nodded gratefully.

With a smile, Amelia looped her arm through mine and led me away to look at fabrics on the opposite wall. "What color do you like best?" she asked.

I studied the folded fabrics. They were organized by color, starting with red and ending with purple. Some were printed while others were plain, but all were beautiful. "My maid dresses me in green."

"Do *you* like green?" Amelia asked.

"I've never really thought about it," I admitted. I looked over the column of green fabrics, considering. There were many shades—evergreen and celadon and emerald and everything in between. I ran my hand over the bolts of fabric, thinking about their potential.

The evergreen was so deep and dark it was almost brown, like the slimy silt at the side of a riverbank or on a frog. And the celadon was so bright it almost looked yellow, like the first buds that appeared in spring. My fingers trailed over the emerald fabric. It matched my mourning ring.

I withdrew my hand and dropped it to my side.

The fabrics were all lovely. But even if they carried the potential to highlight the green in my otherwise muddy eyes or matched Mama's ring, none made me feel beautiful.

"No, I do not suppose I do like green," I said to Amelia.

"Then you must select something else. What color do you like?"

"I really don't know."

"Well, what color makes you feel happy?"

"Whatever the opposite of green is, I suppose."

"Red," Amelia said matter-of-factly. "The opposite of green is red."

"Hmm." Most of the fabrics in this store were pale pastels and creamy whites—as was most fashionable and appropriate for young, unmarried women—but there was also a sizable selection of patterned prints—most likely imported from India—too. Mama had always loved to dress in bright colors no matter what was in fashion.

"Then I think I like red the best."

"For a minute, I worried you were about to say dark blue was your favorite." Amelia laughed a little, then, glancing at her mother and the modiste measuring out the blue print, sighed. "Truly, mothers can be so infuriating."

"I suppose mine was too," I said quietly.

Amelia grimaced. "I should not have said that. I wasn't thinking."

"It is fine, really."

"I'm sorry if I have upset you."

"On the contrary. I love talking about my mother. Most people don't feel comfortable talking of those who have passed, but I wish they would."

"Does your father speak of her?"

"On occasion but usually with heartache."

"May I ask . . ." She hesitated. "How did she pass?"

"Of course." I allowed my gaze to roam over the brightly colored fabrics, trying to imagine which one she would have selected for herself, which one she would have chosen for me. "Mama took ill just after my thirteenth birthday, but her illness progressed slowly. Papa hired the best doctors he could afford. We even moved to Bath in hopes of finding a cure, but nothing could alleviate her symptoms. She persisted as long as she could, but just after my coming-out, she took to her bed, and there was nothing to be done."

"You must miss her greatly."

"I do. So much."

"Lady Winfield and your mother were close?"

I nodded. "They grew up in the same town. And as girls, they were inseparable, but then they married very different men—Lady Winfield's rank rose, and my mother's fell—and the only thing that remained fast from their former lives was their friendship. They wrote letters often, and Mama and I visited Summerhaven every summer. My fondest memories are of those days."

Our conversation lulled, and we returned to the task of choosing a fabric. Amelia held up a deep shade of ruby.

"Too matronly," I said, and she returned the fabric to the wall.

"What about this one?" she asked a moment later. She held up a bright shade of crimson this time.

I scrunched my nose and shook my head. The brighter shade was closer to what I wanted, but I wanted to impress Ollie, not scare him.

We searched all the red fabrics and were about to reach the orange section when a bolt of fabric caught my attention. It was almost invisible, wedged between two heavy fabrics, but I tugged free the fabric, then held it up. It was perfect!

"Amelia." I touched her elbow, and she turned. "I think I have found it."

"Coquelicot," she said with a smile. "The color suits you."

I glanced at the bright poppy-colored bolt and bit my lip. "Do you really think so?"

"I *know* so."

The bold shade was really only appropriate for a married woman to wear, but perhaps that could work to my advantage; when Ollie looked at me, I wanted him to think of *marriage*. I would ask Lady Winfield's opinion. Amelia and I took the fabric to the cutting table where Lady Winfield and Lady Rumford still stood with the modiste.

"Have you decided on a fabric?" Lady Winfield asked.

"I think so, but I should like to ask your opinion first." I tentatively showed her the fabric.

Lady Winfield touched the fabric. "Your mother would have loved it, and so do I." She took the fabric and handed it to the modiste. "You must also select some trim."

Amelia and I walked toward the front of the store where the notions, lace, and other trim were organized.

We'd been searching through the items for a few minutes when Amelia grew bored and pushed back the curtain to gaze out the front window. "How goes your plan with Lord Jennings?" she asked.

"Damon can be rather irritating at times, but our ruse does seem to be working in regard to making Ollie jealous."

"I believe it," Amelia said. "But I was actually inquiring after Lord Jennings's commitment to your deal. See there." She indicated out the window.

I followed her gaze. Damon stood in the lane with a man whose clothes were well-worn and his grooming lacking. He did not appear Damon's equal, yet the pair stood in the shadows, close together, conversing.

"Do you know who that man is?" I asked Amelia.

She shook her head. "I've never seen him before."

The man said something, articulating with one hand.

Damon nodded, then glancing around, he reached into his coat pocket. He turned his shoulder inward as if trying to hide his actions, but from my vantage point, I saw him pull out a small parcel.

The man took the bundle and pulled back the paper, revealing a tidy sum of bank notes. He hurriedly tucked the package in his own coat, then limped away, disappearing between two shops.

Damon straightened his cravat and then his cuffs, then he stepped back into the lane as if nothing nefarious had taken place.

Worry pooled in my stomach. I resumed my search for trim, but it was impossible to focus. Had Damon taken gambling too far? Was he in some sort of trouble?

"Oh dear," Amelia said a moment later.

"What is it now?"

"See for yourself."

I glanced out the window. Damon stood with an elegantly dressed young woman and another older woman.

"Who are they?" I asked Amelia.

"Miss Digby and her matchmaking mother." Amelia groaned.

I squinted through the glass to get a clearer view of her. It was the same honey-haired woman Ollie danced with at the ball. I frowned. Why was Damon conversing with her?

As if he could feel us staring, his gaze moved in the direction of the shop window where we stood.

Amelia quickly let the curtain fall closed. "I think we are caught." She grinned.

"No. You hid us just in time."

After a moment, we peeked out the window again.

Damon smiled at Miss Digby as she spoke. They were standing near one another, but not improperly so. Still, I felt a twinge of jealousy. Not because I had developed an affection for him, of course, but because he should not be speaking with Miss Digby; Ollie had all but declared his suit for her, and Damon had promised to pretend to only have eyes for me.

"I should go to him," I said, setting down the fistful of trim.

"He appears to be doing more than fine on his own," Amelia said.

"Yes, but running off all the would-be Lady Jenningses is part of our bargain. If I *don't* go to him, by the time I've won over Ollie's affections and our charade is over, Damon will be all but off the marriage market. And where will that leave you?"

As if to prove my point, Miss Digby looked up at Damon through her lashes, and Damon rewarded her with another smile. "See there, how Miss Digby bats her lashes at him?"

"She is rather obvious about her interest, isn't she?" Amelia said.

"To be fair, she is rather young, and subtlety *is* an acquired virtue," I said.

We giggled.

"Come on then." Amelia looped her arm through mine, and after handing our trim selections to Lady Jennings and Lady Rumford, we made our way outside.

CHAPTER THIRTEEN

WE WAITED FOR A CARRIAGE to pass before we crossed the lane to where Damon stood with Miss Digby and her mother. The lane was well kept on the sides nearest the shops, but the center was a muddy mess.

"Perhaps we should find a better path," I suggested.

Amelia looked down the lane. "There doesn't appear to *be* a better path."

I glanced at Damon. Miss Digby stood especially close to him now, and judging by the way he smiled appreciatively down at her, he didn't seem to mind the proximity.

I clenched my jaw and lifted the hem of my skirt, eager to cut off the connection between Damon and his admirer. "We'll just have to hope the mud isn't too thick then."

I stepped gingerly into the center of the lane. Amelia followed. Mud squelched beneath my boots, but I avoided the worst of it.

"Ah, Miss Kent, Miss Atherton," Damon greeted us as we approached. "I've been expecting you." His eyes flicked knowingly toward the modiste's shop window.

"Lord Jennings." Amelia curtsied, but I was too focused on trying not to sink into the mud to say a proper greeting of my own. It would be my luck to lose my footing and fall in the mud in front of Miss Digby. Not for the first time, I wished it were acceptable for women to wear trousers.

"May I assist you, Miss Kent?" Damon offered.

"Yes." I took his hand, and he helped me across. "Thank you."

"It was my pleasure," he said, and then he returned his attention to the others. "Miss Digby, Mrs. Digby, you know Miss Atherton, but may I present the delightful Miss Kent?"

Miss Digby's bright-blue eyes bore into mine, but she smiled sweetly. "Miss Kent."

"Miss Digby," I returned.

Her gaze roamed over my dress or, rather, Mama's dress that Nora had altered to fit me. I smoothed my skirts, and Miss Digby grinned. What Ollie saw in her, I would never know. I already dreaded the picnic I would have to endure in her company.

"Are you visiting the modiste?" Amelia asked Miss Digby.

"Yes. It is our second visit this month. Mama insists I have a new dress for every social event."

"Only the *best* will do for my daughter," Mrs. Digby said, and she looked pointedly at Damon.

Did she think Damon was best for her daughter? What about Ollie? Miss Digby should be so lucky as to have a man as wonderful as Ollie.

"Miss Kent and I have looked through every bolt of fabric," Amelia said. "And we found the most beautiful dark-blue print that I think would suit you. You must let me show you."

Miss Digby glanced at her mother and then up at Damon, as if realizing her moment with him had come to an end. After a quick farewell, they allowed Amelia to lead them away.

"You were quick to vacate the modiste's shop just now," Damon said to me. "That wouldn't have anything to do with *me*, would it?"

"Don't flatter yourself. I was only living up to my half of our bargain—to drive away unwanted young women and their mothers."

"Miss Digby's company was hardly unwanted." Damon smirked.

"Oh? What a dreadful mistake I've made. I will call her back for you." I stepped toward the modiste's shop.

Damon caught my elbow. "That won't be necessary."

"I thought not." For as much as Damon had seemed to enjoy flirting with her, I believed him when he said he had no intention of marrying anytime soon.

We continued walking toward the carriage and passed the spot where he'd stood earlier with the unknown man.

"Damon, who was the man you were speaking with before?" I asked as we walked.

"What man?"

"The man you were huddled with just over there." I pointed to the shadowed spot between shops as we walked by it. "You gave him a small parcel."

The only indication Damon heard my question was the slight tension in his brow.

"Won't you tell me?"

Damon led me around a small puddle. "He's a business contact."

That man was *not* a man of business, at least not a reputable one. Damon was lying. Why? "What sort of business contact?" I pressed.

"The details would bore you."

"That's unlikely."

"Did you find an acceptable fabric?" He changed the subject without apology.

I gave him a pointed look. "If you don't want to tell me your business, then I am under no obligation to divulge mine."

"I take this to mean no acceptable fabric was found?"

"I'm afraid the details of my visit to the modiste would *bore* you."

"No doubt," he said, "but I am very good at feigning interest."

I met his gaze. "As am I, *my lord.*"

"Touché," he said, and we continued down the lane. "What shall we speak of then? The fine weather or perhaps the quality of shops in this town?"

"I have no interest in idle chatter."

"Then let us discuss more important matters. Why did you hide in your room last night?"

"I'd rather not discuss it," I said.

"And I'd rather you didn't hide from me."

"What makes you think I was hiding from *you?*" He really was arrogant.

"Weren't you?" There was a softness to his voice that made me want to tell him the truth. Perhaps if I were honest with him, he would be honest with me.

"It was Ollie I couldn't face," I said quietly.

"Why would you hide from Ollie?"

"Our ride yesterday bothered him."

Damon's head tilted to the side. "Was that not our express purpose?"

"It was, but it doesn't make me feel better."

"Do you regret our arrangement?"

"Only when you keep things from me. I would feel better if you weren't so private."

Damon shook his head. "I'm sure you would not."

Why was Damon always so obstinate? He could be forthcoming about his feelings regarding things I did not care to know but silent when it came to things I did. For once, I wanted to be on the upper hand of our conversation. I searched my mind. There had to be something . . . Ah. Yes. I knew just the thing to lure him into conversation.

"Red," I said.

"Pardon?"

"The color fabric I chose is red. Poppy to be exact."

"Poppy? I would have expected you to choose a subtler shade. White or pale green perhaps."

"Yes, well. I wanted to select a color that would be noticed."

"That color will—" He paused to clear his throat. "It will suit your complexion nicely."

"Thank you. Now it is *your* turn to be forthcoming."

"You want a confession." He shook his head with a small laugh. "Very well then. The night you wear such a dress will surely be the end of our little charade. Ollie and every other man in the room will be captivated by you."

My cheeks burned. No man had ever paid me such a direct compliment.

Damon smiled to himself as if pleased by my stunned reaction. This wouldn't do. If he wanted to play games, then I would be a worthy opponent.

I took a steadying breath, sliding into character. "I didn't choose the color to please your brother."

"Oh? Who did you buy it to please?"

I looked up at Damon through my lashes and smiled coyly like I'd seen Miss Digby do. "Myself." That was only partially true—I'd chosen the fabric because I liked it but also because I hoped the bold shade might make Ollie see me in a different light—but Damon needn't know that.

He didn't laugh like I'd expected. Instead, he held my gaze and in a low voice said, "How foolish of me to have hoped."

Was he teasing me again? No matter how well I thought I was faring at commanding our conversation, he *always* managed to get in the last word. Damon did not play fair.

At long last, we reached the carriage. A footman scurried to meet us at the door, but when he moved to open it, Damon held up his hand, stopping him, and he opened the carriage door himself. "Miss Kent." He held out his hand to assist me up.

I hesitated. He'd only dismissed the footman and offered me his hand so people nearby would see the gesture. I *knew* this, and yet it *felt* like more.

Damon leaned close. Too close. Close enough that I could smell the musk of his shaving soap. "The polite thing to do when a gentleman offers you his hand, Miss Kent, is to accept it."

I made a show of looking around.

Damon followed my gaze. "What is it?"

"I was searching for the *gentleman* to whom you were referring."

Damon grinned. "It is a good thing I don't pride myself on titles or I would be offended." He laughed deeply, and the bellowing sound drew the attention of several passersby, including Lady Winfield, Lady Rumford, and Amelia, who'd all emerged from the modiste's shop.

"Damon, hush. You're attracting attention."

"Good," he said. "Now. Shall we try this again?" Once more he offered me his hand, and this time, I quickly took it.

As soon as I was safely inside the carriage, I attempted to pull my hand from his, but he held it tight. Then bowing over my hand, he placed a kiss on my gloved knuckles.

I tried not to react, but once again, my cheeks betrayed me.

With a knowing smile, Damon turned to wait politely at the carriage door for his mother.

Drat!

This was *Damon,* I reminded myself. The same boy who had teased me so mercilessly. His act was only part of our plan to avoid entanglements; I needed to remember that no matter how quickly my heart now beat. He was a man now—a rather handsome man, I hated to notice—but still just as untrustworthy. Damon had likely assisted many young ladies into carriages—he was obviously practiced at the art. He'd probably flirted and teased them as he had me today.

I frowned.

I didn't like the thought.

And it bothered me that I didn't like the thought.

A few moments later, I heard Lady Winfield approach, and then the carriage jostled as Damon handed her up. Once we were all seated inside, we began the journey home.

"Hannah and I had the most successful visit to the modiste," Lady Winfield said. "How went your business, Damon?"

Damon glanced at me. "It was . . . informative."

"I saw you conversing with Miss Digby."

"Indeed. Her mother accosted me in the street."

"Damon," Lady Winfield said reproachfully, but she pressed her lips together as if to hide a smile. Did she not approve of Miss Digby?

"Thankfully," Damon continued, "Hannah saved me from the wiles of the lovely Miss Digby."

"Speaking of Miss Digby, that reminds me," I said. "Ollie suggested we all picnic together. Miss Digby, Miss Atherton, and her brother, in addition to Ollie, you, and me."

"*Ollie* suggested I attend?" One of Damon's shapely eyebrows rose. "How did you cajole an invitation for me?"

"Nobody cajoled anyone," I said. "It was simply a matter of numbers."

"Ah. So it was you. I thought as much."

Lady Winfield shook her head. "What is it with you boys? As children you two were inseparable."

"Those days are long gone."

Lady Winfield sighed.

"You'll come though, won't you?" I asked Damon.

"Will you be in attendance?" he asked me, and I nodded. "Then so shall I."

The carriage dipped, and I rested a hand on my middle.

"I almost forgot." Damon reached into his pocket and pulled out a small brown bag tied with twine. "This is for you."

I eyed the bag. A trick?

When I made no move to take the little bag, he untied the twine and tilted the bag so I could see inside.

Amber-colored candies. Perhaps they were made from bugs or were excessively spicy or—

"It's candied ginger. Sailors use it to curb seasickness," he explained. "I thought it might help you."

Oh. He was being thoughtful.

Lady Winfield's gaze moved between Damon and me with curiosity. An emotion I also felt.

My fingers brushed over his palm as I took the candied ginger, and I apprehensively placed the confection in my mouth. The smooth, sweet candy had a bit of spice, but it wasn't hot, only pleasantly warm. It melted in my mouth until only a pleasant taste remained.

"Do you like it?" he asked.

"Very much. Thank you."

The carriage suddenly jerked, and I flew forward and landed in Damon's lap. Luckily, Lady Winfield had been resting her arm on the window ledge, and she braced herself in her seat. The carriage came to an abrupt halt, tilted at an extreme angle.

Damon gripped my waist, his eyes searching me as if looking for injury. "Are you all right?"

I hardly knew. Everything had happened so fast, so violently. But nothing hurt. "I think so."

His grip loosened, but only slightly. "You needn't throw yourself at me to get my attention," he whispered, his breath tickling the sensitive skin of my ear. A pleasant shiver ran down my neck and arms. "I assure you, you already have it."

My lips parted, but no words escaped my mouth.

He finally released his hold, and as I sat back in my seat, I risked a glance at Lady Winfield. Thankfully, she was preoccupied with something outside.

"It seems we are stuck in a rather large puddle of mud," she said.

The footman confirmed as much a moment later, and after some discussion between him and Damon, it was decided we needed to evacuate the carriage if we were to become *un*stuck. Only one wheel was trapped, so the two men should have been able to dislodge it without further assistance.

Damon alighted from the carriage first, and his Hessian boots sunk deep into the fresh mud. He carried his mother to the side of the road first and then returned to help me.

He held out his hand, but I searched for another way to the side of the road that would not involve Damon carrying me. I was having trouble thinking straight today, and Damon's nearness wouldn't help matters.

But there was nothing for it; it was either risk a ruined hem or be carried.

"I won't drop you if that's what you're worried about."

That was not my worry at all. "I'm sure you will not. At least not with your mother standing watch."

"It's true," he said. "I would never tempt that woman's wrath."

I laughed a little. Lady Winfield was the epitome of kindness and grace. There was not an unkind bone in her body.

Tentatively, I placed an arm around his broad shoulders. Damon slid one arm behind my back and the other under my knees, cradling me against his chest. Warmth radiated through his coat.

"See?" he said. "You can trust me."

"Can I?"

Damon held my gaze as he set me gently on the ground. "Always."

I wanted to believe him, but he held his secrets closer than a hand of cards. He didn't wish to marry, but he would not tell me why. And who was the man he'd been speaking with? Why had he flirted with Miss Digby when he knew his brother was attempting to court her? And Ollie had called Damon opportunistic. What had that meant?

Damon walked back to the carriage to assist the footman.

"Damon," Lady Winfield called, "leave your coat."

"I had thought not to scandalize Miss Kent by removing any articles of clothing today, but seeing as this is my best coat, perhaps you're right, Mother."

Lady Winfield rubbed her forehead. "Never have sons, Hannah. They will turn you gray before your time."

"Mama said the same thing about daughters," I confessed.

Damon retraced his steps to the side of the road and stood in front of me. He pulled open his coat and relaxed his broad shoulders, freeing first his right arm from his sleeve and then his left. His shirt sleeves clung to his thick arms, his waistcoat to his tapered torso.

Swallowing hard, I forced my gaze to his cravat. Where it was safe. Where it was proper.

He gathered the garment into his hands and held it out to me. "If you'd be so kind, Miss Kent? I know how much you admire the fine cut of my coats, so I believe it will be safe in your care."

I grabbed the coat, a bit more forcefully than I'd intended, and his mouth twisted into a satisfied grin.

I narrowed my eyes at the infuriating man. Must he always tease me so?

"Come, my dear," Lady Winfield called to me. "Let us wait in the shade."

I turned on my heel and followed her to a copse of willow trees. I sat on a log and laid Damon's coat on my lap.

From my position, I had a clear view of the carriage. Damon and the footman worked together to wedge a long branch under the stuck wheel. And with his jacket removed, Damon's strength could not be hidden. The thin material of his shirt strained across his shoulders and arms.

"Did you enjoy our visit to town today?" Lady Winfield's voice startled me.

Had she seen me watching Damon? Oh dear. I truly did not have a good explanation for that.

"I-I did, yes. Thank you so much for buying me such a beautiful dress."

She waved me off. "Truly, it was my pleasure." Lady Winfield sat on the opposite end of the log and adjusted her skirts. "It was nice of you to invite Damon to Ollie's picnic."

"I could hardly do otherwise." At least not if our little *arrangement* was to work to *my* advantage.

"I suppose I worried that after the way you parted so many years ago, things might be strained."

"That was such a long time ago."

"It was," she agreed. "Much has changed since then, hasn't it?" Lady Winfield's gaze turned studious.

Having no idea what she was searching for, I straightened, trying to appear a lady.

"Hannah, I must make a confession," Lady Winfield said. "Miss Digby seems to have set her sights on Ollie. And though I'm sure she's a lovely girl, I don't believe she's the right match for my son." She grimaced. "I thought that if I invited you here—or rather, I *hoped*—the pair of you would pick up where you left off. You always were two peas in one pod."

Ah. Lady Winfield was playing matchmaker.

I knew from Papa that Mama and Lady Winfield had once dreamed of Ollie and me marrying one day, but I was surprised she still held that dream.

"I'm just glad to visit."

"I am glad you are here too, but there is more." She nervously clasped and unclasped her hands. "When I invited you to Summerhaven, I did so without Ollie's knowledge or permission."

While I'd guessed as much in the days following his failure to greet Papa and me, I hadn't let myself believe it. The confirmation hurt, but I tried not to let her see my disappointment.

"I'm truly sorry—" Her voice caught, and she placed a hand on her chest beneath her throat. "I apologize if my meddling has caused you heartache."

I shook my head and tried to smile. The truth that Ollie had not been the one to invite me here, that he perhaps didn't even want me here, did bring me pain, but it was not her fault.

"I can't help but wonder though," she continued, "if perhaps things aren't just as they should be." Lady Winfield looked between Damon and me and smiled.

Guilt twisted inside me like a kite caught in the wind.

What she saw between Damon and me was nothing more than a carefully planned charade. Damon had no true feelings for me, and I had none for him. But what could I say that would not ruin our ruse and also not give Lady Winfield false hope?

"Now it is *I* who must confess. I believe I'm better suited to your original machinations."

Lady Winfield's brow furrowed, and her gaze moved to where Damon worked in the road with the footman. They'd managed to wedge the branch under the wheel, but not without effort. Damon's cravat hung loosely from his neck, and his hair fell across his forehead. The most incredible urge to run my hands through the inky strands blew through me like a gale. Sudden and strong.

As if he could feel my stare, Damon looked up and smiled.

I swiftly tore away my gaze.

Lady Winfield smiled. "I might be mistaken, but I believe my Damon would disagree."

I bit my lip. If Lady Winfield believed Damon had developed an attachment for me, then our charade was working. *Too* well.

I didn't want anyone to get hurt—especially not Lady Winfield, who had been nothing but kind to me—but what could be done about it?

Admittedly, I'd reacted to Damon's display of charm, but only because I'd been unprepared for our supposed courtship to be so public. But if I didn't press on, Ollie would likely marry Miss Digby, and I couldn't let him tie himself to a woman such as she. She'd revealed herself today when she'd flirted with Damon; she didn't care one whit for Ollie. She was only using him to win a more coveted prize, the future Earl of Winfield: Damon.

Though I didn't like misleading Lady Winfield, I took comfort that she'd invited me to Summerhaven to win Ollie's heart, and that was exactly what I was trying to do.

My ruse with Damon had muddied the waters, but I had to stay the course. For *all* our sakes.

CHAPTER FOURTEEN

"Good luck, miss," Nora said, stifling a yawn.

A flicker of guilt passed through me for making Nora rise so early, but then she handed me Mama's sheet music, and I felt reassured in my actions. Ollie loved both piano music and the sunrise. And this morning, before the picnic, it was my plan for us to enjoy both. But first, I needed to practice—*without* an audience.

"Thank you, Nora. I will need it today." As excited as I was for the picnic, to spend the whole of the day with Ollie, I dreaded seeing Miss Digby even more. She had been so cruel to me in town. I could only hope she would expose her true colors today.

Nora bobbed a curtsy, then closed the bedchamber door.

The corridor was as dark as a starless sky, the candles having all been snuffed out the night before. I hadn't thought to bring a candlestick, seeing as I never rose this early. I almost turned back to ask Nora to prepare one for me, but she'd already sacrificed enough sleep on my behalf.

I placed a hand on the wall to guide me and padded down the corridor. I'd dressed in a long-sleeved morning dress and thick shawl, but I still shivered. Grim-faced portraits lined the corridor, and although I couldn't see them, I felt their disapproving glares.

Clutching Mama's music to my bosom, I made my way to the grand staircase and carefully descended. The entry hall was as dark and drafty as the corridor upstairs, but when at last I reached the morning room, a fire burned in the hearth. I closed the door behind me, not wanting to wake anyone, then sat at the pianoforte.

As I lifted the lid, I marveled first at the pale-blue Jasperware cameos and then at the keys. This grand instrument contained so many more octaves than

Mama's sturdy square one at home. Finally, I spread Mama's sheet music on the elegantly carved music holder and then laid my fingers on the keys with trepidation.

At home in London, I'd played Mama's melody almost every day, but it had been weeks since I'd practiced. I began with scales to warm up my fingers, then played a few simple songs from memory. Finally, I set my hands on the piano keys for Mama's song. I played the notes correctly, though awkwardly. I took a steadying breath, trying to relax into the song's rhythm, but there was nothing for it; I was a fawn attempting to stand on unpracticed legs.

Mama had taught me to play her square pianoforte as a young girl by placing my fingers atop hers. I had loved sitting with her on the bench, the gentle way she'd guided me through the measures. But as I'd grown into a young woman, I didn't have the patience for practice. I wish I had been able to cultivate it though, because there wasn't a day that passed now that I didn't long for her music. Now, the harder I tried to master Mama's song, the worse I played.

By some miracle, I made it through the first page. But when I reached the second, I hit a wrong note. And then another. And yet another.

"Drat!"

A chuckle came from the door. The *open* door, I discovered with horror.

I peeked over my shoulder. Damon stood in the doorframe. He wore a dark-blue redingote and buckskin breeches and had a riding crop tucked under his arm. He really was handsome.

"Good morning." He smiled amusedly.

Though I was glad Ollie hadn't witnessed me play so poorly, I disliked being the source of Damon's amusement. I shot him a frown and returned to my music, hoping he'd continue on to his obvious errand in the stableyard.

But Damon walked into the room and stood at the end of the pianoforte.

"If you intend to distract me," I said, "it won't work. I play better with an audience."

"Oh. Well, I wasn't intending to stay, but if my presence will help you to play better . . ." He laid his riding crop on a side table and perched himself at the edge of the pianoforte.

"That was not meant as an invitation," I said.

Handsome but annoying. I continued playing.

"Why are you awake so early?" Damon asked. "I have never known you to be an early riser. And it is painfully obvious how much you hate playing the pianoforte."

"If you must know, I was hoping to practice before Ollie rose so I could play for him as we watched the sun rise together."

Damon chuckled. "I doubt my younger brother has seen a single sunrise since before he left for Eton."

My fingers fumbled over the notes. "You must be mistaken. Ollie *loves* the sunrise."

"Perhaps when he was a boy, but my younger brother now prefers sundown and everything that comes after."

I didn't dignify his insinuation that Ollie was a cad with a response.

Damon walked around the body of the pianoforte and sat beside me on the bench.

I made a valiant effort to ignore him, but no matter how far I scooted away from him, I couldn't escape the heat of his arm, the rich scent of his cologne, the gentle press of his knee against mine, and I hit a wrong note. With a frown, I moved my hands back to their original position to start the song over again.

"Why are you starting over?" Damon asked.

"I made a mistake."

"Only a minor one," he said. "You should keep going."

I shook my head. "I want to play it perfectly."

"You don't have to play the song perfectly to enjoy the music. I daresay if you start over every time you make a mistake, you will only ever play the first dozen measures."

I glared at my *un*welcome companion. "Perhaps *you* should like to play."

"Do you want me to?" he asked.

"I do." If only to prove how difficult this song was.

"Very well then. Prepare yourself to experience something delightful."

I rolled my eyes. "Careful, my lord. Pride cometh before the fall."

"Not pride, my dear Miss Kent—confidence." Damon briefly studied the music, then gently, almost reverently, placed his fingers on the keys.

And then he filled the room with Mama's melody. Like a river rushing over smooth rocks, the notes flowed from his fingers as easily as they had from Mama's. It felt as if it had been a lifetime since I'd heard her song played so purely, so perfectly, and I clung to every note. And for the briefest of moments, I almost felt as if she were here again.

Too soon, it was over. The last note hung in the air for a long moment, and then Damon gingerly removed his hands and placed them in his lap.

"That was . . ." I could hardly speak. "That was beautiful." My eyes welled with tears. "I did not realize how much I have missed hearing Mama's melody played properly."

"Your mother wrote this piece?"

I nodded. "Her square piano was a wedding gift from her parents, but music sheets are expensive, so . . . she wrote her own songs."

"It is lovely. Thank you for sharing it with me."

"Thank you for playing it for me." A tear trailed down my cheek. I gave myself a little laugh. "You must think me quite the watering pot."

"That's not what I'm thinking." He raised his hand toward my cheek as if he meant to dry my tears, but then he paused and produced a freshly laundered square from his pocket. Our fingers brushed when he handed it to me, and a warm shiver traveled up the length of my arm.

I swallowed hard. "What are you thinking then?"

"I'm not sure I should say."

"Now you must tell me." I patted my cheeks with his pocket square, then touched my hair to make sure nothing was out of place. "I shall be discomfited until you do."

Damon pressed his lips together, as if trying to hold a secret captive, but after a moment, he conceded the fight with a shake of his head. "I was thinking about how lovely your eyes are."

My heart raced. He sat so near and stared into my eyes so intently. Had I heard him correctly? Was he in earnest? Was it wrong that I wanted him to be? "W-what did you say?"

A noise sounded across the room. The fire? A floorboard? Damon glanced in the direction of the sound, but I could scarcely look away.

"Your eyes," he said more loudly but with less feeling. "They are lovely."

"Don't fall for his words, Hanny. Damon uses that line on all young ladies." Ollie entered the morning room, newspaper tucked under his arm, and sat on the sofa. "He probably played a song for you too."

Damon stood abruptly.

"I thought as much." Ollie snickered and opened his newspaper.

Damon walked to the window and leaned against the frame, his rigid form highlighted by the daylight. "It seems you have chosen the perfect day for a picnic," he said to Ollie. "Hardly any rain clouds."

Ollie lowered his newspaper. "I am surprised you carved out time in your schedule to enjoy it."

"Come now, Ollie. You know I would never pass up an opportunity to enjoy such lovely company." Damon winked at me.

Although I knew this action was for Ollie's benefit and not mine, my face warmed all the same. And I couldn't stop thinking about what Damon had said before Ollie had appeared. Did he really think my eyes beautiful?

Yesterday, when Lady Winfield had said she thought he'd developed an affection for me, I was certain she'd only been fooled by our ruse, but now it didn't *feel* like pretend.

There was something between Damon and me. What exactly, I did not know, but he was not the villain I had made him out to be. And I had to admit that I'd come to enjoy the time I spent with Damon. Not only was he an excellent conversationalist, but he was also a worthy opponent. I liked how he challenged me at chess and encouraged me to have my own opinions. And my heart had never felt that kind of stirring as it had when he'd played the pianoforte for me, like a tiny lightning bolt had struck the center of my chest. No, I could not deny that the time I spent with Damon was exhilarating, but it was also confusing and chaotic.

I was not the first to fall for his charms, and I would not be the last. Not to mention the fact that Damon didn't trust me. I'd shared more of myself than he had. He would not even tell me who his business contact was yesterday in town, and although I loved how he'd complimented my eyes, he'd not done it freely. I'd had to drag it out of him.

"Hanny?"

I blinked out of my reverie and looked at Ollie. "I'm sorry. What did you say?"

He set aside the newspaper and stood with a smile. "I asked what song you were playing before I arrived." He walked over to the pianoforte.

"Oh. It was nothing."

Ollie tilted his head to study the sheet music: Mama's notes in the margins and the curled corners of the pages. "It doesn't *look* like nothing. Will you play it for me?"

I glanced at Mama's sheet music and felt cold. I couldn't explain why. I'd risen early for this exact purpose, but I had no desire to play for him. Or I did . . . didn't I? Just not now.

Feeling out of countenance, I leaned forward and collected the sheet music. "I'm actually quite hungry. Perhaps another time." I rose and replaced the bench. "Shall we all go to breakfast?"

Ollie hesitated briefly but then nodded in agreement. He retrieved his newspaper from the sofa and moved toward the door.

I glanced at Damon, but he remained at the window and said nothing. "Will you join us, my lord?" I asked.

He shook his head. "I have delayed my morning ride long enough. Ares requires exercise."

I had the sudden longing to feel the wind on my skin, to smell the fresh scent of flowers and field and sky.

But no.

I'd come to Summerhaven to be with Ollie, and though things had not gone precisely to plan, it seemed I was finally being granted my wish to spend time alone with him, so I pushed away my frenzied feelings.

"Enjoy your ride," I said to Damon, then I walked to Ollie's side where I belonged.

CHAPTER FIFTEEN

AFTER A PLEASANT BREAKFAST WITH Ollie, Nora helped me change into my finest day dress—a creamy muslin gown patterned with tiny green flowers—then I donned a pale-green pelisse for warmth and matching bonnet to highlight the color of my eyes. Heaven knew I needed all the help I could get to stand out against Miss Digby today.

When I came downstairs, Damon and Ollie were waiting for our guests on the steps outside; Damon stood nearer the left, and Ollie the right.

I hated to see them so at odds. My pretending to have feelings for Damon didn't help their relationship, but hopefully once Ollie and I were happily settled, and he knew how Damon had helped bring us together, their relationship would mend.

As it was, I had no choice but to stand between them.

Ollie was too distracted by his fob watch to notice me, but Damon tipped his hat to me in greeting.

"How was your ride this morning?" I asked him.

"Bruising." He squared his shoulders as if to stretch the ache out of them. "And your breakfast?"

"Delightful," I said, and though Ollie was still too preoccupied by his watch to voice his agreeance, it *was* true. I felt better than I had in a week.

Ever since Lady Winfield had insinuated that Damon had developed a *tendre* for me, I'd felt off-balance. At every turn, I'd scrutinized Damon's words and deeds, constantly wondering if his feelings for me went beyond the terms of our ruse. Truly, it was no wonder that this morning, as I sat next to Damon at the pianoforte, I'd imagined meaning between us that didn't actually exist.

But thanks to a little distance from Damon and some time alone with Ollie this morning over breakfast, I knew now that I'd only been caught in the current of Mama's melody and that nothing more than friendship—and a tentative one at that—existed between us. He was merely helping me turn Ollie's head, and I was helping him avoid an unwanted marriage contract.

So why had he complimented my eyes *before* Ollie had come to the morning room?

He had only been trying to pacify a crying woman, and I shook away the thought; we were nothing more than friends.

Indeed, the only worry I had now was Miss Digby.

A cool breeze rustled through the aspens, and I was glad I wore my warmest pelisse.

Ollie craned his neck to see down the drive. I didn't see any conveyances approaching, but he descended the stairs anyway.

"Methinks my brother is overeager to greet his guests," Damon whispered.

I hated to notice, but he did seem it. If only Ollie had come to town with us last week, then he would have seen how Miss Digby had batted her lashes at Damon. But he hadn't. I could only hope that Miss Digby would reveal herself today so we could put this ordeal behind us.

At last, a pair of grays appeared at the gate. They pulled a dark-blue carriage—the Rumfords' carriage. Even if I had not seen it in town last week, the gold letter R decorating the doors would have given it away.

"Try not to stare," Damon said as the carriage came to a stop. "It will only encourage him."

"I don't understand."

"You will soon enough."

A footman scurried to open the door.

A ruffled cuff and an ornately carved walking stick appeared first, followed by a pair of buckled shoes and a pair of bright-yellow brocade breeches. Amelia's brother, Mr. Atherton, was the walking definition of a *fop*. The only thing missing was a powdered wig and painted face.

"You are staring," Damon said.

I forced a blink.

"Mr. Atherton," Damon greeted.

"Lord Jennings." He tucked his ornately carved walking stick under his arm and strode toward Damon and me, his coattails swishing as he walked, looking like a strutting peacock with all its plumes on display.

"It has been too long," Damon said.

"And yet, not nearly long enough." Mr. Atherton sighed theatrically. "Last we met, you stole a good deal more than your fair share of my money."

"*Won*, you mean." Damon gripped Mr. Atherton's shoulder, but spoke to me. "Mr. Atherton is terrible at the card table, and he is bitter I played his failings to my advantage."

"It is true." He laughed. "I am a terrible hand."

The two men jested as only old friends could, and I smiled politely, trying to hide my disapproval; far too many fortunes had been lost to gambling.

Mr. Atherton turned to me. "But what I lack at the tables, you lack in manners, Jennings." He tipped his head toward me.

"Forgive me," Damon said, taking up his gentlemanly bearing again. "Miss Kent, may I introduce the incomparable Mr. Atherton?"

Mr. Atherton removed his hat with a flourish and dipped into an overly low bow over my hand. "It is a privilege and an honor, Miss Kent."

I glanced at Damon. He looked near to hysterics. This could prove to be a long afternoon.

"Frederick!" Amelia leaned out of the carriage. "You must help me with these." She held two baskets out the carriage door.

Mr. Atherton straightened with a sigh and replaced his hat. "I'm sure Mr. Jennings is equal to the task."

"Mr. Jennings is already assisting me with *those* baskets." She indicated to Ollie, who was carrying a towering load to the handcart that would follow us to the picnic destination. Amelia huffed. "Really, Frederick. You could at least pretend to have manners."

"Not at the expense of my new waistcoat." He touched the covered buttons that ran down the center, then straightened the ruffled cuff of his sleeve.

"Allow me." Damon walked to the carriage, leaving Mr. Atherton and me alone.

Mr. Atherton turned to me. "How is it you have the unfortunate occasion to know our Lord Jennings?" he teased with a smile.

"Our mothers were the best of friends."

"So that makes you and Lord Jennings old friends too then?"

"Not exactly. He tolerated me at best. It was Mr. Jennings who was my friend."

Mr. Atherton pursed his lips. "But now it is Lord Jennings who is your *friend*?"

"I like to think them both my friends."

"Ah," he said. "I believe I understand you perfectly. It is hard for me to choose between them too." He winked.

My eyes widened. "You misunderstand me, sir."

"Do I?"

I was ready to tell him how wrong he was, but if I did, I would give away the ruse. It was better to let him think what he would.

Thankfully, Damon and Amelia were almost upon us.

"Hannah looks as pale as a bedsheet." Amelia frowned. "What have you said to startle her, Frederick?"

Mr. Atherton held his walking stick to his chest. "Your lack of confidence pains me, sister. I was only inquiring how Miss Kent knows our dear Jennings brothers. A perfectly amiable topic of conversation, I assure you."

"You don't expect me to believe that, do you? You must not make fun at Hannah's expense or we will never be invited back to Summerhaven, and I will never forgive you."

Damon nodded. "Hannah does tend to hold onto offense, Mr. Atherton. Best make your apologies now."

"I do *not* hold onto offense," I protested.

"You do." Damon grinned, and he reached out to touch the curls that framed my face. "Should I provide a few examples?"

I batted his hand away with a frown.

"That won't be necessary, Jennings," Mr. Atherton said to Damon, then he turned to me. "Miss Kent, please accept my most heartfelt apology."

"No need, truly."

Amelia tugged me to her side. "My brother can be intense, but underneath all his fancy clothes, he is a kind and gentle soul."

"As soft as custard." He patted his trim stomach. "I'm completely harmless."

I believed him. For all his frills and frippery, he didn't seem to take himself too seriously.

Ollie finally returned from his errand of loading the baskets and directing footmen, but he didn't contribute a single word to the conversation. I searched my mind for a topic that might interest him, but then a second carriage appeared and commanded his attention.

He separated himself from our group and stood tall to greet Miss Digby. It was the ball all over again.

Amelia and Mr. Atherton followed a few steps after Ollie to greet Miss Digby.

"Breathe," Damon said.

I hadn't even realized I'd been holding my breath. I forced air into my lungs.

"That wasn't so hard now, was it?" Damon said.

I narrowed my eyes at him.

He only smiled. "Even your glare is beautiful."

My eyes widened, and I glanced at Mr. Atherton and Amelia, who stood close by. And although neither seemed to have overheard him, we had to be careful. We wanted people to believe we were *beginning* to form an attachment, not about to have the banns read. I pulled him a few paces back and lowered my voice. "You shouldn't say things like that."

"Shouldn't I?"

"No. You should not. When you speak like that to me in private, it confuses things." It confused *me*.

"Go on," he said.

"Our goal was to make Ollie and all the marriage-minded mothers believe our ruse, but *your* mother believes you've developed a *tendre* for me."

"Would that be so awful?"

"Seeing as I am in love with your brother and you with bachelorhood, yes it would be quite awful indeed."

He laughed.

"It isn't funny, Damon. I don't want anyone to get hurt."

"Nor do I." He sobered.

"You'll watch your words then?"

He tilted his head side to side as if considering. "I promise not to say anything in front of Mother that is not true."

"Thank you." I sighed in relief, feeling much better knowing we understood each other.

I turned my attention once again to Ollie.

Drat! I'd been too distracted to see him greet Miss Digby. I needed to be more focused if I was going to turn this picnic to my advantage.

Miss Digby's pale-pink gown brought out the color in her cheeks, and her expertly curled blonde ringlets bounced on her shoulders as she walked at Ollie's side to join our group.

Damon stepped forward. "Miss Digby, how good of you to endure my brother's presence for one afternoon."

Ollie shot daggers at Damon.

Miss Digby smiled coyly at Damon. "It is a small price to pay to be invited to Summerhaven, my lord. I've been waiting such a long time for an invitation."

She and every other young lady of the *ton*. No wonder Damon needed the protection of our ruse.

Ollie offered his arm to Miss Digby, then led the company northwest toward our picnic destination. We walked the well-worn path in pairs, Ollie and Miss Digby, followed by Damon and Mr. Atherton, and finally, Amelia and me. I didn't know the location he'd selected, but it really didn't matter; with wildflowers decorating the rolling green hills, all of Summerhaven was beautiful.

Amelia looped her arm through mine and leaned close. "Lord Jennings is in rare form this morning—smiling, laughing. I honestly didn't think him capable of such levity."

"Levity is his favorite form of irritating me, I'm afraid." I told Amelia about all that had happened in town after we'd parted: the carriage getting stuck in mud, Damon carrying me to the side of the road, and the meaning Lady Winfield had inferred.

"*Has* he formed an attachment to you?" She eyed Damon's back.

"I had considered the possibility," I admitted quietly, and I almost told Amelia about how he had played Mama's melody for me this morning but decided against it; the last time we'd spoken of Mama in the modiste's shop, it had made her feel bad. "But no. He is as content in his bachelorhood as he ever was."

"Has *your* attention shifted?" She squinted at me.

"Heavens no. My heart lies with Ollie."

"You are certain?"

"But of course I am certain. I've loved Ollie for a lifetime." I set my gaze on Ollie ahead of us. He was pointing out the river in the distance to Miss Digby. She nodded, though her wandering gaze did not make her seem overly impressed.

"It would be okay," Amelia continued. "If you have developed feelings for Lord Jennings, you can tell me."

"There is nothing to tell," I said. "Truly. We are nothing more than co-conspirators."

"If you're sure," she said, and we continued on our way.

Several more minutes passed before Ollie announced we'd reached our destination.

I could only blink.

How could he?

I knew every branch, knot, and protruding root of this tree. This was *our* tree. The tree we'd spent each summer climbing and playing under. The tree we'd hid in so I wouldn't have to go home to London. The tree where he'd first kissed me.

"Will this location do?" Ollie asked Miss Digby.

Her ringlets bobbed in approval, and Ollie motioned for the servants to set up the picnic.

With haste, servants scurried to spread the blanket and arrange food on a table. Cold meats and cheese, finger sandwiches, and fruit made a veritable feast.

If only it weren't set under *this* tree, I might have been able to enjoy it.

The others went to the table to make their selections, but I needed a moment to compose myself.

A hand on my shoulder startled me. "Are you all right?" Damon asked.

"Why wouldn't I be?" My gaze traveled up the tree branches.

"I'm not sure," he said, "but I can see something is wrong."

"Well, I'm fine," I said.

"You don't have to pretend with me, Hannah."

"Isn't that what we do?"

He looked at me for a long moment, his eyes unsure.

"Never mind," I said, and I walked to the table where the food was laid. I selected a finger sandwich, a few berries, and cheese.

I sat on the opposite corner of the blanket from Ollie and Miss Digby, next to Amelia, and Damon and Mr. Atherton joined us a few moments later.

Miss Digby daintily fed herself one tiny bite at a time as if she were a little bird. If only she would fly away. But seeing as she would not, perhaps it would be best if I discovered more about my competition.

"Miss Digby," I said, "do you enjoy reading?"

"No." She laid her plate in her lap. "I am far too busy with my art and dance lessons for leisure."

She was probably also exceptionally talented at the pianoforte as well.

"Hannah lacks the patience to master such fine arts." Ollie took a bite of meat.

I frowned at Ollie. While it was true, there was no need to voice it.

"You know each other so well," Miss Digby said. "I didn't know. Why have you not mentioned Miss Kent before, Mr. Jennings?"

"There wasn't much to mention." Ollie shrugged. "Miss Kent and I haven't seen each other for a *very* long time."

"I see. Where are you from then, Miss Kent?" Miss Digby asked.

"London."

Her face scrunched. "But Mr. Jennings lets a set of rooms at Albany. If you are such close friends, then you must have seen one another last Season."

"Hannah only returned to London last year," Ollie said. "She hasn't had a proper Season."

I'd not told him that. I mean, I *had*, but only in a letter. Which meant he'd lied.

About everything.

Ollie had received my letters, and he'd known I had been living in London, and he'd not called on me. He'd not even written me.

"No Season?" Miss Digby said. "But you live in London! How dreadful."

"Not really. I much prefer quiet nights at home, reading by the fire." I could have explained why I'd not had a Season, but I refused to share any part of Mama with Miss Digby.

I glanced at the man I'd once considered my best friend and felt . . . betrayed? Humiliated? Angry?

"It is true we haven't seen each other for such a long while," I said to Miss Digby. "But Summerhaven was my home every summer of my youth. We all practically grew up together."

"Quite so," Damon said. "Those were the best days of my life."

Miss Digby's face pinched, and she looked at Ollie as if waiting for further explanation.

Ollie gave her an easy smile. A dimpled-chin smile. *My* smile. "It's true," he said. "We were like siblings."

My anger kindled. If *that* was how he remembered our relationship, then perhaps he needed me to refresh his memory. "That is not at all how I remember things, *Oliver*."

He tensed when I used his Christian name and glanced at Miss Digby.

"In fact," I continued, "it was under this tree that we—"

"Played," Ollie cut off my sentence.

So he *did* remember. This knowledge made his betrayal sting even more.

"Hannah used to tie her skirt between her legs so she could better climb," Ollie continued.

"You *are* like siblings." Miss Digby giggled behind a gloved hand.

"That is not even the half of it," Ollie said.

"Ollie," Damon warned with a shake of his head.

But Ollie pressed on. "Hannah was always trying to compete with Damon and me. I think she wished she'd been born a boy."

"Mr. Jennings, you are wicked," Miss Digby laughed openly.

My anger became a roaring fire. How could he be so cruel? He wanted to impress Miss Digby, but this was beyond the pale.

"I believe we all sometimes wish we could be someone we are not," Damon said.

"Yes," Amelia agreed, laying her hand on mine. "My brother, for instance, wishes he'd not been born a gentleman but rather a common man so he could be a Bow Street Runner."

"It is true," Mr. Atherton said. "Or at least it *was* true until I discovered the profession would require a wardrobe completely devoid of any color."

Amelia continued speaking, but I didn't hear a word.

Ollie glanced at me with a sorrowful expression, but I averted my gaze. He'd laid me down to raise himself up, and it was unacceptable.

"Please excuse me," I said. "I need to stretch my legs." And I stood and walked toward the riverbank without a backward glance.

CHAPTER SIXTEEN

THE PATH THAT LED TO the river was overgrown with tall grass; blades whipped my arms, and my half boots slipped in the soft soil, but I refused to stop walking until I reached the bank.

Why had Ollie been so cruel? So unfeeling? He'd said he wanted me to like Miss Digby, but he didn't seem to care much what her opinion was of me.

As I neared the shore, I yanked off my gloves and set them on a boulder, then stooped to gather a handful of pebbles. I flung a rock into the water, trying to skip it across the surface, but it sank immediately.

I turned back to the water, and with as much force as I could muster, I flung another rock. Again, it sank without skipping. Could *nothing* go my way today?

Behind me, footsteps squelched in the mud. I peeked over my shoulder, expecting to see Ollie, but I found Damon instead. He silently joined me at the bank.

"If you're planning to tell me what I'm doing wrong—"

"No," Damon said, cutting off my words. "If I recall correctly, *you* were always better at skipping rocks than both Ollie and me combined." He stooped to search out a handful of flat stones, handed several to me, then effortlessly skipped a few across the river's surface.

I *had* been better at skipping rocks. Much better, in fact. As children, the three of us had stood in this same spot. I'd been so good at skipping rocks, but the boys had been terrible at it. I'd shown them how to pick out the perfect stone, flat and light in weight, and how to fling their wrists just so, but they never could master it.

Until today, that memory had brought me joy, but all I could see now was a little girl with her skirt tied between her legs.

I sank another rock.

Ollie had treasured our friendship back then. What had changed? I couldn't make sense of his cruelty. Had I made some unknown social blunder and caused him embarrassment? Perhaps he wished to distance himself from me? Was I really so flawed?

The sharp edges of the remaining stones dug into my hand. "What is wrong with me, Damon? I know I'm not as lovely as Miss Digby, but what special trait does she possess that I lack?"

"Two thousand pounds."

My head jerked back in surprise. Whatever I was expecting him to say, it was not this. "You mean to say that Ollie is interested in Miss Digby because she is . . ." I couldn't even bring myself to say what Damon was insinuating.

"Wealthy?" Damon supplied. "Yes. That is precisely what I'm saying."

"You're wrong." I shook my head. "Ollie doesn't care about things like that. He would never pursue someone based on their income."

"He does, and he is. I thought you knew." Damon walked to the large boulder where I'd laid my gloves and sat. "Unfortunately, he has little choice in the matter."

"There is *always* a choice."

"Not if you are the second son of an earl," Damon said simply. "He is expected to maintain his position in society but given no means to do so."

"I understand well that his position in society is precarious."

"You understand that his position is precarious, but do you understand why?"

"Of course I do. He is a second son and therefore will not inherit Summerhaven, nor the title that comes with it. But that hardly matters. He will inherit Winterset Grange from your mother."

"Yes," Damon said. "But the grange will only give Ollie a toehold with which to stand in the world and nothing more."

"What of his allowance? Your father doesn't intend to cut him off, does he?"

"No. But the entailment on Summerhaven only ensures a modest allowance for second sons. It is enough to run the grange and provide a humble living, but in order to enjoy the abundant life he has become accustomed to, he will have to marry someone of means like Miss Digby, or he will have to earn his keep through employ."

Everything suddenly made sense. Why Ollie had been so intent to court Miss Digby and why Miss Digby obliged. *He* needed her money, and *she* needed his good surname. Ollie cared more about riches than he did about love.

I gritted my teeth.

While I knew that other men married for money, it being a practical way for second sons to secure the life they'd grown used to, I'd always thought our love would raise us above the system. The way Mama's and Papa's love had lifted them.

All I had ever wanted was to be happy in my marriage the way my parents had been happy in theirs. I wanted to marry for love and love alone. I'd thought Ollie had wanted the same, but I'd obviously been wrong. Ollie had weighed his options and decided me worth very little.

I was so mad at him, and I was mad at Society too. It wasn't right that a person's standing in Society should have the power to dictate who married whom.

The coldness of the boulder beneath me seeped into my bones. Water lapped the shore, and the tall reeds of grass rustled in the breeze.

I glanced up at Damon. "Doesn't it seem wrong to you that Society dictates who a person can or cannot marry?"

"Criminal," Damon agreed. "But that is the way of things."

"It should not be so. Such intimate and enduring relationships should be decided by the individuals themselves. It isn't fair." I huffed.

Damon made a noise that sounded suspiciously like a laugh.

"Is something funny?"

"Not at all. In fact, I agree with you completely. I was just remembering how you made that same sound that last time we stood here."

How he could laugh about that day, I had no idea. "You have no need to remind me of that awful day. I remember it well."

"Do you?"

I gritted my teeth. "Of course I remember." That horrid day stained my mind like black tea on a white dress.

"What is it you *think* you remember?"

"You know very well." I touched the curls that framed my face. "And I'd prefer not to discuss it."

"I am not a mind reader, Miss Kent. But I do believe we remember a few things differently."

I glanced up to frown at him, expecting to see a teasing glint in his eyes or smile on his lips, but I only found sincerity.

"Very well then, I will tell you what I remember. But you should know that my memory does not paint you in the best light."

"As I am well aware."

"We were skipping rocks just over there." I pointed to a shady spot on the riverbank. "I thought I saw a school of fish, but then you corrected me, saying they were tadpoles, nearly frogs, and I was so disappointed."

He made a face. "No, you weren't. You were excited. Don't you remember? You could scarcely tie up your skirt fast enough. And even though you didn't know how to swim, you walked right into the river. The water came right up to your waist."

"Even then I was headstrong."

"No," Damon said. "You were *fearless*."

I shook my head, confused. "I actually do remember that. But it doesn't make sense. I hate frogs."

"You didn't use to," he said quietly. "What else do you remember about that day?"

"Ollie grew bored of skipping rocks, so I suggested we play hide and go seek in the garden."

"And I agreed."

"Yes, but only if we played in the east wing. Ollie said no because your father had forbidden us from entering that wing, but you goaded him until he acquiesced."

"I was trying to impress you with my bravery," Damon said.

"You wished to impress me?" I looked at him askance.

"Is that so hard to believe?"

"It is actually. You were always playing so many pranks on me."

"I assure you, none were intended as such. Please go on."

"We ran across the great lawn toward the house. You were in the lead, but Ollie was close behind. I ran as fast as I could, trying to keep up, but I'd untied my skirts, and my foot caught the hem. I tripped." I shook my head. "You see? Ollie can hardly blame my dislike of skirts. They've caused me ire since girlhood."

"Yes." Damon laughed. "I suppose they have."

A memory came into my mind like a dream.

Damon rested his hands on his knees, breathing hard from running. "Are you hurt?"

I frowned up at him. "Skirts are stupid."

"I don't think so." He smiled.

"That's because you don't have to wear one."

"You're probably right," Damon said. "Come on. I'll race you back to the house." He helped me to stand, and then I chased after him all the way back to the house.

I blinked at Damon. "You ran back for me," I said. "Why did you do that? You hated me."

"Never," he said in a low voice. "Do you remember anything else of that day?"

My memories were fuzzy. The only things I could remember with clarity were the very things I'd tried so hard to forget. "You locked me in a traveling trunk," I said.

"To protect you from my father. He'd returned early from London, and I didn't want him to find you in the east wing."

"But you left me there all day." I truly thought I would die in that trunk.

"I would have come back if I could, but Father—" He shook his head. "I sent Ollie."

"He never came for me," I said. "I was locked in that trunk for hours; it was a housemaid who finally found me."

"I didn't know," he said in a low voice.

"And that night at dinner, you put a frog in my drinking glass."

"I'll admit putting that poor creature in your drinking glass was ill-conceived, but it was not malicious."

I raised an eyebrow at him.

"I went back to catch it for you. I wanted to make you smile."

"What?" I shook my head, feeling like my mind had been tied in a knot. For so long, I'd seen the circumstances from one point of view, the images sketched in plain black and white. And although the events *did* happen, Damon was coloring my memories with new meaning. He'd not hated me. And if what he said was true, he felt quite the opposite. But there was one thing that remained.

"What about my hair?" I asked. There could be no explanation for that action. "You cut it so close to the scalp that I had to disguise my baldness with bonnets and bows for months."

Damon's gaze fell to his mud-encrusted boots. "I never meant to cause you pain," he said quietly.

"Why did you do it then? Have you no further explanation?"

"I do." Damon swallowed hard. "But first, you must promise to hear me out."

I nodded.

"There was a footman," he said tentatively. "Thomas was his name, and he was desperately in love with a scullery maid. She was leaving, though I can't remember why now. Thomas didn't want to forget her, so she gave him a lock of her hair . . ."

"Go on."

"Well, it was nearing the end of summer, and you, too, were leaving Summerhaven soon, and I would be leaving for Eton, and I thought that if I had a lock of *your* hair, I would never forget *you*."

The same warmth of desire that I'd felt earlier this morning while he'd played Mama's melody rushed up at me.

"The night before you were to return home to London, while we all slept in the nursery, I crept over to your bed with a pair of scissors, intending to cut a small lock of your hair. But instead of trimming the end like I should have, I cut near the scalp.

"I knew right away that I'd made a mistake," he continued. "I ran back to my room and prayed the whole night for a miracle, that your hair would grow back. I will never forget how you screamed the next morning, how you shouted your hatred for me." Damon looked at me, his eyes regretful and sad. "I'm sorry," he whispered.

I hadn't thought it possible but knowing why he'd done what he had bled me of any anger and lingering resentment, and for the first time in a long time, I saw the man sitting beside me for who he really was: a true friend.

Damon had always treated me like a friend and equal—he'd encouraged me to skip my own rocks, to catch my own frogs. And when I had tripped and fallen, it was Damon—not Ollie—who'd run back for me. Damon had locked me in the traveling trunk to protect me from his father; he'd caught me a frog to make me smile; and he'd cut my hair because he hadn't wanted to forget me.

Damon had cared for me, and I had cared for Damon. I'd cared for him as much as I cared for Ollie. How had I forgotten that?

"I forgive you," I said.

Damon let out a long breath, as if he'd been holding it for a very, *very* long time.

"What did you do with the lock of hair?" I asked softly, so he would know that I wasn't asking out of malice, but because I was honestly curious.

"You can hardly expect me to remember." He laughed lightly. "I was just a boy."

"You seem to remember everything else about that day," I said, but he said nothing in return. "Well, will you at least tell me if it worked?"

"Did what work?" Damon asked.

"Did my lock of hair help you to remember me?"

Damon's eyes flicked up to meet mine, and he smiled uncomfortably. "We had best rejoin the others now. We have been gone a long while."

Damon stood and held out his hand to assist me from my seat on the boulder.

I placed my hand in his, and without a glove, our skin touched. His hand was warm, his palms rough, his grip strong. My half boots slipped in the slick soil, and Damon's arm came around my waist.

I looked up at him through my lashes.

Damon loosened his hold, testing my balance. "Can you stand?"

I nodded, and he released me to retrieve my gloves, but in truth, I was more than a little off-balance and not because of the soggy soil.

We started back toward the picnic in silence. It was as if my life's entire foundation had been upturned one stone at a time. Everything I thought I knew was now opposite. Damon was not the villain I'd made him out to be. He maybe even cared for me, or at least, he had when we were children. And Ollie did not care for Miss Digby as I'd worried, but he was trapped by his circumstance.

We were *all* trapped by our circumstances.

When we came upon the path that led back to the old oak tree, I stopped walking. "I think I will walk back to the house," I told Damon.

He studied me as if looking for injury. "Is something the matter?"

"I am well," I said. "I just have no interest in providing any further entertainment for Ollie or Miss Digby today. Will you please tell the company I have a headache and have gone to lie down?"

"May I see you safely back to the manor first?"

"That is gentlemanly of you, but I prefer to walk on my own just now."

Damon glanced uneasily toward the manor, but he seemed to understand I wasn't voicing my opinion but rather my decision, because he didn't follow me when I turned and walked away.

CHAPTER SEVENTEEN

When the first glimpses of daylight lit my bedchamber, I sat up in bed.

Yesterday, I'd been angry that Ollie had chosen to court Miss Digby instead of me and for caring more about what Society thought of him than what I thought, but what if he didn't realize he even had a choice?

I'd come to Summerhaven expecting us to pick up where we'd left off, but we'd not spoken of our feelings for many years. Perhaps he wasn't certain I still loved him. But if he *did* know the feelings of my heart and that I didn't care about wealth or status or about anything but being with him, perhaps he would marry me.

It would be a sacrifice in some ways, but true love *required* sacrifice. Mama had sacrificed a life of luxury to marry Papa, and they had been happy. It stood to reason that so, too, could Ollie and me.

The thought of confessing my affection for him made me feel like a tree without leaves, naked and exposed, but it was the only way. The time for games and subtleties had passed; if I wanted Ollie to choose me, then first, he needed to know that I chose him.

When Nora at last entered my bedchamber, the sky was still dark; the sun had risen some time ago, but clouds hung low, blocking out any light. How I missed the warmth of the summer sun.

Nora helped me into a blue dress (Ollie's favorite), and then she styled my curls into a loose plait (my favorite). I dabbed a bit of rose water onto my wrists and neck, pinched a little color into my cheeks, then stood from the vanity with determination.

As I walked down the long corridor toward the grand staircase, I wondered if Damon would also be downstairs this morning or if he would already be out riding Ares. A sudden urge to ride the hills with him flitted through me. Perhaps I could delay my conversation with Ollie until after I'd ridden with

Damon. Perhaps I could get him to tell me more about—no. What was I thinking? I didn't want to ride with Damon. He was irritating and proud, and even though we'd had *some* good experiences together this summer, it was *Ollie* I wished to spend time with. It was Ollie I cared for. And Ollie I needed to speak with this morning. Not Damon. I'd loved Ollie since I was a young girl, and it was time to make my feelings known to him.

I found him in the morning room, sitting on a sofa by the window, reading *The Morning Post*. An image came into my mind of the two of us sitting close together and reading the newspaper. He would take the political section, and I would read current events or perhaps the other way around. It didn't matter, so long as we were together. I just had to convince him.

I straightened my posture. This was it. This was the day my life would change forever. Pulse pounding, I stepped into the room.

Ollie looked up from his paper. "Good morning."

"Morning," I said, but that was *all* I said. How did one bring up the feelings of one's heart?

"I would have thought that after such a sudden and terrible headache yesterday you would have slept later."

"Headache?" I asked.

"That was the excuse Damon provided for you not returning to the picnic."

"Oh. Yes, of course." I sat on the opposite end of the sofa from him and neatly folded, then refolded, my hands in my lap.

"Miss Digby was disappointed you didn't return," Ollie said.

"Was she?"

"Yes, she was. It was quite rude of you not to return to the picnic."

"Rude of *me*? A headache is a perfectly valid reason to leave a picnic."

"Only if one truly exists."

I clenched my jaw. After the way Ollie had treated me yesterday, he had little right to lecture me on manners. But I did not wish to quarrel with him today. I'd come here to speak to him of my feelings, and I would not be deterred.

Still, I hadn't the faintest idea how to broach the subject. I searched the recesses of my mind for an example of how to proceed. Surely, one of Miss Radcliffe's or Miss Edgeworth's heroines had declared her suit to a gentleman, but I could not think of one example.

"Well, I hope you're feeling better today," Ollie continued, "because Miss Digby is coming to call on you."

I stiffened. "I'm not feeling up to the visit."

Ollie released a heavy breath and set his newspaper on the side table. "May I ask why not?"

I gathered my courage and looked him in the eye. "Because I have no wish to watch you court her."

Ollie's head tilted to one side, and his brow creased in the center.

"Do you care for me, Ollie?"

"Of course I do. You are one of my dearest of friends, Hanny. That is why it's so important to me that you and Miss Digby become friends."

"No, Ollie. Do you care for me as more than a friend? Because . . . I do."

His eyes widened in surprise.

"When the letter arrived inviting me to Summerhaven," I hurried to explain, "I thought it had been written at your behest. I thought you wanted to court *me*."

"Hannah, I—" He cut off his words with a shake of his head. "This whole summer you have only had eyes for Damon. You played chess with him, rode horses with him, you danced with *him*. I thought you were enamored with him just like all the other young ladies of the *ton*."

I bit my lip, knowing I should not confess to mine and Damon's ruse—if Ollie knew, it could further alienate the brothers—but how else could I explain my actions? How could Ollie know for certain that my heart lay with him and not his brother? I *had* to tell him.

"It was a ruse," I said.

His eyebrows dipped low, furrowing his brow. "*What* was a ruse?"

"Everything. What you saw between Damon and me . . . Our relationship was a ruse."

"Why would you—"

"Damon needed to delay marriage, and I needed you to see me. It was a charade."

"A charade?" he repeated.

I nodded. "The only reason I allowed Damon to pretend to court me was to turn your head."

Ollie blinked.

"You made me a promise," I pressed on. "Years ago, under the old oak tree. You said we would always be together."

"I made that promise to you when we were *children*," he said softly. "You must understand that we can never be anything more than friends."

"You're wrong. That is what I'm trying to tell you. You don't have to court Miss Digby. You will inherit the grange. We will be happy there. If you are worried about living in reduced circumstances, you needn't. I don't care about being wealthy or possessing a title. I only care about *you.*"

"And I, you," Ollie said. "Indeed, every happy memory of my childhood includes you. Your letters helped me survive Eton. But when I entered Cambridge, and I finally understood what our exchanging letters might mean, I stopped writing to you. I thought you understood. I'm so sorry, Hanny, but I have never thought of you in that way." His eyes pinched at the corners with pity.

My hands began to tremble as the truth of his feelings sunk into my soul. He did not love me. He had *never* loved me, at least not in the way I loved him. Eight years I had loved him. Eight years I had waited for him to send for me. Eight years I'd written to him. And although I'd never declared my love, the truth had been there, between every word, sentence, and paragraph. How could he not have known? Unless . . . he *had* known. It suddenly seemed so obvious. He had known of my affection for him, but he did not feel the same for me. That was why he stopped writing to me. My eyes stung with embarrassment. "Do you love her?"

Ollie was quiet for a long moment. "We are a good match," he finally said. "I have a good name, which she needs, and she has a—"

"A sizable dowry, which you want. Yes, I know."

He winced. "Please do not think poorly of me. I am only doing what—"

I held up a hand, stopping him. "But do you *love* her?" I asked again.

"With time, I hope to."

My heart broke with those words. He did not love her, but he also did not love me. There was nothing more to say, nothing more to be done. He'd made his choice, and it was not me. "Then I wish you every happiness." I stood to leave.

"Wait," Ollie said.

But I fled to the entry hall. Servants were milling about, and I tried to avoid their gazes, but it was impossible. I needed to leave. Now. But to where?

"Miss Kent, up early two mornings in a row."

My gaze snapped up to where Damon descended the stairs. As soon as our eyes met, he took the steps two at a time and didn't stop until he stood before me. "What is wrong?"

My breaths came in short bursts now, and tears threatened to fall from my eyes, so I merely shook my head.

Footfalls sounded behind me. "Hanny," Ollie called after me.

Damon glanced over my shoulder and then back at me with a furrowed brow.

"Take me away from here," I whispered.

Without a word, Damon tucked me under his arm and led me toward the door. But Ollie met us in the middle of the room and blocked our way.

"Hanny, *please*," Ollie said, bending his knees to look into my eyes.

I leaned into Damon's shoulder.

"I could be wrong," Damon said, "but I don't believe she wishes to speak with you."

"*You*." Ollie glared viciously at Damon.

But Damon did not seem to care. He carefully ushered me around Ollie and out the front door.

The cool air bit my cheeks as we walked down the outside steps to a curricle already waiting in the drive. Damon handed me up and then climbed up himself. He gathered the reins in his hand, and with a flick of his wrist, the pair of horses jolted down the lane for the gates.

CHAPTER EIGHTEEN

I made the mistake of looking back.

Ollie stood on the front steps, watching Damon and me go, his shoulders drooped, his hat fisted in his hands.

I trained my gaze on the barren road before me again. What would become of me? Without Ollie, I didn't know. I'd placed all my hopes for the future in marrying him, but those hopes had been in vain. I had nothing now. No dowry, no name, no prospects.

The curricle bumped along the road, and I gripped the edge of my seat to steady myself. I breathed in the crisp country air, inhaling in short staccato bursts.

Damon shifted the reins into one hand and produced a handkerchief from the inner pocket of his great coat.

"Will you tell me what happened?" Damon said in a gentle voice.

I dabbed the moisture from my cheeks. "I would not know where to start."

"The beginning is generally advisable," he said with a small smile.

"That is the problem. I don't know the beginning of my and Ollie's story, only the end. And to recount that would be much too humiliating."

"Would you have me guess what's transpired?"

I shook my head. "It is best we both forget the entire scene."

Damon ably maneuvered our conveyance around a large mud puddle. "I'm afraid you ask the impossible. You ran from the drawing room crying with my brother in full pursuit. Seeing as he thinks *we* are in the prelude to a relationship, I have half a mind to call him out."

Ollie did *not* think Damon and I were in a relationship anymore, but I did not have the capacity to handle Damon's ire just now. I would tell him everything later when my emotions had settled. I lifted my gaze to him. "You would not call out your own brother."

"As a gentleman, I don't rightly have a choice. Unless you tell me otherwise."

He was only trying to make me smile, but I wasn't in the mood to be teased. "I will tell you what happened. But from this day henceforth, we will never speak of this again." I took my time folding Damon's handkerchief, considering my words. But there was no way to make this story any less mortifying.

"Yesterday, after what you said about Ollie's circumstance, I thought perhaps you might be wrong. I hoped that if he knew he had another choice in life, if he knew that I loved him, then he wouldn't wish to marry Miss Digby. I thought—" My voice wavered. "It doesn't matter what I thought. This morning I confessed my feelings to Ollie, and he informed me he does not feel the same. You were correct." I paused. "He is determined to marry Miss Digby even though he's admitted he does not love her. I shouldn't have doubted you. I must apologize."

"Please don't." Damon glanced away from the road to look at me. "You must know I take no delight in your pain." Damon spoke with sincerity, but I heard only pity.

How silly I must seem to him. How naive. I spoke of love and marriage to a man who did not value them.

"Do you want to know what I think?" he asked. I shook my head, but he continued anyway. "I think you are in love with the *idea* of love."

A laugh burst from my mouth. "That is absurd."

"Is it?"

"Yes!"

"You love Ollie, to be sure, but you love him as a little girl loves a puppy—with naive innocence and far too much idealism. It is admirable you wish to save my brother from a loveless marriage, but he is his own man and must make his own decisions."

I frowned. "Have you no words of comfort?"

"I promised to always tell you the truth."

"Yes. But must you put it so bluntly?"

"The truth is often painful, but not without virtue. That is to say, now that the truth is out, you are free to move forward."

"I don't want to move forward. Not without Ollie."

"Forget Oliver," Damon said brusquely. "If he cannot see the strong, opinionated, *beautiful* woman before him, then he does not deserve you."

Warmth bloomed inside me like a rose on a summer day. No man had ever spoken such kind things to me before.

"And forgive me for saying this," he continued, "but is Ollie truly the man you want to marry anyway?"

"You know he is."

"I know he *was*, but my younger brother is not the same person you knew as a girl. *You* are not that same girl. Life, and all that it requires, has changed all of us," Damon said. "I fear my brother would censure the things that make you *you*."

I shook my head. "He would never."

"He already has, Hannah. First at the ball, then in the stable with your choice of horse, and even yesterday at the picnic."

With evidence laid so clearly before me, it was impossible not to see the truth: Ollie was not the boy I'd once known, and he did not love me.

The evidence had been there all along; I should have guessed his feelings when his letters began to dwindle and when he'd not been present to greet me at the beginning of the summer. And even if I'd not guessed the truth then, I should have seen it when he'd chosen not to dance with me at the Rumfords' ball and when he'd missed the opportunity to walk with me in the garden. At every turn, Ollie had revealed his true self, but I'd not believed him.

How could I have?

Ollie was my dearest childhood friend. My foundation. The dream upon which I had built all other dreams. He was the man Mama had wanted me to marry, the man Papa approved of. If Ollie was not the man for me, then I didn't know where that left me.

And what of my ruse with Damon? We'd been seen together on a number of occasions now—even Lady Winfield believed us to be forming an attachment. And although Damon had given me his word as a gentleman that he would sooner marry me than allow my reputation to be tarnished, I had no desire to trap a man into marriage—especially one who abhorred the institution.

I trained my gaze on the unfamiliar rock-strewn road before me. I didn't know where we were going or even how long it would take to get there. "How much farther to our destination?"

"Are you feeling ill?"

"Only mildly. Riding in the open air is easier. Your boots are in no danger."

"To be safe . . ." He produced a small linen bag from his coat pocket and loosed the twine at the top to reveal a ginger candy. "May I interest you in a confection?"

"Do you regularly carry sweets in your pocket?" I asked, taking the sack.

"Only recently, Miss Kent."

The curricle suddenly felt much too small for two people, and not knowing what to say, I ate another piece of ginger.

"And to answer your original question," Damon said, "I have no destination in mind."

"Ollie said—" My voice caught on his name, but I pushed passed it. "That is, your brother said you had business."

"I was going to visit my father's tenants to check on the harvest," Damon said. "But now we are merely enjoying a leisurely ride together. We can return to the manor whenever you wish."

"I have no wish to return anytime soon." I was not prepared to face Ollie, nor Miss Digby, who was apparently coming to call upon me. "I would much rather join you in seeing to your affairs."

Damon bounced the reins in his hand, his jaw tight. "You would not."

"On the contrary, I am intrigued to learn what it is you do all day, and I should like to see your father's holdings. In all the years I have been visiting Summerhaven, I have never been to the corner of your estate that houses your tenants."

"That was not an accident, and we won't be going there today."

I frowned. "Then what do you propose we do? I refuse to go back to the house, and you refuse to go forward."

"I suppose we shall have to drive the curricle in circles."

"Without a chaperone? What will your mother think?"

"What she thinks is not my concern right now. Luckily, we are riding in an open-air curricle and have not ventured from my family's estate. While our situation may not be strictly appropriate, it is also not entirely *in*appropriate."

"Yes, but your mother requested we have a chaperone, and I don't want to disobey her wishes. Perhaps if we are seeing to your errand and surrounded by people, our offense would be much less severe."

"Hannah," Damon warned with a shake of his head.

"Damon." I raised my chin. "Whatever it is you are hiding, I can handle it. I am not some helpless child you need to protect."

He glanced at his handkerchief damp with my tears and the linen candy bag in my lap, then looked at me questioningly.

I quickly rearranged my hands over them. "I know you probably think me nothing more than a proper young lady who will swoon at the sight of sadness, but I'm certain Summerhaven is incapable of producing anything to rival the atrocities I've encountered in London with my service with the church. I've seen injured men returning from war, widowed women struggling to survive, and hordes of hungry, dirty children. So your tenants—even if they are struggling during this uncommonly rainy season—at least have a roof over their heads, fertile land to farm, and a wise and generous landlord."

"I wish that were so," Damon said. "Please allow me to spare you from this."

"I am afraid I'm far too *headstrong* to allow you to turn us back now."

"I feared as much." He chewed his lip. "I see that I can't win this, but I hope you will at least remember that I did try." He clicked his tongue, and the horses sprang forward.

CHAPTER NINETEEN

AN ODOR PERMEATED THE AIR as we neared a small stone cottage. It did not have as potent an aroma as London, but it *was* distinct—like sheep and earth and rain.

"We can still turn back," Damon said.

I squinted at the cottage in the distance, and though it was partially blocked by a hill, I saw nothing that warranted us turning back. The road was rough with rocks, but it was not in disrepair, and the stone cottage, although small, appeared sturdy enough.

"Let's continue," I said.

We passed a field, and sheep looked up from their grazing—though I wasn't sure what they were eating as the field was mostly void of vegetation.

The road became increasingly rutted, and the horses slowed their pace. Damon clicked his tongue to urge them on, but they were reluctant as we came around a curve.

Slowly, the cottage came more clearly into view. Up close, with a crooked frame and a roof that boasted more holes than cover, the house did not even look fit to house livestock. Stagnant water pooled at the bottom of the stone structure, and there was evidence of rodents too.

The tenants emerged from the cottage: a bedraggled woman with a baby on her hip, followed by a limping man. His form was familiar, but I could not place where I'd seen him before.

Damon pulled back on the reins, halting the horse.

"M'lord," the man said and bowed as best he could. "We weren't expecting you."

"Mr. Turner," Damon greeted in return. "My father has sent me to check on the harvest. But are *you* well? Why aren't you at work in the field?"

"I am well enough," the man said. "But the crop . . ." He glanced at the barren, soggy field behind him, then swallowed hard, his Adam's apple rolling the length of his too-thin neck. "There was an early frost and . . . the crop has failed, sir."

Damon surveyed the land with a bleak expression.

"And the rain is soon to fall," Mr. Turner continued. "Roof won't hold without shorin'."

Damon lifted his gaze to the roof. "You received the supply of thatch?" he asked, and the man nodded. "But I see you have not made use of it."

"I've spent day and night trying to save the crops, sir."

Damon nodded. "You are a hard worker, Mr. Turner. And a smart one too. But I was told to remind you that Michaelmas is only a few weeks away and your payment is due."

The man lowered his head, out of deference or defeat I couldn't be sure. "Yes, m'lord."

"I will not take any more of your time then," Damon said.

"Thank you, m'lord." Mr. Turner nodded for his wife to go back into the cottage, which she promptly did, and then he hobbled to the side of the house where there was a large pile of thatch. After securing a bundle onto his back, he moved toward a ladder leaning against the front of the house.

"Surely, he doesn't intend to climb that ladder," I said. "Is there no one to assist him in repairing the roof?" I asked, though I already knew the answer. He wouldn't be risking his life to climb that ladder if he had any other option.

Damon shook his head.

I held my breath as the man climbed the wobbling ladder one rung at a time. At the top, he shakily transferred onto the roof. But by the grace of God, he made it safely.

"We have to help him," I said, my voice barely above a whisper.

"If I could, you must believe I would."

"You *can* help them. Send word to your father immediately. His steward has obviously not informed him of his tenants' living conditions."

"He knows," Damon said, and he stared down at the reins in his hands, and his vibrant blue eyes were now stormy and gray.

"And . . . so did you," I realized. "This was the reason you didn't want me to join you today."

"Please do not look at me that way," Damon said.

"You must help them," I said again but more firmly this time. "This roof will not hold out any moisture. The Turners will become ill. They could die. Damon, think of the baby."

He pressed his eyes closed for a long moment, and I thought he was seeing reason, but then he slowly shook his head. "I can do nothing more for these people."

"These people?" Anger boiled inside me. How could he speak so dismissively? "*These people* are *your* tenants, Damon."

"They are my father's tenants."

"And one day yours," I snapped back.

"I know how this must seem to you, but if I were to get down from this curricle and assist those poor souls—" Damon gritted his teeth. "There are forces at work here that you don't understand."

"Then tell me." I wanted to believe that Damon, the kind man I'd come to know these past weeks, who had saved me at the Rumfords' ball and carried me across the mud puddle and played Mama's song so reverently on the pianoforte, was *also* a kind landlord. But the dilapidated home and farm before me provided no evidence. "Please." I pleaded with him to tell me, to *trust* me.

"I am not in a position to help them," he said.

I shook my head, disappointed. "You *are* in a position to help, and I must insist you do so."

"I am sorry, but my hands are tied." He flicked the reins to encourage the horses forward.

"No!" I grabbed the reins and pulled back with all my strength.

Damon reached as if to retrieve the reins from my grasp, but I held them tight. As soon as we came to a halt, I flung the reins back at him and stood.

"What are you doing?" Damon reached out to steady me.

"What *you* will not." I gathered my skirts, preparing to climb down from the curricle without assistance.

"But it is about to rain."

"As I am well aware. Please return to your grand home where you will be warm and dry by the fire."

"Lud, Hannah. Is that what you think I want?"

"What else can I think, *my lord*?" His proper title sounded like a curse.

Damon swore under his breath, and as I moved to step down, he caught my wrist. "I am content to offer my back, but I will not risk yours. I will assist Mr. Turner with the roof, and you will wait here."

"I most certainly will not." I attempted to snatch back my arm, but he held it tight.

"Though quarreling with you is a most enjoyable pastime, I cannot allow you to win this argument." And he tugged my arm, drawing me back into my seat. "I will work more quickly knowing you're safe. Please. Wait here." Damon swung himself down from the carriage and secured the horses to a nearby post.

I frowned at his back as he disappeared around the corner of the house where the thatch was piled. If he thought he'd won this debate simply because he'd managed to speak the last word, he was gravely mistaken. I awkwardly alighted from the carriage. My half boots sunk into the mud almost to my ankles, and I quickly lifted my hem.

"I told you to wait in the curricle." Damon's voice was gruff behind me, and when I turned to face him, I found his expression matched his tone.

"You did, but I never agreed."

Damon gave me a stern look, but he didn't send me away. Mr. Turner and his family needed as much help as they could get, and Damon knew it. "Thatch," he finally said. "Carry it from that pile there"—he pointed toward the side of the house—"and bring it to me here on the ladder."

With a nod, I hurried toward the pile, and Damon went in the opposite direction to the ladder. I retrieved a large bundle, and when I turned back, he was already waiting on the ladder. I handed him the thatch and then turned back to the pile. I tried to move briskly, but heavy mud already caked my hem, slowing me. I held up my skirts as best I could as I gathered another bundle of thatch, but there was nothing for it. I simply could not hold up my hem and carry the thatch at the same time.

A most unladylike idea came to me. Ollie would not approve, but he wasn't here, and my promptness was more important than my pride at present. I dropped the thatch and bent to tie up my skirt.

With the thatch in my arms once again, I rushed to where Damon descended the ladder.

His gaze dropped to my exposed ankles, and he raised an eyebrow.

I thrust the bundle at him, then rushed back to the pile again.

It didn't take long for sweat to gather on my forehead and my arms to feel heavy. They ached desperately and would surely fail me at any second, but I vowed to press on until they did. Rain began to fall, making my errand all the more difficult, but I wouldn't stop, *couldn't* stop, until the men had what they needed to cover every hole in this roof.

"You should go inside now," Damon called from the roof.

"Not until you have enough thatch." That poor baby *would* sleep in a dry bed tonight.

I repeated the same process what felt like a hundred times, retrieving thatch, handing it to Damon, and then running back to the pile to do it all over again. Finally, Damon said they had enough.

I turned toward the curricle to wait for Damon.

"Won't you come inside, miss?" the woman—Mrs. Turner, I presumed—called to me from the door. "You can warm yourself by the fire."

I hesitated. As wonderful as that sounded, my dress was soaked through and my half boots muddy. But I didn't know how much longer Damon would be at work, and now that I had stopped moving, I was already beginning to feel chilled.

"Thank you," I said, and I attempted to wring water from my dress, but it made little difference; I was as wet as a fish.

"Make haste now. I don't want the children to catch their death."

CHAPTER TWENTY

INSIDE THE COTTAGE, I WAS surprised to find three more children and an older woman. It was a small space for so many people—not even as large as my room at the Winfields' estate—but obvious efforts had been made to improve the home: a rug on the dirt floor, simple curtains over the windows, and a vase of fresh wildflowers on the table.

On the left side of the room, a fireplace and sideboard made for a kitchen; in the center were a table and chairs; and on the left side of the house was a door that appeared to lead to a single bedchamber.

"Thank you for inviting me into your home, Mrs. Turner," I said, stepping around a bucket full of rainwater.

"What little we have, we have to share," she said. "And please call me Betsy. Mrs. Turner is my husband's mum." She nodded toward the fire where the older woman was tending a large pot of what smelled like stew.

"We have a visitor, Mum. This is . . ." Betsy looked at me.

"Hannah Kent," I supplied.

"This is Miss Kent, Mum. She's come for a visit with the master."

Mrs. Turner turned from her task and eyed me with suspicion. Her gaze raked over me, stopping on the hem of my skirt, which was still tied in a knot above my ankles.

I quickly stooped to untie it.

"The master?" Mrs. Turner sneered. "What business has he here? Come to grind our noses further into the dirt?"

"Now hush, Mum. You mustn't say such things." Betsy glanced at me worriedly. "It is Lord Jennings who has come, not Lord Winfield, and he has been good to our family. Even now he is working on our house."

"Is that what all that racket is about?"

"All that racket is fixing our roof," Betsy said. "Now move to the side so Miss Kent can stand by the fire."

With a huff, Mrs. Turner moved ever so slightly to the side and resumed stirring.

I tried to take up as small a space as I could and held out my hands to warm them. The stew smelled of vegetables and herbs and had a savory aroma similar to the recipe Mama and I used to feed the poor. A twinge of guilt coursed through me, thinking about Papa being left alone to serve the community without Mama or me to help him.

"May I stir that for you?" I asked Mrs. Turner.

Her gaze turned skeptical.

I held out my hand to prove that it wasn't an idle offer.

She pulled back with a shake of her head. "I don't want it to burn."

I nodded that I understood and turned my attention to the children who continued playing quietly with their little toys on the floor. Across the room, the baby let out a rasping cry, and Betsy hurried over to the cradle and gently picked the baby up.

"There, there, sweet baby John," she soothed as she sat on a rocking chair and pulled down the neckline of her dress and lifted him to her breast.

My cheeks warmed. I'd never seen a woman feed her child—Mama didn't have any more children after me, and even if she had, she likely would have employed a wet nurse.

Baby John cooed, and Betsy smiled down at him.

I suddenly felt as if I were intruding on something special, sacred even, and I looked away, catching Mrs. Turner's gaze.

"Nothing to be ashamed of," she said. "Perfectly natural, just as God intended it to be. Soon as this here babe is weaned, Betsy will work as a wet nurse."

Wet nurses could make a tidy profit, and sometimes their wages were even greater than what a man could make harvesting the fields. But to work as a wet nurse, Betsy would have to leave her own children. The family would benefit monetarily, but to not see them every day seemed like a great sacrifice.

"She will make a wonderful wet nurse," I finally said.

"Right you are." Mrs. Turner nodded.

As if in agreeance, Baby John let out a full and contented sigh.

Betsy pulled the infant from her breast, and after swaddling him in his little blanket and laying him in his cradle, she returned to the fire to help Mrs. Turner with the stew.

I felt a tug on my skirt. A little boy, no more than five or six years old, with big brown eyes and a tangle of dark curls, stood at my side. "Well, hello there. What is your name?"

"Matthew," the little boy said.

"It is very nice to meet you, Matthew." My hands trembled without the nearness of the fire to warm them, so I tucked them into the folds of my skirt.

"Do you live in the big 'ouse?" he asked.

I shook my head. "No, but I am a guest there."

"What's it like?"

He likely wanted me to tell him about Summerhaven's luxuries, the fine furnishings and the exotic foods, but how could I when he would likely never enjoy those things?

"The manor is lovely, but"—I leaned conspiratorially close and lowered my voice—"the east wing is haunted."

Matthew gaped. "Really?"

"Well, I have never actually seen any ghosts, but that is what Lord Jennings told me when I was your age."

Matthew's face scrunched as if he were considering the truthfulness of my statement.

"The entirety of the east wing is not actually haunted." Damon's voice surprised me from behind, and he joined us at the fire. "Only the hall of portraits. You have never seen so many angry faces." Damon narrowed his eyes and pursed his lips, imitating the paintings of his ancestors.

Matthew laughed at Damon's antics, but I was too distracted by the rainwater dripping from the ends of his hair to be amused. I liked his hair this way, brushed across his forehead. A little looser, freer. I itched to run my hands through the inky strands. It reminded me of the boy I once knew, once liked.

I liked him *now*. Perhaps more than I should.

Damon continued on about the hall of portraits, and I remembered a time we'd stood in that great hall together as children.

"Caught you!" Damon had tagged Ollie's back. "Now it's your turn to count, Ollie."

"I hate this game." Ollie dragged his feet back to the parlor, counting sullenly. "One. Two. Three . . ."

"Come on, Hannah." Damon led me down the long corridor and into the portrait gallery. The black and white tiled floor looked like a chessboard, and the ceiling was painted blue to look like the sky. My gaze roamed over the paintings; some were large, others small, but they were all stone-faced and grim.

"Why do they all look so angry?" I asked Damon.

"Eight. Nine. Ten . . ." Ollie's voice carried into the gallery.

Damon laughed and continued searching for a place to hide. "They aren't angry. They're powerful. And one day I'll be powerful too, just like my father and his father and his father's father and all the previous earls of Winfield. One day a painting of me will hang in this room."

"When they paint you, you should try not to look so stern."

"Fifteen. Sixteen. Seventeen . . ."

"I'll try to remember to smile for you." Damon smiled at me then, and his eyes shone as brightly as the sea on a sunny day. "Now stop talking and hide."

"You're uncommonly quiet, Miss Kent." The sound of Damon's husky voice pulled me back into the present. "Is something wrong?"

I shook my head, chasing away my wayward thoughts. "You're only a little unkempt."

His eyes followed my gaze up to his hairline, and with a small smile, he pushed back the wet strands.

"Matthew," Betsy called. "To the table for dinner."

Matthew didn't move; he remained staring up at Damon. I couldn't blame him. Damon was a captivating storyteller.

"Scurry to the table for dinner now," Damon said, "or your ma will be cross with me." Damon nodded toward the table, and this time, Matthew quickly obeyed.

"Lord Jennings, Miss Kent, you both must sit and eat too," Betsy said.

"That is kind of you to offer," Damon said. "But we—"

I clutched Damon's forearm to stop him from rejecting her invitation. While it was commendable that he didn't want to take food from their plates, I knew from my time serving the poor in London that it would be a far worse crime to refuse. "We would be *honored* to break bread with your family, Betsy," I said.

Damon looked at me in question but quickly fell into line. "May I escort you to dinner, Miss Kent?" He offered me his arm.

A silly gesture indeed, considering the table was not five feet away from where we stood, but also endearing.

Damon helped me with my chair, then sat across the table from me.

Betsy served us each a bowl of steaming stew, and Mrs. Turner watched us anxiously from her perch by the fire.

Damon ate a spoonful. "I daresay Prince George's chef could not create a meal half so delicious."

Mrs. Turner wagged her finger at Damon. "Flattery is a tool of the devil," she said, but her eyes shone brightly with pride.

Betsy continued serving the rest of the family as we ate. Or, rather, *tried* to eat. My hands shook so badly from the cold that lifting my spoon to feed myself proved difficult.

"You are cold," Damon said with concern. He shifted as if to remove his own coat, but then stopped—it was also wet and would do little good.

"I'm fine," I whispered, and I tried to prove as much by eating another bite of stew, but by the time the spoon reached my mouth, most of the broth had fallen back into the bowl.

Damon beckoned for Betsy, and she hurried over. "Miss Kent is in need of dry clothing. Do you have a dress to spare?"

"That really isn't—" I started to refuse, but my sentence was cut off by an admonitory look from Damon.

"Yes, m'lord. And you must also borrow a shirt and trousers from my husband."

"Very good." Damon nodded.

"Truly, this is not necessary," I protested. "I will only become soaked again when we leave."

"We won't be leaving here until the rain stops," Damon said. "We rode here in an open-air curricle, and I will not risk your health for the second time in one day."

"Come with me, Miss Kent," Betsy said. "I will find you something dry to wear."

CHAPTER TWENTY-ONE

As I followed Betsy into the bedchamber, I noted her readiness to obey Damon's command and thought it odd. The Winfields had not provided adequate living conditions for the Turners, but they did not hold any bitterness or resentment toward their landlord. Why?

Betsy undid my ties, retrieved a dry dress, and stood behind me to assist me into it.

"May I ask you a question, Betsy?"

"About Lord Jennings?" Her voice seemed to smile.

I nodded. "Earlier when you told Mrs. Turner that he has been good to your family, what did you mean?"

She slipped her dress over my head, settling the fabric over my shoulders, but didn't speak.

"I was cross with him earlier," I admitted, pulling my arms through the slightly too-long sleeves. "And I am wondering if my scolding was misplaced."

In truth, I *knew* my scolding had been misplaced. I'd reacted impulsively when I'd first seen the condition of the Turner's farm, but his tenants didn't seem to resent him and even spoke kindly of him. And more importantly, I knew Damon. He was intelligent and kind. He was helping them. I was sure of it. But how? And why was he doing it in secret?

"Lord Jennings is a good man," Betsy confirmed as she did up the back of my dress. "He does the best he can for us tenants."

"How does he help?" I pressed her for more information.

"I'm not sure I should say, miss."

I nodded. Though I still didn't understand Damon's exact dealings with his tenants, or why he wouldn't help them openly, I was glad to know that he was helping.

Betsy went back to the trunk and pulled out a set of her husband's clothes and set them on the corner of the bed for Damon. I followed her out of the room to rejoin the others.

Damon looked up from his stew and smiled at me dressed in Betsy's clothes. I smoothed my skirt. It was made from coarse homespun, but I was much more comfortable wearing this dress than the fancier one I'd arrived in.

"I've laid dry clothes on the bed for you, m'lord," Betsy said to Damon.

"I can serve as your valet if you'd like?" Mr. Turner offered.

"You are kind to offer, but I will clothe myself." Damon stood and walked into the bedchamber, closing the door quietly behind himself.

I sat at the table and ate a spoonful of warm stew. It tasted as good as it smelled.

My bowl was almost empty when Damon emerged from the room, and I froze with my spoon in midair as he walked toward the table. Mr. Turner's clothes fit him snugly. The shirt stretched across his broad shoulders, and without a proper cravat, it gaped slightly at the neckline and revealed a portion of his chest.

Damon grinned. "Do you approve, Miss Kent?"

I quickly averted my gaze—embarrassed to be caught admiring him. I gave Damon a polite smile, trying to hide my discomfort, then said loudly enough for the Turners to hear us, "It was kind of our hosts to share their things with us."

"To be sure," Damon said in his low tone, "but that is not what I'm asking. I'd like to know if you find me as pleasing in this attire as you normally do."

"What makes you think I find you pleasing?" I said, but Damon *was* an objectively handsome man no matter what he was wearing, and there was nothing I could do to hide the admiration that was surely written in pink on my cheeks. "I think you should have let Mr. Turner serve as your valet. You seem to have forgotten your cravat."

With a light laugh, Damon relaxed into his seat across the table, and we resumed our meals.

When we were done, Betsy cleared our bowls. "Please enjoy your leisure by the fire while you wait for the rain to pass."

Damon thanked her, and we moved our chairs nearer to the fire.

We sat together in silence for a moment, enjoying the sounds and movement of life around us. The children were quarreling over their little game, Baby John was upset again, and Betsy fussed over him. Mr. Turner had disappeared into the back room—likely to change into dry clothes of his own. And the elder Mrs. Turner had moved to the now-vacant table to eat her own bowl of soup. Noise filled every corner of the home, but there was a comforting rhythm to it, which I found pleasant.

Growing up, it had only been Henry and me. He was several years older than me, though, and more interested in his studies than in me. And since I'd not had any younger brothers and sisters, there was never anyone to play with after dinner. Mama and Papa had wanted more children, but they'd never been blessed with any more. A pang of emotion swelled inside my heart. Was it possible to miss something, *someone* I'd never known?

I missed Mama. So much. All the little things she said and did. The scent of her lavender perfume and the sound of her playing the pianoforte. She was as talented as she was beautiful and likely could have had her choice of husbands, but I was glad she had chosen Papa.

"What are you thinking of?" Damon asked.

"Nothing of import," I said.

"*Nothing of import* would not crease your brow so deeply."

I consciously relaxed the worry from my forehead. "I was pondering whether it was possible to miss something that never belonged to you."

"I know it is." Damon held my gaze for a long moment and then continued. "So you were thinking of Ollie then?"

"No. I was mostly thinking about my mother," I admitted. "And her choice to marry my father. Though they did not have much in terms of possessions, they were happy."

"Could *you* be happy as a poor man's wife?" Damon asked.

"Yes."

He gave me a small smile. "You don't even have to think about it, do you?"

"What's there to think about? My mother married for love, and she was happy. Why not I?"

"Not many are as brave as your mother. Financial burdens often turn the sweetest of couples bitter."

"For some that may be true, but I have never been afraid of living a simple and quiet life."

"You are a wonder, Hannah. My brother does not deserve you."

"I do not wish to speak of Ollie just now."

"Nor I." Damon shifted in his seat and leaned forward, resting his elbows on his knees. "What do you wish to speak of?"

"Your tenants."

"Of course you do."

"This home is in utter disrepair, but the tenants do not despise you. Why?"

A shadow fell over Damon's face. I expected him to tease away the topic, but then he met my gaze and said, "Because I help them."

"That much is obvious. I would like to know *how* you help them."

"Money."

My eyes narrowed. "How is that possible? Everything in your possession is your father's. And seeing as he is aware of the conditions yet refuses to send aid, I hardly think he'd approve of your charity. And if you were to simply take his money without permission, he would notice when his books reflected a deficit."

"You miss nothing, do you?" He shifted in his seat, the wood creaking beneath his weight. "The money I give them I have earned through gambling."

"Gambling?" I frowned. "That cannot be a wise or reliable method of securing funds."

"No," he agreed. "But I am up at the tables more than I am down. And I know horseflesh, so I can usually make a tidy sum at the racetrack. But most importantly, my profits, and the way I spend those profits, are not easily traceable."

"And you freely give your earnings to your tenants?"

Damon glanced at the children playing on the threadbare rug, then lowered his voice again. "They have more need of it than I."

Across the room, a chair squeaked when Betsy stood. "Time for bed, children." They groaned, and Betsy silenced them with a pointed look.

Mr. Turner stood with effort from the table to help, and as he limped toward his little family, I realized where I'd seen him before. Mr. Turner was the man I'd seen Damon give the parcel of banknotes to. At the time, I'd thought they were about something nefarious. Guilt twisted in my stomach for thinking poorly of them.

Mr. and Mrs. Turner ushered their children into the bedchamber, and the door creaked closed behind them.

"How was he injured?" I asked quietly.

Damon glanced around the room. Only Mrs. Turner remained, and she sat across the room in Betsy's rocking chair, looking near to falling asleep. Still, Damon lowered his voice. "War."

I'd seen many war injuries in London, so it wasn't surprising, but it still made me sad. "And when did Mr. Turner become your father's tenant?"

"Before he enlisted. His father, the late Mr. Turner, was our original tenant. Before he passed, it was agreed that the young Mr. Turner would take over the land lease. When he returned from the war injured, Father did not think him equal to the task of working the land and desired to release him from the lease, but Mr. Turner was intent on staying."

"Naturally. This is his home, his livelihood."

"Exactly so." Damon nodded. "Mr. Turner has worked hard, and he has done a fine job, but he will never be able to care for the land like he did before being injured. And with the weather this year, he's fallen increasingly behind on his payments. Father thinks they need to go, but I believe our contract can still be mutually beneficial."

I stared up at Damon in admiration. This was a side of him I hadn't seen before, a side he didn't reveal often. "What you're doing here is good."

"Perhaps, but it is not enough. What our tenants need is for my father to give them more help."

I couldn't disagree. "Will he?"

Damon shook his head. "No. My father sees the Turners' situation not as a failing on his own part but rather theirs. He believes if they had been good stewards of all he has given them, then they would not now be in this position."

"But Mr. Turner's injury was not his fault, and neither is the failed harvest."

"I agree with you," Damon said. "But my father argues that if they had only prepared more in years previous, then they would be able to now save themselves."

"That is madness." Even I could see that the Turner family only lived from one harvest to another. On a parcel of land this size, there would be no surplus to save. "Your father must be made to see reason."

"I have tried. Even going so far as to draw up and present plans to him."

"What sort of plans?"

He shifted in his chair. "You will think me foolish."

"I promise I will not."

Damon rolled the hem of his shirt between his forefinger and thumb. "I have been studying agriculture and talking with other landowners about the most beneficial farming techniques, and with some wise investments, better education, and up-to-date practices, I believe we can give the Turners, and our other tenants, the means to succeed." Damon glanced at me as if gauging my reaction.

"You must do it then."

"It is a great deal more complicated than that."

"Not so. You have the means and the desire; you lack nothing to bring about change."

"Only the authority."

"But one day you will have it. And think of all the good you will be able to do."

"As soon as I inherit, I fear I will become exactly like my father and his father and his father's father. I have been taught my whole life that the only way I can ensure my family's survival is by doing what has always been done."

"You will not be like your father or any of the previous earls of Winfield, and you won't make anyone suffer."

"How can you be so sure?" he asked earnestly.

"Because you got out of the curricle today and because you have been helping your tenants for a long time previous."

"You have too much faith in me." He shook his head.

"How can I not?" I said, and I suddenly realized how much I believed those words. At every turn this summer, Damon had been my savior. "Must I remind you of how you asked me to dance at Rumfords' ball even though it was not in your interest to do so?"

"Ah. But it was."

"We both know you could have found other means of avoiding an unwanted marriage. Your motivations in coming to my aid were purely unselfish."

A humorless laugh escaped his throat. "My motivations for asking you to dance with me were anything but pure, Miss Kent. I am a man, and you should not forget it."

"And *you* must not forget that you are not your father. You are your own man, and you can choose a different path."

Damon stared at me with an unreadable expression. I could not guess his thoughts, but something had shifted between us. Something deep and meaningful and true. I couldn't be sure when it had begun—at the riverbank or at the pianoforte, or perhaps it had started when he carried me across the mud puddle or even earlier when we danced the quadrille at the Rumfords' ball. I only knew that it had begun and grown from there.

Damon blinked, and with a shake of his head, he stood and walked to the window. He stared into the darkness as if his thoughts weighed heavy in his mind.

I bit my lip. Had he taken offense at something I'd said? I hadn't meant any, but even if he had been offended, I could not apologize for speaking truth.

"The rains have ceased," he finally said. "We must return home with haste." Damon let the curtain fall closed and moved toward the bedchamber. He knocked lightly on the door, and Mr. Turner appeared in the threshold.

Damon explained our leaving, and Mr. Turner hurried outside to prepare the horses and curricle.

Damon turned to the elder Mrs. Turner, who was awake now but still looked tired. "I'm sorry to ask this of you, Mrs. Turner. I know the hour is late, but we require a chaperone if we're to avoid ruining Miss Kent's reputation."

She nodded her understanding.

"You will have a room with us for the night and be compensated for your generosity."

"Very good, m'lord."

Betsy emerged from the bedroom. "I will gather your wet garments and a few things for Mum." She moved to lay the baby in his cradle, but he let out a barking cry.

"I can hold him," I offered.

Betsy nodded and handed the bundled baby to me. He was so warm and his cheeks rosy. His breathing was so fast. I'd never held a baby before, but I was sure his little chest wasn't supposed to rattle the way it did. I rubbed his back through the blanket, and I was glad, if nothing else, that he had a dry home to sleep in tonight.

I glanced at Damon. He watched me with a soft gaze. He didn't say anything, but he also didn't look away. Nor did I.

Betsy returned with our things and a shawl for her mother.

I handed the baby to her, then followed Damon to the curricle waiting outside. Damon assisted Mrs. Turner into the curricle first, then me, and finally climbed in himself. It was a snug fit, but I didn't mind sitting close to him. I even relished his nearness.

Damon clicked his tongue, prompting the horses into motion. It didn't take long before my eyes became heavy with sleep. I blinked several times, trying to keep myself awake, but it did little good, and I closed my eyes.

CHAPTER TWENTY-TWO

"Hannah," a deep voice murmured.

I blinked awake and found Damon smiling down at me.

"We are home." He brushed hair from my cheek.

Realizing my *other* cheek rested on his shoulder, I quickly sat upright and smoothed my hair and face. "Forgive me. I must have fallen asleep."

"Right you did," Mrs. Turner said. "Nearly as soon as we left the farm. Not that Lord Jennings seemed to mind none."

Damon gave me a private smile and alighted from the curricle. He handed the reins to the groom, then reached up to help me down. Our ungloved hands touched. His were rough from work, but his hold was gentle. A pleasurable shiver pulsed through me. Did he feel it too?

The butler appeared at the door and quickly descended the stairs to where we stood on the drive. "Are you well, my lord?"

"Quite well, Caldwell," Damon said to the butler. "Better than I have been in some time. If you will please take our guest inside." Damon gestured to Mrs. Turner. "And see that she has all she needs for the night."

"Yes, my lord." Caldwell bowed politely, then helped Mrs. Turner alight from the curricle. Caldwell guided her around the back of the manor toward the servants' entrance.

Damon offered me his arm, which I readily took, and he tucked my hand into the crook of his elbow.

"Do you think anyone will still be awake at this hour?" I asked.

"I do not think so, else Father would have met me at the gate to read me a lecture. I'm sure Ollie told Mother you were with me, and since I was on Father's errand—I do not think we were missed."

We entered the darkened manor through the front door. Only a few candles burned in the entryway. I breathed a sigh of relief and moved toward the stairs.

"Good night," I whispered.

"Wait." Damon caught my hand. "I want to show you something."

I glanced around, worried that perhaps someone might see, but everything was still and quiet. He led me down the darkened corridor toward the east wing. And although we were adults now and entering this part of the manor was no longer forbidden, it still *felt* forbidden.

Damon pushed open a door to reveal a breathtaking ballroom. I'd seen it before but never like this at night.

The curtains were tied back with thick tassel ropes, and moonbeams flooded through the large arched windows, bathing the great hall in light. The hall was prettily papered, gilded frames hung on the walls, and overhead were several glittering chandeliers. "It is beautiful." I glanced at Damon and found him watching me.

"Yes," he agreed, his voice solemn. "May I be so bold as to ask you to dance?"

"You wish to dance with me? Now? Here?"

"This is a ballroom, is it not?"

"Yes. However, nothing about this situation is proper. Not the hour, not the setting, not even our clothing."

"Is something wrong with my clothing, Miss Kent?" He quirked a teasing brow at me. "You must tell me what is amiss so I can remedy my appearance to your satisfaction." He made a show of lifting his arms wide and turning in a slow circle.

"Hmm," I said, and my gaze roamed over his too-tight shirt, where it strained across his broad shoulders and gaped at the neckline. The sleeves, too, were short and exposed his muscled forearms. But it was his tousled hair and the wild way it fell across his brow that had me captivated.

"Well?" he said. "What is your measure of me?"

"On second thought, your clothing is fine. But your hair is—um—rather rumpled."

He looked up at his hairline. "Seeing as I have no mirror to remedy the defect, perhaps you might assist me."

I stepped close, and Damon lowered his head obligingly. He smelled good, like polished leather and oranges. Rising onto my tiptoes, I ran my hands through his thick hair. I combed the strands with my fingers until they lay neatly in place, but I left a few strands free to fall across his forehead.

Damon leaned into my touch, bringing our faces close together. His breath tickled my cheek, and my fingers stilled. We were standing so close. Close enough to kiss.

I *wanted* him to kiss me.

The realization startled me, and I lowered from my tiptoes and moved to withdraw my hands. "It is better now."

Damon caught my wrist and rubbed his thumb across the sensitive skin, and I was certain he could feel my hammering pulse.

"We should probably go," I said. "If someone sees us . . ."

He shrugged. "As you've said, I have never cared one whit for my reputation, and I do believe your quadrille could use some practice."

I gave him a teasing frown. "You'll be pleased to know Nora acquired some papers with dancing steps for me to study. I am now quite proficient."

"And what of your waltz?"

Heat crept up my neck and bloomed in my cheeks just thinking about the scandalous dance, and I was glad the chandeliers were not lit. "I know the forms," I admitted. "Though, as you know, I am not the best dancer."

"Nonsense." He extended his hand to me. "Dance with me," he said, and this time, his request was made in a serious tone. Moonlight cast shadows on his face, highlighting his cheekbones and straight nose. Even in dim light, and wearing clothes not befitting his station, he was extraordinarily handsome.

I could not resist him.

Stepping forward, I placed myself in front of him. He bowed, and I curtsied. Our introductory forms were slow and precise, our first touches feather-light and timid. And when at last we came together, our opposite hands clasped above our heads and our arms lightly rested on the other's shoulder in an *almost* embrace.

Our silent dance progressed. And even without music to guide our steps, we kept an easy rhythm, circling and swaying. We all but floated around the ballroom.

"I think you were being modest," he whispered. "You dance beautifully."

"If that is true, it is only because I have found the right partner."

His hold tightened. I stared into his eyes, and a feeling washed over me. A feeling I had waited my entire life to experience. A feeling both dangerous and delightful.

I was in love with Damon.

The realization was sudden and sure, like a flash of lightning and the first fall of rain.

I gripped the rough material of his shirt, and he pulled me closer. The heat of his body warmed me despite the coldness of the room.

I wished to never dance with another man again. Never hold or touch or whisper to anyone but him. I felt safe in his strong embrace.

We danced for several more minutes, but too soon our steps slowed and our dance ended. Damon released his hold of my back but not my hand, and then bowing low, he placed a lingering kiss on my hand and then my cheek.

"What the devil is going on here?" a deep voice bellowed from the doorway.

Damon tensed at the sound of his father's voice.

I quickly stepped away, putting an appropriate space between us. Though no matter how much space I put between us, it would not change the fact that Damon and I were alone in a darkened ballroom.

Lord Winfield's imposing figure filled the door's threshold. His flickering candle illuminated his tight lips and gruesome stare, making him look like an angry caricature from the *Post* come to life. "Miss Kent, you will return to your bedchamber forthwith. And Damon, my study. Now." He did not move from the door but waited for compliance.

Damon squared his shoulders as if bracing himself for a certain scolding.

I, on the other hand, shrank. In truth, I wished I could melt like a candle and seep into the very floorboards beneath my feet.

"You are not to worry," Damon said, his voice low. "Father is cross with me, not you. I will speak with him and explain the situation."

"What exactly is our situation?" I asked quietly.

Before he could answer, Lord Winfield coughed loudly behind us, a deep, gravely sound that echoed through the ballroom and made his displeasure that we were still standing here known.

Damon gave me a small, strained smile, and then we followed Lord Winfield through the threshold and into the entryway. Lord Winfield continued toward his study, and Damon led me to the base of the grand staircase. "Thank you for the dance, Miss Kent. I shall never forget it." And then he followed his father into the study.

I turned to walk up the stairs but only got so far as the first step before I looked back. Lord Winfield's study door was slightly ajar, and his deep voice seeped through the crevice.

I glanced up the stairs, knowing I should return to my bedchamber as Lord Winfield had instructed, but how could I sleep when I knew Damon was being punished? I couldn't. I padded toward the study, hiding myself to the side of the door so that if it opened, I would at least be partially hidden.

"Why, pray tell, are you dressed in peasant clothes?" Lord Winfield asked, his voice low and angry.

"I am wearing Mr. Turner's clothing because he kindly loaned them to me when we were caught in the rain," Damon said.

"I sent you there this morning. You should have returned hours before the weather turned. Where have you been tonight?"

"At the Turner farm," Damon repeated. "Our tenants needed assistance fixing their roof."

"You *labored* with them? Of all the absurd, vulgar things you have done, this outdoes them all."

"They needed help," Damon said. "Urgently."

"I do not deny it, but a gentleman cannot work his own land. It is simply not done." Lord Winfield released a heavy sigh, as if his anger had bled from him, and he was suddenly exhausted. "Damon, you cannot be both lord and friend. I have tried to teach you this principle time and again. Had someone seen you, you would have been shunned by the *ton*."

"I could not care less about the *ton*."

I smiled, so proud of Damon for speaking his convictions, and leaned toward the door to better hear.

"Oh, you do not?" Lord Winfield said. "What about your sway in the House of Lords when the time comes? You have a desire to see reform in a number of laws, do you not? What about making an advantageous match? You must want for a beautiful and well-bred wife. And if you do not care about yourself, which, given your behavior tonight, it seems you do not, then you must at least consider your mother and how she will be treated in her social circles. And what about your brother's standing? Are you content to ruin him as well? You have led with your heart, not your head, again, and you simply cannot afford it, not if you wish to have any standing in Society."

"Hang Society," Damon spat back. "I refuse to turn my back on our tenants as you have."

"Is *that* what you think of me? That I have turned my back on them?" Lord Winfield laughed humorlessly.

"I could hardly think otherwise. The Turners have been good, hardworking tenants, yet you will not fix their roof, invest in better farming equipment, or extend their payment."

"What has happened to Mr. Turner is regrettable," Lord Winfield said, "but I did not deal him the blow. War did. And while I wish I could house and feed every hungry man, woman, and child, I am running an estate, not a charity. I must see to the needs of my *own* family, and so must you. Soon you will be lord and master of this estate, Damon. You must learn to act like it."

"Must act like *you*, you mean."

"Indeed."

"I am not you, Father. And I do not want to run Summerhaven in the manner you have. I want—"

"It does not matter what *you* want," Lord Winfield interrupted. "In order for the estate to survive, you must do what has always been done."

"I do not want it to merely survive. I want the estate to thrive. My education has taught me there is a better way."

"Then perhaps it is time for a *re*education," Lord Winfield said.

"Perhaps it is," I agreed, "but not for me—for *you*. Times are changing, Father, and you must change too."

Father raised one brow, surprised by my boldness, then gave me a stern look of warning.

My stomach clenched, but I would not back down. "I recently borrowed a book from the lending library and have been studying agriculture," I said. "I believe if we were to teach our tenants new farming techniques and invest in better machinery, we *all* could benefit."

He shook his head. "The only sure way for this estate to survive is by doing what has always been done."

"I disagree. Our tenants are suffering, Father. Doing the same thing will only bring about death. For the estate to prosper, we must evolve. We must try something new."

"Trying something new might work, but it might not. I am not willing to risk ruin."

I looked Father directly in the eyes and said, "Risk nothing, gain nothing."

Father stilled and silently appraised. There was a long beat of silence before he continued. "This is Miss Kent's doing. She has a bleeding heart like her mother had, and her beliefs are unduly influencing you."

I clutched my hand to my chest, covering Mama's ring. He'd meant it as an insult, but nothing could be more of a compliment.

"Hannah has nothing to do with this," Damon said.

"*Hannah?*" Lord Winfield repeated, his words softer now, almost pitying. "Oh, Damon. A *clergyman's* daughter? You cannot be serious. She is so far beneath you, it is laughable. A summer tryst before you finally take up your familial obligations is one thing, but you should be grateful I discovered you tonight. If it had been anyone else, you would have been forced into an undesirable marriage with the chit." Lord Winfield's voice grew quiet, and I imagined him letting out a great sigh, though I couldn't hear it.

I leaned toward the study door, straining to hear Damon's response, but either he'd spoken too quietly for me to overhear, or he hadn't said anything at all.

I pressed myself into the shadows, feeling small. Perhaps, like both Lord Winfield and Ollie, Damon deemed me undesirable. He was a lord after all, and I *was* only a clergyman's daughter. Not to mention the fact that Damon had only suggested our ruse because he wished to avoid marriage.

But that had changed . . . Hadn't it?

I removed myself from my hiding spot behind the door and hurried up the stairs. And as I padded down the corridor to my bedchamber, I felt the disapproving glares of Damon's ancestors staring down at me.

CHAPTER TWENTY-THREE

"MORNING, MISS. OR PERHAPS I should say good afternoon." Nora fluttered about my bedchamber, preparing for the day.

"Good morning, Nora," I croaked.

Nora looked at me funny. "You feelin' unwell, miss?"

"I'm—" *Fine*, I started to say, but my throat burned, and my head felt full, like the London fog had rolled into my room overnight and taken up residence.

Nora walked to my bedside and held her hand to my forehead. "You are warm. Best spend the day resting in bed. I will fetch a tray from the kitchen for you."

"No," I said, and I attempted to push myself up to a sitting position, but my muscles were too weak and achy. "Ooh . . . Perhaps you are right. Will you please assure Lady Winfield I am well? I do not want to worry her."

"Of course, miss. But first you must tell me, was it terribly romantic? Getting caught in the rain with Lord Jennings?"

Oh dear. Nora's question meant gossip was circulating belowstairs. I tried to think of a way to answer her honestly without actually answering her question at all. "Rain produces mud, and I have never thought mud to be romantic, have you?"

Nora's face scrunched. "Well, no, but—"

"Me neither," I said, relaxing back into bed. "Would you mind collecting that tray now? My throat hurts, and some tea might help."

With a quick curtsy, Nora quit the room.

I rolled over in bed, hoping to catch the last wisps of sleep, but when I closed my eyes, all I could see was Damon wearing Mr. Turner's shirt and the way it clung to his shoulders. All I could feel was the warmth of his lips on my hand and cheek. And all I could hear was his voice, whispering to me in the dark as we danced.

A sigh escaped my mouth, and I smiled. Though our evening had not ended as I would have liked, I already anticipated the next time I would see him again. We would discuss our feelings and come to a solution.

A knock came at the door, and I drew up the covers to hide my nightdress. "Come in," I said, raising the pitch of my voice so as not to sound like a frog.

The door swung open, and Lady Winfield entered the room. She took one look at my face and said, "Oh my dear, you *are* flushed."

I was certain that I was, but not for the reasons she believed.

Lady Winfield walked to my bedside and sat on the edge. Her brow pinched with concern as she studied my face. She pressed a cool hand to my forehead. "You are warm but not hot. That is good."

A movement at the door drew my attention. "Ollie," I said in surprise, and I drew up my blanket even further.

"Forgive my intrusion," he said from the corridor, "but your maid said you are feeling unwell, and I had to see that you were okay."

"I am only a *little* under the weather," I reassured him, though it burned my throat to say it.

"Still," Lady Winfield said. "Your maid was right to encourage you to stay in bed."

"Is there anything you need?" Ollie asked.

Damon, I wanted to say, but I didn't. He was no doubt still out on his morning ride, exercising Ares, and as soon as he returned and heard I was unwell, he would surely send up a comforting note or forsake propriety and come to wish me well.

A chill shivered through me. "Nora is bringing up a tray, so I will have everything I need soon, but thank you for checking on me."

Ollie nodded, but he lingered in the doorway.

"I will let you rest then." Lady Winfield rose from the bed. "I will come back to check on you in a few hours."

I nodded, grateful.

Lady Winfield walked toward the door. "Come, Ollie."

"I need a moment alone with Hannah," he said.

Lady Winfield glanced at me, her expression wary, then back at her son. "Please," Ollie said.

"Only a moment," she said. "I will wait for you in the corridor."

He nodded, and Lady Winfield stepped out of my bedchamber.

Ollie stepped inside my bedchamber, and the light from the window exposed dark circles under his eyes, rumpled clothing, and mussed hair. Had he slept at all?

All that had transpired between us yesterday rushed back at me. My confession of love, fleeing from the room, Ollie's pained look as he watched me leave with Damon. So much had happened since then—Damon and I had repaired the Turners' roof, he'd told me his secrets, we'd danced in the moonlight.

"I must apologize for how I responded to you yesterday in the morning room."

"You have no need to apologize. You acted as a gentleman."

"Yes," he said. "I mean, no. That is not what I am apologizing for." He ran his hands through his hair, mussing it further.

"Please," I whispered. "Let us not speak of it."

"I have no desire to cause you any further distress," he said, "so I will not press the subject, but may we please talk of it another day?"

The conversation had been embarrassing enough to live through once, and I had no desire to resurrect it, but I nodded to placate him.

"Are you sure there is nothing I can do for you?" he asked.

"I am sure," I said, "but thank you."

He nodded and started to turn away, but then something caught his eye behind me, and he stopped.

I followed his gaze to the bundle of lavender tied to my bedpost.

"I should have walked with you in the garden," he said. "I am sorry you had to pick those alone."

I frowned. I thought *he'd* picked them for me and sent them to my room the night I'd pretended to have a headache. It had been these flowers, a small but sure token of his affection in my mind, that had encouraged me to persist in my ruse with Damon. But they hadn't been from Ollie at all. And I knew, even without asking, that the flowers had been from Damon. For it had always been Damon who'd seen me, Damon who ran back to help me when I fell as a girl, and Damon who'd asked me to dance as an adult. The realization that it was *always* Damon brought clarity and confidence in my growing feelings.

Nora appeared at the door with a tray.

Ollie quickly stepped aside to allow her to enter, then he removed into the corridor. "Feel better," he said, and then he left.

Nora set the tray on my bedside table. "Do you require anything else?"

"Actually, yes. A bit of paper and a quill. I believe when Lord Jennings learns of my illness, he will feel responsible. I would like to write him a note, telling him not to worry. Would you be so kind as to give it to him?"

"I would," Nora said. "But he is gone, miss."

"Yes, I know. You should give him the letter when he *returns* from his morning ride."

She shook her head. "No. I mean he left for London early this morning with his father. I overheard a footman telling a housemaid in the kitchen."

"Oh." I tried to hide my surprise with a small smile. "Did the footman say why they left? Or when they will return?"

"No, miss. I'm sorry," Nora said, and with a bob, she quit the room.

Damon was gone? And without word or warning.

Undesirable marriage.

I touched my cheek where Damon had kissed me and tried to push the words from my mind. Lord Winfield had spoken those words, not Damon, but they continued to fester. Although we'd shared candid conversations and a romantic dance yesterday, we did not have an understanding.

CHAPTER TWENTY-FOUR

EVERY DAY FOR THE NEXT week, Ollie sent something up to my room to aid in my recovery. Some days he sent a book and other days he sent flowers. And finally, after a week of rest, my fever abated, and I regained my health.

But still, Damon did not return, nor did he write.

Sitting at my vanity table while Nora fixed my hair, I wondered what he might be doing in London. Perhaps he was seeing to matters of business with his father? Or this could be a social visit. Perhaps Lord Winfield was trying to entice Damon into taking up his *familial obligations* to marry a *beautiful* and *well-bred* young lady. Whatever the reason for his visit to London, the marriage-minded mothers would no doubt make the most of the future earl's stay in the city. Would Damon dance with other women? Attend dinner parties? Go to the theater? I tried to shake the intrusive thoughts from my mind, but after a week of lying in bed, they'd become a near-constant plague.

"There," Nora said. "All finished."

I thanked her and walked to the breakfast room.

Lady Winfield looked up from her meal when I entered. "Hannah." She brightened. "I am so glad you are well. This house has not felt the same without you up and about." She motioned me over to the table.

A footman stepped forward to help me with my chair and then my food, and as he served me, I couldn't stop myself from glancing at Damon's empty chair.

I missed him terribly. It was so strange; I'd lived years without him crossing my mind, but now I could hardly go a single moment without thinking about him. I felt silly that my feelings could be so changeable, but I could not deny that they had changed. Though *changed* did not feel like quite the right word to describe what had happened. It felt more like I'd discovered something that had always existed.

How could I have been so blind? And for so long.

"Hannah," Lady Winfield said, pulling me out of my reverie. "I have invited Lady Rumford and her daughter over for tea, thinking Miss Atherton might lift your spirits after your illness, but perhaps I was overeager. Are you feeling well enough for a social call?"

"Oh yes. I am more than ready for some company and conversation." I was a bit nervous too. The last time I'd seen her had been at the picnic, and so much had transpired since then. Would she understand?

"Wonderful," Lady Winfield said. "I think I will have a table set for us in the rose garden. It's such a lovely day."

"It *is* a lovely day, Mother." Ollie walked into the breakfast room with a newspaper tucked under his arm and a stack of letters in his hand. He sat in his usual seat at the table across from me. "I passed Caldwell on the way in," he said and gave her the letters.

She riffled through them. "Thank you, Oliver."

I hoped there would be one addressed to me from Damon, but no. Lady Winfield set the stack aside and opened the first letter. Ollie returned to his paper and I to my breakfast.

"Hanny," Ollie said, drawing my attention. "Seeing as it is such a nice day, might I entice you to walk with me in the garden after breakfast?"

I blinked at his invitation. Although he'd been attentive to me while I lay in my sickbed, now that I'd recovered, I fully expected him to return to his normal behavior of ignoring me and courting Miss Digby. But I welcomed the chance to strengthen our friendship. "I would like that very much. Thank you."

"The pleasure is all mine," he said and opened his newspaper.

Gentlemen commonly read the *Post* at the table—even Papa enjoyed the habit—but when I wasn't participating in the activity, I found I quite disliked being ignored.

"Oh!" Lady Winfield exclaimed, looking up from her missives. "We have received an invitation from the Garretts. They are hosting a ball at the end of the week."

Ollie lowered the corner of his newspaper and met my gaze. "Perhaps we can finally have that dance I promised you so long ago."

My brow tightened at his words, and it took me a moment to respond. "That would be nice." I smiled at him across the table, but I could not help wondering why he was acting so strangely. First with an invitation to walk in the garden, and now he wished to dance with me? Perhaps my illness had worried him more than I'd realized. But whatever the cause, I would not turn down the opportunity to mend our friendship.

Lady Winfield opened another letter and skimmed the contents. "And more good news! The modiste says your dress will be ready to be fitted in time to wear to the Garretts' ball."

"That is wonderful news," I agreed. It would be so nice to have a new dress to wear. What would Damon think of it?

Lady Winfield's final letter was sealed with red wax, and pressed into the center was the Jennings family crest.

My heart gave a little jolt, and my fingers itched to snatch it.

Lady Winfield read silently between sips of tea, her face giving nothing away. And then she sighed. Heavily.

I held my breath. Was something wrong?

"What is it?" Ollie asked.

She shook her head. "Damon writes that he and your father are to remain in London for another fortnight so he can continue his lessons with a man named Mr. Rowley."

A fortnight. But that was so long. And who was Mr. Rowley?

"Pity they will miss the ball," Ollie said.

The ball and more. If they remained in the city that long, Damon and I wouldn't even *see* each other before I returned to London.

Had he designed it that way?

"It won't do," Lady Winfield said. "If your father and Damon do not attend the ball, the Garretts may view their absence as a slight. I must write back immediately and convince them to come home. Please excuse me." She rose from the table and quit the room, and I could only hope her efforts to persuade them to come home proved successful.

"It really is a lovely day for a stroll, is it not?" Ollie said as we walked down the garden path.

"Lovely," I agreed, though I had to admit my mind was more focused on where Damon was than where I was at present. What was he learning from Mr. Rowley? And when would he return? And while I had no right to expect him to write me, it hurt that he did not even ask after my health in his letter to his mother. "Do you know Mr. Rowley?"

"Mr. Rowley?" Ollie asked.

"Damon's letter to your mother said he was learning business from a Mr. Rowley."

"No, I cannot say that I do."

"Do you find it odd that your father and brother plan to be away from Summerhaven so long?"

"Everything my brother does is odd."

With a frown, I turned my attention to the lavender stalks dancing in the breeze.

"Hanny, there is something I wish to speak with you about."

"What is it?"

"Well, I hoped we could discuss what you said last week in the morning room."

I stiffened. "Oh. I do not think that is necessary."

"But it is. I am mortified by my response. As soon as you fled, I knew I had made a mistake. I was cruel and blind, and I hope someday you'll be able to forgive me."

My shoulders relaxed. "I forgive you now. Truly. If anyone has need to beg the other's forgiveness, it is I."

Ollie's eyebrows furrowed. "Whatever for?"

"There are so many things to choose from, aren't there?" I sighed. "Perhaps I should apologize for the fact that even though you made your intentions for Miss Digby known to me, I did not respect your decision." If only I had listened to him in the beginning, I would have saved us both a great deal of trouble. "Or perhaps I should apologize for cornering you in the morning room." I cringed even thinking about that conversation. "I really am so very sorry for that."

"Seeing as your only mistake was in caring for me, I cannot accept your apology." He stopped walking and turned to face me. "And . . . I have a confession of my own."

I braced myself, knowing he was about to announce his engagement. Although I didn't approve of his choice of bride, it was his decision to make, and I would pray for their every happiness.

Ollie took a deep breath. "Miss Digby and I have ended our courtship."

"What?" My forehead tensed. "But why?"

"We did not suit. In fact, she rather brought out the worst in me, don't you agree?"

"I cannot argue with you on that point," I mumbled, and he laughed lightly. "But you seemed so certain of her. In truth, I thought you were days away from announcing your engagement."

"I was," he said sheepishly.

Confused, I shook my head. "I don't understand. What has changed your mind?"

"You."

"Me?" I squeaked.

"Yes, my brave girl. *You*." Ollie stepped forward and took my hands in his. I froze at his unexpected touch. "When you came to me in the morning room and said what you did, I will admit you caught me off guard, but you have opened my eyes. I see now that I had become so intent on proving my worth to others that I lost myself. I thought more money, better clothes, and friends in high places would make me worthy, would make me *happy* . . . but no. I was only caught up in the chase of what I thought was a more valuable and worthy life. When you confronted me about only courting her for her dowry, the way you *looked* at me—" He grimaced. "I have never felt more worth*less*."

"I'm sorry, Ollie. I should not have said that."

"You have no need to apologize. In fact, I am grateful for your candor that day. I daresay you saved me from a lifetime of misery."

Had I? I'd saved him from a loveless marriage perhaps, but had I also condemned him to a life of destitution? "W-what about the grange? Do you not *need* a wealthy wife to see to your future estate's survival?"

"Some sacrifices will have to be made, it's true. I will need to give up my set of rooms in London and probably my account at the haberdashers too." He sighed, then chided himself with a shake of his head. "But provided no further extravagant expenditures are made, the grange will survive and so will we."

"*We?*"

He ran his thumb over my knuckles, and his gaze softened as he looked into my eyes.

I snatched back my hand in sudden understanding. He had not come to a conclusion about his relationship with Miss Digby; he'd come to a conclusion about me. About *us*.

Ollie frowned. "Is something wrong?"

"No. Nothing. I only wish to continue our stroll."

"Of course, if that is your desire, but let us also continue our conversation."

"Perhaps we should not," I said and started down the path again. "There is nothing so nice as the sounds of nature." I'd longed for this show of affection from Ollie most of my life, but now I had the sudden urge to hide in the same hedgerow we'd played in together as children.

Ollie glanced at me sidelong. "Have I said something to offend you?"

"Not at all. The lavender bushes are inordinately beautiful this year. So full of blooms and fragrant too, don't you think?"

"Yes, but Hannah, I am trying to tell you something important."

I knew he was, and I could guess what about, but I did not wish for him to continue. I took a steadying breath and slowed my step to face him. "I know," I said. "But I am not prepared to have this conversation."

"Are you feeling unwell?" he asked.

"No, it's not that. It is just . . ." I bit my lip.

How could I ever explain my change of heart after he'd given up his courtship with Miss Digby for me? I glanced around for an escape.

"Amelia!" I all but cried her name with relief when I saw her entering the garden path.

"Good day, Miss Kent. Mr. Jennings," she said as she approached, and then when she joined our circle, "I hope I am not intruding."

"Not at all," I said quickly.

"No," Ollie agreed, though much less emphatically. "In fact, it is good you are here. I have some business matters to attend to, and I should hate to leave Miss Kent without a companion. If you will excuse me." He touched the brim of his hat in a curt goodbye, then left the way we'd come.

"It appears things are going well with your Mr. Jennings," Amelia said once he was out of sight.

"It would appear that way, wouldn't it?"

"Yes. You were standing so close. Did he finally declare his suit?"

I feared he had been trying, but . . . "No. We were only continuing a conversation from a few days ago."

"Well, he looked as if he wished to," she said. "How does Lord Jennings feel about this development? Is he ready to be cast aside for his younger brother?"

"I would not know. Damon is in London learning from a Mr. Rowley."

"Mr. Rowley?" Her nose scrunched.

"Do you know him?"

"Thankfully no, but Frederick wrote of him often last Season. I am surprised you have not heard of him. He has quite a reputation among the *ton*."

"Oh?"

"Yes, well. We do not need to speculate on Mr. Rowley or on Lord Jennings's less respectable diversions, but I do hope Lord Jennings will get any ungentlemanly conduct out of his system before we wed."

I lost my footing and stumbled.

Amelia grabbed my arm, catching my fall. "Are you unwell?"

"I am still a little weak from my illness," I lied, but the truth was the idea of Damon gallivanting about London made me feel almost as ill as the thought of him marrying Amelia. I'd known of her plan to avoid love and marry Damon almost from the very moment we met—and since I rather disliked Damon at that time, I had not been bothered by her plan—but now . . . everything was different.

"You are looking a little pale. Let us sit until you have recovered." She led me to a bench and fanned my face. "Mother received a missive from the modiste that my new dresses are ready."

"Mine is ready too," I said.

"We must wear our new gowns to the ball," she said.

I agreed, and Amelia continued fanning my face.

Though we'd only known each other for a short time, I was grateful for Amelia's friendship. It had been so long since I'd had a friend to talk to about inconsequential things like this—since before Mama took ill. I missed it more than I'd realized.

I wanted to be honest with Amelia about everything that had happened between Damon and me. But what would I even tell her? I had developed feelings for Damon, but I didn't know if he felt the same for me. We'd shared some meaningful moments and candid conversations—or at least I thought we had—but he'd disappeared to London without so much as a goodbye or note of explanation, and I did not know when he would return.

Still, I held on to hope. Until Damon returned and we had a chance to speak, I would not know how he truly felt. And it did not seem prudent to talk of things I did not yet understand. Not to mention unkind. Amelia had been hurt by a friend before, and I did not want to cause her any more pain by dragging her needlessly through a similar situation.

No. I would wait to say anything to her until Damon returned.

"You are still looking a little pale," Amelia said. "Perhaps you need refreshment. Shall we find Lady Winfield and my mother in the rose garden?"

I nodded. "Yes, let us go."

She threaded my arm through hers, and we made our way around the back of the manor.

CHAPTER TWENTY-FIVE

Two days later, as I dressed for dinner, a carriage clattered up the drive. And although I could not see the drive from my window, I could hear voices outside. Lord Winfield and Damon.

"Nora," I called. "Help me dress."

She did, and I rushed down the stairs.

I found Damon in the portrait gallery. He stood in the middle of the black and white marble floor with his back to me. Hands clasped behind his back, he stared up at a painting of the first Earl of Winfield with so much intensity that he did not even seem to hear me approach.

"Damon."

At the sound of my voice, he turned to face me. His gaze was direct, but his eyes were as cold as the marble statues surrounding us. "Miss Kent," he greeted with a bow of his head.

Surprised by his formality, I bobbed a quick curtsy. "I see Mr. Rowley was able to educate you in gentlemanly behavior."

"Indeed. I found my lost manners in London." He gave me a weak smile, then turned back to the life-sized painting before him.

I stood at his side and stared at the imposing portrait. Damon had told me the first earl's story so many times as children that I would never forget it. He had been given the earldom by King Henry VIII after the siege at Boulogne for his bravery and valor and was bestowed with Summerhaven.

Damon rubbed the back of his neck, then dropped his hand back to his side. A flash of gold caught my attention. A signet ring on his smallest finger.

"What is this?" I asked.

He followed my gaze to the ring, then looked up at me. "Hannah," he said, his voice heavy. "My trip with Father to London was not an educational endeavor as he led everyone to believe."

I waited for him to say more, but he only looked at me with a pained expression, his eyes hooded, his lips pinched. "Is everything all right?" I asked.

He shook his head and bit down on his lower lip as if to stop himself from saying anything more.

My first thought was that their journey had something to do with their tenants. That perhaps Lord Winfield had found some way to punish the Turners for Damon's aid, or that Baby John's condition had deteriorated and the worst had happened. But how would London fit into either of those equations? It wouldn't. "You're scaring me. Why did your father take you to London?"

"He was there to secretly see a doctor who specializes in consumption of the lungs." A shadow crossed Damon's face. "Hannah"—his voice broke—"my father is dying."

A memory, sudden and sharp, of Mama lying in her sickbed filled my eyes with tears. "Oh, Damon. I am so sorry." I laid a hand on his forearm, wishing there was something I could do to spare him from the agony of losing a parent.

He clutched my hand and wove our fingers together. A moment passed, and he did not loosen his grip. He clung to me like I was the only thing holding him to the earth. "Father's condition has been worsening for some time," he continued. "I didn't know he was even ill. I only learned of his illness on this trip. He never said anything. He's been trying to prepare me to take up my duties, always pushing and prodding me to do more, to be more, and I hated him for it. What kind of son doesn't even notice how ill his own father is?" His words came out in a rush, one sentence after another like he was still trying to make sense of it all.

But having lost Mama, I knew there was no sense to be made. Death was a thief in the night that offered no explanation. I squeezed his hand, and in a sudden motion, Damon turned into me and fell into my embrace. His arms circled my waist, enveloping me, and I held him tightly so he would know he was not alone.

"He was hopeful this particular doctor might have a cure. That's why he didn't say anything sooner. But the doctor said there is nothing to be d-done." His voice caught, and he buried his face in my neck.

I rubbed his shuddering shoulders, and he clutched the fabric of my dress. "How long does he have?" I asked quietly.

"No one rightly knows. His symptoms are worsening, but the man is stubborn. He will probably live forever—or at least until I have found a suitable wife."

I stiffened. "A *suitable* wife?" I stepped back, putting enough distance between us so that I could look into his eyes.

"Hannah." He clutched my arms. "I didn't mean—"

I took another step back out of his reach. His hand lingered in the air a moment before dropping to his side.

"I thought—" I paused to choose the right words. "After all that has transpired between us this summer, I thought we were very near to an understanding."

"We were. I want desperately to make you a proposal of marriage, but Hannah, my father is dying and—" He pressed his eyes closed and shook his head. "You will never know how sorry I am, but I cannot marry you."

"I don't understand." I stared up at him in a state of shock. "We danced in a darkened ballroom together. We shared soft words. We *held* each other."

"I'm sorry," he said again.

I shook my head, unwilling to accept his apology. "Was this all a ruse to you? Am I nothing more than a plaything for you to trifle with?"

"No," he said. "No. You must know that you are not."

I knew nothing. My heart raced with panic. I could not lose him. Not now, when I was so close to having everything I had ever wanted; love and happiness were only a breath away. "Your father wants you to marry a well-bred woman who is your equal. I understand that, but, Damon, if you care for me as much as you claim to, how can you abandon me?" I could not lose another person I held dear.

"I did not want to tell you like this." Damon pulled in a long breath. "My father's failing health is not the only thing he revealed."

"Go on."

"In an effort to build up Summerhaven, to add wings and servants and status, he has accrued many debts. He has tried to pay off his creditors by cutting expenses where possible and investing in ventures overseas, but his ventures failed and so did the crops. Summerhaven is on the brink of ruin, Hannah. And because of Father's worsening health, he has passed the responsibility of seeing the estate through this dark time onto *me*."

I sucked in a breath. "Summerhaven is . . . ruined?"

"Very nearly." Damon nodded, his expression grave.

I lifted my gaze, taking in the vast portrait hall. The portraits, the statues, the tapestries. All of this, all of *Summerhaven*, now fell on Damon's shoulders. I could not imagine the weight of it.

"What will you do?" I asked quietly.

"What else *can* I do?" He paced the floor in front of me, pushing his hands through his hair. "In order to save Summerhaven, I must set aside my own desires and do as my father did and his father and his father's father and so on, in order that I might ensure the estate's future."

"Even if saving it comes at the expense of others?"

He stopped suddenly and looked at me. "Not at their expense, but for their *survival*. Hannah, I am all that stands between my family, my servants, and my tenants and certain ruin. I *must* marry for money."

I did not have it in me to cease hoping. I could not accept it. "Surely there is some other way, some investment you can make—"

"If Father had saved in times of plenty, perhaps, but investing takes both time and capital. I have neither."

"Perhaps a distant relative could make you a loan until circumstances improve."

"I promise you I have gone over every possibility no less than a hundred times since Father told me of his failing health and the estate's dire circumstance. There *is* no other way." Damon's gaze moved to the wall where the Jennings family crest hung. "*Conservabo ad mortem*," he read aloud. "'I will preserve it until death.' My father is dying, Hannah. From this day until the day I die, Summerhaven is my responsibility. I cannot be the weak link."

The gravity of the situation settled in me like an anchor falling to the sea floor, and I knew what he said was true. He could choose me and lose his estate or choose another and save it. I knew what he must do, but . . .

"What about me?" I said weakly.

In two swift steps, Damon stood before me again. "You will be fine. Mother wrote that Ollie has become quite attentive in my absence."

My throat tightened. "You would have me return to Ollie?"

He looked at me for a long moment, his jaw taut. "No," he said finally. "If he is what you want, I could not speak against it. But he will be one among dozens of suitors. You are beautiful and intelligent and kind. There is no doubt in my mind that you will find someone who will love and care for you."

I stared at him in disbelief. "After all that has passed between us, how can you say that?"

"Because I must. People are depending on me, Hannah." He swallowed hard. "All I have ever wanted is to be loved by you. You once asked what I did with your lock of hair, and I told you I didn't know where it had gone. But I lied." His sentence trailed off, and he reached into his pocket and pulled out a lock of hair. The fine strands were light and curly, and the little bundle was tied together with a green silk ribbon. He absently fingered the hair, a self-soothing motion that was likely born out of years of habit. And when he looked at me again, his eyes welled with tears. "I have loved you my whole life." His chin trembled. "I will *always* love you."

He loved me.

I'd waited my whole life to hear those words. They meant everything and yet held no meaning; he loved me, and I loved him, but no matter our affection, we could never be together—not if Summerhaven was to endure. Tears clouded my vision, and I dropped my gaze to the floor so he would not see my swell of emotion.

"Please try to understand." His voice broke. "I don't want this separation, but I have no choice."

"There is *always* a choice," I whispered. There had to be.

"You have no idea how much I wish that were true." He reached out as if to touch my cheek.

I shook my head. "Goodbye, my lord." I dipped into a shallow curtsy and fled the room.

CHAPTER TWENTY-SIX

I HAD NO DESIRE TO rise from bed the next morning, but today was my dress fitting at the modiste. Still, I was careful to leave my bedchamber only when Lady Winfield would already have risen and there was no chance that I might find myself alone with either Damon or Ollie.

Breakfast was served informally in the morning room, and I was relieved that all the Jennings men had already come and gone. Though I had no appetite, I picked at breakfast, forcing myself to eat a few bites of toast and a little fruit.

A few hours later, Lady Winfield and I settled into the carriage. "Are you excited to see your dress?" she asked as we started toward town.

"I am," I admitted, though I was a bit nervous too. I had felt brave when I'd chosen the bright poppy-colored fabric, but I was feeling decidedly less so now. Even if I didn't like my new dress, Lady Winfield had been so generous to purchase it for me, so I would have to wear it to the Garretts' ball.

My nausea began only a few minutes into our ride, and I longed for one of Damon's ginger candies.

When at last we reached town, I alighted from the carriage, and thankfully, as we walked to the modiste, my stomach settled.

A bell rang overhead as we entered.

"Welcome," the modiste greeted in her thick French accent, then she led us to the back of the shop where my dress hung.

I gasped when I saw it. "It is beautiful. Thank you."

"You should not thank me until you've tried it on, miss." She led me into a small room in the back of the shop, and a maid helped me changed into the gown. I stared at myself in the mirrors, smoothing the soft silk below the stylishly high empire waist. The dress had small puff sleeves that capped my shoulders, and intricate trim lined the bodice. It was the most elegant dress I'd ever worn, but it was difficult to muster enthusiasm. When I'd selected this bright fabric, I'd done so because I had wanted Ollie to think of marriage, but now the only person I wished would look my way was Damon. He couldn't. And even if he did, it would only make things harder.

I followed the maid back to the front of the shop to show Lady Winfield and to be fitted by the modiste.

"Oh, Hannah," Lady Winfield said when I walked out. "It is even lovelier on you than I imagined."

I studied my reflection. "Do you really think so?"

She nodded. "Oh yes, my dear. It brings out your complexion so nicely. Truly, it is gorgeous. You were right to trust your instincts."

Her words sounded just like something Mama would have said, and I tried to take comfort in Lady Winfield's compliment. But in truth, there was a part of me that wished I'd chosen a creamy white fabric for my new ball gown so I could blend in with the crowd of other young ladies at the Garretts' ball instead of standing out.

The modiste made note of several alterations, then pinned parts of the dress that needed to be taken in. When she was finished, I changed back into my green dress.

"Do you really like it?" Lady Winfield asked when we exited the shop.

"I do. Thank you for your kindness and generosity," I said, and I meant it too, but when I attempted a smile, the expression felt false.

"The pleasure is all mine," Lady Winfield said. "You have no idea how often I have longed for a daughter to dress and spoil. But . . . I must admit, you seem a bit out of countenance today. Are you all right, my dear?"

I bit my lip, wishing that I could confide in her, but of course I could not. I'd made such a mull of things, and there was nothing to be done about it. "I am only a little worried Ollie won't approve of my dress."

"Oh, is that all?" She smiled kindly. "Well, I do not think you need to worry whether or not he approves of your dress. He will not be the one wearing it after all."

A light laugh broke through my melancholy.

"I do understand your concern, though. Ollie has always been overly obsessed with Society's opinion of him," she said. She glanced at me, her eyes narrowing slightly. "Damon is quite the opposite though, don't you think?"

"In almost every way," I said quietly, a lump growing in my throat.

"It is an interesting thing to mother sons. I wish so desperately for each of their happiness." Lady Winfield grew quiet for a moment. "I hope you will forgive my impertinence, but I must ask, do you love my son, Hannah?"

I sucked in a surprised breath. Was she asking if I loved Ollie or if I loved Damon? She had spoken of both men in this conversation. "W-which son are you speaking of, my lady?"

"*That* is my question."

My cheeks burned under her observation. Not knowing how to answer, I bit my lip. Lady Winfield had invited me to Summerhaven in hopes of Ollie and me forming an attachment. When that had not gone according to her plan, she'd hinted that she wished for Damon and me to form an attachment. And we had, however impossible our union might be now.

"Forgive me, Lady Winfield. I should like to answer your question, but—" my words caught in my throat, and I only barely willed my chin not to quiver.

She gave me a small, sympathetic nod as if she somehow understood. And as we walked to the carriage in silence, my heart had never felt heavier. Not only was I losing the man I loved, but I was also losing Lady Winfield—another connection to Mama.

Back at the manor, I retired upstairs to the library, wishing to be alone, to be close to Mama. Dark wood bookshelves lined the walls, and two large windows supplied the room with an abundance of light. I could almost picture Mama sitting in the window seat with a book in her hand. On the north side of the room, next to an unlit fireplace, was an armchair and a small table. On it was a thickly bound green book—the one I'd often seen Damon studying.

Curious to know what he'd been reading all summer, I crossed the room. I ran my fingers over the gold-embossed title on the cover, *Agriculture and Industry* by A. Wilson Smith. I smiled wistfully. Damon had been trying to help his tenants all along.

I sat in the armchair and leafed through the book. Bits of torn paper with scribbled notes were tucked between the pages. I pulled one out and read a detailed note he'd scribbled about the best practices for crop rotation. I rubbed the slip between my fingers. What he'd chosen to sacrifice for his family and for Summerhaven was admirable, but that did not make this any easier.

"I know what you are doing," a deep voice came from the door.

I quickly closed Damon's book and whirled in my seat, hoping to see Damon standing in the threshold, but no, it was Ollie.

"What is it you *think* I'm doing?" I asked.

"Avoiding me," he said. "And quite well too. May I join you?"

"Of course."

Ollie strode into the library and sat on the window seat. "Do you remember how our mothers used to sit here and watch us play in the garden?"

"I was thinking of it just before you walked into the library. It is one of my fondest memories."

"Did you know they used to plan for our nuptials?" A smile tugged at one corner of his mouth.

"Yes." My cheeks warmed. "Papa told me the story before I came here this summer."

He turned away from the window to face me. "I know I've made many mistakes this summer, but I would like to mend things between us. I cannot bear to have you hate me."

"Hate you? I could never *hate* you, Ollie."

"Then why are you hiding in the library?"

Ollie knew me so well. I looked at Damon's book in my lap, ashamed. "Because I'm . . ." *heartbroken*, I wanted to say, but not wishing to hurt Ollie further, I settled on, "Confused."

"How could you not be?" he said. "Damon lured you into a ruse and then abandoned you when it no longer suited him."

"This is not his fault." None of this was his fault; we were both victims. "He did not lure me. I entered freely into our charade."

"The fact that you believe that only proves how convincing he was in his deception." Ollie leaned forward, resting his elbows on his knees. "I knew you were spending time together, but after everything he'd done to torture you as a girl, I thought you were immune to his *charms*." He sneered. "I had no idea how deeply he'd sunk his claws into you. How he'd used my blindness and your sadness to his advantage. I will never forgive him." Ollie clenched his jaw. "But I hate myself too. If I hadn't been so caught up in securing an advantageous life, if I hadn't been so blind, you never would have had to enter into a ruse."

"Please don't blame yourself, and you mustn't hate Damon either. He—" What could I say about his situation that would not betray Damon's trust? "He is trapped in an impossible position."

"Oh yes, being a lord of a grand estate is quite impossible," he muttered.

"Don't be petulant."

"I am sorry, but my whole life I have come second to Damon. Second born, second son, second in line. I never thought I would be second in your heart too," he said on a heavy breath.

"It is not a competition, Ollie."

He huffed a laugh. "*Everything* is a competition when a future earl is your brother."

"It didn't used to be," I said. "What happened between you two? You used to be so close."

A wistful look clouded Ollie's expression. "He was my best friend before he went away to Eton," he admitted.

"And after he returned?"

"He was different. Contemptuous, superior. For years, I wondered what I had done to make him hate me, but I didn't learn the answer until I attended school myself: I was inferior. I would never be titled, nor wealthy. I was beneath him." His voice grew small, childlike.

What injuries had he endured as a boy at the hands of his classmates to make him shrink this way? My heart ached for little Ollie, remembering the homesick letters he'd sent me from Eton. I touched his shoulder, wishing to comfort him.

Ollie laid his hand atop mine and gave me a feeble smile before resting his hand back on his knees. "Have you noticed how Damon struts around now like everything is below him? He won't even step into a ballroom unless someone of elevated station is in attendance. He merely hides away in the card room, spending his future fortune."

The truth pressed against my lips, and I wished I could speak for Damon and make Ollie understand that Damon was not the scoundrel Ollie thought him to be. But I couldn't say anything without revealing *everything*. And I could not do that to Damon. He had disclosed his father's failing health and Summerhaven's dire situation to me in confidence, and I would not betray his trust. All I could do was listen to Ollie and try to explain what little I could.

"I do not mean to be childish," Ollie continued. "But you cannot know what it is like for me to walk daily among the peerage and to have to live with the knowledge that I will never be one of them. Even within my own family, I am nothing more than a spare."

"Your family loves you," I said.

"Yes, but my life will never hold the value that Damon's does, and I confess, that truth has driven me a little mad." Ollie let out a heavy breath. "From my time at Cambridge forward, everything I did, everything I said, was done to impress and improve my standing in Society . . . including courting Miss Digby." He glanced at me. "I have been so blinded by my desire to make more of myself that I did not even realize how selfish I was being . . . until your confession." His eyes softened on me.

I clutched Damon's book in my lap, bracing myself for whatever Ollie meant to say next.

"Hannah, when you ran from me that day in the morning room and got into the curricle with Damon, I have never felt more heartbroken." He pressed his eyes closed like the memory brought him fresh pain, and when he looked at me again, his gaze was earnest. "And during the torturous days that you lay in your sickbed, I was in agony. I remembered how we used to make fun of the *ton*, and I realized that I'd become everything we'd sworn we wouldn't. And worse, I wasn't even happy. I tried to remember the last time I'd been happy. And do you know when it was?"

I shook my head. "When?"

"It was the last summer we spent together. The summer before I went off to Eton. Hannah, I don't want to be one of those people we made fun of . . . I want—I want—" He paused, swallowed hard, and then looked me in the eye. "I want to be a man worthy of you. I don't want to lose you."

"You won't," I said, meaning to reassure him that we would always be friends.

"I'm worried I already have." He gave me a sad expression, then rose from his perch at the window seat and walked to the armchair where I sat. He knelt in front of me, bringing us at eye level.

I sucked in a breath.

"I made a mistake, Hannah. A grave one. My behavior toward you this summer was unforgivable. I was an imbecile," he continued, "a complete and utter cad."

I smiled a little. "Don't forget fool."

"The *biggest* of fools. You should never, ever forgive me."

"Perhaps I should not," I teased, but when he looked at the ground in shame, I knew I'd taken it too far. "But I, too, did many things I am not proud of, and I should hate to allow one summer to tarnish a lifetime of memories."

"I want to be a man worthy of your affection. If you would allow me to court you as I should have from the beginning, I promise you will not regret it."

"Ollie, I—I am glad you feel you are on a better path now, but what I thought I wanted . . ." My sentence trailed off, and I gave him a sad smile.

"Our conversation in the morning room made me realize some things too. We were only meant to be friends. I should have known that years ago when you stopped writing to me, but it took you rejecting me for me to finally understand."

He shook his head, and his uncommonly unkempt curls flopped to one side. "I have given you every reason to doubt me, but let me show you that the dreams we once had can still come true. Walk with me tomorrow in the garden."

He was offering me everything I'd always thought I wanted, only I didn't want it anymore. I touched Mama's ring on my finger and shifted my gaze to the window bench. Mama had known both Damon and Ollie, and she had wanted Ollie for me. But I couldn't bring myself to do it. I'd fallen in love with Damon, and it could not be undone.

"Hanny?" Ollie said softly.

I met his hopeful gaze and was overcome with guilt. "I don't wish to hurt you, Ollie, but I see now that my affection for you was naive. A childhood dream. But we have grown up and grown apart. We do not even know each other anymore."

"That is entirely my fault," he said. "I have been blind and selfish. But please don't give up on me."

His words tugged at me, but after the experiences I'd shared with Damon this summer, I would never be the same. My heart had bloomed like a rose, and it could never again be a bud.

"I will walk with you tomorrow, but I can only offer you friendship."

"I understand," he said in a low voice, nodding. "I do, and I will walk with you tomorrow only as friends. But, Hannah, I do hope that rekindling our friendship will eventually lead to more."

I shook my head, but he rose before I could say more. And with a polite bow, he quit the room, leaving me alone to sort my feelings.

CHAPTER TWENTY-SEVEN

THE NEXT MORNING, I STAYED in my room until I saw Damon ride out on Ares. It was a cowardly thing to sit in my window seat, waiting for him to leave. And I could not avoid him forever, but I was not ready to face him yet.

Ollie was already in the breakfast room, reading *The Morning Post* when I entered. He smiled and stood. "Good morning, Hannah. You look lovely this morning. I trust you slept well?"

"I did. Thank you." I walked to an empty chair across from Ollie and sat.

Ollie remained standing. "May I serve you something to eat?"

I nodded, and he filled my plate with an assortment of fruit, breads, and breakfast meats, then sat and resumed his newspaper.

I tried to content myself with eating in silence, but I could not help frowning at the black and white text between us. And when he turned the page, he saw as much.

"I am being a rather dull breakfast companion, aren't I?"

"Hmm," I said between bites.

He moved to set the newspaper aside, and I almost let him. But how were we ever to regain our friendship if I did not act as my true self? "Actually, I don't mind if you read at the table. I only dislike being excluded."

His brow twitched, as if he hadn't the faintest idea what I meant. "Would you like me to tell you about what I am reading?"

"No." I shook my head. "I should like to read with you."

"You want to read the *Post*?" His face scrunched as if a woman wanting to read the newspaper was absurd. But when I nodded, he quickly smoothed the expression. "All right. I am sure there is a section that would appeal to you in here somewhere. A fashion column perhaps."

"I'm sure I would be happy to read *any* column," I said as he flipped through the pages.

"Ah. Here we are." He handed me the fashion section, and I stifled a sigh. He did not understand me. At least not yet. But today was about progress, not perfection. And although I didn't prefer to read the fashion columns, his willingness to let me read with him was a start and something we could build upon.

After we finished eating, Ollie and I parted for the remainder of the morning with a promise to meet later before luncheon for our walk. I passed the morning by reading a book, and at midday, Nora helped me change into a day dress, pale-green pelisse, and simply trimmed bonnet.

When at last it was time for our walk, I met Ollie downstairs. He wore a finely cut jacket and stylish top hat. His hair had gotten a bit longer since the beginning of summer, and a few of his dark-blond curls peeked boyishly out the sides. And in his hands, he held a blanket and a basket.

"What's this?" I asked.

"Only a small picnic, which I had Cook prepare. Nothing elegant, mind you, only a few finger sandwiches and pieces of fruit. I thought we could walk to the river and enjoy a meal on the bank like old times."

I felt a bit wary after the last picnic he'd planned for us, but I pushed past the feeling with a smile. "That sounds nice."

He held the door open for me as we walked outside. After descending the steps, we continued across the great lawn and past the stableyard toward the meadow. I hadn't noticed it earlier, but heavy gray clouds gathered in the distance.

"Do you think the rain will hold off?" I asked.

Ollie looked up at the sky. "I believe so. There is only a slight breeze, so hopefully the rain will take its time arriving."

I nodded and continued toward the river in silence. If only we could find a topic of conversation that did not feel so forced. Something that would help us become reacquainted. I tried to think of a subject that would interest him, but I doubted he wished to speak of toy soldiers like he did when he was a boy. But he *had* recently expressed a love for London. Perhaps we could find common ground there.

"So, you have been living in London," I said. "Do you miss it?"

"Very much. I love the excitement and energy of the city. What about you?"

"I miss Papa," I said. "But not the city. It is so dirty and loud and . . . pungent."

"It is that," he agreed with a huff of amusement. "But it has a certain charm, don't you think?"

I scrunched my nose. "I much prefer the country."

"I suppose the country has its appeal too." He bent to pick a yellow wildflower and handed it to me with a smile.

"Thank you," I said, and our fingers brushed as I took it from him, but my pulse did not skip as it might have had Damon given it to me. I knew I should not compare the brothers, but it could not be helped. I pushed the thought from my mind, and as we walked on, a question tugged at me. "If I ask you something, will you answer me honestly?"

He glanced at me sideways. "Do you think I would not?"

"I think everyone likes to avoid unpleasant topics of conversation, but we mustn't if we are to move forward in our friendship."

"You are worrying me, but I do wish our relationship to progress. I promise to answer you honestly."

"Thank you," I said, and as we continued down the footpath, I asked, "Why did you stop writing me when I moved to Bath?"

He bit down on his bottom lip. "It was not a conscious choice so much as it was—I don't even know—*life* getting in the way, I suppose."

I twirled the wildflower between my finger and thumb, watching the petals dance in the wind. "I can understand that, but why did you not visit me in London? Did you truly not know I was living there, or did you just choose not to?"

"To my shame," Ollie exhaled deeply, "I did know you had returned. And I *had* intended to call on you when I received your letter, but I always allowed myself to be diverted."

It hurt that he'd not made me a priority, but it was not a surprise. I was glad to know the truth, if only so that we might move beyond it. "Thank you for your honesty."

He nodded, looking more than a little ashamed.

A breeze ruffled through the trees, creating a small symphony, and in the distance was the faint sound of the trickling river.

"I should like to make it up to you," he started, hesitantly. "When we return to London, if you will allow it, I should like to call on you."

My shoulders tightened. I'd often dreamed of Ollie coming to call on me, but now, I wasn't sure I wanted him to. He was such a well-heeled gentleman, from his clothes to the friends he kept, that I couldn't even imagine him setting foot in Cheapside, let alone Papa's cramped parlor. What if Ollie turned up his nose?

"I could take you for a ride in my curricle at Hyde Park," he said, smiling.

"Perhaps," I said, but truthfully, parading around Town for all the *ton* to see did not sound enjoyable in the least.

"Or . . . maybe you would prefer to show me what you enjoy doing?"

I highly doubted Ollie would want to sit with me in the parlor and read, but there was one place he might appreciate. "I spend a few mornings a week serving the poor with the church. We could always use another hand during meal times."

He hesitated, then said, "I daresay I would not have any idea what to do."

"I would teach you," I said. "It's not so difficult."

"All right." He nodded slowly. "We can give charity by day and attend the theater by night. Watch your step." He placed a hand on the small of my back and guided me around a patch of mud. His touch was familiar, but it did not cause me to burn as Damon's had.

"The path gets slicker the closer we get to the river," he cautioned.

"As I well know."

"What was I thinking? Of course you do. Shall we race to the bank like we used to?"

"My skirts are a great deal longer than when I was a girl. I would probably trip."

"You could tie up your hem if you would like. There is no one around to see."

Except him. "No. I would *not* like." My answer came out far more curtly than I intended. "And it was ungentlemanly of you to suggest it."

His cheeks turned pink. "I was only remembering how you used to do that when we raced as children, but of course, it was not proper for me to suggest that to a young lady. Forgive me."

Drat! He had been trying to forge a connection based on a shared memory, and I had cut him down to size. Would we never get this right? "I'm sorry. I know you did not mean anything dishonorable. I was only remembering what you said to Miss Digby about me tying up my skirts as a girl, and I was upset."

"You cannot know how sorry I am for that."

I thought hearing him apologize would make me feel better, but making him feel bad only made me feel worse. "We are spending a great deal of our time together apologizing for what's passed when we should be looking toward the future. Shall we start over?"

He let out a relieved breath. "I would like that very much."

"Me too." We walked a few paces farther down the trail. Fallen foliage and small sticks crunched beneath our footfalls. I missed the way things used to be between us. I missed my friend. The easy way we'd laughed and played and teased one another. Perhaps *that* was what we were missing. I purposefully slowed my step. "Do you hear that?"

He stopped in the middle of the path, as I knew he would, to listen. "I don't hear anything."

I made a show of setting my hand on my hip and turning to look behind us. "Oh. Look there." I pointed at a random spot in the distance. "Do you see that?"

Ollie set the basket at his feet and cupped a hand over his eyes as he squinted into the distance. But no matter how hard he looked, he would not see the fictitious thing I'd invented to distract him.

I slowly stepped back out of his line of sight and gathered up my skirt. And then I ran as fast as my feet—and dress—would allow.

"I don't see anyth—" he started to say.

But I'd already raced away several paces. I glanced back over my shoulder at him. He picked up the basket, but he seemed to be having a difficult time running and keeping the contents inside at the same time.

The river grew louder and louder as I neared the bank. The footpath wound around, and I followed it to the water's edge. "I win!" I shouted breathlessly.

He came up beside me only a few moments later. "Only because you cheat."

"You are just jealous that I thought of the scheme and not you."

"Without a doubt." He laughed and laid the blanket on a patch of dry ground, then set down the basket. "Your victory lunch, madam," he said in a stuffy, upper-crust tone and dipped into an overly dramatic bow.

I stifled a laugh at his antics, remembering the way we used to pretend to be proper adults as children. "Why thank you, sir." I sat and spread my skirt around me like a proper lady.

"Finger sandwich or fruit?" he asked.

"Sandwich first, then fruit."

"An excellent choice," he said, but then he looked into the basket and frowned. "I think our little race has fatally wounded your lunch." He held up a flattened sandwich.

With a giggle, I took it from him to inspect it myself. "It is only a *little* injured," I said, taking a bite. "Yes. It's perfectly edible, I assure you."

"So you are a *cheater* and a *liar*." He shook his head. "What kind of company have you been keeping, Miss Kent?"

I shoved his shoulder, and he pretended as if the light motion caused him injury, lying back and clutching at his pretend wound. I rolled my eyes, and he propped himself onto his elbow.

Silence fell around us as we ate, but this time, it felt light. Leaves rustled in the breeze above us, and the stream trickled before us, and finally, it felt like old times. But then, in the distance, I heard what sounded like a horse neighing. I stilled to listen.

"You are not going to fool me again." Ollie wagged his finger. "So if you mean to steal my sandwich—"

"One smooshed sandwich is enough for me, thank you. I truly thought I heard a horse."

"Perhaps." Ollie shrugged. "This is an easy enough place to water an animal before heading back to the stableyard."

My stomach squeezed. Damon had ridden out on Ares this morning. I did not know where he'd gone, but it was certainly possible that he could return this way. I was not ready to see him, but the sound of hooves beating the earth grew ever louder.

I set aside my sandwich, my appetite gone.

"Would you like a piece of fruit?" Ollie asked.

I shook my head, worried my voice would come out shaky. He shrugged and continued eating his own food.

A flash of black appeared on the footpath, and then horse and rider came into view.

Damon.

He sat high in his saddle, his hair windswept and cheeks flushed. He gripped the riding crop, directing Ares down the footpath toward the river. And when he looked up and our eyes met, my heart pounded in my chest, causing an ache that quickly spread through my body.

"So you *did* hear a horse," Ollie said to me, and then gruffly to Damon, "Brother."

Damon reined Ares to a halt. And as his gaze slid between Ollie and me, taking in our little picnic, his expression darkened. "Pardon me. I did not mean to interrupt." He tugged Ares's reins, steering him in the opposite direction of the water.

Ares snorted unhappily but complied.

As soon as they reached the path, Damon kicked the horse's flanks, and they rode swiftly away. Damon did not look back, but I could not tear my gaze from him.

CHAPTER TWENTY-EIGHT

THAT NIGHT AT DINNER, OLLIE assisted me with my chair.

"Thank you, Ollie," I said, trying not to let my gaze wander to Damon across from me. But whether I looked at him or not, it really didn't matter. His presence filled the entire hall.

"The meal you've had prepared smells delicious." Lord Winfield smiled approvingly at his wife.

"Roasted duck with fennel and mint," Lady Winfield said. "Your favorite in celebration of your return. Thank you for coming home early. The Garretts will appreciate your attendance at their ball."

"You were right to request it of us," Lord Winfield said around a bite of food. "No matter how glum Damon was about it."

"Oh?" Lady Winfield looked at Damon.

I could not help glancing at him too.

He stared at Lord Winfield and gripped his fork with a fierceness more befitting a battlefield than a dinner table.

"I daresay our son met his future wife while we were in London," Lord Winfield continued when Damon said nothing. "The Duke of Maybeck's daughter Lady Margaret. He was quite taken with her. They spoke the entirety of the duke's dinner party and nearly all the way through a performance at the theater."

Ollie looked at me askance, pity in his eyes.

I trained my gaze on my plate. Damon had met—and spent time with—another woman in London. A duke's daughter who was no doubt as beautiful as she was wealthy.

Damon's gaze burned hot upon me, but I couldn't bring myself to meet it.

Had he already known about his father's failing health when he was flirting with this Lady Margaret? Or had he met her before? Either way, her existence no doubt made Damon's decision to fall in line with his father's wishes that he marry a wealthy woman that much easier. But I should not think of things I could not change. Whatever had existed between Damon and me was now over, and it did not serve me to be jealous.

"I would thank you to keep my private affairs *private*," Damon said in a low voice.

"Marriage is not a private matter," Lord Winfield said. "It affects the whole family."

"As you have made me painfully aware," Damon said.

"So long as you *are* aware, I am satisfied."

Damon dropped his fork to his plate. Startled, I looked up. He watched me with a steely gaze. In it was sorrow. Apology. After a long moment, he pushed back in his seat as if to leave.

"Please don't go." Lady Winfield laid a gentle hand on Damon's arm. "I have had Cook prepare your favorite dessert."

Iced oranges.

Damon seemed to soften at his mother's touch, and he scooted his chair back to the table. He glanced in my direction, but I looked away before our eyes met.

I couldn't let him see how much his spending time with Lady Margaret hurt me.

When the meal resumed, I glanced at Lord Winfield. Did he know that Damon had told me about Summerhaven's dire circumstance and about his failing health? I doubted it, or he likely would have sent me back to London by now. And it really didn't matter what I knew anyway, as I was not in a position to do anything with that knowledge. But when would he tell Lady Winfield?

Perhaps he wouldn't.

If Damon married a woman of means like Lady Margaret, Lord Winfield would not need to. The estate would be secured, and his death would come whether or not she knew of his poor health. At least if she didn't know, she wouldn't have to worry. No. Lord Winfield had no reason to concern his wife—so long as Damon came to his rescue.

I glanced at Damon and found him still watching me, his eyes filled with an anguish that matched my own.

I returned my gaze to my plate.

Life was as cruel as it was unfair.

After dinner in the drawing room, Lady Winfield played a lilting melody on the pianoforte. Lord Winfield stood behind her, turning the pages of her music sheets when necessary.

I stood near the hearth with Ollie. He stood quite near and was animatedly sharing a story with me about a prank one of his friends had pulled on him back in London. Something about a chicken being set loose in his room. I didn't know because my mind was attuned to Damon, who sat on the far end of the sofa reading his book. His dark hair curled against the curve of his neck. The way he licked his fingers before he turned each page—

No. I refocused on Ollie.

"Would you care to play chess?" Ollie asked once he'd finished his story.

Ollie did not love the game, but I was pleased he'd suggested a diversion he knew would interest me. "I would be glad to." Truly, I needed something to anchor my thoughts to, and a game of chess was the perfect distraction.

We sat and set our pieces on the chessboard. I studied the layout and decided to move one of my pawns two spaces forward.

Ollie mirrored my move with little thought. "I forgot to mention it yesterday on our walk, but Mother said your new dress is lovely."

"Your town's modiste is very skilled," I said, attempting to brush away his compliment.

"Indeed. Although I daresay it is your beauty which makes the dress, not the reverse."

Damon shifted on the sofa.

"We shall see tomorrow at the Garretts' ball," I said.

"Ah yes, the ball. I've been strategizing how I might steal both your first set *and* your supper set."

"Is that a question, Mr. Jennings?"

He laughed lightly. "It is if you will have me, Miss Kent."

"I will," I said, grateful that I would not have to begin the ball alone. Then I claimed one of Ollie's pawns.

Across the room, Damon slammed his book closed, and then his footsteps fell loudly on the floor as he crossed the room.

I peeked over my shoulder.

Damon stood with his back to me at the cellaret where the bottles of alcohol were stored. He'd removed his coat and wore only his waistcoat and shirt sleeves, and his cravat hung misshapen around his neck.

I wished I could retie it for him. Wished I could pull him back into my arms and tell him that everything was going to be okay. But everything would not be okay. We'd been put in an impossible position by his father, and we had no recourse.

Damon pulled the stopper off a decanter of brandy and poured himself a drink. He stared at the amber-colored liquid for a moment, then drained the glass. He refilled his glass once more, then replaced the stopper. When he finally turned back to face the room, his steely gaze landed on the chessboard between me and Ollie. Damon's jaw tightened, and I knew he was remembering the game we'd shared at the beginning of the summer.

I gave a slight shake of my head, trying to tell him that there was nothing to be jealous of. But Damon quit the room anyway. I stared at the threshold for a long moment, hoping he would rejoin us, but it remained empty.

Ollie cleared his throat behind me. "It is your turn, Hannah."

"Forgive me," I said, turning back to our game. I searched the board, and my eyes landed on the knight. Its windswept mane looked so much like Ares's. I left the piece where it was and studied the board for another advantageous move. There were far too many for how long we had been playing. "Either you are a remarkably terrible opponent, Mr. Jennings, or you are playing poorly on purpose."

"I am not playing poorly on purpose, but even if I was, you never used to mind when I let you win." He flashed me a dimpled smile.

He was trying to make me smile, but it had the opposite effect. Win or lose, I wanted to do so on my own merit, not because he *let* me. "Challenge me, Ollie."

A muscle in his jaw flexed. "I *am* trying, Hannah, but I am not as good at this game as my brother is."

"Pardon?"

"Damon," he said. "You were comparing how well I play chess to him."

"I wasn't."

"You were," he insisted, and my irritation grew. "Never mind. Let's just finish our game."

And so we did. In silence. Until I captured almost all of his pieces and had to say, "Checkmate."

Ollie let out a humorless breath. "It seems I'm no match for you, Hannah. Perhaps we should stick to other diversions to pass our time together."

"Perhaps so."

That night, I went to bed with a heavy heart.

CHAPTER TWENTY-NINE

Nora laid my new poppy-colored gown on the bed. I ran my fingertips over the intricately beaded bodice and delicate cap sleeves. The soft silk gown was even more beautiful than I'd dared to dream. I had no desire to put it on and pretend to be happy, but there was nothing for it.

"You are quiet this evening," Nora said as she helped me change.

"I was only thinking about tonight."

We moved to the vanity table. Nora pinned my curls into place, framing my face with ringlets, and then accented the arrangement with a ribbon and pearls. I dabbed a little rose water onto my neck and was ready.

My skirts swished as I walked down the corridor and descended the grand staircase. Halfway down, I noticed Damon standing alone in the entryway, looking at his fob watch. My heart leapt traitorously at the sight of him. Dressed in a crisp white shirt and formal black tails, he was the picture of a well-heeled gentleman.

Damon looked up from his watch. "Hannah." His gaze raked over me unguarded. "You look . . ." His sentence trailed off, and he swallowed hard.

I continued to the bottom of the stairs. "Your silence is uncharacteristic. Disconcertingly so. You must tell me as a gentleman, does this shade not suit me?"

"You know it does," he said in a low voice. And stepping nearer than was proper, he brought his mouth to my ear. "As I once said, every man in the ball-room will be yours for the taking."

My pulse quickened, but I could not allow myself to feel this way. I set a hand on his chest and stepped back an appropriate distance. "Not *every* man, my lord."

"Please don't call me that," he said quietly.

"We have had this conversation before," I said sadly. "This time, I must insist on propriety." It was the only way for me to endure this separation.

Damon looked at me for a long moment, his gaze full of yearning. "Dance with me tonight," he said as if he could not resist.

"You know we cannot."

"I have been in agony these last days," he whispered. "Please. Dance the first set with me."

I wished I could accept him, but I did not think my heart could abide it. "Damon, I—"

"She has already promised that set to me," Ollie said, and my gaze flashed up to where he descended the stairs, looking handsome in his formal attire. "Perhaps if Lady Margaret is in attendance, you might ask her instead."

Damon glared daggers at Ollie as he took his place at my side, but Ollie did not look away. And a moment later, Lord and Lady Winfield entered by way of the drawing room.

Lord Winfield clenched his jaw when he saw my gown. He clearly did not approve of it, but Lady Winfield smiled.

"Oh, Hannah, you are a vision." Her eyes filled with tears as she crossed the hall, and standing in front of me, she touched my cheek. "I just cannot believe how much you resemble your mother."

"You could not have given me a greater compliment. Thank you."

"Look at me." She withdrew her hand from my face and waved it in front of her own as if to dry her eyes. "Such a watering pot. Come, let us go and enjoy the ball."

The cool night air nipped at the exposed skin on my neck. I pulled my shawl tighter around me, but it did little good.

Lord Winfield helped Lady Winfield into the carriage, then sat on the bench opposite her. Ollie handed me up next, then slid in next to his father. Damon entered last, and instead of taking the rear-facing seat like the other gentlemen, he sat improperly next to me.

Lord Winfield grunted his displeasure.

I folded my hands in my lap, trying to take up as little space as possible, trying not to touch Damon, but there was nothing for it; our legs and arms brushed with every breath.

Memories of sitting next to Damon at the pianoforte invaded my mind as the carriage bounced down the drive. I banished the thought with a shake of my head, but another memory of riding home from the Turners' farm in Damon's small curricle quickly took its place.

The carriage swayed as we exited the gate, and the force of the turn pulled me into Damon. I quickly righted myself, but his nearness combined with the jostling of the carriage was excruciating.

My stomach churned.

I looked out the side glass, but the darkness did not offer an easy distraction. I sucked in a breath, and the scent of Damon's cologne nearly undid me. I rubbed my neck.

"Are you feeling well?" Ollie asked.

I nodded, though it must not have been convincing because Lady Winfield said, "Perhaps you would prefer to switch seats with me and sit by the side glass?"

"You are kind to offer," I said, and my voice wavered. "But I do not think it will help."

Damon shifted beside me, the motion only making me feel worse, and then he held out his hand to me. In his gloved palm, a ginger candy.

I met his gaze and took the amber-colored sweet from him with a quiet, "Thank you."

Damon nodded and looked at me with concern. No, it was more than that. It was longing.

Lord Winfield cleared his throat loudly, and Damon averted his gaze.

Lady Winfield filled the remainder of the drive with idle chatter. Lord Winfield and Ollie made a few comments, but Damon and I remained silent.

At last we arrived. As we walked up the stairs, Ollie extended his arm to me. I hesitated to take it, knowing it would only cause Damon pain, but there was nothing for it. Damon and I would never be married, but Ollie and I could be friends.

A gray-haired butler announced our company at the ballroom door. Though the hall was not so big as the Winfields', it was ostentatiously decorated; pink-papered walls were highlighted by half a dozen glittering gold chandeliers, and flowers graced every surface that was not already occupied by a lavish spread of desserts. And it looked as if all of England had been invited to enjoy it.

Damon disappeared almost immediately, likely to the card room, but Ollie remained at my side. He smiled at me as we pressed through the crush. "I neglected to tell you earlier; you look lovely tonight. Your dress is quite . . . eye-catching." His tone *sounded* sincere, but the way he glanced at the sea of white gowns surrounding us made me unsure whether his comment was intended to compliment or criticize.

I searched for Amelia, scanning the faces of the seemingly endless number of guests, but it was her brother, Mr. Atherton, I saw first. Dressed in light-blue tails and a brocade waistcoat, Mr. Atherton was nearly impossible not to see. Amelia stood at his side in her stunning new yellow gown.

"Mr. Atherton, Miss Atherton." Ollie tipped his head in greeting, and our friends returned the gesture.

"Where is Lord Jennings tonight?" Mr. Atherton asked.

Ollie shrugged. "He has probably slithered off to the card room."

Everyone laughed, and I had to bite my tongue to keep from speaking on Damon's behalf. No one else knew the aid he gave his tenants or what he was sacrificing to secure his family's future. And no one ever would. Except me.

The first set was announced a few moments later.

A spindly gray-haired man walked up to our group. "Miss Atherton," he said. "Will you dance the first set with me?"

Amelia stared at the spittle pooling on his graying beard. Mr. Atherton elbowed her, and she blinked. "Yes, of course, sir."

The man moved toward the dance floor, but Amelia did not follow. She turned to her brother. "If I have to dance, then so do you."

"I do not actually." He adjusted his ruffled cuffs.

"Do not be silly, I know how much you love a stage."

"A crowded ballroom is hardly a stage."

"So you would rather be left alone for all the marriage-minded mothers to pick at you?" Amelia raised an eyebrow.

"On second thought, perhaps I shall ask Miss Moore to dance."

Amelia grinned at her brother, then walked to join her partner on the dance floor.

Ollie offered me his arm. "Shall we?"

I nodded and walked forward with him, then we lined up across from each other. I executed the forms with precision but not enjoyment, and when the set was over, I happily left the floor.

"I will get you a refreshment, my dear," Ollie said.

I tensed. The endearment did not feel right falling from his lips.

"Mr. Jennings looks positively besotted," Amelia said as he walked away.

I held a hand to my forehead, feeling faint. "It is a bit warm in here, don't you think?"

"I daresay *all* ballrooms are warm," Amelia said. "But look, Mr. Jennings is returning with your drink already."

"Your refreshment," he said.

"Thank you." I took the glass and sipped the lemonade, but it did little good.

At the front of the room, the next set was announced. A quadrille and then a waltz. I tried not to think of Damon, but our previous dances drifted through my mind like a dream . . . how he had guided me through my first quadrille with whispered words and our waltz in the darkened ballroom at Summerhaven.

"Might I convince you to stand up with me for another set?" The dimple in Ollie's chin appeared.

I felt as if I might be ill. Dancing two sets in a row would say something about our relationship that I did not mean. "I—"

"Actually, little brother, this set belongs to me."

My stomach caught at the sound of Damon's deep voice behind me, and when I turned, my heart leapt at the sight of him.

"Perhaps you might convince Miss Atherton to stand up with you," Damon said.

Ollie gritted his teeth, but he quickly smoothed the angry expression and turned to Amelia. "Miss Atherton, would you care to dance?"

Amelia glanced at me with narrowed eyes, then turned to Ollie. "I would be happy to, Mr. Jennings." And the pair moved away.

"Miss Kent?" Damon offered me his arm.

I tentatively took it, and we walked through the crush of people toward the dance floor. "You should not have asked me to dance," I whispered.

"One set is not a sin, Miss Kent."

"Then why does it feel like it?"

We formed a square with three other couples. We were thankfully in a different group than Ollie and Amelia; I did not think I could dance with Damon with them watching.

The music began, and I was glad that most of the dance was spent crossing through the square with the gentleman opposite me and then circling in the center with the other ladies. But when the quadrille ended and the waltz began, there was no one to come between Damon and me.

Damon's arm circled my waist and mine his. Together we raised our arms to form an arch above our heads. Heat prickled between us, and when our eyes met, the memory of our stolen waltz overwhelmed me.

"I can't—I can't do this. Excuse me." I pushed my way through the crush, leaving him alone on the dance floor, and I did not stop until I'd reached the portico outside. People were milling about, but I found a semi-secluded spot at the railing and sucked in a gulp of cool air. My eyes filled with tears. I gripped the balcony railing and tipped up my chin to keep them from falling. It did not work. A drop slipped down my cheek and then another.

"Are you unwell?" Damon's voice startled me from behind.

"I'm fine," I said, but my voice was threadbare and shaky.

He stood beside me at the railing. "You look as fine as I feel, which is to say, not at all." He produced a handkerchief from his coat's breast pocket and silently offered it to me.

Our hands brushed as I took it from his grasp. "Thank you." I dabbed the sensitive skin beneath my eyes, but it did not stop new tears from falling. And so long as I stood this near him, there was little hope I would be able to compose myself. I pushed off the railing, away from Damon, and hurried down the steps toward the garden.

"Miss Kent," he called after me, but I did not stop.

Lanterns illuminated the garden path and led to a gazebo. It was not so far away from the manor as to be indecent, but the covered roof would provide privacy from prying eyes. I just needed a moment to regain my composure.

"Hannah," Damon called again, his quick footfalls quieting as he slowed to a stop behind me.

I opened my mouth to beg for a moment of privacy, but my voice clogged in my throat, and only a whimper escaped. I turned away from him, wanting to conceal my face.

"Please don't hide from me." Damon walked to where I stood in the middle of the gazebo and touched my elbow, turning me to face him. The moment he saw my tearstained face, he pinched off his gloves and brushed his fingers across my cheeks to dry them.

In a moment of weakness, I leaned into his touch, relishing the heat of his palm, the scent of his wrist.

"Hannah." My name fell from his lips in a whisper. "I'm sorry," he said. "I'm *so* sorry."

"Me too." I lifted my hand to his chest. His heart was beating so fast and hard. And when he stepped closer—so close that the toe of his boot brushed the hem of my skirt—my heart returned the same rhythm.

But as exhilarating as it was to stand so near him, we should not be so careless; the ball was going on not so very far from where we stood. I moved to drop my hand, but his hand darted from my face and held mine in place. "Stay with me. Please. Just one more moment."

I wanted to, but . . . "We shouldn't. You have an obligation to your family, to Summerhaven."

"I know," he said, hoarsely. "But I don't think I can carry this burden without you."

"You can," I said, even though it pained me to do so. "You *must*." I understood that now. As much as I wished he could choose otherwise, Damon's life was not his own; it belonged to all those who depended on him and always would. I pulled my hand from beneath his and removed his palm from my cheek.

A sad expression stole across his face, and he hung his head. "I am in love with you, Hannah."

"And I love you, Damon." They were the truest words I'd ever uttered, and yet, I should not have said them; voicing our feelings would only make them harder to deny.

"You . . . *love* me?" He searched my face.

"More than I have ever loved anyone," I whispered. How could he not know?

He pressed his eyes closed as if savoring my words, and when they reopened, his gaze landed on my lips. His mouth dipped toward mine as if he had no power to stop it. Pleasure rippled through me in anticipation, but only a breath away, he stilled.

We could never marry. He knew it, and so did I, but we *could* have this moment. I raised onto the tips of my toes and pressed my lips to his.

Damon didn't hesitate.

He gathered my face in his hands and kissed me deeply, *desperately*. It was as if the dam that contained months of restraint had suddenly broken. His mouth moved against mine with purpose and passion.

He tasted of citrus and smelled of balsam.

I circled my arms around his neck and traced the lines of his shoulders with my fingers, memorizing their strength and slope. I never wanted to forget this moment so long as I lived; I would think of it every day and dream of it every night.

My knees became weak, and just when I thought they might give out from under me, Damon wrapped his arms around my waist and backed me up against the gazebo. He braced his weight on the post behind my head and feathered kisses on my lips, my cheeks, my jaw.

Consumed by the sensation, I lost sense of time and place and reason. All that existed was him and me and our kiss.

And then someone gasped.

Damon tensed but did not move away, instead shielding me from view with his body. But there was no point in hiding; we'd been discovered and now must face the consequences.

I gave Damon one last lingering look, then stepped out from behind him.

"Hannah?" Amelia said, her voice stricken.

"You need not worry, Miss Atherton," Ollie said evenly, though he glared daggers at Damon. "What you see is only a charade. One with which my brother has taken far too many liberties."

Amelia looked at me, her gaze pleading for me to give her some justification for what she had witnessed.

But there was nothing I could say to ease this blow. I could only offer her the truth and hope she would understand.

"It is not a charade," I whispered. "Not anymore. Our feelings for each other are real."

Her eyes widened with betrayal. "How could you?"

I opened my mouth to explain, but she held up a hand, stopping me. "I don't want to know. You have hurt me enough already." And she turned and strode away.

I stared after her, knowing she deserved a full explanation and apology, but first, I needed to explain my actions to Ollie before the rift between the brothers became a chasm. I turned back to Ollie.

"After all that he has done to tease and torture you," Ollie said, "you must know that a daring dress and quick kiss will only entertain him for so long. How could you let yourself fall for his act?"

"It is *not* an act," Damon said in a stern voice.

Ollie trained his gaze on Damon. "Oh? Do you intend to marry her then?"

I knew Damon's answer before he said it, but it still hurt when he said, "No."

Ollie lunged forward, grabbing Damon by his lapels, and pushed him up against the same post that Damon had just braced himself on to kiss me. "You are a blackguard, Damon. A self-serving scoundrel and a cad. Just because you are a lord, that does not mean you can treat her like this. She is not beneath you."

"You're right," Damon said, and he pushed Ollie off of him and stood in front of me. "I should not have dishonored you. I'm truly sorry, Hannah."

"I know," I said.

"Your apology counts for naught if you refuse to do the honorable thing and marry her, brother." Ollie pushed past Damon, knocking his shoulder. "Come, Hannah. We must return if your reputation is to remain intact. I will tell Mother you have swooned and need to return home. I'll have the carriage brought around straightaway."

I glanced at Damon. His shoulders drooped, and his eyes were cast downward. I hated to leave him in this state, but Ollie was correct that I needed to return. I reluctantly moved toward Ollie.

"No." Damon stepped forward, blocking my path. "I cannot endure this. We will find another way to save Summerhaven." He said it only loud enough so I could hear. "Together." He spoke with desperation, and it broke my heart, but I could not let him do something now that he would later regret.

"You know there is no other way. Please do not make this any harder than it already is. I will leave Summerhaven tomorrow morning at first light."

I moved to one side, and so did he.

"Damon, if you care for me as much as I care for you, then you will let me go."

And this time when I moved to walk away, he let me pass.

CHAPTER THIRTY

THE NEXT MORNING, LADY WINFIELD stood on the drive. Her sorrowful expression brought me fresh pain.

"Your carriage is ready, Miss Kent," Caldwell said when my trunk was stowed.

"Are you sure you wish to leave early?" Lady Winfield asked.

"Yes," I said quietly. "Thank you for having me as your guest this summer. I'm so grateful for your kindness and generosity."

She gave me a warm embrace, and it felt like a final goodbye.

Caldwell helped me into the hired coach and shut the door.

The carriage jolted harshly down the drive, and I leaned forward in my seat, taking one last look at Summerhaven. It seemed impossible that I would never again see my most treasured place in the world. There would be no more morning rides on horseback, no more afternoons skipping rocks on the river. I would never listen to Damon play the pianoforte again, nor be challenged by him at chess.

I turned away from the window.

The coach wasn't as comfortable or as well-sprung as the Winfields' carriage, and it did not take long before my stomach tied in a knot. I wished for one of Damon's ginger candies, Lady Winfield's gentle voice, Ollie's smile. If only I could hear Papa's reassuring words or have one more embrace from Mama. Oh, how I longed for Mama.

But I was alone.

I'd lost everything.

CHAPTER THIRTY-ONE

SITTING ON THE SMALL BAY window seat of our London townhouse, I rested my head against the wood frame. The parlor was dark and damp and cold. Outside, rain pelted the window and trickled down the glass in dirty rivulets, and carriages carved deep scars into the muddy lane.

Since returning from the country nearly four weeks ago, London had been cloaked in perpetual shades of gray and black and brown, the rain torrential and unending.

I had not received word from anyone in the Jennings family or from Amelia. I did not expect I ever would. I could hardly blame them for hating me.

I hated me.

In my selfish pursuit to win Ollie's affection, I'd caused everyone so much anguish. Worse still, I'd believed my actions justified.

I'd told myself that I had to do whatever was necessary to turn Ollie's head and convince him to marry me, not only because I loved him but also because I wanted to save him from a loveless marriage with Miss Digby. I believed her the worst sort of person, but I was no better, was I? We had both used people to get what we wanted. She used Ollie to get close to Damon, and I used Damon to get close to Ollie. We were one and the same, she and I.

In my anxious pursuit, I'd also hurt Amelia. It had not been my intention to betray her trust, but that hardly mattered. Time after time, she'd asked me if my feelings for Damon had changed, and I had not confided in her. I'd hurt her the same way her friend Rose had. Though I'd not meant to fall in love with Damon, I had. And I should have told Amelia the truth as soon as I knew it myself.

I deserved to be miserable.

But Amelia did not.

I moved to the escritoire situated in the corner of the room and pulled out a slip of paper, then set to work trimming my quill. I should have written this letter of apology as soon as I arrived home, but I had been too sad and ashamed and afraid.

My hand trembled as I dipped the quill into the inkwell, and then I painstakingly laid out my heart. Page after precious page, I detailed the entirety of what happened—how the ruse came to be, what happened during that time to change my heart, and finally, the mistakes I'd made in not disclosing everything to her sooner. I prayed my words would soften her feelings toward me so we could mend our friendship, though I did not expect it. I had not been a good friend to Amelia, and she was justified in her anger.

I folded and sealed the letter, then set it on the mail tray for Mrs. Potter to post. Sitting in the window seat again, I tucked my legs underneath me and stared outside at the falling rain.

Papa laid a blanket on my lap, startling me awake.

"Sorry," he whispered. "I did not mean to wake you."

"It is quite all right." I shifted in my seat, turning away from the window to face him.

Papa sat in his cushioned armchair across from me. "A letter came while you were sleeping."

"Oh?" My pulse quickened. Could it be from Summerhaven? Or perhaps Amelia?

Papa watched me from his chair and laid the letter in his lap.

"Bad news?" I asked.

He shook his head. "On the contrary. Henry and Georgiana are coming through Town to visit on their way to Captain Bromley's house party. Never did understand the lure of large social gatherings myself, but they seem pleased."

"When will they visit us?" I asked, feigning interest.

"In ten days."

"And for how long will they stay?"

Papa glanced over the letter. "A week." He smiled.

With a sigh, I nodded. While I was excited to see Henry again, my new sister-in-law could be a challenge. I wasn't social enough for her liking, nor was I interested enough in fashion. She'd probably faint if she saw my unfashionably bright poppy-colored dress. But for Papa's sake, I would do my best to evince eager excitement.

"That is wonderful," I said. "It will be good to see them, and I'm sure a house party will be just the thing."

"I am glad you think so; Henry and Georgiana have also secured an invitation for you."

"For *me*?" I blanched but quickly composed myself. "That is to say, how very kind of them. I do hope they will not be displeased with me when I refuse."

"But why would you refuse? I thought you enjoyed the country."

"I did. I *do*."

Papa adjusted his spectacles and set his newspaper on the side table. "I am worried about you, Hannah. You have not been yourself since returning home early from Summerhaven. It has been several weeks now. Will you tell me what happened?"

I wished to avoid this topic more than anything but knew it could not be escaped. Not forever. "Oh, Papa. I have made such a mess of things."

"It cannot be so bad."

"Whatever you are thinking, I am sure it is worse."

Papa's brow furrowed.

Guilt filled me, but it was time to confess all the mistakes I had made and all the people I'd hurt.

My voice quivered, but I intended to tell him everything, beginning with how I'd misinterpreted Lady Winfield's invitation and then confessing how I'd hoped for an engagement with Ollie but was mistaken.

Papa interrupted me almost immediately. "I daresay Mr. Jennings is at fault. All those letters he sent to you while your mama lay in her sickbed . . ." Papa shook his head disapprovingly.

"He sent them to comfort me, not court me," I said and hurried to continue my story. "As soon as I discovered the truth of Ollie's feelings for me, I was ready to return to London. But then, Damon told me he was in a difficult position as well, and he made me a proposition."

Papa's eyes narrowed.

"Nothing indecent," I quickly added. "Lord Winfield was demanding that Damon marry, but he wasn't ready to take up the obligation, so he suggested we pretend to court. And I agreed, thinking it would make Ollie jealous and turn his head." Saying the words out loud brought new shame.

Papa rubbed his forehead.

"Our charade didn't go according to plan though. The more time I spent with Damon, the more I grew to care for him."

"And what of your feelings for Mr. Oliver Jennings?" Papa asked. "I thought you liked him."

"I do care for Ollie. He's my dearest childhood friend, and the letters he sent me while Mama was sick lifted my spirits, but . . ."

"But you don't love him," Papa said.

I shook my head.

"Do you love Lord Jennings?"

I nodded. "He is a good man, Papa: hardworking, generous, and kind. I love him more than I have ever loved anyone."

"Does he not return your feelings?" Papa frowned as if confused.

"He does, but for reasons I can't say, we cannot be together. I have made so many mistakes, Papa. I've hurt so many people." I then told Papa how I'd lied to Amelia and deceived Lady Winfield.

He grimaced. "It is not like you to lie, Hannah."

"No," I agreed, "but you cannot know how desperate I felt. The future I'd dreamed of my whole life was slipping through my fingers like water. And I could not give it up, not without trying. I am not excusing my actions—what I did was wrong. I'm only trying to explain why I did what I did."

"Love can make a person do things they never believed themselves capable of," Papa said sadly.

"I hate that I have let you down. If only I had been constant to Ollie like Mama had wanted."

Papa's face smoothed with sympathy. "Dear girl, your mother did not want you to marry Mr. Jennings because *she* loved him. She wanted you to marry him because she thought *you* loved him. If your feelings changed, she would not have wanted him for you."

"But she knew me best. Even better than I knew what I wanted for myself. Perhaps if I had followed her wishes, I would not have lost everything."

Papa shook his head. "Your mother was a wise woman, but she did not know the workings of your heart. First and forever, she wanted you to be happy."

Papa's words warmed me like a cup of tea, and I knew what he said was true. Mama had known what I'd wished for as a child, but she was no longer here. What was best for me now weren't the dreams of my childhood, and I did not need to cling to them to please her. She would never want me to sacrifice my future happiness for her past dreams.

"I only wanted a love match like you and Mama had," I said.

Papa's head tilted to the side and he frowned. "I loved your mother more than life itself, Hannah, but we were not a love match."

I blinked. "What?"

"Well, *I* was enamored with her from nearly the first moment I saw her, but I daresay my feelings were not reciprocated." He chuckled. "I had a good name and a secure income, which enticed your grandparents into arranging the marriage. But as a second son of a second son of a second son who spent his days in service to the church, I fear I was a rather dull prospect for your fiery mother."

"But Mama loved you," I said. "I saw how much she cared for you with my own eyes."

"Yes, well. With enough time and care, love can grow even when planted on stony ground."

I shook my head. "I cannot believe your marriage was arranged."

"Things were different back then." He lifted one shoulder. "Love matches were not as common."

How was this even possible? They had appeared so happy, so in love.

"Don't be glum. I loved your mother, Hannah, and she loved me. How we began is not so important as the fact that we arrived."

I nodded, but I had spent my whole life idolizing their relationship and wanting to emulate their love in my own life. And to find out they had not even chosen their marriage for themselves . . .

It was as if the painting of my life had been ripped from one frame and put into another. The painting was the same—the brush strokes of love, the same image—but somehow everything looked completely different now.

CHAPTER THIRTY-TWO

HENRY AND GEORGIANA ARRIVED ON a Monday, the boot of their carriage stacked high with trunks. Georgiana wore a light-blue traveling dress and a handsome hat adorned with peacock feathers, and Henry wore a simple coat and trousers: opposites in every way.

Papa embraced Henry and then Georgiana. "How was the journey?"

Georgiana frowned. "Rather bumpy," she said and gave Henry a displeased look.

"Hopefully we will have a more comfortable carriage by this time next year," Henry said.

Georgiana sighed heavily and ascended the stairs to the top step where I stood. She kissed my cheeks, first the right and then the left, in the way of the French. I found this habit of hers endlessly amusing, seeing as how she'd never actually been to France because of all the wars.

After brushing our boots clean on the scrape, we walked inside to the parlor. Henry and Papa sat comfortably in the cushioned armchairs, and Georgiana took my usual seat on the window bench. She fanned out her skirt into a lovely blue puddle, then beckoned me to sit on the sliver of unoccupied space beside her. Not wanting to wrinkle her, I perched myself on the edge.

"How are you, Hannah?" Georgiana asked.

"I am well enough."

"You are a bit pale."

"Thank you for your concern," I said, "but I am not ill."

"Perhaps not, but you are not well," Georgiana said. "A weekend at Captain Bromley's country house will do you good. Your father was right to write me."

My nose scrunched. "I thought *you* wrote to *Papa*." I glanced in his direction, but he was suddenly very interested in the cuff of his sleeve and would not meet my gaze.

"No," Georgiana said. "Quite the opposite. Your papa wrote to Henry that you have become quite morose."

"Georgiana," Henry snapped, his gaze flashing to me and then back to his wife.

"What? Even if Papa had not written, her state is hardly a secret," she said. "Look at her, Henry." Her gaze moved from my un-styled hair, down my wrinkled dress, and finally landed on my worn—but comfortable—slippers.

Well, whatever Papa was about, I wanted no part of it. "It was kind of you to think to invite me," I said. "But I do not want to impose."

"Don't be silly. Henry has arranged everything. Haven't you, dearest?"

"Everything," Henry nodded, and a teasing glint shone in his eyes. "I daresay after *all* the trouble it took to procure you an invitation, it would be quite unfortunate if you did not now attend."

I raised an eyebrow at Henry. "And just how did you beg me an invite?"

"I asked Captain Bromley."

I huffed a laugh. "That is all?"

"That is all it took." He shrugged. "Indeed, when he learned you were young and unmarried, he seemed quite eager to extend the invite."

I gripped the edge of the seat so I did not fly off it and strangle him. "You didn't."

"No." He laughed. "I didn't. Though my wife wishes I would have made you such a prelude."

I sighed. Georgiana was nothing if not a matchmaker.

"Captain Bromley and your brother have become quite good friends," Georgiana interjected. "They play cards together every Thursday."

Papa shot Henry a look of disapproval.

"I attend Captain Bromley's weekly gathering for the company, not the cards," Henry said.

Papa nodded, pleased, then looked at Georgiana. "Perhaps I was a bit too hasty in writing you. Hannah has just returned from a visit in the country, and I assumed she was longing to return. But perhaps she was only weary from traveling."

Georgiana studied me.

"Henry mentioned you'd gone to the country," Georgiana said. "How was your little stay, Hannah?"

"Lovely," I said.

"And the company?" she asked. "Did you meet anyone in particular?"

Any particular *gentleman*, she meant.

I smiled, hoping it would suffice as an answer, and folded my hands neatly in my lap.

"Perhaps a new topic of conversation is in order, my dear." Henry gave me an apologetic look. "I believe Hannah does not wish to speak of her visit."

"How right you are," I said.

Georgiana frowned and reluctantly conceded the conversation.

"Why don't we discuss what diversions you want to fill your time with while you're here," Papa suggested.

"We actually do not have much time to fill," Georgiana said.

"Nonsense," Papa said. "A week is plenty of time."

Henry straightened. "Unfortunately, we cannot stay that long. We should like to, of course, but the roads are in such poor condition because of all the rain, and so it is probably prudent to depart London early so we can arrive on time."

"We *must*," Georgiana corrected, "if we do not want to sleep in the attic with the servants. Captain Bromley runs his parties with the same precision he runs his ship. He has a reputation for rewarding guests who arrive early enough to attend his notorious welcome luncheons with the best rooms."

"I understand." Papa smiled, but the sentiment did not reach his eyes.

I felt bad for Papa, but I was not surprised that Georgiana wanted to arrive at the house party early. She loved social events with a ferocity that I could never hope to understand. I often marveled how she seemed to derive energy from the same social events that left me feeling drained.

Henry chewed his lip. "I would have written to you about the change of plans, but my letter would have arrived after we did."

Papa patted Henry's knee. "We will make the most of the time you have. How long will you be staying?"

"Two days," Georgiana answered curtly.

Two days was still one too many, in my opinion, but not for Papa. He'd been anticipating their arrival since reading their letter and had planned more than enough diversions to fill a fortnight. Though he tried not to let his disappointment show, it still bled through.

Georgiana touched my arm. "Perhaps you could play something uplifting on the pianoforte for us, Hannah."

"I was just thinking how much I missed your playing, *sister*."

Georgiana bristled at the term of endearment. It was not very Christian of me, but I took a strange sort of pleasure in her discomfort. Henry had fallen for Georgiana almost as soon as we'd arrived in Bath, but Georgiana had not accepted Henry until after her fifth Season when all her other prospects for marriage had withered, and though she had finally come to accept Henry, she'd never fully accepted the rest of us.

"Perhaps *you* could play?" I suggested. "Papa is tired of my pecking, and besides, you are a better musician than I am." Georgiana was only barely proficient at the pianoforte, but I played her pride to my advantage.

"How kind of you to say. I would be delighted."

She chose a fast-moving, scattered piece that was as unwelcome as a nightingale's song at midnight. The second piece was even more cacophonous, and by the third, I considered holding pillows against my ears.

I glanced at Henry to see if perhaps he could extricate us from the misery, but he was smiling adoringly at his wife. Love was as deaf as it was blind, I supposed. And Papa was no help at all; he only appeared pleased to have a full house again.

When at long last Mrs. Potter announced dinner, I sprang from my seat and followed the scent of roast beef to the kitchen. Henry's favorite.

Without a footman to assist, Henry pulled out his wife's chair and helped her settle into her seat. Watching Henry care for his wife felt odd. As a boy, he had been so ill-mannered at the dinner table, chewing with his mouth open, resting his elbows on the table, and even tipping back in his chair so far that he fell over a few times. But he seemed to have matured into quite a refined gentleman.

"Tell me more about this house party," Papa said to Georgiana.

"Well." She patted a napkin around her mouth. "Captain Bromley amassed quite a fortune during the war, and now that he is home on half-pay, he apparently means to enjoy it. He has invited some of London's finest families and planned an endless supply of entertainment. Hannah will have such a diverting time that she won't want the weekend to end." Georgiana subtly tipped her head in Papa's direction.

Worry lines framed Papa's eyes and scored his forehead. I had been so entrenched in my own heartache that I hadn't realized I'd been causing him pain too. I had no desire to go to Captain Bromley's party, but if I stayed home in London, Papa would continue to worry over me. He'd endured enough worry these past few years already. I did not wish to be the cause of any more.

"I daresay I will find it diverting." I smiled at Georgiana. "Thank you for inviting me to come with you."

She gave me a subtle nod of approval.

The conversation swirled on around me, but I had little to contribute.

After dinner, Henry and Georgiana retired to their bedchambers, tired from the day's journey. And Papa moved to his study to work on his sermons. Wanting to be close to Mama, I went to the pianoforte. I wished she were here to comfort me, but her music would have to suffice.

I laid out her music sheets and set my fingers on the keys. I played the first notes with some trepidation, wanting to get them correct, but then I remembered what Damon said about not having to play a song perfectly to enjoy the music, and I pressed on.

Slowly, her song flowed from my fingers. Note after note, measure after measure, the pleasure, if not perfection, of playing the pianoforte unfolded itself to me. As the song continued, I imagined Damon sitting beside me, his strong, steady hands on the keys, the warmth of his arm against mine. His encouragement to keep going.

It had been a month since I'd physically left Summerhaven, but my mind was still there. Still with Damon. The ache of losing love would likely never go away, but with time, I hoped the pain would dissipate. In the meantime, I needed to find a way to go on with my life without causing Papa pain.

When the song ended, I let my fingers linger on the keys, allowing myself to remember one last time how it felt to sit next to Damon and hear him play Mama's melody so perfectly, and then I closed the lid.

I would go with Henry and Georgiana to Captain Bromley's party and allow it to renew my spirits. And when I returned, I would busy myself with serving the poor, visiting the sick, and caring for the church with Papa.

CHAPTER THIRTY-THREE

THE ROADS WERE INDEED AS bad as Henry and Georgiana had feared, but I armed myself with a plethora of ginger candies from the confectioners, so I felt only mildly ill as we rattled up to Captain Bromley's estate.

The gray stone manor was not nearly so large as Summerhaven, but it boasted of an expansive lawn, and a number of people were already gathered there. It seemed that even despite Georgiana's scheming, we had arrived right on time, if not late.

"Oh dear." Georgiana wrung her hands as she looked at the crush of people already gathered on the front lawn. "We should have gotten here earlier."

"If we had arrived any earlier, my love, we should have been asked to help the staff ready the rooms."

Georgiana's nerves momentarily gave way to a small smile.

"We have arrived just in time to be fashionably late," Henry continued. "See there, the duke and his daughter, Lady Margaret, have also just arrived."

"The duke." Georgiana craned her neck to see him out the side glass. "I had no idea he was coming. What a wonderful surprise!"

But I was more focused on the name Lady Margaret. Wasn't that the name of the woman Lord Winfield wished for Damon to marry? She was *here*? A pit formed in my stomach.

"Do you think we can meet His Grace?" Georgiana asked eagerly.

"Perhaps after we have said hello to Captain Bromley," Henry said.

"Yes." Georgiana bit her lip. "I have gotten a bit ahead of myself, haven't I? I should not allow myself to be so excitable."

"Your excitability is one of my favorite things about you." Henry smiled at her.

Our carriage came to a stop, and a footman opened the door. Henry hopped out and turned back to assist Georgiana and then me.

I smoothed my hair and dress, bidding myself a moment before entering the lion's den.

"Come along, Hannah," Henry said. "We must introduce you to Captain Bromley so he will not think you are an interloper."

I *was* an interloper but hopefully a welcome one. As we walked toward the fountain where Captain Bromley held court, I was surprised to find Captain Bromley was younger than I'd imagined—closer in age to Henry than Papa. I knew almost nothing about my host, I realized, other than he was a captain in the Royal Navy, was on half-pay, and apparently enjoyed hosting house parties.

"Mr. Kent, Mrs. Kent," Captain Bromley greeted Henry and Georgiana around a bite of food. "I am delighted you are here and right on time too."

"The pleasure is all ours," Henry said, then he turned to me. "Hannah, allow me to present Captain Bromley."

"I should be honored," I said.

"Captain Bromley, my sister Miss Hannah Kent."

"Ah, Miss Kent." Captain Bromley dipped a polite bow. "Your reputation precedes you."

My tongue suddenly felt swollen, and dread washed over me. Had he heard gossip about what had happened between Ollie, Damon, and me at Lord Garrett's ball?

"You look as if you have seen a ghost, my dear. Forgive me. A lady's reputation is nothing to trifle with. I did not mean to frighten you." He cleared his throat. "Lord Rumford said you have quite the refined palate."

I released a relieved breath. "You have heard about the frog legs."

"Frog legs?" Georgiana's nose scrunched.

"Yes!" Captain Bromley chuckled. "Your sister-in-law was the only young lady at Lord Rumford's supper table who did not turn up her nose at the fare. Miss Kent, I do hope you will find my culinary selections this weekend just as delectable."

"I am sure I will. Thank you."

"Please enjoy yourself." He gestured toward a gazebo, where an assortment of food was laid on a table.

I excused myself, leaving Henry and Georgiana to continue the conversation, and made my way to the table, where I hoped to find no frog legs. Thankfully, there were none, but I did find some*one*.

Amelia.

She was selecting a few slices of cheese and grapes. She looked up when I approached but didn't speak.

"Did you receive my letter?" I asked tentatively.

She nodded, but her expression gave nothing away.

I had hoped my letter would soften her feelings toward me, but perhaps she was still angry. She would be justified in her feelings, of course, but perhaps I could bring her some measure of comfort by offering her a verbal apology.

"Amelia, I am *truly* sorry."

"You need not continue, Miss Kent," a male voice said behind me.

I whipped around to find Amelia's brother, Mr. Atherton. Oh dear. I'd expected it to be difficult to face Amelia, but I had not planned on facing her brother too.

"You see, forgiveness would be quite impossible seeing as you have nothing to apologize for."

Amelia gave me a sheepish look. "Frederick is right. You have no need to apologize for love."

"I don't?"

She shook her head. "You can hardly help who you fall in love with. I even suspected as much the day of our picnic. The way he followed you to the river, and when he returned, he was very put out of countenance. He gave Ollie quite a tongue lashing on your behalf. Like a knight in shining armor, he defended your honor."

Mr. Atherton tucked his bespoke walking stick under his arm. "I think I will leave you ladies to converse. If you will excuse me."

"Happily, brother," Amelia said, and with a tip of his hat, he strode away. Amelia looked at me again, her eyes soft and sad. She opened her mouth to say something, but a gentleman walked into the gazebo where we stood.

"Perhaps we can explore the garden and speak privately?" I pointed to the far corner of the garden where fewer people meandered, and she nodded.

A few moments passed as we walked with nothing to fill the silence but the swishing of our skirts. I didn't know what to say—I hardly knew what to think—so I waited.

"I was embarrassed," Amelia admitted. "You wanted to marry for love, and I wished to avoid it. In the beginning, I loved that dichotomy of our friendship, but when you found love with the very man I had set out to entangle . . . Well, I feared you would think very poorly of me."

I shook my head. "I promise I did not."

"And I will admit, I was hurt that you didn't tell me about your feelings for Lord Jennings. I asked you as much at the picnic, but you didn't confide in me."

"I did not know my own feelings then," I said. "But I should have told you when you came to visit me after my illness. I am sorry I didn't."

"Yes, I know. You spelled it all out rather poetically in your treatise."

I laughed a little. "I confess my letter lacked brevity. But I wanted you to know that I didn't mean to use our friendship to my advantage."

"I know you are not Rose," she said quietly, "but when I found you in Lord Jennings's arms, it took me back to the time when I discovered Rose's feelings for Mr. Wheaton."

I nodded. "I'm sorry I didn't confront my own feelings sooner and that I didn't tell you the truth of them at the first possible moment."

"And I am sorry I allowed my past to steer the future course of our friendship," Amelia said. "I am glad you wrote to me, and I'm glad you are here now."

"As am I."

"Now what of you and Lord Jennings?" Amelia said.

My heart felt as if would break all over again just hearing his name, but I tried not to let the emotion show on my face. "We have not spoken. Nor do I expect we will again."

"Not spoken?" she said. "I rather expected to hear the banns read in church."

I bit my lip. "I was worried there had been talk among the *ton* about what happened at the ball."

"Only whisperings," Amelia said. "No one else saw anything that happened in the garden gazebo, so there was only a tiny bit of talk about your sudden departure, both from the ball and Summerhaven the next day."

I bit my lip, worried, not only for my own reputation but also for Damon's. Though a man's reputation was much more robust than a woman's, it was not impenetrable. In order to marry a wealthy daughter of a peer, surely his name would need to be free of blemish.

"Do not worry," Amelia said. "Lady Winfield silenced all talk by explaining that you only left because you were so homesick for your papa in London."

I breathed a sigh of relief. "That is good." Though I hated to think of Damon marrying someone else, it was his duty, and I did not begrudge him happiness.

"But what of you and Lord Jennings?" Amelia asked again.

"I am afraid there will be no banns read. Even though we care deeply for each other, he has a duty to his family, his estate, and to his tenants to marry a wealthy woman."

"Oh, Hannah. I am sorry. Truly. What will you do?"

"I suppose I will try my best not to think of him until the sting of losing him has passed."

Amelia bit her lip. "And what if Lord Jennings decides to attend Captain Bromley's party?"

"Damon will not be here." I shook my head. "You must trust me; my sister-in-law would have made it *abundantly* known if an unmarried future earl was planning to attend."

"Oh, he will be here," Amelia said with an air of confidence I could only hope to possess one day.

"What makes you so sure?"

"My eyes." She batted her eyelashes and then pointed behind me. "Is that not him alighting from his family's carriage?"

I glanced over my shoulder, and my heart fluttered like a leaf caught in a breeze.

Damon.

CHAPTER THIRTY-FOUR

Top hat in hand, Damon emerged from the carriage wearing buckskin breeches, a dark coat, and a snow-white cravat. It had been over a month since I'd seen him, but my feelings had not lessened. If anything, they'd only grown stronger.

A moment later, Ollie alighted.

"Did you know they were attending?" I asked Amelia.

She shook her head.

I suddenly realized why they were here, or at least why *Damon* was here. "Lady Margaret," I whispered. "He is here to court Lady Margaret."

"You don't know that." Amelia laid her hand on my shoulder. "It will be all right."

"I am sure you're correct," I said, and it was true. Everything *would* be all right, though not in the way she meant. If Lady Margaret consented to marry Damon, Summerhaven would be saved. I knew this was his plan; I just did not think I would have to watch it happen. I took a steadying breath and met Amelia's gaze. "I had best return to Henry and Georgiana. May I find you later?"

"You had better not leave me with only Frederick for company."

We parted with a quick goodbye, and I rejoined Henry and Georgiana, who were still conversing with Captain Bromley by the fountain, knowing that Damon and Ollie would be moving in the same direction to greet their host.

"There you are, Hannah," Henry said. "I was wondering when you would return."

"I was just saying hello to an old friend."

"Old friends are the best of friends," Captain Bromley said.

"Quite right," I said, and I snuck a peek in Damon and Ollie's direction. The brothers rapidly approached our circle, but they had yet to notice me.

I smoothed my dress and surreptitiously bit down on my lips to add a little color to them.

"Lord Jennings, Mr. Jennings," Captain Bromley said. "Welcome."

"Captain Bromley," they both returned with a polite bow.

"Your timing is impeccable, gentlemen. We were just discussing the merits of old friends. I believe you both know Mr. Kent and his sister, Miss Kent," he said, and I stepped out from behind Henry. "But have you met—"

"Hannah?" Damon blinked, and then as if remembering himself, he shook his head. "We are not friends, Captain Bromley. That is to say, you were correct in your original assertion; Miss Kent and my brother hold the association, not I." And then to me, "Forgive me for speaking so informally, Miss Kent. It will not happen again."

I managed a nod, but Damon's words cut me deeper than a knife; gone was the man who had kissed me in the gazebo, who had held me and begged me to be his. This was how things had to be for the good of everyone, but I wished it could be otherwise.

Georgiana gingerly cleared her throat.

"Forgive me, Mrs. Kent," Captain Bromley said. "Please allow me to introduce to you Lord Jennings, the future Earl of Winfield, and Mr. Oliver Jennings, the current Earl of Winfield's second son."

Georgiana curtsied to both men, looking more than a little pleased to make their acquaintance.

Ollie fully returned the courtesy, but Damon gave her the barest nod. "A pleasure, Mr. and Mrs. Kent. If you will please excuse me, I see someone I must greet." Damon strode toward a distinguished-looking man and an elegant young woman.

Lady Margaret. It had to be. Her clothing was the latest fashion, and her jewelry whispered of wealth, and she held herself with an air of confidence. And why wouldn't she? With hair the color of ravens' wings and an ivory complexion, she looked every bit the daughter of a duke and future wife of an earl.

My heart clenched when he took his place beside her, and she smiled at him.

"You must forgive my brother," Ollie said, pulling my attention back to those around me. "He lacks a certain social skill."

Captain Bromley laughed. "House parties are not for everyone."

Ollie smiled at me. "May I steal you, Miss Kent? Captain Bromley has a fine collection of French roses I think you would enjoy."

"The Provence roses are most exquisite this time of year," Captain Bromley agreed.

Georgiana gave me an encouraging nod.

"Thank you, Mr. Jennings," I said. "I would be glad to walk with you."

With one hand, he indicated the garden path to his left, and we continued that way, exchanging the expected pleasantries. We entered the rose garden through an arch, and I felt as if I'd stepped into the Garden of Eden. The English countryside was home to some of the most beautiful gardens on earth, but this was extraordinary. Low boxwoods were used to define arc-shaped planters in a circular arrangement, filled with varying heights and colors of French roses. The effect was nothing short of stunning.

"I knew you would like it." Ollie smiled.

"I daresay you could bring any young lady here, and she would like it."

"Perhaps, but I brought *you*," Ollie said. "I hate how we left things, Hanny."

"Me too."

"I am glad you are here." Ollie nodded, looking down at his Hessian boots. "I miss you, Hanny. So much."

"I miss you too, Ollie."

"Since you've been gone, I've often found myself wishing we could go back to the days when we were children."

"Those were good days," I agreed. Carefree and easy.

"Did you ever think we would grow up and attend a stuffy house party?" He raised his nose in the air and glanced down at me.

I stifled a laugh. "Never."

The gravel crunched beneath his boots as we continued down the path. "What do you think everyone would think if I were to chase you through this garden?"

"I daresay it would cause quite a stir. But it would be diverting, wouldn't it?"

"Indeed." He rewarded me with a smile, the dimple in his chin fully on display. He slowed his step as we neared the most beautiful red-rose bush. "And what do you think they would say if I were to pick you a rose?"

I glanced at him sideways, trying to decipher whether he was still only trying to be funny or flirting.

He flashed me a capricious smile, and I knew it was the former. Relief flowed through me like a river. "Well," I said in my snootiest voice, "they are quite lovely. You could hardly be blamed."

"In that case . . ." He made a show of selecting a rose, then gave it to me with a flourish.

"Why thank you, Mr. Jennings."

"It is my pleasure, Miss Kent."

And before I knew what was happening, he took my hand in his and placed a whisper of a kiss on my knuckles. It was not lingering, nor did it contain any hint of love, but from a distance, it might look that way.

I glanced around to see if anyone had observed his childish antics, and my gaze immediately landed on Damon. He'd seen. His gaze lingered on me a moment, and then he turned his attention back to Lady Margaret. But he'd seen.

Ollie straightened.

"It looks like the company is moving inside. I'd best go change for dinner," I said.

"May I escort you into the dining hall tonight?" he asked.

I nodded. "I would like that."

"As would I." He offered me his arm, and as we made our way back toward the manor, and though my heart still hurt from seeing Damon in his new life, there was a tiny spark of hope that perhaps Ollie and I were on the path to regaining our friendship.

CHAPTER THIRTY-FIVE

DIRECTLY AFTER THE WELCOME LUNCHEON, Henry, Georgiana, and I were shown to our rooms.

"Oh, Henry! It is lovely," Georgiana exclaimed. "Captain Bromley must think highly of you, husband. We are so close to the grand staircase. And look! There is even an attached room for Hannah."

I followed Georgiana into the antechamber. It had most likely been used originally as a sitting room or a nursery for a new baby. Though neither room was large, both were well maintained and decorated in the latest fashion.

"Are you satisfied, my love?" Henry asked Georgiana.

"Exceedingly." She smiled.

"I am glad to hear that because your maid has already unpacked all your trunks."

Georgiana removed her hat and gloves, then sat on a settee. "Hannah, come sit with me." She patted the bench, motioning for me to join her.

I glanced at Henry, hoping he'd swoop in to save me from whatever conversation Georgiana planned to entrap me in, but he'd moved to the window, and his back was to me.

There was nothing for it. I untied my bonnet and sat beside her.

"I must say I am rather surprised by you, Hannah."

I could only imagine how I had disappointed her. "How so?"

She smiled. "You have positively blossomed in the months we have been separated. Last Season you were—well, perhaps we should not speak of it. But now, you have so many friends. Miss Atherton, Captain Bromley, Mr. Jennings. You even hold an acquaintance with Lord Jennings. Although apparently you are *not* friends." She studied me for a moment. "How *have* you made such fine acquaintances?"

Her question, although a bit rude, was not undeserved. Last Season, when Georgiana had taken it upon herself to serve as my chaperone, I'd proven quite a disappointment. Not only had I danced with only one gentleman, but I'd also not conversed easily with her friends, leaving her to act not as my chaperone, but as my nursemaid.

"Our mothers were friends," I said simply. If Georgiana knew what happened between Damon and me this summer—the ruse, the ball, our kiss—she would likely fly into a fit of nerves.

"You are being modest." Henry turned away from the window and sat on the sill. "Hannah practically grew up at Summerhaven."

"I see." Georgiana's eyes widened with delight. "But why haven't you spoken of your acquaintance with the Winfields?"

"Because *I* am not well acquainted with them," Henry said. "Mama and Hannah spent a considerable amount of time at Summerhaven, but being older, I usually remained in the city with Papa to focus on my studies. We have a few scattered memories from my early boyhood, but nothing to boast of."

A shadow dimmed Georgiana's joy. "That is too bad. But what a delightful discovery as we endeavor to secure Hannah's future."

I groaned.

"You did not think my wife agreed to let you come along simply for the pleasure of it, did you?" Henry chuckled.

"I had hoped."

"Oh no." He shook his head. "Now that she has experienced the bliss of matrimony, she will not be satisfied until she sees every one of her acquaintances happily settled."

"You say that as though my liking marriage is a bad thing," Georgiana said.

"No, my dear. To be honest, I am relieved. I only thought Hannah might like to know what—or rather *whom*—she is dealing with."

Georgiana scowled playfully at Henry. "You act as if marrying off one's ward is not precisely the goal of every chaperone in attendance. I originally intended Captain Bromley for Hannah, but Mr. Jennings is the second son of an earl and a much better prospect."

My eyes widened, and my gaze flashed to Henry, pleading with him to intercede.

"And isn't he set to inherit a fine house from his mother?" she asked. "I do believe I remember hearing as much from Miss Wilson last Season."

"Winterset Grange." Henry nodded.

"That is right," she said. "A charming estate in the north."

"Your memory is a wonder, my love. But I don't believe Hannah wishes to marry the same boy she waded in ponds with as a child. Perhaps you should focus your matchmaking efforts on some other poor unsuspecting gentleman."

"I disagree. Their amiable acquaintance should lend itself quite nicely to a blissful marriage. Don't you agree, Hannah?"

"Not at all." I shook my head. "Ollie and I—"

"*Ollie*, says she." She glanced meaningfully at Henry.

"*Mr. Jennings*," I corrected myself, "and I do not suit."

"Whyever not? You seemed quite content together in the rose garden this afternoon. He gave you a rose and then kissed your hand, did he not?"

"Yes," I said. "But—"

"I thought so. A winter wedding will be just the thing." Georgiana nodded, undeterred. "Spring would be better, of course, but it is not wise to wait too long." She then rose from the settee and walked to where Henry stood as if everything was done and decided. "Oh!" she said. "I almost forgot. A bit of gossip is already stirring at our little house party. Apparently, Lord Jennings is here on the hunt for a wife, and that is why the duke is here with his daughter. He caught Lady Margaret's eye last month in London. Rumor has it they mean to become engaged before the party's end."

"Wherever did you hear that?" Henry asked.

"Hester Richins," she said, "who heard it from Grace Crenshaw, who heard if from her maid, who heard it from Lady Margaret's maid."

"That is a long list indeed." My brother exhaled.

"Can you imagine if *both* of Lord Winfield's sons become engaged in one weekend?"

"The operative word being *if*," Henry said.

"You are missing the point entirely. The talk of dual engagements will overwhelm the society column. And Hannah will be at the center of it all."

As much as the thought thrilled Georgiana, it terrified me. I had no desire to become engaged, and I did not want to watch Damon begin his new life.

"We must dress you in your finest gown this evening," Georgiana continued. "That new red gown."

I stiffened. "I do not think it would be appropriate." For so many, *many* reasons.

Henry *tsked*. "My wife is a force of nature, Hannah. Once she has set her mind to something, you might as well reconcile yourself to your fate."

Georgiana frowned at her husband. "Your tongue is as loose as your cravat, my love. Here, let me help you." She walked to Henry and set about fixing his knot. "But perhaps Hannah is right. She should wear the dress *after* she and Mr. Jennings are engaged. It will draw attention to their announcement."

Henry opened his mouth as if to protest on my behalf, but Georgiana tugged his knot tighter, cutting him off.

"There," she said. "Much better."

"Quite." He pulled at his collar.

Although we were dressed and ready well before dinnertime, Georgiana had insisted we wait nearly three-quarters of an hour before we went downstairs. *Fashionably late* had worked well in securing us a nice room, Georgiana reasoned, so perhaps the same tactic would also earn us an advantageous seat at the table.

We were among the last to arrive in the drawing room. Ollie met us at the door, but he didn't even have time to utter a greeting before the butler announced dinner, and the company began assembling into a tidy line by rank.

Ollie offered me his arm, and we fell into line.

As expected, Damon was seated near the head of the table with the other lords and Lady Margaret beside him. Damon glanced sideways at us as we walked by. My skin prickled with awareness, though I did not allow myself to dwell on it.

Once everyone was seated, Captain Bromley formally welcomed all his guests.

Ollie behaved a perfect gentleman, taking special care to serve me and then engage me in conversation.

I tried to focus on what he said, but my gaze kept wandering in Damon's direction. I could not actually *see* him from where I sat, but I imagined him serving Lady Margaret. Did *she* enjoy frog legs?

No, I scolded myself, and I pressed my fingers to my temples in an effort to drive away the unwanted thought.

"Are you feeling unwell?" Ollie asked. "You have hardly touched your meal, and you have not said more than a few words."

I looked down at my plate still full of food. "Forgive me. I am not used to large social gatherings, and I am a little overwhelmed."

"Of course. Perhaps tomorrow's schedule will be more to your enjoyment. Captain Bromley has planned for a ride to the ruins tomorrow."

"Oh?"

Ollie nodded. "An old abbey on the northwest corner of his property. I have been told there is a hill nearby it with an old tower that I would like to explore with you. Will you join me?"

Georgiana pinched my elbow. How she heard Ollie's invitation over the commotion in the dining hall, I could not say.

"I would like nothing more," I told Ollie, and it was true. The freedom of riding called me to the hills like a siren called a sailor to the sea.

After dinner, Amelia sidled up beside me, and we walked with the other ladies toward the drawing room. As we passed through the corridor, Amelia told me about dinner. "Lord Jennings behaved a perfect gentleman toward Lady Margaret, but they didn't exchange more than a handful of words."

Perhaps that should have made me feel better—the fact that he was not enjoying himself with her—but the thought of him being miserable in his future marriage only made me feel worse.

In the drawing room, the women had already separated into groups. Georgiana clustered with a small circle of her friends, no doubt to gossip. Lady Margaret sat on a sofa in the center of the room, and several young ladies buzzed about her, no doubt hoping to forge an advantageous friendship. Amelia and I, however, moved in the opposite direction, to a small table and chairs placed near the fire.

We'd only been sitting a few moments when Lady Margaret rose from the sofa and moved toward us.

I sucked in a quick breath.

Had Damon said something about what had happened between us? I doubted he would bring up the whole debacle with the woman he was courting, but why else would she come my way?

Amelia followed my gaze and quickly stood, intercepting Lady Margaret only a few paces away.

Lady Margaret looked a bit confused when Amelia led her in the opposite direction. But to Lady Margaret's credit, she politely followed Amelia away.

I breathed a sigh of relief. I had no desire to learn of all the wonderful qualities of the woman Damon would soon marry.

Sometime later, the men trickled into the drawing room. Captain Bromley and the duke made their appearance first, followed by a few other gentlemen I did not know. Eventually Ollie and Mr. Atherton wandered into the room.

But Damon never showed.

CHAPTER THIRTY-SIX

STANDING AT THE VANITY TABLE the next morning, I checked my appearance in the mirror one last time. Everything appeared in place; my curls were perfectly secured beneath my bonnet, my riding habit free of wrinkle or stain.

Georgiana came up behind me. "Here," she said, handing me a new pair of York tan gloves. "You should have a new pair of gloves for today."

"What is happening today?"

She smiled. "I do believe Mr. Jennings will propose given the right opportunity."

My hands stilled around the gloves. "Why would you think that?"

"How could I not? Upon arrival, Mr. Jennings begged a private audience with you. He has attached himself to your side for nearly the entirety of the weekend."

"We are friends."

"Friends do not kiss your hand in a garden for all to see."

At the time of our walk in the garden, I had thought we were only playing as we used to, but upon closer inspection, I saw our encounter with new eyes. Ollie was a gentleman well versed in the rules of polite society. He would not have made his preference for me so obvious unless he felt something more for me than friendship.

Oh dear. Georgiana was right.

"My dear, you look positively terrified. I assure you, marriage is not something to be frightened of, so long as you are wedding a good and kind gentleman, which Mr. Jennings is."

I shook my head at a loss for words. "I am only surprised."

"Surely you cannot be."

"No." My voice quivered. "I do not suppose I can be." Though I was. "I can't marry him, Georgiana."

"Surely you must wish to set up a household of your own."

I did wish for a household of my own. Summerhaven. But that would never be. I shook my head.

Georgiana's face hardened. "I know marriage is a daunting prospect without your mother to lead and guide you, but you cannot live off your father's charity forever."

Which was to say, if I did not marry, I would become a burden to Papa, and when he passed on, my brother would inherit the encumbrance. I did not want to be an affliction to my family, but neither did I wish to marry without love.

"You must not be selfish, Hannah. I believe Mr. Jennings intends to offer for you, and you must not think of yourself. He is handsome, kind, and most importantly, he will provide you a good life. A fine home. *Children*."

I looked down at the York tan gloves in my hand and nodded.

"Good. We must make haste now," Georgiana said, "or the company will leave without us and we shall have to ride to the ruins with the groom." She went to wait in the corridor, leaving me alone with my thoughts.

Marrying Ollie seemed the logical course in every way. He was all the things Georgiana had said, and our foundation of friendship *would* lend itself well to building a strong marriage. But . . . could I marry without love?

I stared down at Mama's ring on my finger.

All my life, I'd believed that my parents' marriage had been a love match—that they met, fell in love, and married—but their union had been arranged without love or affection. Mama had not even cared for Papa when they married, but they had grown in love together.

A love match had always been my greatest desire, but perhaps love had many faces. There was passionate love, like I'd experienced with Damon, of course, but what about a love of compassion like I felt for Ollie? Surely that also held value.

Everyone thought we would make a good match—Papa, Mama, Lady Winfield, Georgiana—even *I* had once wanted us to marry. Perhaps with time and care, love *could* grow like it had for Mama and Papa. I wasn't sure it was possible, but I hoped it was—if not for myself, then for Damon.

With a steadying breath, I slipped my hands into the gloves.

Henry and Georgiana were waiting for me in the corridor. We walked down to the grand staircase, and I was relieved to find Amelia waiting at the bottom in her own riding habit. I hurried ahead of Henry and Georgiana to where she stood. "Thank goodness you are here, Amelia. I must ask you a favor."

"Anything," she said. "What is it?"

"Please do not leave my side."

Her eyes narrowed. "Is something wrong?"

"Not yet," I said. "But Georgiana believes that Ollie plans to propose marriage to me."

Her eyes widened. "You do not think he will declare his suit while we are out riding *today*, do you?"

"I don't know, and I am not ready to find out. Not today."

She nodded. "I promise not to leave your side."

I breathed a sigh of relief. "Thank you."

"Miss Atherton," Henry said when he and Georgiana joined us. "Will your brother be coming with us today?"

"Not likely," Amelia said.

"Does he not enjoy riding?" Georgiana asked.

"Not at all. In fact, he rather despises how saddles wrinkle his clothing. I expect he has hunted out Captain Bromley's library and is halfway through reading a book."

"An honorable pastime indeed," Henry said. "Well then. Let us be on our way to the stableyard."

Unlike at Summerhaven, the horses here were kept nearer to the main house and required only a short walk.

As soon as we entered the stableyard, my gaze found Damon. He looked dashing in his dark riding coat; the deep color brought out the blue in his stormy eyes.

"Ah," Georgiana said, pointing toward the far end of the yard. "There is your Mr. Jennings."

"He is not *my* anything."

"He will be soon." She smiled. "And look, he is standing with His Grace's daughter, Lady Margaret. It is only too bad his dreary brother, Lord Jennings, is there too. We shall have to hope he is good-humored today." Georgiana moved as if to leave.

"Georgia—" I reached for her elbow, but she evaded my grasp.

"I thought my wife planned to see you engaged by the end of this house party," Henry said. "But it seems she is intent to have you married by sundown." With a chuckle, he strode after her.

I reluctantly followed, my half boots sinking into the soft soil.

"Miss Kent," Ollie said as we approached. "I was beginning to worry you had abandoned me."

"Forgive my lateness." I glanced at him and forced myself not to look at Damon. "As much as I would like to say that I have never been tardy before, I must confess to having been told that Napoleon could have prepared an entire regiment for war in the amount of time it takes me to get ready." The words slipped out before I could stop them.

Damon's eyes flickered up to meet mine, his brow furrowed.

"Miss Kent," Ollie said, reclaiming my attention. "I do not believe any of your party has had the pleasure of meeting Lady Margaret. Allow me to make your introduction."

She was even more beautiful up close. Her lips curved in a perfect Cupid's bow, and not one hair appeared out of place.

"It is a pleasure to finally meet you, Miss Kent. I have heard so many wonderful things about you that I was beginning to wonder whether you were fact or fiction."

I gave Ollie a disapproving look. "Mr. Jennings has a habit of embellishing things, I'm afraid."

"Mr. Jennings?" She frowned. "Don't you mean—"

"Lady Margaret," Damon cut in, "it looks as if the horses will be ready soon. Might I assist you in choosing your mount?" He held his arm out to her.

"You should like to help *me* choose a mount?" She looked at his proffered arm with a raised eyebrow.

"Please," Damon said, his voice low.

She glanced in my direction, then allowed him to lead her away.

"It appears Lord Jennings's mood has *not* improved," Georgiana whispered to Henry.

Several minutes later, Captain Bromley walked up behind us. "What a fine-looking group," he said. "Let us see if we can get you paired with the right horses."

We followed him to where the groom stood with Damon and Lady Margaret. Many horses were already saddled.

"Lady Margaret," Captain Bromley said, "seeing as your father is a man of horses, do you have a preference in your mount?"

"I should like to ride a filly. One with a little spirit."

"Very good." Captain Bromley nodded and turned to the groom.

"I suggest Honeycut, sir," the groom said.

Captain Bromley nodded his approval. "And Miss Atherton?"

"I would never pretend to be the equestrienne that Lady Margaret is," Amelia said. "A mare with very *little* spirit will do nicely for me."

"Take heart, Miss Atherton," Captain Bromley said. "Few of us are as accomplished on horseback as Lady Margaret."

Georgiana requested the gentlest mare Captain Bromley stabled, and he happily obliged. "And Miss Kent. What of you?" he asked.

I knew precisely what kind of horse I wished to ride, though I worried that the others would think me unsuited to my choice. "I should like to ride a stallion."

"A stallion?" His face stretched into a smile. "You are a woman after my own heart, Miss Kent. There is no better way to explore the countryside than on the back of a thoroughbred."

Damon's gaze burned warm on my cheek, but I forced myself not to meet it.

"Perhaps the Godolphin Barb," the groom suggested.

"Yes," Captain Bromley nodded. "I believe you will enjoy the mount, Miss Kent."

"Is it safe?" Georgiana asked. "Hannah is a Londoner and not so accomplished on horseback."

"I believe Miss Kent is capable, madam," Damon said.

My heart jolted. I had not expected anyone to speak for me, least of all Damon. But when I looked at him, his expression was stony, and he quickly averted his gaze.

"I am glad you think so, Lord Jennings," Georgiana said. "But as her chaperone, I am not so sure. Captain Bromley, do you have a horse better suited to an unexperienced young lady? A gentle mare, perhaps?"

My cheeks warmed with embarrassment.

"Might I suggest a filly, madam? She is quite safe but perhaps a bit more exciting."

"Hmm," Georgiana said. "Perhaps if Hannah had an accomplished companion at her side, my fears would be alleviated." Georgiana's gaze slid to Ollie. "Mr. Jennings, would you be willing to see to Hannah's safety?"

"It would be my honor," he said, giving me an open smile. "So long as Captain Bromley has a horse equal to the task."

"I have a fine Darley Arabian that should suit you, Mr. Jennings," he said. "For you as well, Lord Jennings and Mr. Kent."

Georgiana's lips curled at the corners, and she nodded as if pleased. "Miss Atherton," she said. "Seeing as our mounts will be well matched, you are welcome to ride at my side."

Amelia shot me a regretful look, then to Georgiana she said, "Thank you, Mrs. Kent. I will."

Damon assisted Lady Margaret onto the mounting block. Their hands were both gloved, and the contact between them did not linger. Still, I burned with jealousy. I tried to push away the feeling, but it would not be moved.

Once all had mounted, Captain Bromley led our party out of the stable-yard. And the horses, like people walking into a dining hall, seemed to know their inherent rank and passed through the gate accordingly. Captain Bromley, Damon, and Lady Margaret led the party; Ollie and I fell into place near the middle; and Henry, Georgiana, and Amelia were behind us. The groom followed with the rest of the party in the reverse.

In the meadow, Captain Bromley pointed out the abbey in the distance. "Any who would like may go on ahead," he said. "I will remain here with those who wish to go at a leisurely pace."

Needing a moment of reprieve, a moment to forget my jealousy, I encouraged my horse into a canter. She readily obeyed, but her speed was not fast enough to flee from my feelings.

With a frown, I tightened my legs around the saddle horn and leaned forward. "Come on, girl. Faster."

I kicked her flank with one leg and tapped her other side with my riding crop, and she leapt forward. The wind whipped across my cheeks and twisted through my hair. Every part of me felt alive. My body, my mind, my soul.

"Hannah," Ollie called after me. "Be careful."

When we came to a rolling hill, I expected my mount to slow, but even without encouragement, she swiftly pressed on. The ground flattened out again on the other side, and the world passed by in a blur of green grass and blue-gray sky.

Before I knew it, the abbey ruins loomed before me. Crumbling gray stone walls and arches that reached heavenward were all that remained. Still, it was awe-inspiring.

I reined in my horse, and she gave an unhappy stomp of her hoof.

Ollie came up beside me, and his eyes shone brightly. "I did not know you could ride like that," he said. "I could not take my eyes off you. You were magnificent."

At his words, I went cold.

I glanced behind me for the other members of our company, but there was not a soul in sight. Not Henry or Georgiana, not Amelia, not Damon. We had raced here too quickly. I was alone with Ollie, the very thing I'd told myself I would not let happen.

"Hannah, I—"

"Race you to the top of the tor," I said, and without waiting for his reply, I rushed up the large hill toward the tower at the top. At the peak, I reined in my horse and took in the view. I felt as if I could see all of England.

Ollie came up beside me a moment later. "I do believe we may need to have a discussion about the proper way to begin a race, madam. That is twice now you have begun a race without a proper start," he teased, the look of love in his eyes replaced by a boyish smile.

"Do try not to be a sore loser, Ollie," I tossed back.

He only grinned and dismounted. After helping me do the same, we tied our horses to a post and walked inside the tower. The walls of the tower stood sturdy and tall, but there was no roof.

Ollie said something, but I could not make out his words over the wind that whirled and moaned around us. He pointed at the opening, where a door should have been, and I nodded. Back outside, we sat on a bench that was protected from the wind.

We sat for a few minutes, and an uncomfortable feeling descended upon us. I tried to think of something to say or do to lighten the moment, but no game, no joke, no distraction could lessen this discomfort.

"Hannah," Ollie said, tentatively reaching for my hand. "We have known each other almost our whole lives. That relationship has primarily been one of friendship, but lately, I have desired more." He bowed over my hand as if to kiss it, and I reflexively snatched it away. He looked at me with a pained expression.

"I'm sorry," I said. "This is all just so sudden."

"Sudden?" He laughed a little. "As I said, we have known each other our entire lives. No relationship could be *less* sudden than ours."

"We have known each other an entire lifetime, it is true, but, Ollie, nothing is as it was before."

"I know I was blind and that the ruse with Damon hurt you. But all that is behind us now."

My heart jumped into my throat, and I felt as if I might suffocate.

He took my hand again. "Hannah Kent, will you do me the honor of becoming my wife?"

I looked into Ollie's eyes, and I could see our future. We would marry and move north to live at Winterset Grange. In time, children would be born to us. They'd inherit Ollie's blond curls and my muddy eyes. It would be a good life, a blessed life.

He was offering every dream I'd ever had, but I felt no stirrings of happiness, no elation, no passion. My heart did not soar, and my bosom did not burn. There was only sadness where there should have been joy.

And in that moment, I knew.

I could never give my heart to Ollie because it already belonged to Damon.

"Ollie," I whispered, and I moved to pull my hand from his.

He clasped my hand tighter between both of his. "Please don't reject me, Hanny. I can make you happy. I know I can. Please." His voice caught and he swallowed hard. "*Please* let me."

"I am so sorry, but I can't."

"Why not?" He searched my eyes as if looking for answers. "Because of Damon?"

I hung my head, not because I was ashamed for loving Damon, but because I could not bear the sight of hurting Ollie. "Yes."

He shook his head. "I know I will never be a great lord like Damon. I will not inherit a grand estate or a vast fortune, but I will have the grange, and it will provide us with a sufficient living."

"I do not love Damon for his estate or his fortune, Ollie."

His brows knit together. "You . . . *love* him?"

"I do."

"Hannah." He took a deep breath. "I do not believe Damon was genuine in his affection toward you. What he did to you, luring you in with that ruse, was unacceptable, but abandoning you when the ruse no longer served him was unforgivable."

"I know how it must seem to you, but we *do* love each other."

Ollie looked deep into my eyes, and his voice was quiet when he said, "He will never marry you."

"I know," I said quietly.

"You just need time. I understand. I will wait for you. As long as you need."

I might be able to nurture my feelings for Ollie, but it would never be enough; one look from Damon produced more excitement in me than Ollie's proposal of marriage. Although I cared for Ollie immensely, I did not love him the way a woman should love the man she intends to marry.

I *loved* Damon.

No matter how impossible it might be, it was Damon I wanted to come to my sickbed and ask after my health, to dance with me and ride horses together and challenge me at chess. And even though our circumstances prevented our union, I could not relegate Ollie to second place in my heart. To do so would be cruel. "You deserve to be more than my second choice."

"I was your *first* choice. And had I not been so utterly blind, we would even now be planning our nuptials. I am guilty of many things, perhaps blindness most of all, but I have always loved you, Hannah. Marry me." His eyes pleaded with me to love him, to *marry* him.

But even if I could convince myself to marry a man besides Damon, I could never marry Ollie. I could not live forever in orbit around Damon but never be allowed to touch him, never be allowed to kiss. I could not do it. Not to Damon, not to myself, and not to Ollie.

"I am so sorry, Ollie. But I cannot marry you."

He scrubbed a hand down his face. "But if *he* will not marry you, and *you* will not marry me, then what *will* you do?"

"I will return to my life in London—I will serve the poor with Papa and look after the church."

"And what of your future?"

"I do not know yet. I only know that it is better this way," I said.

"You're wrong."

"How can you say that? We are opposites in every way. I hate London; you love it. You enjoy sport, and I prefer to read—not only novels, but also the newspaper. Particularly political columns."

A reflexive frown puckered Ollie's lips, but then he smoothed his face into a neutral expression. "A lady improving her mind is not a bad thing."

"I am a bluestocking through and through. What you desire is an accomplished young lady who should like to go with you about Town."

"You make me sound like a peacock whose only goal in life is to be admired."

"That was not my intent. I only meant to say that we are different, both in what we enjoy and what we hope for in the future. We would make each other miserable."

"It is *I* who will be miserable without *you*."

"Don't say that." I touched his arm, meaning to comfort him, but he flinched away, and I withdrew my hand. "You will not. Not forever. One day you will meet a beautiful young lady, and she will make you exceedingly happy."

"Is there not anything I can say to change your mind?"

I shook my head. "I am sorry, Ollie."

Ollie rose from the bench. "As am I." He silently assisted me onto my saddle, then mounted his own horse.

We walked them safely down the tor toward the ruin.

The rest of our company had just arrived. Captain Bromley led everyone through the largest of the remaining arches into the space where the chapel would have existed if the church had remained.

It was sad that something once so beautiful, so strong, had been reduced to crumbling stone. I glanced at Ollie. Is this what would become of our relationship?

Captain Bromley's voice carried through the dilapidated abbey as Ollie and I approached the courtyard. "It is said that this abbey is the birthplace of Christianity in England. For thousands of years, pilgrims and seekers came to this sacred site for spiritual renewal . . ."

"Your brother and sister-in-law should be just inside," Ollie said. "I will wait to make sure you are safely with them before I ride back."

"Will you not also come inside?"

"It is better if I return to the manor."

My emotions felt as if they would crumble. I hated to part in this way, but there was nothing I could say in this moment to bring him consolation. With time, I hoped we could rebuild our friendship, but like this ruin, I worried that our relationship would never be what it once was. I directed my horse toward the sound of Captain Bromley's voice.

"Unfortunately," our host continued, "the church had more money than the king. As you can imagine, this was a considerable political obstacle for King Henry. An obstacle that he remedied by dissolving the monasteries and destroying many churches."

When the rest of our company came into view, I glanced back at Ollie. He gave me a curt nod and rode away toward the stableyard.

Damon and Lady Margaret were right behind Captain Bromley, and I doubted they even noticed me as the rest of the company continued through an arch to another part of the ruins. But Henry and Georgiana were situated in the back and walked their horses to where I waited on mine.

"Is Mr. Jennings unwell?" Georgiana asked when the three of us were alone.

"In a matter of speaking," I said, my voice weak. "I have denied him."

"Denied him?" Georgiana stared at me. "But why? He is a fine match. Possibly your only. You must ride after him! Take back your refusal. Tell him you were only surprised."

"No."

"Hannah, if you do not accept Mr. Jennings, you may never have another opportunity to marry," Georgiana said. "You must know that I only want for

your happiness. To see you settled. It is obvious Mr. Jennings cares for you. He
is a good man and a handsome one too."

Henry loudly cleared his throat.

"Not as handsome as your brother, mind you. But marrying him would
better your life in every way."

Except one. He wasn't Damon. I shook my head.

"Make her see reason, Henry."

My brother looked at me pityingly. "I know you are decided against him,
but Mr. Jennings *is* a fine match for you. I believe you would have a good life
together."

If Ollie had offered for me at the beginning of the summer, I would have
said yes without reservation. But now . . . "I cannot pretend to feel something
I do not."

"I believe you are making a mistake that you will live to regret," Georgiana
said.

"Would you like to ride back?" Henry asked me.

I nodded weakly.

"I will continue on with the rest of the company and make your excuses.
Hopefully we will avoid the worst of the gossip." Georgiana guided her horse
away.

Henry and I walked our horses back toward the stables. My horse chomped
at her bit, wanting to run, but I reined her in, needing the quiet of the meadow
to think about what had just happened.

"I don't understand your reasons for denying Mr. Jennings," Henry finally
said. "But I believe Mama would be proud of you for following your heart."

"Do you really think so?"

"I know so," Henry said. "When I was attempting to court Georgiana, you
may remember that she was not at all interested in me. Season after Season, I
tried to win her affection, but she saw me only as a friend." He shrugged. "I
tried to feel something for other young women, but my heart would not be
moved. I was ready to give up, but Mama told me that love was worth working
for, and that I would only ever be truly happy by being true to my own heart."

"And you won Georgiana."

"Not without a great deal of effort and humility on my part, but yes. I
know you must be frightened about your future, but I want you to know that
you will always have a place with Georgiana and me."

"Thank you, Henry," I said, and I locked his words away in my heart. Even
if I forever remained unmarried, at least I would not be alone.

CHAPTER THIRTY-SEVEN

OLLIE DID NOT COME DOWN to dinner that night, and I relied on Henry to escort me into the dining hall. Once seated, he served food first to his wife, then to me, and finally, for himself. And as we ate, he and Georgiana both made an effort to include me in their conversation, although I had very little to say, and they eventually left me alone.

Was this how the rest of my life would be? Would I always have to rely on others? I hated the thought of being the poor spinster sister, of being a burden.

I would have to find some way of supporting myself; perhaps I could secure a position as a governess. I was sure I could find some measure of happiness in caring for children, even if they weren't my own. Or I could try my hand at writing like Miss Edgeworth, my favorite author. She was unmarried and seemed to find joy in the craft. Why not I?

I had no appetite, but I forced myself to take a bite of food. I glanced at Damon. He sat near the head of the table with Lady Margaret at his side. And though he did not smile at her as they spoke, he also did not look unhappy. She was a beautiful young lady and seemed kind. And most importantly, she would save Summerhaven, which meant, in the end, she would save *him*.

After supper, as Georgiana and I were walking through the entry hall to the drawing room, Ollie appeared on the stairs. His hair was mussed, his eyes dim, and he was not dressed in dinner attire but, rather, traveling clothes.

Georgiana and I slowed.

"Mrs. Kent," Ollie said to Georgiana. "Might I have a word in private with Miss Kent?"

Georgiana looked at me, and her gaze held the smallest glimmer of hope that perhaps Ollie and me would reconcile. "Don't be too long," she cautioned, and then she left us alone in the entry hall.

"You are leaving," I said.

He nodded, then stared at me for a long moment. He reached into the inner pocket of his greatcoat and pulled out a letter. He looked at it in his hands for a few moments and then handed it to me.

I ran my fingers over my name penned in elegant script.

"This letter is from Damon to you. I intercepted it from the tray a few weeks ago when I went to post a letter of my own."

"A few *weeks* ago? How could you?"

His gaze fell to his boots. "I believed Damon's show of affection for you was only a plot devised to spite me. Or worse, to deprive you of virtue. So I intercepted his letter and kept it in an effort to protect your honor and save you from heartbreak." He sheepishly met my gaze. "I see now that I have only caused it."

I looked down at the letter and turned it in my hands. The wax seal on the back was broken.

"I'm so sorry," Ollie whispered. "I didn't know."

I only nodded, not trusting myself to speak.

"I didn't read the letter until tonight after we returned from our ride at the ruins. I thought that it might possess some insight that would prove the truth to you. But . . ." He shook his head. "I didn't know, Hanny. Not of my father's health or of Summerhaven's circumstance or your feelings for each other. I didn't know."

I could only stare at him.

"I'm so sorry, Hannah. I hope one day you will be able to forgive me," he said, and then he continued past me through the front door.

Standing alone in the entry hall, I rubbed the letter between my fingers. I should join the other women in the drawing room. Georgiana would worry. Amelia too. But I could not bring myself to move in that direction.

Down the corridor, in the direction of the dining hall, came the sound of voices. Deep voices. The men must have finished their drinks.

Knowing I would not be able to enjoy the evening without first reading Damon's letter to me, I hurried up the stairs and down the corridor to my bedchamber to read it. I sat on my bed and laid his letter in my lap. Was I brave enough to read the contents? Whatever this letter contained, it would surely change the course of my life.

CHAPTER THIRTY-EIGHT

My dearest love,

It has been four weeks since you left Summerhaven and four weeks that I have been in agony. You told me that if I cared for you at all, that I must let you go, but my heart demands otherwise.

First, you must understand one thing. I am in love with you, Hannah. Every beat of my heart, every breath of my lungs—they are yours. I am yours, however unworthy.

From the day you bettered me at skipping stones across the river as a girl to the night you ate frog legs at Lord Rumford's table, my admiration for you exceeds all others. You see the world not as it is but as it should be, and you work fearlessly toward that end. You make me want to work fearlessly toward that end. And your brave example, your encouragement to serve my tenants openly, gave me the courage to be the man I always wished to be, regardless of my title.

My whole life, I have been loved not for who I am but for what I am and what I will one day possess. To my great shame, even I am guilty of reducing my identity and worth to my title and possessions. Would God give me the opportunity, I would go back to that day in the portrait gallery when I told you about Father's failing health and my responsibility to Summerhaven, and I would beg you to be mine, no matter the sacrifice.

But seeing as I cannot, I have worked in your absence to do all I can to secure Summerhaven's future and win you back. I have sold almost every rug, candlestick, and piece of furniture. My curricle is also gone, as is my pocket watch. I daresay the only thing that remains of any value are my ancestors' portraits that hang on the walls.

I have limited the number of staff to only the most essential. I have written to family, friends, and foes, begging for their assistance.

But it was not enough to pay off Father's debts.

I petitioned the government and pled to have the entail on the estate removed so that I might sell a portion of the land and secure the remainder's future. My request was denied.

You have never known a man more desperate.

And then one day, as I was riding Ares one last time before he was to be auctioned at Tattersall's, an idea came to me. It was something you said, actually. About me having a passion for horses.

Not two weeks earlier, I'd met Duke Maybeck in London. Father had arranged the visit in hopes that I might marry his daughter Lady Margaret, but it was her father I spent the majority of my time with, discussing his habit of breeding horses. It is a pastime for him, of course, as he is wealthier than the Prince Regent himself, but it is a lucrative one. One that I might undertake in an effort to save Summerhaven.

I raced back to the manor and wrote to the duke, explaining the dire situation and my plan. By the grace of God, he took mercy on me and supplied a loan. Work has already begun on the new stables, and horses are being acquired even as I write. For the first time in weeks, I have hope. I do not know what will become of my efforts, but it is my most fervent prayer that my endeavor will succeed.

As a betting man, I know the odds of this venture prospering are not favorable. But I will never give up trying to do what I can for Summerhaven, for my family, for you.

You may think me a coward for confessing my feelings in a letter, and perhaps I am, but I cannot endure another day without you, my love.

Please write and tell me I will not have to.

If I do not receive word from you, I will let you go, even as you requested, and I will wish you every happiness.

Ever Yours,
x Damon Jennings

With a trembling hand, I laid the letter in my lap and smoothed my hand over his words, my fingers lingering on his name. His penmanship was exquisite, his words beautiful. Careful. Honest.

What he must have thought when I didn't write him back.

I could hardly stand to think of him waiting day after day after day for my letter that never arrived. It was no wonder he had turned his attentions to Lady Margaret—he had no reason not to.

A tear slipped down my cheek and fell onto the letter. And although I quickly dabbed it away, a few of his precious words were lost forever.

I clutched the letter to my chest with one hand and wiped my face with the other.

Damon loved me.

Or . . . at least he *had* loved me. If only I had received his letter sooner, I would have written to him, and perhaps he would not have courted Lady Margaret.

But I had *not* received his letter, and he *had* courted Lady Margaret, and it was much too late. He could, even now, be making her a proposal of marriage. She was certainly expecting one after the time they'd spent in each other's company this weekend.

My heart clenched, and it felt as if it might stop.

I hated that he would never know that I had not received his letter, that after all he had sacrificed so that we might be together, he did not know that I loved him, that I chose him.

No. I couldn't just sit here. It very well might be too late, but if there was even the slightest chance that it was not, I had to find him and confess the feelings of my heart.

I rose from my bed and ran from my bedchamber. My feet flew down the corridor to the stairs and carried me to the drawing room.

A footman scurried to open the door.

My gaze flitted around the room. Henry, Georgiana, Amelia, and Mr. Atherton sat at a table, playing a card game. At the hearth, Captain Bromley stood with a small group. But I did not see Damon.

"Miss Kent," a velvety voice said behind me. I turned and found Lady Margaret. "I must say, you are an incredibly difficult person to gain an audience with. I have been trying to speak with you all weekend."

"You have?"

"I have. Although a force named Lord Jennings seemed rather intent on preventing it."

"I had noticed that. Perhaps we should have a word with him. Do you know where he is?" It was a sorrowful attempt to learn his whereabouts.

She smiled knowingly. "I *do* know where he is, but I am not sure I should tell you. He has been quite distraught these past few days, and I believe that is, at least in part, due to *you*." She took a step closer. "Miss Kent, time is of the essence, so I must ask you to be candid. Do you care for Lord Jennings?"

The answer to this question was almost assuredly the key to her telling me Damon's whereabouts. Tell her the truth of how much I loved him and she would not tell me where he was; lie and she might tell me. But . . . I couldn't do it. No matter the consequences, I loved Damon and would not deny him.

"You *do* love him, don't you?" Wonder touched her words.

"Yes." I nodded. "I'm sorry. I know you love him too."

"I'm sure I *could* have loved him—he is quite handsome and wise—but it really was a lost cause from the start, seeing as the man is completely besotted with *you*."

My eyes widened in surprise.

"*That* is what I have been wanting to talk with you about," she said. "But why, pray tell, if he loves you and you love him, have you been gallivanting about with *Mr.* Jennings?"

"I—" My sentence hung in the air. I had no idea what she did or did not already know. To explain everything that had transpired this year between us, as well as all that had happened with Lord Winfield and Summerhaven, would take a considerable amount of time indeed. "It is complicated," I finally said.

"Relationships between men and women often are." She sighed, and I got the distinct impression that she knew this fact to be true from personal experience. "Thank you for being honest. Lord Jennings has become a friend, and I did not want to cause him anymore pain. But now that I know you are in earnest, there is no more time to delay. He left directly after dinner, intending to travel home. You must catch him before he is gone."

Needing no encouragement, I uttered a hasty, "Thank you," and hurried from the drawing room.

Outside, I hoped to find the Winfields' family carriage, but the drive was empty, and Damon was nowhere in sight.

No!

I stared down the drive, dark but for a few lanterns. I had missed him, but he could not have made it far. If I hurried, perhaps I could still catch him.

Heart racing, I ran down the steps and across the drive. A full moon illuminated my way across the grass to the stableyard. The gate was closed but not locked. I pressed the door open, and it clanged loudly against the wall.

A horse startled, and a groom rushed to calm the animal.

"A horse," I said. "I need a horse."

"Are you all right, miss?" the groom asked.

"I must catch a guest who has just left."

"Perhaps you should wait until morning, miss."

"This cannot wait." I could not be parted from Damon another moment. I could not endure the thought of him believing I had rejected him. "Please," I pleaded. "Help me."

A man stepped out from one of the stalls, reins in hand. At first, I thought him to be a groom, but when he emerged from the shadows, I realized it was Ollie.

"Hannah?" he asked. "What are you doing here?"

"I read Damon's letter. He is returning to Summerhaven . . . I must ride after him."

Ollie glanced at the groom.

"I've already told her that it is better to wait until morn'," the groom said. "It is dark, and horses are easily spooked."

"Hannah is capable," Ollie said.

"I'm sorry, sir, but I cannot risk it. Although Captain Bromley is a kind and fair master, I do not think he would be understanding if I put his guests in harm's way."

"I understand," Ollie said to the groom, then he turned back to me. "You can take my horse, Hannah."

"Are you sure?"

"He is ready and saddled."

"Aye," the groom said. "With a gentleman's saddle."

"I do not need a lady's saddle," I assured him. "If you will only adjust the footholds on a man's saddle, I will tie up my skirts and ride astride."

"It is not safe, miss."

"I will risk it," I said, already stooping to tie up my skirt.

And despite the groom's continued protests, Ollie led me outside to the mounting block, adjusted the footholds himself, and assisted me onto my mount.

"Thank you, Ollie. You don't know what this means to me."

"Be happy," he said, and then he handed me the reins.

I directed my horse through the stableyard in the direction of the gate. At the lane, I kicked its flanks, and my mount sprang forward.

At the sudden increase of speed, my hands tightened instinctually around the reins, but I remembered Damon's instruction to give my horse its head and loosened my grip.

The horse charged into a powerful gallop.

We continued at a feverish pace for what felt like eternity with no carriage in sight. Had I gone the wrong direction? Had Damon left earlier than Lady Margaret thought? I did not know, but I clung to hope and pressed on.

Finally, in the distance, a carriage came into view. I could not tell whether it was the Winfields' carriage, but I hoped.

I chased after it, and when at last I came upon it, the Winfields' crest came into view. I nearly cried out with happiness.

"Stop!" I shouted, but the driver couldn't hear me over the sound of the horses' hooves beating the earth and the clamor of the carriage.

I encouraged my horse to gallop along the side of the speeding conveyance. "Stop!" I shouted again.

The driver startled when he saw me, then pulled back on the reins, slowing the pair of horses. Finally, the carriage came to a stop.

A moment later, the door swung open, and Damon leaned out. "Have we thrown a whe—" he started, but he stilled when he saw me. "Hannah."

A footman hurried to let down the stair, and Damon stepped out and walked directly to my side.

"Is something wrong?" He searched me for injury. "Has something happened?"

"No, nothing. All is well. Help me down?"

A footman took the reins from me, and Damon helped me down. I quickly stooped to untie my skirts.

"If you are looking for Ollie—"

"No," I interrupted. "Not Ollie."

His eyes narrowed.

I pulled his letter out of my pocket. "I did not receive your letter until this evening after dinner, and I did not think my response should be anymore delayed."

He swallowed hard. "What is it you want from me, Hannah?"

"Everything," I whispered. And gathering my courage, I stepped toward him. "I want your ginger candies and to race you on horseback. I want to skip rocks with you across the river and best you at chess. I want to worry you will make me eat frog legs, and I want to dance every single quadrille and waltz with you at every single ball." My chin quivered, and my voice caught. "I want *you*, Damon."

"You have no idea how much I wish I could believe you. To the limits of reason, I assure you. But you have been at Ollie's side constantly—walking in the garden, sitting next to him at dinner, riding alone with him to the ruins." Damon dragged both hands through his hair, then gripped the back of his neck. "At every turn, I have had to watch you love him. And I cannot do it anymore." His arms hung limply at his sides, and his chin dipped toward his chest. He looked utterly defeated.

"I do love him," I admitted. "But *only* as a friend, which is why I have refused him."

His eyes flashed to mine. "But today at the ruins. I thought—" He shook his head. "You refused him?"

I nodded.

"Do you regret it?"

"No."

Damon stepped tentatively closer. "Are you sure?"

"Are you trying to talk me into it?" I laughed lightly.

"No! But a man can never be too certain of a lady's mind." A slight smile tilted his lips.

"As you have told me before," I said. "I mistook friendship and fantasy for love. But because of you, I now know the true meaning. I love *you*, Damon."

"And I love you, Hannah," he said, and then he gathered me into his strong arms, making me *feel* loved.

We stood like that for a long while, my cheek pressed to his chest in a gentle embrace. We were standing as close as two people could stand, but it was not enough. My eyes flicked to his lips. We had waited so long for this moment; to not only be free to voice our true feelings to each other but also to indulge them.

Damon was in no rush though.

He took his time brushing back my hair and then cradling my face in his hands. And when his thumbs caressed my cheeks, a warm sensation shivered down my spine that made me ache for more.

Clutching the lapels of his coat, I rose onto the tips of my toes, willing him to kiss me. Only a breath remained between our lips now, but he did not move to close the space.

"Hannah," he whispered in a low voice. "As I wrote in my letter, I do not know what will become of Summerhaven. Of me. But I promised myself that if I was ever given another opportunity, I would not hesitate to ask you to be mine. You once said you could be happy being a poor man's wife. Is that still true?"

I chose my next words carefully, so there would be no room for misunderstanding. "As long as that man is *you*, Damon Jennings, nothing could make me happier."

"Then marry me, Hannah. Promise me that I will not have to endure another day without you by my side."

"Yes, I promise. For richer or poorer, I am yours."

And then ever so slowly, he lowered his lips to meet mine in a kiss.

EPILOGUE

One year later

SUNLIGHT FILTERED THROUGH THE WINDOW of the morning room, and a fire crackled in the hearth. I loved this time of day, when everything was so fresh and bright and new. I opened *The Morning Post* and was just about to read when Damon walked into the room.

He wore a redingote and had a crop in hand.

"How was your morning ride, husband?"

"Ares was in a mood today." He strode into the room and over to the sofa where I sat.

"He is probably anxious for his colt to be born," I said.

"In that case, I understand completely." With a soft smile, Damon sat beside me and placed a gentle hand on my swollen abdomen. The baby kicked against the light pressure, and Damon's smile grew.

I laid my hand atop his. "We need to decide on a name."

"Or perhaps *names*," he said. Damon was convinced we were having twins due to the incessant motion of my stomach. I had thought him mad at first, but every day, my stomach seemed to expand, and I wondered if he wasn't correct.

"Twins." I sighed. "Can you imagine?"

"Yes." He smiled. "And I cannot wait."

I bit my lip. I was already anxious to bring one child into the world, let alone two.

"If it is a boy, I should like to name him Zeus," Damon said.

I laughed. "You may name Ares's colt Zeus if you would like, but not our baby."

"Hmm," was all he said. "If it is a girl, what about Anne, after your mother?"

Tears pricked my eyes, and I nodded. I wished Mama were here with me at this happy time, but I could not ask for a better companion and example than Lady Winfield, and I was glad she was close.

After Lord Winfield passed last winter, and right after our nuptials, Lady Winfield moved into the dowager house on the northwest side of the estate. Damon and I had tried to convince her to keep her rooms in the manor, but she said newlyweds needed privacy. Thankfully, she was near, and we saw her almost daily.

Papa, too, visited often, for which I was glad. And also Amelia—who had decided to be the very best aunt our baby would ever have, though I didn't think she had much competition in Georgiana, who did not have much interest in babies or children.

The only person I hadn't seen much of was Ollie. He'd returned to London to live in his set of rented rooms at Albany directly after my marriage to Damon, and when he returned to visit his mother, Amelia took up much of his time. They both claimed only friendship, but I could not help wondering if it was more. Soon, he would move to Winterset Grange. I hoped the change would give him purpose and passion and provide him a new beginning.

Caldwell appeared at the morning room door. "Lord and Lady Winfield—"

"Lord Jennings, please," Damon corrected. He refused to make use of the Winfield title since his father's passing. I wasn't sure whether his decision was due to grudge or grief, but I would not press him. He would take up the title when he was ready, or he wouldn't. It made no difference to me.

"Of course, my lord. Forgive me. Mr. Tobine has arrived to discuss painting your portrait. He is waiting for you in the gallery."

"Thank you, Caldwell," Damon said politely, but as soon as he'd quit the room, Damon turned to me and groaned.

"Oh stop." I nudged his ribs with my elbow. "You have known about this for weeks."

"And I have tried to forget it for just as many. You know I have no wish to have my portrait painted. So many hours of sitting and someone staring at you."

"Alas, the day is upon us, and you must act graciously or he will paint you to look grim and gruesome."

Damon made a grotesque facial expression, scrunching his nose and contorting his mouth. He leaned close, nuzzling into my cheek.

"That is enough." I laughed and playfully pushed him away. "Now help me stand."

He rose with a sigh, then helped me stand. "I actually have an idea," he said, tucking my hand into his arm as we walked toward the portrait gallery. "What if instead of me getting my portrait painted, *we* get *our* portrait painted?"

I looked up at him in question.

"Summerhaven is *our* home, after all, and I do not think I could smile without you by my side."

"You are a gentleman through and through, Damon Jennings, and it was kind of you to ask."

"Why do I feel like you are about to refuse me?"

"Because I am." I laid a hand on my stomach. "I do not think I should like to be remembered looking as large as an elephant."

Damon stopped us right in the middle of the entry hall and turned me to face him. "You are beautiful, my love, and I should very much like to remember you this way."

"Well, I do not, so either you will have to sit for your portrait alone, or Mr. Tobine will have to use his imagination and paint me a girlish figure."

"Does this mean you will sit with me?"

"On one condition," I said. "No, two."

"Go on."

I held up one finger. "First, you do not name our first son Zeus."

He laughed. "And two?"

"You smile in our portrait."

"I do so swear it," he said, pulling me tighter into his embrace. "Although, for our agreement to be legally binding, we must seal it with a kiss."

"Is that how business is done in the House of Lords?"

A smile tugged at his mouth. "Only in the house of Summerhaven, my love, and only with you."

"Well, then." I rose to my tiptoes. "Perhaps you'd best kiss me."

"Perhaps I shall."

THE *Making* OF AN *Earl*

A SUMMERHAVEN NOVELLA

PROPER ROMANCE

TIFFANY ODEKIRK

SHADOW
MOUNTAIN
PUBLISHING

CHAPTER ONE

One month before the start of Summerhaven
June 1817

THE RAUCOUS CHEERS OF THE race-mad crowd filled the spectator stands. I glanced around, not looking for anyone or anything specific but wanting to take in the whole of it: the streaming standards, the sophisticated silk toppers, even the stinking scent of horses.

"Damon," Father snapped. "The race is about to begin. Face forward. *Focus.*"

I had half a mind to turn and sit facing the opposite direction on the bench if only to antagonize him, but that would hurt no one's back but my own.

Besides, I'd looked forward to Royal Ascot since the start of the Season several months ago, and I didn't want to miss a moment of the culminating race—the Gold Cup competition. My excitement was due partly to the race and partly to what the race signified: the end of the social Season and my forced participation in the Marriage Market.

The only damper to my contentment was Father, who sat fuming beside me. He'd bet a significant sum in the Windsor Forrest stakes and lost, so he was in a foul disposition. Although, when was he not these days?

The horses stood at the starting line, their eager jockeys clothed in their employers' colors. When the flag dropped, the horses shot off the line. The crowd sprang to their feet, gentlemen and ladies alike cheering for their favorite horses down the length of the track.

Father barely blinked, his gaze intent upon his pick—Sir Richard, which was currently in the lead. Father fisted his hands, and his signet ring—a symbol of his stewardship and status—shone in the afternoon sun.

I'd placed my bet on Ares, a fine Friesian, not because I thought he would win but because I knew he wouldn't. What better way to subvert Father than to place a losing wager?

Ares was as rare as he was beautiful, but unlike Father's pick, he was not a Thoroughbred. In fact, Ares was the first Friesian ever to be entered in the competition—and likely the last if he lost today, which he appeared to be doing.

Ares had been quick off the line but was falling behind. While he had the spirit and stamina of a racehorse, he did not have the speed. He *was* fast, just not fast enough.

What had Sir Gottfried been thinking when he'd entered Ares in the competition?

Perhaps he'd been baited—Gottfried was nothing if not proud, and his foes loved to leverage this character flaw against him.

As the horses rounded the last bend, the crowd swelled with excitement.

"Steady!" Father said as the horses approached the finish line, Sir Richard neck-in-neck for the lead.

Ares, on the other hand, only fell farther behind.

When Sir Richard crossed the finish line first, I wasn't sure whether to be glad. The more Father won, the more he thought himself good at gambling— as though one could be good at games of chance. But when he lost, he would gamble all the more to earn back what he'd squandered. It was a vicious cycle, to be sure.

Father turned to me with a gloating grin. "Did you see that, Damon?"

"Hard to miss."

"*That* is how you win a horse race. Remember this: risk nothing, win nothing."

"I daresay I did. Had I risked more, I would have lost more."

Father frowned. "You would not have lost had you listened to my counsel and placed your wager on the correct horse. A gentleman should carefully weigh his options and be discerning in all decisions. Best remember that, boy."

I hated when he called me that. I was not a *boy*.

We stood from our seats, and as we started down the stairs, Father said, "I saw Duke Maybeck and his daughter sitting lower in the stand. I would like to make your introduction to him."

To *her*, Father meant. Lady Margaret. Father had pushed a parade of women in front of me all Season. Daughters of barons and viscounts and earls, and now the daughter of a duke?

I had no desire.

I felt like a horse at Tattersall's, waiting to be auctioned to the highest bidder.

When we reached the base of the stairs, Father was swept into a circle of congratulators, so I slipped out of sight and headed for the stableyard.

People strolled down the stretch of stalls, though not as many as I would have expected.

Grooms were already washing down their masters' mounts, massaging the horses' tired flanks. They paid me no mind as they worked, and I watched jealously.

If I could have been born anything, it would not have been an heir to an earldom. I would have chosen a much simpler life, a life of choice and freedom, a life that looked a lot like my younger brother, Ollie's. I envied his freedom; he envied my inheritance. Perhaps it was the nature of man to never be satisfied with his lot in life.

Had I the choice, I would have wanted to work with horses—I'm not sure in what capacity, but I enjoyed being near them. They were calming.

Well, *most* horses were, anyway.

A few stalls down, one horse was making quite a ruckus. I followed the sound and found Ares.

Of course.

The black stallion stomped his hooves and neighed loudly. It was as if he knew he'd lost the race and was throwing a tantrum. Friesians generally possessed calm, steady personalities, but this Friesian was named after the Greek god of war. How could I expect anything less?

A groom tried his level best to rein Ares in, but the horse was too spirited to be subdued.

Heavens, he was beautiful.

Sleek and strong, Ares had a long neck, short ears, and sloping shoulders. He was tall too—sixteen, perhaps even seventeen hands. He had a flowing black mane that would make most young ladies jealous, a tail so long it touched the ground, and thickly feathered fetlocks.

I'd never seen an animal more elegant, and that was to say nothing of the way Ares moved.

He seemed to possess equal parts grace and strength—something I suspected the struggling stableboy did not appreciate at the moment.

Ares's owner, Sir Gottfried, entered the stable and stalked to Ares's stall. "Whip!" he shouted at a stableboy and held out his hand. As soon as he had the instrument, he did not hesitate to use it on his horse.

Ares stood in the corner of his stall, straight and still, enduring it.

I felt every strike.

"Stop," I said promptly, stepping forward. When he did not, I shouted, "For heaven's sake, *stop!*"

Sir Gottfried turned to glare at me. "This horse cost me a small fortune today, and he will pay for it with his flesh." He raised his hand to deliver another set of strikes.

I grabbed his wrist, stopping him again. "How much?"

"Pardon me?"

"How much did he cost you today? I will buy him from you for that amount."

Gottfried eyed me from head to toe. "Not for sale."

"Surely there is some amount that will satisfy you."

"I will not be satisfied until this horse has suffered enough to learn his lesson," he said, punctuating his sentence with another pelt of his whip.

I gritted my teeth, knowing exactly how the bite of the whip stung. "It is your reputation that will suffer if you don't bridle yourself." I nodded toward a small crowd watching from several stalls down.

Sir Gottfried glanced in their direction, then threw the whip at the stableboy and stalked outside.

I remained, staring at Ares.

I didn't know how yet, but I would make him mine.

CHAPTER TWO

WE WERE EXPECTED AT ANOTHER ball later that night. With the end of the Season in sight, the *ton* seemed intent on filling every second with social events before retiring to their family seats in the country.

Father and Mother were already waiting in the carriage when I climbed inside.

Father leveled me with a stare. "A gentleman never keeps company waiting, Damon."

I sat back in my seat with a sigh, exhausted by his endless lectures. He was constantly pushing and prodding me to learn and observe, but never allowing me to actually *do*. I sat through interminable meetings and looked over countless ledgers, but Father never let me have any real responsibility. He seemed certain I would fail. Perhaps I would. But how else would I learn?

"I was disappointed that you disappeared today," Father said. "Duke Maybeck and his daughter wanted to meet you."

"Lady Margaret?" Mother said with a smile, and Father nodded. "Oh, Damon. She is a lovely young lady. I think you would like her. Beautiful, talented—"

"A *duke's* daughter," Father interjected. Of all Lady Margaret's fine qualities, which I didn't doubt were many, of course he thought her advantageous birth the best.

But was she kind? Could she carry on a conversation? Was she witty? Did she have any interests or pastimes? Or possess a sense of humor?

Father did not seem concerned about any of those qualities, though, only about how to elevate our social status.

"Can you make Damon's introduction tonight?" Mother asked Father with far too much enthusiasm.

"Sadly, the duke and his daughter will not attend tonight's ball," Father said.

Mother's face fell. "That is too bad. Well, I'm sure many other fine young ladies will be in attendance tonight. Is there anyone you are interested in dancing with, Damon?"

"No."

"What about Miss Featherstone?" Mother tried. "You appeared to enjoy dancing with her at the last ball."

"I'm glad it appeared that way."

Immune to my habit of making snide remarks, Mother rattled off the names of several eligible young ladies, but they all blurred together. In truth, my heart had only ever been interested in one girl—for that was what she had been back then: a girl, not yet grown into a young lady. But many years had passed since that time. How could I even know whether what I'd felt back then had even been true interest?

"Perhaps you should give me a list of ladies you would like me to dance with tonight so I might fulfill my duty," I said.

"Excellent idea," Father said.

"I was being sarcastic."

"Well, *I* wasn't. It is past time you take up your duties. In fact, I will give you until the end of the year to choose a suitable young lady to marry, or I will choose for you." Decree delivered, he turned to Mother. "Make your list of suitable young ladies for our son to choose from, Elizabeth. Preferably girls with pretty faces, but good breeding and pedigree is imperative."

Father spoke as if I were to select a horse, not a wife.

We'd had this same conversation countless times, but Father had never given me a deadline before. What had changed? And if I refused his options, how would he strike at me?

Mother gave me a sorrowful smile. "Speaking of young ladies . . ." she said, and I sensed her steering the subject in a new direction. "I would like to invite Hannah Kent to stay with us for the summer."

My attention heightened upon hearing Hannah's name.

"With the end of the Season," Mother said to Father, "Oliver will be returning home, and I thought a visit from her might do him good. You don't mind, do you, darling? You remember how close they were as children."

All *three* of us had been close—would that we still were.

"Not at all, my dear." Father raised Mother's gloved hand to his lips and kissed it.

For as fearsome of a father as the Earl of Winfield was, he was as doting a husband. The dichotomy never ceased to amaze me, but I was thankful for Mother's sake.

"You remember Hannah, don't you, Damon?" Mother asked me.

"Of course I do." My hand went to the talisman in my pocket. Even if I wanted to, which I did not, I could never forget Hannah. The last time I'd seen her, we'd been children, and I had made more than a few mistakes. Now I could only wonder what she was like, and I did, more often than I should admit. I was certain Hannah didn't think of me, though, at least not with any affection.

Father and Mother continued in conversation, but I remained quiet, lost in memories of happier days.

When we arrived at the ball, my parents alighted first, and I followed behind, forever in their shadow. Before we were even announced at the door, matchmaking mothers and their hopeful daughters glanced my way. Their gazes slid down my person, seemingly measuring me for my marriage suit.

Over the last several weeks, the ladies' efforts to ensnare me had become more aggressive. With the Season coming to a close, I guessed they were becoming desperate to secure a husband. More than one lady had conspicuously dropped items, such as handkerchiefs and fans, in my presence, requiring me to pick them up and make their acquaintance. One bold lady even exited her carriage in a downpour, counting on me to share my umbrella. The young women always took these moments of forced interaction to hint that they would like to repay the favor by dancing with me at the next ball.

Thankfully, the eager husband-seekers would stop their scheming soon, or so I hoped.

The young ladies at the ball fluttered their fans and looked up at me from under their lashes, as though a simpering smile were all I wished for in a wife.

It was not.

I wanted a wife who had a mind of her own, who challenged me, one who could carry on a proper conversation, yes, but also a young lady who could laugh with me, who could laugh *at* me. I wanted someone who wanted to marry *me*, not my eventual earldom.

Still, I did my duty and danced with every eligible young lady Mother suggested that night. The young ladies were nice enough, pretty enough, talented enough—but for all their efforts, I felt nothing.

After supper, I retreated to the card room. I didn't have any interest in gambling, but it was better than being sized up all evening.

Father was holding court at a card table in the corner, so I walked in the opposite direction and found my friend Frederick Atherton at an almost full table. I nearly laughed when I saw him. There were dandies, there were fops, and then there was Frederick Atherton. Dressed from head to toe in a teal-blue brocade pattern that reminded me of a peacock, he looked purposefully ridiculous; like a blasted Macaroni. All that was missing was a powdered wig and plume.

"Nice ensemble." I smiled and sank into the chair beside him.

"Why, thank you, Jennings. My father did not think so." He grinned.

"I'm sure he did not." Whereas I found small ways to subvert my father, Fred rebelled openly against his father through fashion. I did not understand it, but it seemed to work well enough.

No sooner than I relaxed back into my chair, Sir Gottfried entered the card room. He scanned the room for an empty seat and paused when he saw me watching him.

Perhaps this was the opportunity I'd hoped for.

Holding Gottfried's gaze, I tipped my head to the empty seat across from me, issuing him a challenge.

Smirking, he stalked over and took the seat.

With the table now full, cards were dealt, and we placed bets.

My first few hands were worthless, but instead of folding, I increased my wagers, baiting Gottfried and feigning frustration as I lost bet after bet to him. If he thought he was on a winning streak, he might get reckless.

I bided my time, hoping for the right hand but knowing it might not come. Unlike Father, I held no delusions about games of chance. I might win; I might not. But tonight, for Ares's sake, I hoped I would.

With every win, Gottfried got greedier and more careless.

A crowd gathered around the table, Father among them. How much had he lost? I hoped not all his winnings from Royal Ascot.

And then it happened. I got the hand I'd been hoping for.

"Wagers," the dealer called.

Frederick frowned his displeasure at his hand and slapped down his cards. "Fold."

Gottfried was up next. He glanced at me, looking as though he were debating what to do, and I squinted at my cards, pretending to be nervous. He grinned and raised the stakes.

I had him.

"Don't do it, Damon," Frederick said.

But it was Father's voice that rang in my ear: *Risk nothing, win nothing.*

Against my better judgment, I took Father's advice. I met Sir Gottfried's gaze and said, "With the way my luck has run tonight, I should probably quit, but where's the fun in that?" I pushed all my chips to the center of the table. "All in."

Gottfried looked at his cards again, then glowered at me. "You play like a child instead of winning like a man."

"Can you match the wager, Sir Gottfried?" the dealer asked.

"I can't match that sum," he ground out.

"Then, you will have to fold, sir."

Gottfried glared at me over his cards. He hated to lose. I'd been counting on it. This was my moment. "Your horse," I said. "Wager Ares, and I shall consider our bets even."

He didn't even pause to think about it. "Fine."

Someone produced a paper for Gottfried to sign to confirm his wager.

Gottfried laid down his cards first.

"Good hand," I said, and he grinned.

"A *very* good hand," Frederick muttered next to me.

"But not good enough," I said and watched Gottfried's face pale as I laid down my winning hand.

The crowd swelled with excited conversation. Even Father's frown was replaced with smug satisfaction.

"No," Gottfried sputtered, staring at the cards in shock. "No! I demand a rematch!"

"You have nothing left to wager," I reminded him. "Besides, I've already won what I want." I stood and plucked the paper he'd signed from the table.

Gottfried's glare sharpened. "You bet all this"—he indicated to my considerable earnings—"for *Ares*?"

"I did. And if one hair on his body is hurt before he is handed over to me, I won't hesitate to call you out."

"Welby Park," Gottfried said. "I'll wager Welby Park for what you've won tonight."

I blinked. "You'd bet your entire estate to win back a horse you do not want? What of your wife? Your children?" I shook my head in disbelief. "I don't want Welby Park. Go home, Gottfried."

I'd won.

Ares was mine.

CHAPTER THREE

One week later, I stood on the stone steps of Summerhaven—my family's seat in the country—waiting for Ares to be delivered. I'd hoped to ride my new horse home from London instead of riding in the carriage with Father and Mother, but Gottfried had delayed the day of the delivery. I suspected he'd not wanted the *ton* to see me riding his horse out of the city.

At last, I saw Ares.

As a groom led the mount down the long drive, I couldn't look away from the eye-catching movement of Ares's lofty trot and the way he held his head high. Once the mount of medieval knights, the noble Friesian heritage Ares boasted blazed in his every inch.

I hoped Ares would have a calm and steady personality but also drive and discipline. Friesians were known to be loyal, willing, and cheerful—hopefully, Gottfried's abuse had not broken him.

I met the groom at the base of the stairs and walked to Ares. I ran a gentle hand down his neck.

"An impressive win, Damon."

At the sound of Father's voice, I found him staring at me with a funny look. It took me a moment to place his particular expression because it had been such a long time since I'd last seen it: pride.

"But," he continued, "you should have fleeced the fellow and taken Welby Park too."

I turned my attention back to Ares. "No matter how much I dislike Sir Gottfried, I could never turn his wife and children out of their home."

"They are not your concern." Father's lips pursed in displeasure. "*Your* concern is to build up the earldom. You missed a golden opportunity."

"I showed restraint."

"You showed weakness. A gentleman knows that difference. You are not ready to take up your duties, Damon."

"And whose fault is that?" I shot back. "How am I expected to be an earl if you won't give me any real responsibilities?"

He studied me for a long moment, working his jaw. "Perhaps you have a point. I've granted you a life of luxury and ease for far too long. I have given you all the pleasures of your position but demanded no responsibility. Have a groom saddle your horse. You will ride out with me and Mr. Bancroft today to visit our tenants, the Turners, and *you* will take charge."

"Truly?" I asked, and Father nodded, surprising me. Perhaps my win had improved his confidence in me.

"If you want more responsibility, I will give it to you," Father said. "But you had better not disappoint me, Damon."

"I won't," I promised.

"Good," Father said. "Mr. Bancroft arrives within the hour. Be ready."

The road that led to the Turners' farm was deeply rutted and riddled with rocks. The small stone cottage was located on the outermost edge of the estate and was hidden partially behind a hill, so I had not seen it in many years.

As we approached, the air smelled strongly of sheep and something else . . . stagnant water? When the cottage came into sight, we stopped at the top of the hill and took in the sight.

Heavens, what had happened here?

Everything was in utter disrepair. The cottage was crooked, the thatched roof nearly gone, and the field barren.

"It is even worse than I remembered." Father heaved a breath.

"Mr. Turner is four months behind on his payment," Mr. Bancroft told Father. "He has requested more time to—"

"More time?" Father scoffed. "To what, further decrease the value of my property? Certainly not." He shook his head and turned to me. "Damon, you will deliver a notice of eviction today and demand the Turners vacate the premises within a month."

"But, Father, the welfare of our tenants is *our* responsibility. If they are struggling, we must help them."

Father shot me a look of warning. "This is a failing on *their* part, *not* mine. Had the Turners been wise stewards of everything I've entrusted to them, had they prepared in years previous, they would not find themselves facing evic-tion. They have not taken care of the cottage, which I have entrusted to them, and they have fallen behind on their payment. Therefore, these tenants must be evicted. Do you have the fortitude to do what must be done?"

Did I?

Wasn't this what I wanted? The chance to act as an earl. To learn and try my mettle.

The Turners had held the land lease longer than I had been alive. But it was obvious they were struggling to survive here; perhaps they would be better suited to city living.

"Thirty days," Father said again. And this time, I nodded. "Can you do this on your own, or do you need my assistance?"

"I can do it," I said.

Father nodded his approval. "I'll leave you to it, then." Father and Mr. Bancroft returned the way we'd come, leaving me alone to carry out the task.

I guided Ares down the hill and dismounted. My hand felt heavy as I raised it to knock on the door.

I heard voices behind the door, but it took a long time for it to be opened. When it finally did, Mr. Turner stood on the threshold. Behind him stood a woman, likely his wife, with a baby on her hip and three young children clutching her skirt. One of which, a little boy, had wide, worried eyes and a tangle of curls that reminded me of Ollie's.

"M'lord," Mr. Turner said, bowing his head respectfully.

"Mr. Turner," I returned. "Might you come outside so we can have a word in private?"

While I had to deliver the eviction notice, I could at least spare him the indignity of doing so in front of his wife and family.

He hesitated briefly on the threshold, seeming to steel himself for what was to come, then stepped outside, or rather, *limped* outside.

"You're injured," I said.

"Waterloo." He held his head high.

"Is this why you've failed to care for your cottage? Why you've fallen be-hind on your payments?"

"No, m'lord."

"Why, then?"

"The crops failed, sir. The weather last year—this year, too"—Mr. Turner sighed—"was terrible, hardly any sun and buckets of rain. I've lived here my whole life and never seen anything like it."

I nodded. "That might be true, but a man must still see to his affairs." I sounded so much like Father that it scared me. I swallowed hard and started again, softer this time. "Have you no savings, Mr. Turner?"

"We did have, but me mum got sick and required medicine."

"I am sorry to hear that. Is she well now?"

"She is. That is her voice you hear inside."

That meant seven people lived in a cottage smaller than my bedchamber, seven people I would be evicting from their home. How could I do it?

"I know why you are here, m'lord," he said, his voice rough with emotion. "If you deliver the eviction notice, we will be gone in the time you require."

Even in the face of defeat, he held his head high. I admired his honor and pride, but how could I accept it?

"You said you've lived here your whole life, Mr. Turner. Where will you go?"

He shook his head. "I don't know, but that's not your concern."

Wasn't it?

His family had been our tenants for two generations. He'd worked hard to save his crops. It felt wrong not to come to his aid in his time of need. But how could I help him? Even if I convinced Father to give Mr. Turner more time to make the payment, I did not think it would help.

I pulled the eviction notice from my coat pocket and glanced at the bottom line. The total amount due was nearly identical to the sum I'd won at the gambling table. How carelessly I had placed my bet that night at the ball; I'd wanted something, and to get it, I'd bet a significant sum without a second thought.

I did not deserve my inheritance.

Mr. Turner, on the other hand, had worked hard his whole life to provide food and shelter for his family. He'd even fought for our country, and he was about to be evicted.

He did not deserve this blow.

But he held out his hands anyway, asking without words for me to deliver him the notice.

As I stood before him, guilt rushed through me for having begrudged my birthright, for having despised the duties that came with the privilege of one day becoming a peer. And I felt sick as I handed him the paper and said, "You have until Michaelmas to make your back payment, Mr. Turner."

He nodded, chin held high even as it quivered. "I understand, m'lord. We will see that we are gone."

But as Mr. Turner turned to open the door, I could not go through with it. "Perhaps it doesn't have to come to that," I said, stopping him. Mr. Turner looked at me in question. "You are my father's tenant, Mr. Turner, and one day, you will be mine. You have not reached this point because you are careless, nor even because of your injury. I wish to help you."

His gaze turned cautiously hopeful. "How?"

"I will give you a loan, free of interest, to cover your past-due payments to my father. I will tell him you had some savings, and I convinced you to use it to pay your debt. When you can, you will pay me back."

"I will, m'lord. I swear it."

I knew he would. He conducted himself with pride, and I did not doubt his honor. "Also, your roof needs repair. If you will supply the labor, I will have thatch delivered immediately."

Again, he nodded.

"In return, I ask two things: first, you do all you can to save the crops." Father needed to see that his tenant was trying to do all he could to ensure income.

"Of course, sir."

"Second, this agreement stays between us. You may tell your wife, but no one else, not my father, nor his manservant, no one." If Father found out about my assisting them, I didn't know what he would do to the Turners, but I was certain their fate would be far worse than it was now. "Are we understood?"

"Yes, m'lord." He blinked back tears. "Thank you, m'lord."

I nodded. "I will give my father the necessary funds to settle your past-due payment, and soon, I will supply you with a small loan so you can purchase whatever supplies you need. I will send word on where to meet me."

"Thank you, m'lord. You don't know what this means to me."

That night, I gave Father the money I'd won gambling to pay for Mr. Turner's past-due rent. Father seemed skeptical of my story but could not argue with the stack of banknotes I set on his desk. I walked out of his study, head held high, and as soon as I shut the door, I breathed a sigh of relief.

CHAPTER FOUR

THE BOOT OF OLLIE'S CARRIAGE was piled high with trunks.

"How many things does one man need for a single summer?" I asked Mother.

She fought a smile. "Several, it seems."

"Do you think he's planning a *coup d'état*? Smother me in my sleep so that he might inherit Summerhaven?"

Mother gave me a disapproving look.

"You're right," I said, shaking my head in mock disappointment. "What was I thinking? Ollie wouldn't dare dirty his hands. Perhaps he means to poison my meals."

"Damon," Mother scolded.

"Again, you are right. Poisoning me would require far too much planning and effort. Perhaps he'll push me from my horse while I'm at full gallop."

"What has gotten into you today?" Mother turned fully to face me. "Go easy on your brother. You know how difficult it is for him to be here."

I *did* know. It was hard for me, too, and for precisely the same reason: Father. One might think this commonality would bond us as brothers, but it did not.

With a sigh, Mother turned back to the drive as the carriage came to a stop.

It hadn't been long since I'd seen Ollie—a month, at most. We'd attended several of the same social events this past Season. But it had been a long time since we'd truly talked. A very, *very* long time. I disliked the distance between us and longed for the closeness we'd once shared as children, but I didn't know how to repair our relationship or even *if* it was repairable.

A footman opened the carriage door, and Ollie alighted. As always, he was impeccably dressed: Hessian boots, crisp cravat, and a sophisticated silk top hat, which he perched elegantly atop his head as he ascended to the house.

Mother held out her arms to him, and they embraced.

She would never admit it, but Ollie was her favorite. Their personalities were similar—easy and serene. But part of her affection seemed based on the fact that he was the spare; it was as though she were trying to make up for Father's *lack* of care toward his second son.

Ollie would likely claim that I was Father's favorite. His favorite target, perhaps. Father's attention toward me had nothing to do with me and everything to do with my being born first. I was his *heir*.

If only Ollie and I could put our birth order aside, we might build bridges between us instead of barricades.

When Ollie and Mother parted, I said, "Welcome home, Ollie."

Ollie's gaze raked over me, and I was sure he was cataloging all my faults. With cold austerity, he said, "Damon."

When he turned his back to me, over his shoulder, I mouthed to Mother, "*Coup d'état*," and mimicked choking to death.

She frowned at me, then softened her face to smile at Ollie.

"Where is Father?" Ollie asked.

"Inside," she said, her tone apologetic. "He wanted to welcome you, but he was in the middle of a task that he could not break away from."

Hurt shone in Ollie's eyes.

"Come, let's go inside to see him," she said, and Ollie offered her his arm.

As luck would have it, Father was walking out of his study when we stepped inside the entry hall.

"Darling," Mother said, and Father looked up. "Ollie has arrived."

Ollie straightened.

"So he has. About time too." Then to Ollie, "Cutting it a bit too close to our guests' arrival, don't you think?" He spared Ollie no more than a glance, then turned to me. "Damon, I need your assistance in my study with something important." Without another word, Father stalked back to his study.

Ollie shrank.

Father had not even said hello to Ollie. It had obviously hurt Ollie, but since Father spoke only in lectures these days, Ollie should count himself lucky.

As usual, Mother stepped in to smooth things over. "Ollie, I also need help with something. Lord Rumford is hosting a ball. If I write Lady Rumford a note requesting that they include the Kents, would you be willing to deliver it? I know you are probably tired from traveling, but if you leave soon, you will be back in time for Hannah's arrival this afternoon."

"Of course. I should be happy to help you, Mother."

"Wonderful!" Mother clapped her hands together. "I will write a quick note to Lady Rumford, and you can deliver it right away." Mother disappeared into the library, leaving Ollie and me alone in the entrance hall.

"Don't you have something *important* to do?" Ollie asked.

I shrugged. "I thought I'd wait with you while Mother writes her missive so we can converse."

He eyed me, searching me as though I had some ulterior motive. "I don't need you to entertain me. You are not my keeper, Damon."

Ollie could be overly dramatic at times. I disliked his ire toward me, but I understood it. I was the one who had planted the seeds and watered them, after all. Father's setdown hadn't helped his mood either.

As though reading my thoughts, Ollie glanced—or rather, glared—at Father's study door. "It must be nice being seen," he said.

"You mean scrutinized? I assure you, it is not so pleasant as it appears."

"I'm sure it is better than being *beneath* his notice," Ollie said, and somewhere in the slump of his shoulders, I saw the younger brother I used to know. "Well, I suppose that is the price you must pay for one day owning everything." He made a show of glancing around the expansive entry hall, then back at me. "Forgive me if I do not feel bad for you, *my lord.*"

"You have no idea what my life is like," I said. If he did, he would not be jealous.

"Yes. Well. You ensured that, didn't you?"

He wasn't wrong. I *had* been the one to demand distance in the beginning, but it was a decision I regretted. We'd been close as children, but as we'd grown, Father had begun using our affection to force me to do his will. He knew hurting Ollie would hurt me far more than any punishment he could inflict upon me. I could still hear the snap of the ruler coming down on Ollie's knuckles.

I'd started keeping my distance to protect Ollie. If Father believed we weren't close, he would stop trying to hurt me through him. And it had worked; mine and Ollie's relationship had withered.

A few years later, when Ollie started school at Eton and I'd been in my last year, we'd had the opportunity to rekindle our bond as brothers. But no matter how far from home we might have been, Father's hold on me was absolute. I was afraid.

And so I'd warned Ollie to keep away from me at school. For the most part, he had, until one day, he'd approached me in the schoolyard crying. To my ever-living shame, instead of offering him help, I'd given him the cut direct.

From that day forward, he'd started calling me *my lord* to demonstrate his dislike of me.

I'd deserved every inch of Ollie's derision back then, but now that we were adults, I hoped we could reconcile—but Ollie seemed to only want to lengthen the divide. "You are much changed, Ollie."

"And *you* are exactly the same."

I'd been wrong. We could not build a bridge between us.

Mother stepped back into the entrance hall and handed Ollie the missive. He kissed her cheek and strode to the door.

Father's important task was *not* very important at all: a stack of paperwork. Father wanted me to read the documents, summarize them, and show him where to sign. The tedious task took more than two hours to complete.

"Sir." Caldwell, our butler, stood at the study door. "Your guests are arriving."

We stood and joined Mother in the entrance hall.

"Where is Ollie?" I asked Mother.

"He hasn't returned yet," she said with a shake of her head.

After Father's cold greeting and our tepid conversation, I understood why Ollie might not want to hurry home, but did he not wish to be here to greet Hannah?

Caldwell opened the door.

Father held out his hand, and Mother placed hers on top. As always, I trailed behind them.

The servants, dressed in green livery, stood on the steps in a show of Father's status and superiority. I hoped Hannah would not interpret it as such.

My pulse raced with anticipation. It had been so long since I'd seen Hannah. Hopefully, time had not changed her as it had Ollie. I squared my shoulders and lifted my gaze to the carriage waiting on the drive.

And then, there she was: Hannah Kent.

She sat forward in her seat next to the side glass and craned her neck to see around me, likely looking for Ollie. It had been some time since a young lady had looked around me. I both hated it and loved it.

Mr. Kent alighted first, then handed down Hannah.

I sucked in a breath as she stepped down.

She was even more beautiful than I remembered.

"Welcome," Father greeted.

"The pleasure is all ours." Mr. Kent bowed respectfully.

Father barely tipped his head in return.

They entered a mundane conversation, but I didn't hear a word. I could focus only on Hannah. Her hair was darker than it used to be but still curly. I was happy it had not changed much; I'd always loved her hair. Her hazel eyes, which were forever shifting shades, were more green than brown today, and I liked how they studied me with meticulous curiosity.

Gads, she was gorgeous.

"Hannah," Mother said, warmth in her voice as she looked Hannah over.

Hannah dropped her gaze, appearing embarrassed. "I'm afraid the journey was rather long, my lady."

"Oh, no, my dear. I was only amazed at what a beautiful young woman you've become. You look so much like your mother." Mother embraced Hannah, and Hannah softened.

Finally my turn, I stepped forward. Hannah's eyes went to my watch key and seal—something I had not worn when we'd been children—and I wondered what she was thinking.

"Miss Kent," I said.

"My lord." She sank into a shallow curtsy.

My lord? I winced. To her, I'd always been Damon. "I see someone has managed to make a lady out of the wild girl I once knew," I said, trying to tease a smile from her lips, and when it did not work, I added, "A pity."

A delicate line formed on her forehead.

"Do try not to scowl, Miss Kent. It will crease your lovely brow."

"Damon Jennings." Mother's eyes were as wide as a startled mare's, shock galloping across her face. "You have been taught better manners."

"My apologies, Mother. Teasing a beautiful woman is one of few things that has yet to be lectured out of me."

Hannah's mouth all but hung open, and Mother was stunned. I could understand her confusion, considering all the conversations we'd had of late about my having no interest in any of the young ladies of the *ton*, but I could not help myself. I felt like flirting for the first time in a very, *very* long time.

"I promise I did try to teach him proper decorum, Hannah."

"You must not blame yourself, Mother. I'm certain it was not the teacher but the pupil who is to blame."

"Quite right," Mother said.

"You have no idea how he tortured me as a boy," Mother said to Hannah.

"Oh, but I do." Hannah held my gaze.

"How could I have forgotten how mercilessly he teased you." Mother grimaced.

Hannah looked embarrassed again. "Forgive me, Lady Winfield. I'm rather out of countenance from the journey." She set a gentle hand on her stomach. "Carriage rides do not agree with me."

"Oh, you poor thing. Let's get you settled into your room. Damon, please escort Hannah inside so I can speak to Cook about preparing a tray."

Mother quickly disappeared to do so. Father and Mr. Kent had also already gone inside, leaving us alone. I'd had to be so careful over the last several months not to be alone with a young lady—so zealous were their attempts to entrap me—that I felt momentarily off balance.

"Allow me to escort you indoors." I offered her my arm.

She glanced at my arm like it was a snake. "No, thank you," she said and started up the stairs.

I stepped in front of her, blocking her path, and her glare was glorious. It had been so long since a young lady had not censored her true feelings around me, and I found it wonderfully refreshing. "No, thank you?" I raised an eyebrow.

"I am quite able to manage on my own, my lord."

I frowned. "Are you to *my lord* me all summer?" I didn't think I could stand hearing it. Not from her. I wanted her to see *me*, not my title.

"Are you going to *be* here all summer?"

Apparently, she was not as excited about this arrangement as I was. "You could at least attempt to hide your displeasure."

"I can call you by another name if that is your desire. Although I do believe you will find *my lord* to be more agreeable."

My lips twitched. *There* was her fire. "It seems I have some work to do in repairing my reputation."

"Please don't waste your effort." She stepped around me and started up the stairs. "I thought Ollie would be here to greet Papa and me." She glanced over her shoulder at me. "Do you know where he is?"

"I am not my brother's keeper, Miss Kent." My words came out more forcefully than I'd intended, and Hannah pushed past me with surprising force for someone so small.

"Perhaps his absence is for the best," I called after her. "My brother is much changed."

She whipped around, facing me fully. Her eyes, full of fire, hit me straight in the heart. "Even changed, Ollie is *twice* the gentleman you could ever hope to be, *my lord*." She turned swiftly and swayed, unsteady on her feet.

I hurried to her side and grasped her arm. "Are you all right?"

"I am fine," she said.

But she was *not* fine.

And then neither were my boots.

Her stomach emptied in spasms, and once it finally settled, she looked up at me with wide eyes, her gaze filled with shock and mortification.

I silently handed her my handkerchief and removed my boots. "Will you now allow me to escort you inside?" I once again offered her my arm and found it funny that she still looked like she wanted to refuse. Thankfully, she finally took it, and the warmth of her hand sent a pleasant shiver up my arm, and if I had not already, I would have fallen in love with her right then and there.

Heavens. I still loved her.

I'd thought that once I'd seen Hannah, I might realize my feelings had been nothing more than a boyhood crush. But my feelings had only matured. All this time, I'd never stopped loving her, which was problematic, seeing as she quite obviously disliked me.

CHAPTER FIVE

THAT NIGHT, I CAME DOWN to dinner and found Hannah hovering at the drawing room door, staring at Ollie. "If you don't close your mouth," I said in her ear, "you will catch flies like a frog."

Hannah closed her mouth, then shot me a scathing glare. "It is rude to sneak up on a person, *sir*."

"Sir." I smiled. "An improvement from *my lord*, I think."

"Do not flatter yourself." Hannah spared me a scowl before strutting into the drawing room.

I followed in her wake. Mother, Father, and Mr. Kent occupied one sofa, so I sat alone on the other.

The book on agriculture I'd borrowed from the lending library was still sitting on the side table from when I'd been reading earlier, so I retrieved it and tried to read. But try as I might, I could not concentrate.

Ollie and Hannah were standing across the room so I couldn't hear their conversation, but the way he smiled down at her and the way she smiled up at him was . . . distracting.

What was he saying to make her smile so sweetly?

A few minutes later, they moved to stand at the hearth, and there, by the light of the fire, I saw Ollie's eyes skim down her form. My grip tightened on my book.

"You *look* very well," Ollie flirted. "The country air suits you."

"I'm not sure Damon's boots would agree with you," Hannah mumbled, and I smiled to myself. "But I admit, I'm glad to be free of London."

Did she dislike London? I thought most young ladies loved the city.

Ollie seemed to miss her meaning entirely and expounded on all the benefits of living in the city. With every word he spoke, she seemed to become more and more subdued.

Did he not see how she shrank from the subject?

Could *she* not see how much he'd changed?

I returned my focus to my reading. Perhaps it was a fool's errand, but I wanted to find some way to help the Turners. It seemed impossible in the time remaining before Michaelmas, but I couldn't not try.

Then suddenly, silence. I glanced up. Hannah seemed sad. At least this time, Ollie seemed to notice it too.

"Tell me, Hanny. What is wrong?" he said.

Hanny. I rolled my eyes. I'd hated it when Ollie had called her that when we were children, and it was no more endearing now that we were grown.

With their voices low, I caught only snippets of their conversation. "You were living in London, same as me . . . You didn't call on me."

"I thought you were still living in Bath," he said, even though I was sure it wasn't true. I hoped she knew it too. "A simple misunderstanding." Ollie ducked to catch her eye. "Forgive me?"

I could not hear her response, but she appeared more than happy to.

Not long later, dinner was announced at the door, and I set my book aside.

Ollie offered his arm to Hannah, and she did not hesitate to take it, as she had hesitated with mine earlier. I frowned at the fact as they fell in line behind me, and Hannah must have taken my reaction as reproof because the look she shot me was severe.

"Is Damon always so . . . superior?" she asked Ollie, and though her voice was hushed, I heard it.

Superior. Was that really how she saw me?

"*Always*," Ollie replied. "My brother is a great lord, you know. Superiority, it seems, comes with the title."

I frowned at him over my shoulder, and as soon as I faced forward, they laughed.

I had hoped that time would dull the sting of yesteryear, that somehow, the three of us might have a happy summer together. Like old times. But I'd been naive. Too many mistakes had been made. Too much time had gone by.

In the dining room, I took my usual seat and found myself sitting across from Hannah.

"I hear the weather has all but ruined the Season," Father said to Mr. Kent. "Tell me how this affects your dealings with the church, Kent."

"We have seen a slight decrease in the size of the congregation on Sundays," Mr. Kent said.

"I daresay God sent the rain to ruin us all," Father grumbled.

"Or perhaps he intends for us to reflect, not bring us to ruin, my lord." Mr. Kent corrected him—he probably did not even realize he'd done so, but Father's disdain was obvious.

"Spoken like a true man of God." Father gave a derisive laugh, which dissolved into a deep cough.

"My lord?" Mother said. "Are you all right?"

"I have no need of a nursemaid, Elizabeth."

"Of course not," she said, then masterfully maneuvered the conversation to a new topic: the Rumfords' ball. "Just this afternoon, Ollie requested the invitation be extended to our guests."

Hannah brightened and leaned toward Ollie. I couldn't make out their hushed words, but I knew from her smile that she was thrilled.

Mother offered to serve as Hannah's chaperone, so her father could enjoy the card room. But again, Mr. Kent voiced his disapproval. He didn't seem to realize he was delivering Father a setdown, but I would relive this entire miserable night to see Father scolded.

Again, Mother navigated around the sensitive subject. "Seeing as I am now in your employ," Mother winked at Hannah, "Oliver will be glad to dance the supper set with you."

Ollie held Mother's gaze for a long moment, and I was sure Hannah saw the silent standoff as she shifted in her seat as though uncomfortable.

Finally, Ollie came to his senses. "What say you, Miss Kent? Would you—"

"I would," she replied far too eagerly, and for the life of me, I didn't understand what she saw in this spoiled, selfish version of my younger brother. His fine smile? His fancy clothes? Ollie's tower of trunks suddenly didn't seem so silly.

I took another bite of food.

"Damon," Mother said. "Who will you dance the supper set with?"

Not this again, and from Mother, no less. "No one," I said, staring at my plate, hoping to avoid another inquisition.

But of course, Father wouldn't miss a chance to give me a dressing down. "Not dance?" He snorted. "How *absurd*."

He thought everything I did these days was absurd. No matter how hard I tried, I could not ever please him.

Mother touched my arm. "There is always a shortage of eligible men. There must be someone who could entice you into dancing at least one set."

"No," I said and shoveled another bite into my mouth. The sooner I finished my food, the sooner I might leave.

"*No?*" Father said. "You *will* dance tomorrow night and fulfill your obligations. I will not pass my title to a dead line, Damon."

He spoke as though he had a choice in the matter. He did not, and neither did I. Whether he liked it or not, I would be the next Earl of Winfield.

"If you refuse your duty to this family," he continued, "you also refuse the benefits. Do I make myself clear?"

"Often and rather forcefully." My back held the scars to prove it.

"Good." Father nodded. "You'll dance the first set with Lord Rumford's daughter."

Amelia Atherton was Fred's sister. She was pleasant and pretty, but she was far too much like Fred for me to be able to envision anything more than a friendship. But it was pointless to argue. Father had decided, and that was that.

When dinner was done, the ladies retired to the drawing room. Father usually lingered at the table and slowly sipped his port, but tonight, he downed the glass and swiftly stood. Apparently, he was done being lectured by Mr. Kent. Pity, that. It had been quite entertaining.

As we walked to join the ladies, I touched Ollie's elbow, holding him back. "Where were you this afternoon?"

"What's it to you?" he said.

"Hannah was disappointed that you weren't here to greet her."

"If you must know, I was making the acquaintance of Miss Atherton."

"What of Hannah?"

He frowned. "What *of* her?"

"You must have guessed that Mother invited Hannah here to make you a match."

"You think Mother wishes to match me with *Hannah?*" Ollie scrunched his nose and shook his head. "You must be mistaken."

"I don't think so. I should know the signs, seeing as Mother spends significant time trying to make *me* a match."

He rolled his eyes. "I'm sure she does, *my lord.*"

"Would you please stop calling me that?"

"It *is* your title, is it not?"

"I am your brother first and forever."

"*First* being the most important word in that sentence."

Lud, I wanted to shake him. But seeing as I would not advance on that front tonight, I retreated to my original objective and said, "You shouldn't dance with Hannah, Ollie."

"Whyever not?"

Had he not heard a single word I'd said? "You *know* why not."

Ollie opened his mouth, but before he could respond, Hannah stepped into the corridor, her eyes ablaze.

"Hannah," I sputtered. How much had she heard? "I thought you were otherwise occupied in the drawing room."

"I am certain *that* is true." She angled her body toward Ollie, cutting me from the conversation. "Shall we take a stroll in the garden tomorrow morning? From my window, I can see that the lavender is in full bloom. I would love a bouquet to scent my room."

"I would enjoy that very much," Ollie said, and then they turned their backs to me, and I felt all of twelve years old again, loving her and watching her love him.

Unwanted, I grabbed my book from the side table and retreated to my bedchamber.

CHAPTER SIX

I DRESSED NICER THAN NORMAL for the ball tonight. I did not usually dress to impress, seeing as I wished to avoid attention not attract it, but I didn't want to look like a slump standing next to Ollie.

"You look especially handsome tonight, Damon." Mother watched me descend the stairs with a smile. And when I reached the base, she stepped away from Father and Mr. Kent to stand with me. "Perhaps someone has managed to catch your eye. Miss Atherton, perhaps?"

"For all your tireless attempts to make me a match, you are not very good at guessing where my interest lies."

"So there *is* someone who interests you." Mother's eyes sparkled with delight.

I frowned, hoping to discourage her, but the damage was done. I'd opened Pandora's box, and Mother would not be content until I stood at the end of an aisle and said *I do*.

Ollie came down next, looking ever the well-heeled gentleman. How did he manage to wear such stiff collars? Mine were half as high and likely a quarter as stiff, yet I felt as if I might choke.

"I daresay the young ladies will be beside themselves when they see the pair of you tonight."

Then, at the top of the stairs, Hannah appeared. I swallowed hard. Dressed in green and hair elegantly styled, she was stunning—without a doubt, the most beautiful woman I'd ever seen.

But of course, she had eyes for only Ollie—even despite the fact that he'd failed to walk with her in the lavender garden today as they'd planned.

He, however, had not even noticed Hannah standing there.

Hating to see her disappointed, I nudged Ollie and nodded to where she stood on the stairs.

To my surprise, he produced a small sprig of lavender from his coat pocket. Too little, too late, I thought, but Hannah tucked it into her hair. How was it that he could do no wrong in her eyes and I could do no right?

I tugged at my cravat, loosening it a little.

"Look at the pair of you," Mother beamed at them. "All grown up. Quite a lovely couple, aren't they, dear?" she asked Father, but he barely responded before announcing that it was time to leave for the ball.

With a sigh, I pushed myself off the wall and walked to the carriages. As soon as we were seated—our family in one conveyance and Hannah and her father in the other—Father started in on me: how to sit, who to dance the supper set with: one of the daughters of the peers—the wealthiest, preferably.

I glanced at Ollie, hoping he would see that being Father's heir wasn't all he thought it was, but Ollie was looking out the side glass into the darkness. I realized Father hadn't said a single word to him all night, and I wondered which was worse: being beneath Father's notice or being his sole focus and forever feeling like a disappointment.

Luckily, we did not have to listen to Father's lecture for long. The Rumfords' residence was not far from Summerhaven, and we arrived quickly. As soon as the carriage came to a stop, I braced myself.

Stepping into a ball felt like being thrown into the lion's den. And as an eligible bachelor, *I* was the prey. I felt the matchmaking mothers' stalking stares and their daughters' hungry gazes.

I trained my gaze straight ahead, hoping not to get bitten.

After being announced at the door, I immediately went to the card room to hide. I scanned the room and found Fred. I sat beside him and was about to take my first full breath when Father's hand clamped down on my shoulder.

"It seems my son is a bit too content in his bachelorhood to do his duty," he jested.

The older gentlemen at the table snickered, and Father pulled me from my seat, all but pushing me back to the ballroom.

"You've promised to dance the first set with Miss Atherton. A gentleman should never keep a lady waiting."

"I promised her nothing. *You* did."

"Alas, you will do your duty and dance with the chit."

He was right. I would.

I had no desire to hurt Amelia, but neither did I wish to court her, much less marry her.

Thankfully, Miss Atherton was not difficult to find, with her fiery red hair, but I had not noticed Hannah standing behind her. She watched as I extended my hand to Miss Atherton, and I would have given anything to know what she was thinking.

As we danced, Miss Atherton engaged me in polite conversation. She was flirtatious and funny, and for a moment, I wished I could return her interest. It would make things so much easier with Father. But I felt nothing, and I would not toy with her. When our set was finished, I thanked her and returned to the card room.

I played several hands before the supper set was announced. A collective sigh sounded, knowing we must all do our duty as gentlemen and ask the young ladies to dance, lest we be labeled scoundrels and seated alone for supper.

I scanned the crush in search of one of the young ladies on Mother's list so that I might satisfy Father. Instead, I saw Hannah. She stood alone and looked nervous.

Ollie had promised to dance this set with her. Where was he?

It did not take long to find him flirting with Miss Digby.

Miss Digby was beautiful, but beyond her generic good looks, I did not know what Ollie saw in her. The young lady was insufferable. But that besides, he had promised to dance this set with Hannah. Surely he wouldn't risk Hannah's reputation by spurning her for a pretty face. I held my breath, hoping he would do the right thing.

Finally, he made his way to Hannah, and Hannah looked relieved. But when he reached her, they spoke for only a few moments before Ollie walked back to Miss Digby. Hannah's face fell. I hated to see her sad, but perhaps it was better that she knew the truth.

She glanced around the ballroom—whether looking for a partner or an escape, I didn't know—and we locked gazes. I silently tried to tell her it would be all right, that I would dance with her, that I wanted to, but she fled to the balcony before I could reach her.

I followed her, wading through the gossip that stirred in her wake.

There were so many ways this could end badly—every other interaction between us had—but there was nothing for it. Hannah needed my help, and whether she wanted it or not, I would come to her rescue.

As soon as I stepped outside, I saw the sprig of lavender Ollie had given her on the ground and knew that she saw him for who he was. I offered her a sad smile, and she turned away as though embarrassed.

Unfortunately, we did not have time for feelings, not if we were to save her reputation. So I donned a happy tone and said, "There you are, Miss Kent. I have come to claim my set."

Her eyes narrowed slightly. "I beg your pardon, but—"

"Are you feeling faint?" I stepped forward and steadied her, then lowered my voice. "The only way to silence the whispers that have already begun to circulate is if we give them something more interesting to talk about. Now, take my arm, and do try not to frown as I lead you to the dance floor."

She'd always been a terrible actress, so her voice was stilted when she said, "I was feeling a little flushed, but I am recovered now."

"I am glad to hear it. I have been waiting all evening to dance with you."

It was true, so it was easy to say. It was the reason I'd dressed nicer than usual and worn cologne. I had not thought I would be granted this opportunity, but selfishly, I was grateful for it.

As we entered the ballroom, her eyes searched the room for *him*, and I felt a surge of annoyance.

"Looking for Ollie undermines the purpose of our dancing together," I whispered as we made our way to the dance floor.

"I wasn't looking for Ollie," she said. "I was searching for an escape."

Of course she was. "Am I really so loathsome?"

"Yes. I mean, no. Damon, I cannot do this. I can't dance the quadrille." She hurried to explain that she'd not completed her dancing lessons due to her mother's illness and had never learned the quadrille.

Lud. She looked as though she might be ill right here in the middle of the dance floor.

"Do exactly as I say," I said only loud enough for her to hear as we took our places at the head of the square.

She nodded up at me, eyes wide with fear.

I gave her a reassuring smile, and then we were dancing.

I hated seeing her scared but also relished the feeling of her looking to my lead and trusting me as she had when we were children. I never thought she would look at me this way again, and I did not want it to end, but of course it did. Our dance was not without mistake, but we avoided major errors.

"You did well," I whispered.

"Thank you for assisting me, Damon. Truly."

"I had little choice, Miss Kent. You were looking quite green, and my boots can handle only so much abuse."

She glared up at me, but her eyes did not hold the same contempt for me as before. At least, not until I offered her my arm and she realized she was stuck sitting next to me for the supper set.

We were seated near the head of the table, which, unfortunately, also meant we were seated near Father. Ollie sat closer to the middle of the long table, though the distance did not prevent her from looking in his direction.

"Miss Kent," I said, commanding her attention, "you appear to be searching for a particular dish. The *grenouilles*, perhaps?"

"Yes," she said uncertainly. "The *grenouilles*. Thank you."

As I stood to serve her, Mother said, "I didn't know you were fond of frog legs, Hannah."

Hannah's gaze snapped to me, and I grinned.

"I am also fond of frog legs," Lord Rumford said. "Miss . . . ?"

"Kent," Father quickly supplied.

"Kent," Lord Rumford repeated thoughtfully. "Any relation to the Duke of Kent?"

Father looked at Hannah, then spoke on her behalf. "Perhaps distantly." Though we knew there was no relation, distant or otherwise.

"Well, relation or no," Lord Rumford said, "I am happy to have a young woman with such a refined palate seated at my table. Please tell me how you like them, Miss Kent."

"May I?" Damon gestured to the platter.

"You are *too* kind, my lord," she said through gritted teeth, and I served her a large pair of frog legs. "And you must not forget to serve yourself," she said. "I should hate for you to be left out of our enjoyment."

"Unfortunately, my palate is not as refined as yours or Lord Rumford's."

Lord Rumford grinned. "The lady is your superior, Jennings."

"One need only look at her to confirm that fact."

"Hear! Hear!" Lord Rumford held up his glass, and we drank in Hannah's honor.

Hannah's cheeks pinked, and I added humility to the list of characteristics I liked about her.

"Well, Miss Kent, how do you find them?" Lord Rumford asked.

"Fresh and well-prepared. My compliments to the chef. And I thank you, Lord Rumford, for your generosity."

He beamed at the compliment. "The pleasure is all mine."

When he turned away, Hannah kicked my shin under the table. It didn't hurt so much, but it caught me off guard, and I choked on my drink.

"Are you all right?" she asked.

"Yes." I cleared my throat. "Thank you for your concern. It was most heartily felt."

"I am *so* glad." She shot me a mischievous look, and I glanced down at my plate so she could not see how thoroughly her attention affected me.

I wanted this, I realized. I wanted someone to dance the supper set with and to sit next to at the table. I wanted someone to laugh with me and scowl *at* me. I wanted to feel seen. It had been such a long time since someone had looked at me and not my title.

I loved that Hannah didn't smile sweetly at me or say what she thought I wanted her to say. To her, I was not the future Earl of Winfield. I was just Damon. With her, I *felt* like me.

After supper, I escorted her back to the ballroom and then turned toward the card room.

"Are you really not going to dance?" Hannah said, stopping me and glancing at all the unpartnered young ladies.

I felt a twinge of remorse. "I know that you yearn for my company," I said, trying to ease my discomfort by teasing her, "but you really should not be so forthright with your feelings. People will think we have formed an attachment." I winked. "Now that you have had a set with a future earl, I should think you will have more than enough willing partners to keep you occupied. Enjoy the rest of your ball, Miss Kent." I bowed.

She gave me a disappointed frown.

And as I walked away, I felt every inch the cad she likely thought me to be.

I slipped into the card room and found Fred. He handed me a drink as I sank into the seat beside him, and then I distracted myself with the game.

Only a few hands in, I won a particularly large pot. It felt good, I realized. Winning. For a moment, I'd forgotten what was bothering me. I'd forgotten Father's expectations, Mother's matchmaking, Ollie's disgust. I'd even forget Hannah's disappointment. For a few minutes, I'd felt nothing but the win, and I suddenly understood why Father found it addictive.

As my winnings were pushed into my pile, I glanced around the room. I didn't even realize what, or rather *whom*, I was looking for until my gaze landed on Father.

He was sitting on the far side of the room and had a similar stack of winnings. The sight was sobering.

I always thought I would make a better earl than he'd proved to be, if for no other reason than I was more evenly tempered. But as I sat there staring down at my stack of winnings, I saw the truth: if I continued as I was, I wouldn't become a better earl—I would become *him*.

Thoughts of whom I might become in the future plagued me all the way home from the ball. And by the time we arrived home, I was determined to do things differently, starting with Ollie.

I waited for the right moment to approach him, ensuring that Hannah and her father were up the stairs and out of sight. Then, mustering courage, I turned to Ollie. "Can we talk?" I asked.

He sighed. "I know you are vexed with me for making you stand up with Hannah, so you can spare me the lecture, *my lord*."

"I *am* vexed with you," I said. "But that is not the reason I want to speak with you."

Ollie studied me for a long moment. "Go on."

Knowing this conversation could either bridge the gap between us or widen it irreparably, I selected my words carefully and spoke from my heart. "I dislike what has become of us. I want to mend the rift in our relationship."

He narrowed his eyes, searching mine for sincerity. "I don't see how things could be any different between us," he said. "Our positions are unequal. You have everything, and I have nothing."

"My birthright brings with it many blessings," I agreed, trying to see the situation from his point of view. And then wanting him to understand mine, I added, "But in some ways, it is also a burden. My life is not my own. Every hour of every day, I am told where to go, what to do, even who to marry."

"And every day of *my* life, I am ignored and unnoticed," he countered as if this were a competition.

"I envy your freedom, brother."

"Freedom?" Ollie laughed. "You really don't get it, do you? I don't *want* freedom. I want to *belong*." He paused for a second, letting his statement sink in, then said bitterly, "You may not be free, but at least people care about you, Damon."

"As they do for you, Ollie."

He shook his head, pushing back against my perception. "You don't know how it feels to be born into a titled family, to be brought up in a life of leisure and luxury, but given no means to maintain that position in Society."

"No means?" I said. "You will always have an allowance from the earldom. And what about Winterset?"

"You mean my eventual banishment?" Ollie laughed humorlessly. "Yes, I suppose I should be grateful for that."

"You should be," I said despite his sarcasm. Society was not often kind to second sons, but our parents had provided for Ollie's future; upon his majority, he would inherit Winterset. "Most second sons are not so lucky."

"*Lucky?*" Ollie scoffed. "I daresay you would not say so if it were *you* who would one day be exiled to live so far from Society that you'd surely be forgotten."

"How can you think that? We could *never* forget you, Ollie."

"You forget me all the time," he said, his tone a mix of anguish and frustration. "Take tonight, for example: the whole family sat at the head of the table, but I had to sit separately at the foot. Do you have any idea how that feels?" he said, and his words continued pouring out, cutting off any response I might have made. "You don't. You couldn't possibly. Because *your* place in Society and in our family is assured. Mine is not."

I stared at him in disbelief. "Is *that* why you rejected Hannah to dance with Miss Digby tonight? You want to marry a wealthy young woman?" It was well-known that Miss Digby had a decent dowry, and although many men married for money, I thought my brother was above the practice.

Ollie said nothing in reply, but his guilty expression confirmed my suspicion.

"Ollie." I shook my head, disappointed. "How could you do that to Hannah? You hurt her deeply and risked her reputation."

He hung his head. "I feel terrible for that. Truly, I do. But I must do everything I can to secure my future. Mother should not have meddled and made me dance with Hannah."

"She should not have," I agreed, knowing how it felt to be on the receiving end of her matchmaking schemes. "But *you* agreed to the set, and I daresay in doing so, you made Hannah believe you cared for her."

"I have done *nothing* to make Hannah believe I hold any affection for her beyond friendship. If anything, I have discouraged it. So don't you dare judge me for dancing with Miss Digby, Damon. I am only trying to secure a place for myself in the only life I have ever known."

Ollie's words hung in the air, heavy with the weight of his frustrations.

And when he retreated up the stairs, my chest ached, knowing that the division between us had only deepened.

CHAPTER SEVEN

THE NEXT MORNING, HANNAH DIDN'T come down to breakfast, so naturally, I went to investigate.

As I approached her bedchamber, I slowed my steps, not wanting to startle her, and peeked inside. Hannah held up two bonnets, squinting at them as though she were trying to decide which to wear.

I stood at the threshold, watching her. "Wear the blue," I said.

Hannah looked up in surprise, and when she saw me, her face fell.

Not the effect I normally had on women, but it was strangely refreshing. "What are you doing?" I asked.

"Packing," she said and handed the blue bonnet to her maid.

It was then that I noticed her traveling trunk. "Yes, I can see that. Why?"

"Because that is what one does when one intends to travel."

My stomach dropped. "You're leaving?" Mr. Kent had to return home to care for his parishioners, of course, but Hannah was supposed to stay all summer. She couldn't leave. Not yet.

"How observant of you, my lord. You had best leave me to pack. If Papa and I are to reach the inn by nightfall, I must make haste."

Seeing as I did not want her to leave, I leaned against the doorframe.

"It is a shame this will go unused," Hannah said to her maid, staring down at her riding habit. "I was so looking forward to riding the hills."

"Perhaps you should stay, then," I suggested.

Hannah sighed in irritation. "What is it you want, Damon?"

"Originally, I wanted to inquire why you didn't join us in the breakfast room this morning. But seeing as that question has been answered, I'm now here to stop you from leaving."

She frowned. "My mind is made up."

Perhaps it could be *un*made. How, I wasn't sure yet. I just knew I didn't want her to leave, so I made quick work of dismissing her maid and stepped into her room to argue my point. "I had hoped, after last night, that we'd made some progress repairing our relationship," I admitted.

"Asking me to dance was the act of a gentleman, and I thank you for that."

"But . . . ?"

She pinned me with a hard stare. "You made me eat frog legs, and I should never forgive you for that."

The corner of my mouth twitched with a smile. I loved her feistiness. "May I speak candidly?"

"I would prefer it."

It was then that rain began pelting the window. Hannah ran over to it and stared outside for a long moment. When she trudged back to her trunk, she seemed more than a little forlorn.

"Something occurred to me last night during dinner," I said.

"What is that?"

"I will tell you, but first, answer me this: Why did you come to Summerhaven?"

"Because your mother invited me."

I bobbled my head from side to side. Technically, that was true. "But why did *you* accept her invitation?"

"I wanted to be away from the chaos of city life. London can be quite stifling."

I knew something of how she felt. During the Season, I often felt like I might suffocate in London. But again, "That is not why you came. You are here because you wish to marry Ollie."

She gasped, seemingly surprised by my audacity, though she should not have been. "My feelings are much changed after last night," she said.

"Would that that were true, but alas, your feelings for my addled brother are *not* changed. It is only your pride that has been wounded."

Her face pinched with annoyance, and I felt like a fly buzzing in her face that she wished she could shew away. "I'd thank you to leave my room now."

"Don't be cross. I did *try* to warn you."

"What is it you want?" Hannah asked again.

"Your help."

She raised an eyebrow at me in question. "How exactly do you want me to help you?"

"I want you to allow *me* to court you."

She snorted in amusement. "You cannot be serious."

"I assure you, I am in earnest," I said. But she did not seem to believe me, so I explained, "My father is intent that I marry by the year's end. He's seen fit to parade every eligible young woman in this part of the country in front of me in hopes that I'll choose a wife. But if I pretend *you* have caught my eye, that I intend to court *you*, I would not have to court another, you see?"

Technically, that was true. Although my *real* reason for wanting Hannah to stay and allow me to court her had nothing to do with Father and everything to do with my feelings for her. I cared for Hannah, and I hoped she might come to care for me too.

"Oh yes. I *do* see . . . But I will only be here a short time. When I leave, you will be no better off than you are now. Your father will still demand that you court and marry another young woman, will he not?"

Again, I shrugged, and then the strangest thing happened: her gaze roamed over my form—her eyes widening ever so slightly as they slid over the slope of my shoulders—and then she swallowed hard as though she *liked* what she saw.

I *wanted* her to like what she saw. "Much can change in a short period of time," I said.

"Perhaps . . . but I still don't see how our pretending to court would help *me*."

"You wound me." I held one hand to my chest. "But to answer your question, Ollie has always wanted what's mine. If he thought *you* were mine—"

She held up a hand, stopping me. "Ollie is not so juvenile."

He *was* that juvenile and also predictable. I'd bet almost anything that he'd come back to scratch after I retreated to the card room last night. "Ollie came around to you only *after* we'd danced at the Rumfords' ball," I guessed, and Hannah confirmed my suspicion when she bit her lip. "My hypothesis," I continued, "is that when Ollie sees us spending time together, he will become green with envy, just like at the ball, and he will rush in to steal you away from me."

She sighed as though my plan were silly. "There is only one problem with your plan."

"Only one?" I could think of several. "Pray, tell me."

"We don't *like* each other."

"I like you just fine, Miss Kent. That said, many couples don't like each other."

"That may be, but such courtships are generally based on mutual benefit." She returned to the window and pulled back the curtain. She stared outside for a long moment, then sighed and sat on the window seat, crossing her arms in frustration.

"I see you're not convinced," I said.

"It is good to know your eyesight is working properly."

I walked to the window seat. "My plan *would* work, Hannah."

"It would not." She stood from the window seat and pushed past me. "Don't be absurd."

"Absurd?" I bristled at the word. Father had called me absurd so many times over the past months that it was practically part of my identity. But what was so *absurd* to her about me courting her? I followed her to her trunk, standing closer than I should, and lowered my voice. "To say that your affections could have moved on to Ollie's titled and obviously more handsome older brother? Yes. That *would* be absurd."

"Nobody would believe our courtship," she said seriously.

"The Rumfords' ball was a good demonstration of my preference for you, was it not?"

"Must I spell it out for you?" she said. "No one would believe that *you*—a titled gentleman—would be interested in *me*—a woman of no consequence. Perhaps if I stood to inherit a substantial fortune, but I do not."

"Not all marriages are based upon mutual financial benefit. What if what people saw was a love match?"

She dropped her gaze to her slippers. "I'm no great beauty."

"If you believe *that*, perhaps you should have your eyesight checked."

She peeked up at me and gave me a small smile, but then she immediately sequestered herself in thought again, setting a hand on her stomach.

"You look as if you're about to reject your breakfast," I said.

"I suppose it's fortunate for your boots that I did not make it to the breakfast room this morning," she teased me back.

"Quite," I agreed, earning another soft smile.

A long moment passed before she said, "I'm sorry, but I'm going to go home with Papa as soon as the weather permits."

I waited a moment for her to recant her decision, and when she did not, I strode to the door, pausing on the threshold. "I didn't think you had it in you to give up so easily."

"I don't believe your plan will work."

I wasn't sure that the plan I'd proposed to her would work either. I just needed my *actual* plan to work—the plan where she didn't leave my life this morning in a carriage with her father. I desperately needed her to believe me so she would stay. I glanced down the corridor to buy myself a moment to think, and an idea hit me. At least it would give me another day and evening with her. I stepped back into the room. "Let me show you that it will. We will stage an experiment."

Hannah looked wary but curious, so I continued, making it up as I went. "Tonight, after dinner, I'll demonstrate my preference for you, and you will respond to my advances. I will prove to you that a pretend attachment between us will open Ollie's eyes to you. If my plan works, you stay. If it doesn't—"

"I will leave." She quietly pondered my proposal. "Forgive me if I'm wary of your experiments." She smoothed the ringlets framing her face behind her ears, and the talisman I always carried grew heavy in my pocket.

"I saved you at Rumfords' ball," I said. "You owe me this much."

"I owe you nothing," she said, frowning. "One measly set does not make up for an entire childhood of torture."

"Torture?" We'd had an unfortunate parting, to be sure, but *torture*? Really?

"I could hardly call it otherwise." She raised her chin and glanced purposefully at her trunk and then again at me, but for the life of me, I didn't know what she meant by it.

I shook my head. "Call it what you will. The fact remains that until the rain stops and the roads have dried, you are stuck here."

Slowly, she nodded. "You have one night."

"Dinner was delicious," Mr. Kent said to Father as we sat in the drawing room that night.

"Our chef is from France," Father boasted. "He studied under the same master as the prince regent's chef. Isn't that right, my dear?"

"I hardly remember," Mother said modestly. "Shall we have some music on the pianoforte this evening?"

"Splendid idea," Father said a bit too boisterously and coughed. "I would be delighted to hear you play, my dear."

Mother played a lively sonata, during which Hannah kept sneaking glances at Ollie.

I sighed and stood from my seat on the sofa. "Miss Kent?" I said, blocking her view of him. "Would you care to join me for a game of chess?"

"I'm sorry," she blinked up at me. "What did you say?"

"I asked if you would care to join me in a game of chess." I gestured to a small table where a chessboard was set.

"She doesn't want to play with you, Damon," Ollie said. How he heard me from where he stood at the hearth, I had no idea.

"On the contrary," Hannah said. "A game of chess sounds delightful."

"But you hate games of chance," Ollie said.

I internally rolled my eyes. Chess was not a game of chance.

"Chess is not a game of chance," Hannah said.

Ha! Just as I'd thought!

"It's one of strategy," she continued. "One I very much enjoy, given the right opponent."

She allowed me to lead her to the table and assist her with her chair.

"What manners," she said. "Thank you."

"I know this may be surprising to you, but *some* women find me charming," I said as I walked around the table and settled into my seat.

"You are correct," she said.

"That I'm charming?" I waggled my eyebrows at her.

"No." She laughed. "That I find it surprising."

I frowned and pointed at her side of the board. "White goes first."

"As I'm well aware. You have no need to explain the rules." She studied the board as though considering her first move, and *I* considered how I might engage her in conversation.

"Do you know the history of this game?" I asked.

"No," she said, moving a pawn two spaces forward. "But I expect you're about to tell me."

"Indeed." I smiled at her snarkiness and told her what I knew of the history. Miraculously, that led to one of my favorite topics: political reformation, which seemed to interest her too.

As we talked, Ollie took notice.

"Don't look now," I said, "but it seems our experiment is working. Ollie is beside himself with jealousy."

"Truly?" Hannah started to turn.

"I said *don't* look." I glanced at Ollie, and when he looked away, I nodded to Hannah that it was safe to peek.

She did so and seemed sad. "Do you really think Ollie will marry Miss Digby?" she asked.

"Her or someone like her," I said. "If you leave now, he will have no reason not to."

She considered this at length. "Does your offer still stand?" she asked finally.

"Yes."

"You must desperately wish to avoid marriage. Is the institution so bad that you'd truly welcome this arrangement?"

"You have no idea the lengths I'd go to subvert my father," I said, though that was not the point of this charade.

"Then, perhaps we should discuss the terms," she said.

My heart squeezed with surprise and anticipation. Was she really about to agree to my ruse? "You needn't worry over trifles. I shall be the most doting beau." I would shower her with affection, publicly if she permitted.

"Until you are not," she said. "I do believe the siren song of the card tables may prove too strong a temptation for you to keep your promises."

"You think so little of me?"

She gave a partial shrug. "Half a dozen ladies at Lord Rumford's ball tried to catch your eye, yet you did not dance with a single one."

"I danced with you, did I not?"

"You rescued me. It is different."

"Hmm." I returned my gaze to the game, afraid she might see the same look in my eyes that I'd seen on her face when Ollie had walked away from her: desperation. I could feel her teetering on the edge of agreeing to stay. I couldn't let her see how much her decision meant to me.

"You are a man," she explained. "And I've learned of late that a man's heart is as changeable as the weather in England."

"Ollie's heart had little to do with his decision, I'm afraid."

"Yes, well . . . Forgive me if I don't want to be slighted by both Jennings men in one summer."

I would rather die than slight her. "I would never. But to ease your mind, we should promise to only have eyes for one another. I will not entertain advances from other women, and you won't fawn over Ollie."

"I do not *fawn*."

"You do, but you must not if this is to work. You and I must appear to be interested only in each other." How I loathed watching her flirt with my undeserving brother.

She frowned. "If we have eyes only for each other, then how will I encourage Ollie to propose?"

"You won't have to encourage him," I said. "In having eyes only for me, you will drive Ollie so mad with jealousy that it will be impossible for him not to recognize the depth of his feelings for you. I expect he will be so besotted with you by the end of summer that you will receive the engagement you desire."

"And what happens to you when our charade is over? If you were to pretend to court me and then I refuse you for your younger brother, people would talk. No mother in her right mind would allow her daughter within a hundred paces of you."

"That is the point," I said.

"You must promise me, Damon. You can't reject me when our arrangement no longer suits you. Being courted and then rejected by an earl—"

"I am not an earl," I interrupted.

"Not yet, but you will be. And should you show interest in me and then snub me, that would be enough to ruin my reputation."

"I'd sooner marry you. You have my word as a gentleman; the responsibility of ending our ruse will be left to you alone to execute."

"Then, I agree to your terms."

I breathed a sigh of relief that when Mr. Kent left tomorrow morning, Hannah would not be going with him. "I promise you won't regret this," I swore and hoped to heaven that she wouldn't.

CHAPTER EIGHT

THE NEXT MORNING, UPON MR. Kent's departure, I was driven to distraction. Last night, Hannah had agreed to stay at Summerhaven and participate in my ridiculous ruse, but this morning, she seemed despondent.

"Lady Rumford and her daughter are coming to tea today," Mother said over breakfast.

"Oh . . . how nice," Hannah said, but she did not seem to mean it.

Perhaps her melancholy was due to her father's leaving for London this morning. Or possibly her low spirits were owed to Ollie's declining to dance with her at the ball. I hoped it was not because she regretted our charade.

I didn't.

"I must confess," Hannah said, "I'd forgotten about Lady Rumford and her daughter coming to tea. Damon invited me to ride the hills on horseback this morning."

I smiled. I couldn't help it. I *loved* hearing the sound of my name on her lips.

Father did not.

He lowered *The Morning Post*, the crisp paper crinkling in his hands, and looked hard at Hannah. "I am afraid *Damon* is unavailable, Miss Kent."

"I don't recall being previously engaged, Father. You must excuse me from the meeting as I have urgent business of my own this morning." I winked at Hannah.

Father frowned. "More important than seeing to matters of your future estate?" he challenged.

To be honest, I could not think of anything more important than riding with Hannah this morning. Certainly, nothing more that I wanted to do. "No."

Father coughed deeply into his napkin, and when he recovered, he continued, "You will reschedule your business and attend my morning meeting with Mr. Bancroft."

"I'd rather not."

"Must I compel you in *all* matters?" Father's tone turned dangerous.

"No."

"Quite right," Father said, turning his attention back to his plate, effectively ending our conversation.

Father and Mr. Bancroft were already seated when I entered the study. Father frowned and motioned for me to take the chair beside Mr. Bancroft.

Mr. Bancroft had been Father's steward for as long as I could remember. I liked him well enough—he was loyal and wise—but he was stuck in the past. He had a particular way of doing things and did not stray from it.

"Damon will be taking over more of the day-to-day duties," Father said to the steward, surprising me as I took my seat.

Mr. Bancroft nodded. "Very well."

"Damon was able to get the overdue rent from the Turners," Father said.

"Oh?" Mr. Bancroft said, sounding surprised. "Where did Mr. Turner find such a sum?"

I tensed. Father was disconnected from the day-to-day duties. He'd never liked associating too closely with his tenants—*A gentleman should keep his distance,* he always said—but Mr. Bancroft was more intimately involved.

"Don't know," I said with a shrug. "Does it matter?"

Mr. Bancroft eyed me as though trying to discern how I'd succeeded where he'd failed, then shook his head. "I suppose it doesn't matter, so long as he continues making payments."

"When is the next payment due?" Father asked.

Mr. Bancroft consulted a ledger. "Michaelmas, my lord."

"Damon, make sure Mr. Turner knows his next payment is due by Michaelmas and not a day later."

"I will. But there is something else I'd like to discuss before I do." I hadn't forgotten my promise to Mr. Turner to provide him with thatch. Father motioned for me to continue. "The Turners need a new roof. I'm sure there is a reason for the oversight, but it should be rectified immediately."

"You wish me to provide a new roof to an unprofitable tenant?" Father scoffed.

"I do." Just because Mr. Turner had not lived up to his end of the contract did not mean Father should not hold up his. The Turners were our tenants, and we were responsible for their welfare.

Father's face was red with anger, but he held his tongue in front of Mr. Bancroft.

I needed to try a new angle to get him to agree to the new roof. I'd pricked his pride, but I needed to appeal to his pocketbook.

"Even if the Turners are evicted," I said. "The cottage roof would still need to be replaced before it could be let to new tenants."

Mr. Bancroft nodded in agreement. And Father's expression drained of contempt and filled with curiosity.

"If you will allow it," I said, "I will make arrangements for thatch to be delivered to them as soon as possible, and I will ask Mr. Turner to install it."

"Do not ask," Father said. "*Insist*. It is the least he can do to deserve it."

Although I disagreed vehemently that our tenants should have to do anything to *deserve* what I deemed a basic human right, I considered it a win that Father did not outright deny me the assistance.

After the meeting, I found Hannah in the drawing room having tea with Mother, Lady Rumford, and her daughter, Miss Atherton. It took some convincing, but Mother finally allowed me to steal Hannah for our ride.

Still, it took some time for Hannah to change into her riding habit. So long that I wondered whether she'd changed her mind.

Pacing the entrance hall, I checked my pocket watch. Nearly an hour had passed. How much longer should I wait? Perhaps this was payback for making her eat frog legs.

I was nearly ready to walk up to her room to check on her health when, at last, she started down the stairs.

"Ah, Miss Kent. There you are. I was beginning to think you'd changed your mind about joining me for a ride."

"Not at all, my lord. A woman just needs time to prepare."

"Napoleon could have prepared an entire regiment for war in the time it took you to get ready."

Her eyes widened in the most adorable way. "You don't truly mean to compare me to such an abhorrent man as *Napoleon*, do you?"

"The analogy felt appropriate." I shrugged.

I was happy to finally have a private moment alone with her—we'd hardly said two words since she'd agreed to our ruse—but she was quiet as we walked toward the stableyard.

"Are your baskets full?" I asked her.

"Pardon?"

"You were woolgathering," I said. "What has commanded your attention so completely?"

"It is nothing," she said, setting her gaze on the expanse of lawn before us.

But even looking at her sideways, I saw her cheeks redden. "You are a terrible liar." I brushed my gloved fingers across her cheek, and she swatted me away.

"If you must know, I was only admiring the fine cut of your coat."

As much as I wanted to believe that was true, I knew better. "Truly terrible." I shook my head in mock disappointment. "You should not even try."

She bit her lip, then blurted, "I told Amelia of our arrangement."

I'd thought things felt funny in the drawing room but had brushed it off. "I cannot guess at your strategy. May I ask *why* you told her?"

"She was kind to me at the ball, and we became fast friends," Hannah explained. "It did not feel right keeping this information from her, not after she confided in me."

"What did she confide in you?"

"You must know she has set her cap for you," Hannah said.

"If *that* is your criteria for deciding who should know of our plan, then I fear you will have to tell every young lady in England of our scheme."

She rolled her eyes. "You are the most arrogant man with whom I have ever conversed."

I had not meant to brag—young ladies' attention was not something I enjoyed nor was proud of—but I could see how Hannah might think so.

"Are you angry with me for telling Amelia?" she said, sounding worried.

"Anger is a rather unbecoming emotion."

"You did not answer my question."

"I am not angry, but I do hope Miss Atherton is a better liar than you have proved." My plan depended on it.

When we finally reached the stable, I tucked her hand into the crook of my arm and led Hannah inside. Ollie stood in the long corridor, conversing with a groom.

"Brother," I called.

Ollie turned and took in Hannah's riding habit. "I forgot you were riding together today."

Did he? "I'm surprised our readied horses didn't serve as a reminder."

"Yes, well . . ." Ollie cleared his throat. "Seeing as there are two *stallions* saddled and no gentle mare, I could hardly have been expected to remember."

"I see no issue," I said.

"Are you daft?" Ollie frowned. "Hannah cannot ride a stallion."

"Whyever not?" Hannah stepped forward, and I caught a glimpse of the girl who had never backed down from a challenge.

"Because you are a woman. It is not safe, much less proper," Ollie said, and she gave him a fierce glare.

"It is plenty safe," I reassured her.

"But not proper," Ollie said, and I saw her shrink.

"What is *your* preference?" I asked Hannah. "The stallion or the mare?"

"I . . ." Her sentence hung in the air for far too long. "Though I appreciate your faith in me, Damon, Ollie is correct. I'm not so accomplished on horseback. I should be happy to ride the mare."

"A wise and proper choice," Ollie said to her, then gave me a gloating grin.

"I quite disagree," I said, excusing myself to instruct the stablehand.

Hannah and Ollie continued in quiet conversation. I could not hear what they said, but it looked intense. As soon as I rejoined them, Ollie excused himself. What I wouldn't give to see us all friends again.

Outside, the stablehand waited with our horses—Ares and Andromeda.

Hannah frowned at her horse. Compared to Ares, Andromeda was short and squat. Hannah stepped onto the mounting block with a sigh, and the groom assisted her into the saddle.

We rode out of the stableyard together toward the hills. I tried to engage Hannah in conversation, to which she said, "Perhaps we should improve the ride with silence."

"I would rather we speak."

"Conversing was not part of our deal."

"True enough. Shall we wager for it?" I suggested.

Hannah frowned her disapproval. "Can you not leave gambling to the tables?"

"I *can*, but for reasons you needn't concern yourself with, I choose not to."

"Then, we are at an impasse. I do not wager."

"A friendly race, then. To the crest." I pointed to the top of a grassy knoll in the distance. "Whoever reaches it first will decide the topic of conversation—or lack thereof—for the rest of our ride."

She glanced at the crest, then said, "I accept," and kicked Andromeda's flank.

I followed fast behind her for a few moments, then pulled even beside her. I grinned at her for a long moment, then shot ahead to cross the finish line first.

"Conversation it is. When did you first know you were in love with my brother?"

She sighed in obvious annoyance at the question. "It was the end of my twelfth summer. We were standing under the old oak tree saying goodbye; he kissed my hand and then my cheek, and . . . I just knew."

"Is that all it takes for you to fall in love with a man? A kiss on your hand?"

"*And* my cheek."

"Had I known it was so easy . . ." I might have skipped suggesting a charade and jumped straight to kissing her. I laughed under my breath.

"You mock me." Her mouth tilted into a frown in the most adorable display of annoyance. "You have no doubt given and received many kisses. I probably seem foolish or naive to someone like you."

"Someone like me?" I raised an eyebrow.

"An heir to an earldom must have an endless supply of willing women to kiss."

"Ah, yes. The title is quite attractive to your sex. Though to be fair, many women find my estate more alluring."

"Do you deny it?"

"Most emphatically. I am not the libertine you imagine me to be."

"Perhaps not, but Ollie would have let me win the race to the crest."

"Had you ridden the stallion instead of the mare, you would not have needed me to let you win. You could have won on your own merit."

She shot me a severe look and then stared straight ahead. We rode in silence for several minutes, and when I could no longer stand it, I said, "What are you thinking?"

"I was wondering what it would be like to live every day in such a paradise."

"Purgatory," I said before I could stop myself.

She looked sidelong at me. "Do you hate Summerhaven?"

"I will confess to disliking what she requires me to be."

"What does she require you to be?"

"My father's son and heir."

Her brow pulled together. "Why would you hate that?"

"You would not understand."

"Because I'm a *woman*?" she all but spat.

Earlier in the stable, she'd tried to hide her irritation, but I *knew* what Ollie had said bothered her.

"No." I gave her a pointed look. "Because you have a father who adores you."

"As do you."

"As I said before, you would not understand."

"Explain it to me."

I hesitated. Not because I didn't want to tell Hannah how I felt but because I did. More than I should.

"If your father is strict," she said, "it is only because he wants you to be the best lord you can be."

Father wanted me to be him. "You should not speak about things you know nothing about." I searched for a new subject. "Was that your mother's ring?" I nodded toward her hand.

"It was," she said softly. "Papa gave the gold band to her on their wedding day, and this emerald was taken from her favorite necklace." Hannah got a nostalgic look on her face when she told me the story of how she'd come to inherit it.

"It's beautiful," I said. "I remember how close you were. I am sorry for your loss."

Hannah's eyes filled with tears, and I had the most intense urge to leap from my mount and brush them away. But Hannah quickly blinked them away instead. And then, as if wanting to escape her emotions, or perhaps wanting to escape *me*, she nudged Andromeda into a trot and then faster into a canter. But still, she seemed unsatisfied.

"Give your horse her head," I shouted.

Hannah relaxed her grip on the reins, and Andromeda sprang forward.

I followed at a distance, wanting to give Hannah space, but then she smiled over her shoulder at me in an open way that made me think she might want to share this moment with me, and I pulled even with her. Together, we raced over hills and through valleys. She was brilliant like this—unguarded and unrestrained.

Her hair escaped her bonnet, and her face held a fierce expression. I remembered this look well. As a child, whenever she was determined to do something, her mouth set and her eyes focused.

I couldn't look away.

She smiled at me over her shoulder once again. I'd always loved riding these hills. Ares had heightened my experience, but now, riding with Hannah, I soared with happiness.

When we finally slowed, she said, "You are a skilled rider."

"Flattery will not soften me into letting you win our next race."

"Not *flattery*"—she smiled—"an observation. You really are talented."

I straightened in my saddle, unsure how to respond to her softness. I liked how it felt, and I did not wish to do anything to discourage it. "My skill, if I possess any at all, is merely a product of my education." I glanced forward and grimaced. *A product of my education?*

"No one can ride the way you do without some degree of passion."

"You wish to speak of passion, do you?"

But she didn't back down. "You love horses. It is as plain as day. Why deny it?"

"Horses can only ever be a pastime, not a passion." No matter what interest I might have, no matter what talent I might possess, I was only allowed to be one thing: an earl.

"Well, he is beautiful. What breed is he?"

"A Friesian." I rubbed Ares's neck. "I won him at the tables and decided to keep him for myself."

"As opposed to . . . ?"

I glanced at her in question. "Pardon?"

"You said you decided to keep him for yourself, as opposed to what?"

"Oh." I stilled. I'd almost inadvertently exposed that I was currently gambling to earn money for my tenants. "Nothing."

Though she still seemed curious, she let the subject drop.

We slipped back into silence, but it felt comfortable, and as we roamed the hills, my mind wandered back to a time when I used to dream of running away. Sometimes, I still dreamed of it, but now I knew better. No matter how far I might go, I could not outrun my title's obligation. I huffed a laugh.

"Something funny?" Hannah said.

"I was just remembering when I was a boy. I once planned to run away and ride across all of Europe. Rome, Spain, Greece . . ."

She smiled. "What stopped you?"

"You mean, besides England's confinement to an island and being forever at war?"

"Yes." She smiled. "Besides that."

I glanced at her sidelong. She seemed in earnest. If I told her the truth about how heavy the weight of my eventual earldom was, how I wasn't sure I even wanted it, would she understand? "*Conservabo ad mortem*," I said quietly, but as soon as the words were out of my mouth, I thought better of it. Hannah already thought me conceited, and I had no wish to add to her list of reasons to dislike me. "Perhaps you're right." I gave her an easy smile. "Perhaps I do enjoy horseflesh. Let us give our mounts their heads again." And then I spurred Ares into a gallop.

Hannah followed suit, riding right beside me. I liked how it felt to have her here. To have a companion—if only for a moment.

We rode side by side for a long while. And when I finally slowed, I looked at Hannah. She was grinning.

"Never in all my life have I felt so wild, so *free*," she said. Wisps of hair had escaped her bonnet and were blowing gently in the breeze.

"Freedom," I repeated. "Incredible feeling, isn't it?"

"Yes," she agreed, and we shared a private smile. Something shifted between us in that moment. A silent conversation—a seeing and being seen. It was a heady feeling, and I was certain she felt it too. How could she not? It was a soft sensation but powerful. I think it scared her, though, because her expression suddenly shuttered, and her jaw set as she looked away.

"We should return our horses to the stables," she said stoically. "There is no one near to witness our charade, so we need not endure any more time in each other's company."

"Is *that* what we were doing?" Her words stung more than they should have. Perhaps I'd gotten carried away in our charade, but I felt something for Hannah. And I could be mistaken, but I thought she might be starting to feel something for me too. Still, I would not force her to stay with me, so I guided us back the way we'd come.

The rest of the afternoon, I licked my wounds. How had I botched things so thoroughly? Today, I'd been given a taste of what it might be like to not be alone, of what it would feel like to have a partner, and I wanted to feel it forever. I wanted *her*.

Perhaps she was having second thoughts about our agreement. If she gave up on it, she would leave. How could I convince her to stay?

I would apologize. I would tell Hannah I was sorry for making her uncomfortable. I would flirt less and listen more, and she would stay. She *had* to stay, if only for the summer.

But that night, she didn't come down for dinner, opting to take a tray in her room instead. She was avoiding me, and I hated it.

Hoping to make recompense, I picked her a bouquet of lavender, and wanting to respect her privacy and decision to be alone, I intercepted the maid delivering Hannah's dinner tray and bid her deliver it. When Hannah saw the bouquet, I hoped she would know how much I wanted her here. I hoped she would choose to stay.

CHAPTER NINE

AFTER MY MEETING WITH MR. Bancroft, I'd sent a missive to Mr. Turner, asking him to meet me in town so that I might give him money to support his family through this bleak time. Having overheard Mother and Hannah's plans to meet Lady Rumford and Miss Atherton at the modiste, it was the perfect cover.

I found Hannah in the garden. Or rather, I *heard* her in the garden with Ollie. I stopped short before they saw me and remained around a corner, out of sight.

"I'm asking you to dance with me," Ollie said. "To make up for the one I missed."

I rolled my eyes, but perhaps this would work to my favor. Ollie was behaving as predicted, showing interest in what I had. I hoped it was enough to convince Hannah to stay and continue our charade.

"We shouldn't," Hannah said. "What if someone sees us? It could ruin both our reputations."

"You never cared about things like that before."

"There are a great many things I did not care about before. But again, we are grown and must act like it."

"You are even beginning to *sound* like Damon," Ollie said.

"If that is true, then your brother is wiser than I've given him credit for."

I smiled at that and wondered whether she thought it true or if she'd said it for the sake of the charade.

"Damon is a great many things, but he is not *wise*," Ollie said.

"Don't say that. Your brother has been kind to me."

"My brother is opportunistic. Do not mistake that for kindness."

There was a long stretch of silence, and I walked away, not wanting to hear anymore. It hurt how much he hated me.

It was not long before the carriage was brought around, and I heard Mother descending the stairs. I waited another moment, then walked outside, timing my entrance perfectly.

A footman had just handed up Mother and Hannah into the carriage and closed the door. He startled when he turned and saw me standing behind him. "Pardon me," I said and opened the carriage door.

"Mother. Hannah," I said, smiling. "Might I accompany you ladies into town? I must see to some business."

"We would be delighted." Mother moved to make room, but Hannah did not. Why was she so set against me? "Do you think you can *endure* my company, Miss Kent?"

She frowned but said, "I can endure it, my lord. I have a strong constitution."

My mouth twitched with amusement, and I climbed into the carriage, taking the rear-facing seat across from the ladies. I knocked on the roof to alert the driver, and we were on our way.

"You look lovely this morning, Hannah," I said and meant it. "I trust you slept well?"

"I did," she said shortly, and I realized it would take some work to coax her from her thoughts today.

As we continued toward town, Mother brought up mine and Hannah's horseback ride and reminded us of the importance of having a chaperone now that we were adults. Hannah seemed embarrassed, and I apologized, but she remained out of countenance.

I searched for something to say to set her at ease, but then the carriage jolted, and I realized perhaps she wasn't feeling uncomfortable but sick.

"Perhaps I misspoke earlier," I said. "Hannah, your pallor is . . . dare I say, green?"

"Damon," Mother scolded. "That is no way to speak to a woman."

"He is correct," Hannah said, setting her hand on her stomach. "How much farther to town?"

"Only a short distance more," Mother said.

Hannah nodded and turned her attention out the window.

Mother continued chattering, but my attention stayed on Hannah. Carriages did not seem to agree with her. I wished there were something I could do to make her feel better. Perhaps there was . . .

When we arrived in town, I quickly alighted and reached for Hannah's hand to help her. She hesitantly slipped her hand into mine, and as soon as she stepped down, she snatched her hand back. I shook my head amused, then assisted Mother.

Mother inquired after Hannah's health, and with Hannah's reassurance that she was well, Mother moved in the direction of the modiste, but I held Hannah back.

"For our charade to be effective, we must be seen together."

"We rode together yesterday."

"Privately," I said. "And while that may work for your purposes, we must be seen together publicly for our bargain to work to *my* advantage." I touched the brim of my hat and walked away to find Mr. Turner.

I'd told him to meet me across the lane from the modiste. The location was near the edge of town but not so obscure as to be odd.

The banknotes sat heavy in my pocket. I'd wrapped them in paper and tied them together with twine. This way, if someone happened to see me give them to him, they would not know what it was they were actually seeing.

I glanced down the lane but did not see the tenant. Not wanting to loiter and cause speculation, I used the free moment to visit the confectioners. I bought what I needed, and when I stepped back outside, I saw Mr. Turner coming down the lane.

"Mr. Turner," I nodded in greeting.

He bowed his head in respect. "M'lord."

"I trust you are well?"

"I am, sir."

"And your family?"

"They will be fine, thanks to you."

Not wanting to prolong our conversation for fear of gossip, I glanced around for onlookers, then produced the stack of banknotes from my coat. I dipped my shoulder to prevent the exchange from being seen.

Mr. Turner peeled back the paper, and his eyes widened when he saw the stack of banknotes.

"Put that away, Mr. Turner," I said, and he quickly did so. "See that you spend it wisely."

"I will, m'lord. You won't be sorry." He disappeared down a nearby alley, and I glanced around for onlookers.

I straightened my cravat and then my cuffs, which were suddenly constraining, and stepped back into the lane, pretending nothing underhanded had occurred.

But it had.

I only hoped no one had seen.

Then, seemingly appearing out of thin air, Mrs. Digby and her daughter Miss Digby approached.

Lud. If I had been paying attention, I could have crossed the lane to avoid the interaction, but it was too late now. We'd locked eyes, and I could not avoid them, no matter how much I might wish it.

"Lord Jennings." Mrs. Digby grinned. "What an unexpected pleasure."

"Indeed, madam."

"What brings you to town today?"

"Business," I said simply, hoping that if I did nothing to further the conversation, it would end.

"Ah, yes." Mrs. Digby nodded. "I'm sure such a grand and beautiful estate like Summerhaven would require a considerable amount of your time and attention."

"Hmm." I nodded. If she only knew how little Father trusted me to do with it, she would not be smiling at me with stars in her eyes.

"It is a pity you have no one to help you shoulder the load. A wife to confide in."

Right on cue, Miss Digby smiled up at me, batting her long lashes. I hated to notice, but she was lovely with her blonde ringlets and bright-blue eyes. Too bad I preferred brunettes with brownish-green eyes.

Thinking of Hannah, I smiled. The Digbys must have taken it to mean something else though, because they became even more brazen.

Stepping closer, Mrs. Digby lowered her voice. "My darling Daphne is quite talented. She can sing a lovely serenade and paint a calming picture. And when the time comes, she will be a wonderful mother; with four younger siblings, she has developed a patient and nurturing demeanor."

I blinked, stunned. Matchmaking mothers had always paraded their daughters in front of me like show ponies in hopes of catching my eye. But *this* was something else entirely. It was as though I'd stepped into the stableyard at Tattersall's, and Mrs. Digby was attempting to auction off her daughter to me on this very street. How *inhumane.*

Poor Miss Digby.

I'd often considered my own plight in the Marriage Market, but I'd rarely glanced at it from a young ladies' point of view. I did not like being seen for *what* I was, but at least I had a choice. I could not say as much for young ladies such as Miss Digby.

Uneasy, I glanced around, searching for some way to extricate myself from my current situation, and it was then that I saw Hannah and Miss Atherton staring at me through the modiste window across the street. The curtains quickly closed, but they'd seen me.

Had they seen anything more? I hoped not, but the modiste window was directly across the lane from where I'd given Mr. Turner the money, and they had, therefore, had a clear view.

If they *had* seen, how would I explain? I couldn't tell them about Mr. Turner's situation without offending their delicate sensibilities, but I also could not say that I was secretly helping him for fear of Father's retribution.

"Ah, Miss Kent, Miss Atherton," I greeted them as they approached. "I've been expecting you." I indicated the modiste's shop window, so she knew I'd seen her watching me.

"Lord Jennings." Miss Atherton curtsied in greeting, but Hannah was frowning down at the mud, which her boot seemed stuck in.

I fought a smile and failed. "May I assist you, Miss Kent?" I offered her my hand.

"Yes," she said, and her willing touch surprised me in the best way. "Thank you." She smiled up at me, and it was then that I realized it was all for show. I'd told Hannah we needed to demonstrate our interest in one another publicly, and here she was coming to my aid.

I released a breath, more disappointed than I had any right to be.

"It was my pleasure," I said, returning my attention to the Digbys. "Miss Digby, you know Miss Atherton, but I don't believe you've met the delightful Miss Kent."

"Miss Kent." Miss Digby curtsied.

"Miss Digby," Hannah returned.

Neither young lady appeared very happy about the introduction, but I did not allow myself to read more into it.

"Miss Kent and I have looked through every bolt of fabric," Miss Atherton said. "And we found the most beautiful dark-blue print that I think would suit you. You must let me show you."

Miss Digby glanced up at me, then offered a quick goodbye, and she and her mother followed Miss Atherton to the modiste. Miss Atherton was a force. Heaven help the man she fell in love with.

"You were quick to vacate the modiste's shop just now," I said to Hannah once we were alone. "That wouldn't have anything to do with *me*, would it?"

"Don't flatter yourself. I was only living up to my half of our bargain—to drive away unwanted young women and their mothers."

"Miss Digby's company was hardly unwanted," I teased.

"Oh? What a dreadful mistake I've made. I will call her back for you."

"That won't be necessary."

"I thought not," she said and started walking toward the carriage with a self-satisfied smile. I remembered this particular smile of hers. She'd worn it every time she'd done something she was proud of: skipping stones across the river, winning a foot race, hiding the longest.

"Damon," Hannah said suddenly. "Who was the man you were speaking with before?"

It took conscious effort not to react. "What man?"

"The man with whom you were speaking earlier. Over there." She pointed to the shadowed spot between shops, where I'd stood with Mr. Turner. "You gave him a small parcel."

My brow tensed. What should I say? I would not lie to Hannah, but neither could I tell her the truth.

"Won't you tell me?" she asked.

Hannah was about to step in a small puddle, so I placed my hand on the small of her back to guide her around it. My fingers burned from the contact in the best way. "He is a business contact," I said simply.

She frowned at me, her delicate brow creasing in the center. "What sort of business?" she pressed.

"The details would bore you."

"That's unlikely."

What was she? A bloodhound? "Did you find an acceptable fabric for your dress?" I changed the subject.

She gave me a pointed look. "If you don't want to tell me your business, then I am under no obligation to divulge mine."

"I take this to mean no acceptable fabric was found?"

"I'm afraid the details of my visit to the modiste would *bore* you."

"No doubt," he said, "but I am very good at feigning interest."

She met my gaze. "As am I, *my lord.*"

That stung. "Touché. What shall we speak of, then? The fine weather or perhaps the quality of shops in this town?"

"I have no interest in idle chatter."

"All right, let us discuss more important matters. Why did you hide in your room last night?"

I knew she'd hidden because of me, but I did not know what I had done or how we might move past it. Her time here was limited, and I did not wish to waste a second.

"I'd rather not discuss it," she said.

"And I'd rather you didn't hide from me."

She looked up at me. "What makes you think I was hiding from *you?*"

"Weren't you?" I said, honestly surprised that she could be hiding from anything else. She'd fled from our ride so suddenly.

"It was Ollie I couldn't face," she said quietly.

"Why would you hide from Ollie?" Had he done something? *Said* something?

"Our ride yesterday bothered him."

I tilted my head to study her. "Was that not our express purpose?"

"It was . . . but it doesn't make me feel better."

"Do you regret our arrangement?" I asked. I could not—*would* not—ask her to continue this farce if she was uncomfortable.

"Only when you keep things from me," she said, looking at me sideways. "I would feel better if you weren't so private."

"I'm sure you would not." If she only knew what she was asking me to divulge, she would be horrified.

"Red," Hannah said.

I narrowed my gaze. "Pardon?"

"The color of fabric I chose is red. Poppy, to be exact."

"Poppy?" Try as I might, I could not picture it. "I would have expected you to choose a subtler shade. White or pale green, perhaps." That was what she always wore. Always. Since she'd been a girl.

"Yes, well, I wanted to select a color that would be noticed."

Red would definitely be noticed. Gads, Hannah would be stunning in that color. "That color will—" my voice caught in my throat. "It will suit your complexion nicely."

"Thank you. Now it is *your* turn to be forthcoming."

"You want a confession." I laughed lightly and shook my head. Leave it to Hannah to corner me. "Very well, then. The night you wear such a dress will surely be the end of our little charade. Ollie and every other man in the room will be captivated by you." Me, most of all.

Her cheeks pinked with my compliment. Could she see my feelings for her? I wore them so blatantly on my sleeve.

"I didn't choose the color to please your brother," she said, looking into my eyes.

My heart pounded with the possibility that she might finally be starting to see me as I saw her. "Oh?" I managed, doing my level best to keep placing one foot in front of the other on the path before me. "Who did you buy it to please?" *Please say me. See me, Hannah. See me as I have always seen you.*

She looked up at me through her lashes, her beautiful eyes boring into the deepest levels of my soul. "Myself," she said, a self-satisfied smirk settling on her lips.

I longed to pull her into my arms and kiss the smirk off her mouth. But seeing as I could not do that, I lowered my voice and said, "How foolish of me to have hoped."

I held out my hand to help her inside the carriage. She did not take it as readily as she had when we'd stood with the Digbys, and she stared at me now.

I leaned closer. "The polite thing to do when a gentleman offers you his hand, Miss Kent, is to accept it."

My jesting seemed to jog her mind back into the present, and she made a show of looking around.

"What is it?" I asked.

"I was searching for the *gentleman* to whom you were referring."

I threw back my head and laughed. *This woman.* How had I gone so long without her in my life? How would I survive it when she left at the end of summer? "It is a good thing I don't pride myself on titles, or I would be offended."

"Damon, hush. You're attracting attention."

"Good," I said. "Now. Shall we try this again?" I once again offered her my hand, and this time, she quickly took it.

Once inside the carriage, she tried to snatch it back, but I did not release my hold. I couldn't. I *should*, I knew that, but . . . if I could not kiss her lips, I would at least kiss her hand. Ever so slowly, I brought her hand to my mouth and placed a kiss on her knuckles.

I let go and turned away to hide from her inevitable rejection.

Mother was nearly at the carriage now and was staring at me with a strange expression. Had she seen me kiss Hannah's hand? I tried to school my face, but it was an unruly student.

I assisted Mother into the carriage and climbed in, too, careful not to make eye contact with Hannah. I needed a moment to remember myself first. She preferred Ollie, I told myself. She was leaving at the end of summer. And even if, by some miracle, we overcame all that, Father would never allow me to marry her.

"How went your business, Damon?" Mother asked.

I hazarded a glance at Hannah and mumbled some response that I hoped made sense. I didn't know.

"I saw you conversing with Miss Digby," Mother said. And if she meant to saddle me with another conversation about marriage, she would be unsuccessful on this count.

"Indeed. Her mother accosted me in the street."

"Damon." Mother tried to hide her amusement by pressing her lips together, but her smile shone through her eyes.

"Thankfully, Hannah saved me from the wiles of the lovely Miss Digby."

"Speaking of Miss Digby, that reminds me," Hannah said, "Ollie suggested we all picnic together. Miss Digby, Miss Atherton, and her brother, as well as Ollie, you, and me."

"*Ollie* suggested *I* attend?" I raised an eyebrow. "How did you cajole an invitation for me?"

"Nobody cajoled anyone," she said. "It was simply a matter of numbers."

"Ah. So it was you. I thought as much."

Mother shook her head. "What is it with you boys? As children, you two were inseparable."

"Those days are long gone." And no one was more depressed about it than me. If I could go back in time, I would.

Mother sighed.

The carriage lurched over a dip in the road, and Hannah groaned, resting a hand on her stomach.

"I almost forgot." I reached into my pocket and pulled out a small brown bag tied with twine. "This is for you."

She eyed the bag as though I were offering her a snake. She really did think the worst of me, didn't she? I untied the bag myself and tilted it so she could see inside. "It's candied ginger. Sailors use it to curb seasickness," I explained as I took a piece from the bag and put it in my outstretched hand. "I thought it might help you."

Her mouth curved into an *O*.

Mother's gaze moved between us with curiosity.

Hannah's fingers brushed my palm as she took the candied ginger, and after inspecting it thoroughly, she placed it in her mouth.

"Do you like it?" I asked.

"Very much. Thank you."

It was then that the carriage suddenly stopped, and Hannah flew forward. Reflexively, I reached out to catch her, and she fell into my lap. Fortunately, Mother had been resting her arm on the window ledge and had been able to brace herself.

Hannah did not immediately move but blinked at me.

The carriage was pitched at an extreme angle, and I held Hannah's waist, steadying her. "Are you all right?"

"I think so," she said.

I loosened my grasp but only just. "You needn't throw yourself at me to get my attention. I assure you, you already have it."

Her lips parted, but she made no sound.

"It seems we are stuck in a rather large puddle," Mother said.

The footman opened the carriage door a moment later, and we determined to safely remove the ladies before attempting to pry the carriage from the puddle.

I carried Mother to the side of the road first, then came back to carry Hannah.

I held out my hand to her, but she seemed to be searching for another way to the side of the road that would not involve me carrying her. I sighed. What would it take to get her to trust me? "I won't drop you if that's what you're worried about."

"I'm sure you will not. At least, not with your mother standing watch."

"It's true," I said. "I would never tempt that woman's wrath."

Hannah laughed a little, and I had never heard a sweeter sound.

Tentatively, she looped her arm around my shoulders, and I took her into my arms, cradling her against my chest. I walked slower than I had with Mother, savoring every second it took us to reach the side of the road. Hannah smelled sweetly of roses.

"See?" I said. "You can trust me."

"Can I?" She searched my eyes.

I held her gaze, and as I set her safely on the ground, I said, "Always."

CHAPTER TEN

THE MORNING OF THE PICNIC, I rose before dawn. I'd hardly slept, so it had not been difficult to do so. What Mother had said in the carriage about my relationship with Ollie still rang in my ears. We had been close. I wanted us to be again, but I did not know how to mend the past or forge a different path so that we might have a relationship in the future. And that was to say nothing of Hannah.

How had I allowed things to become so tangled?

I needed to clear my head before the picnic. And there was only one way to do that: Ares.

Halfway down the corridor, I heard something. Was that . . . music?

I followed the sound to the drawing room and smiled when I saw Hannah sitting at the pianoforte. She played the first few measures, made a mistake, and reset to the beginning. She did this several times, then, frustrated, said, "Drat!"

I chuckled, and she spun to see me.

"Good morning." I smiled and walked into the room, standing at the side of the instrument.

"If you intend to distract me," she said, "it won't work. I play better with an audience."

"Oh. Well, I wasn't intending to stay, but if my presence will help you to play better . . ." I laid my riding crop on a side table and perched myself at the edge of the pianoforte.

"That was *not* meant as an invitation."

"Why are you awake so early?" I asked. "I have never known you to be an early riser. And it is painfully obvious how much you hate playing the pianoforte." Truly, she was torturing that poor instrument.

"If you must know, I was hoping to practice before Ollie rose so I could play for him as we watched the sun rise together."

I almost laughed. "I doubt my younger brother has seen a single sunrise since before he left for Eton."

She missed a note and reset her hands to start again at the beginning. What *was* she doing?

"You must be mistaken. Ollie *loves* the sunrise."

"Perhaps when he was a boy, but my younger brother now prefers sundown and everything that comes after." I walked around the body of the pianoforte and sat beside her on the bench.

She scooted slightly away and started the song again.

"Why are you starting over?" I asked.

"I made a mistake."

"Only a minor one," I said. "You should keep going."

She shook her head. "I want to play it perfectly."

"You don't have to play the song perfectly to enjoy the music. I daresay if you start over every time you make a mistake, you will only ever play the first dozen measures."

She glared at me. "Perhaps *you* should like to play."

"Do you want me to?" I asked. She'd likely only suggested I play because she thought I deserved a comeuppance, but Father had made sure I was proficient in playing the pianoforte.

"I do."

"Very well, then. Prepare yourself to experience something delightful," I said if only to tease a smile from her downturned lips.

"Careful, my lord. Pride cometh before the fall."

"Not pride, my dear Miss Kent—confidence." I glanced over the music. Just as she'd said, the music was challenging. But I enjoyed a good challenge. I set my hands on the keys, taking a moment to center myself.

Hannah sat stiffly beside me as I started the soothing melody, but as the song progressed, she seemed to soften.

I lost myself in the music. It reminded me of summer—water flowing over smooth rocks, cool grass beneath my feet, warm sun over my head. It felt like happiness, like Hannah.

Too soon, the song was finished. I held the final note and looked at her for approval.

"That was . . ." Hannah swallowed. "That was beautiful. I did not realize how much I have missed hearing Mama's melody played properly." Her eyes filled with tears.

"Your mother wrote this piece?"

Hannah nodded. "Her square piano was a wedding gift from her parents, but music sheets are expensive, so . . . she wrote her own songs."

"It is lovely. Thank you for sharing it with me."

"Thank you for playing it for me." A tear spilled down her cheek, and I had to physically grip the bench to keep myself from brushing it away. Her eyes shone like gemstones and were the most beautiful eyes I'd ever seen. If only she'd let me, I'd be content to look into them for the rest of my life.

"You must think me quite the watering pot." She laughed at herself.

"That's not what I'm thinking." I produced a handkerchief from my pocket, and when I handed it to her, our fingers touched, sparking warmth in my soul.

Could she not feel the fire between us too?

"What are you thinking?" she asked.

"I'm not sure I should say."

"Now you must tell me." She self-consciously pinched her cheeks, then patted her hair. "I shall be discomfited until you do."

I shook my head. No matter how much I might want to tell her how I felt, it wouldn't be fair to her. "I was thinking about how lovely your eyes are."

"W-what did you say?"

A noise sounded across the room, and I glanced at the door.

Ollie.

The look on his face told me that he'd heard what I'd said, and I knew, for both her sake and his, that I needed to salvage this. "Your eyes," I said woodenly. "They are lovely."

"Don't fall for his words, Hanny. Damon uses that line on all young ladies."

I gritted my teeth. Two things: One, I hated how he called her Hanny. Two, how would he know what I said to young ladies? He was never home to hear it, and when he was, he made it a point to stand far from me.

Ollie glanced at the pianoforte, and I wondered if he was remembering *that* day. The day Father had found us here, the day I'd decided to sever our relationship. Ollie met my gaze and, speaking to Hannah, said, "He probably played a song for you too."

I stood abruptly.

"I thought as much." Ollie snickered and opened his newspaper.

I stood at the window for a long moment, trying to regain my composure. I had so many conflicting emotions that they were impossible to sort. "It seems you have chosen the perfect day for a picnic," I said. "Hardly any rain clouds."

Ollie's newspaper crinkled as he lowered it. "I am surprised you carved out time in your schedule to enjoy it," he said.

"Come now, Ollie. You know I would never pass up an opportunity to enjoy such lovely company." I winked at Hannah, earning a scathing look from Ollie.

"What song was that anyway?" he asked Hannah, and when she did not reply right away, he said, "Hanny?"

She blinked up at him. "I'm sorry. What did you say?"

Ollie set aside the newspaper and stood. "I asked what song you were playing before I arrived." He walked over to the pianoforte.

"Oh. It was nothing."

Ollie looked at the well-worn sheet music. "It doesn't *look* like nothing. Will you play it for me?"

Instead, she collected the sheets and hugged them close to her. "I'm actually quite hungry. Perhaps another time." She rose and replaced the bench. "Shall we all go to breakfast?"

Ollie retrieved his newspaper and stood from the sofa, moving toward the door.

Hannah stood too. "Will you join us, my lord?"

While I did wish to spend time with Hannah, I didn't think I could stomach sitting at a table with them this morning. "I have delayed my morning ride long enough. Ares requires exercise."

An expression crossed her face, but she hid it before I could decipher its meaning.

"Enjoy your ride," she finally said, then taking Ollie's arm, they quit the room.

It took two hours of hard riding to clear my head. Ares might not have been as fast as a Thoroughbred, but he was enduring. I arrived home with just enough time to bathe and dress for our picnic—I thought—but when I came downstairs, only Ollie was waiting on the outside stairs.

He glanced at me as I stood beside him, then down at his pocket watch.

"Do you like her?" I asked. "Miss Digby?"

"Well enough." Ollie shrugged. "What does it matter?"

"If you are considering spending your life with her, I'd say it matters a great deal."

"Not everyone has the luxury of a love match like you do, Damon."

Hannah joined us before Ollie looked at his pocket watch again, and I bowed in greeting.

"How was your ride this morning?" she asked me.

"Bruising. And your breakfast?"

"Delightful," she said.

Ollie craned his neck to see down the drive. A conveyance was approaching, and he quickly descended the steps.

"Methinks my brother is overeager to greet his guests," I whispered, and Hannah sighed. "Try not to stare," I said as the carriage came to a stop. "It will only encourage him."

Hannah looked at me in confusion. "I don't understand."

"You will soon enough."

Fred's buckled shoes glinted in the sunlight as he stepped down from the carriage. He wore a pair of yellow brocade breeches and carried an ornately carved walking stick.

Hannah's mouth all but hung open. I could not blame her. He'd really outdone himself this time.

"You are staring," I said, and Hannah clamped her mouth closed as I turned to greet Fred. "Mr. Atherton," I said.

"Lord Jennings."

"It has been too long."

"And yet not nearly long enough." Fred frowned and fixed his frilly cuff. "Last we met, you stole a good deal more than your fair share of my money."

"*Won*, you mean." I directed my next statement to Hannah. "Mr. Atherton is terrible at the card table, and he is bitter that I played his failings to my advantage."

"It is true," he said. "I am a terrible hand. But what I lack at the tables, you lack in manners, Jennings." He tipped his head toward Hannah.

"Forgive me. Miss Kent, may I introduce the incomparable Mr. Atherton?"

Fred removed his hat with a flourish and bowed over her hand. "It is a privilege and an honor, Miss Kent."

Hannah glanced at me, and I fought to hold in a laugh.

Miss Atherton, who was still somehow in the carriage, called for Fred's help alighting. He made some sorry excuse about ruining his clothes, so I excused myself to help her.

While I did, the Digbys' carriage entered the gate. Ollie separated himself from the group to greet Miss Digby.

I paused to admire one of the Athertons' new horses as the groom secured it, and when I glanced toward the path, I saw that the party was several paces ahead of me. I watched Hannah giggle at something Miss Atherton said. Her laughter was like sunshine, and I basked in the warmth of it, even though it wasn't intended for me.

"You've got it bad for her, don't you, old boy?" Fred's voice startled me. He'd been waiting for me on the path and seen my unguarded expression. We fell into step behind the others, just out of earshot.

"I'm sure I don't know what you mean."

"Amelia told me about your charade. At first, I thought you were clever in finding a way to put off unwanted courtships, but now I see you're as much a fool as any man in love."

Apparently, my ride this morning hadn't cleared my head after all. Fred was right; I was a fool.

I gave him a half shrug and a lopsided grin. Then, not wanting Fred to say anything more about how I felt and have Hannah overhear, I searched for a change of subject. "I daresay your outfit is brighter than the sun, Fred. I believe we all will be blinded by the end of the day. Could you not have chosen a subtler shade of yellow?"

"I *could* have, but my father might not have noticed—I believe his eyesight grows worse by the day—and then all my efforts to vex the man would have been wasted."

We laughed and continued down the path.

When we reached the old oak tree, Ollie instructed the servants to spread the blanket and arrange food on a table. The feast they produced was more extravagant than I thought necessary for a simple picnic, but the ladies seemed pleased.

Well, everyone but Hannah, who seemed out of countenance.

I set a hand on her shoulder, and she startled. "Are you all right?" I asked softly.

"Why wouldn't I be?" She set her jaw.

"I'm not sure, but I can see something is wrong."

"Well, I'm fine," she said.

"You don't have to pretend with me, Hannah."

"Isn't that what we do?"

I looked at her for a long moment, trying to ascertain what had happened.

"Never mind," she said. She moved to the table and selected food: a finger sandwich, a few berries, and cheese, then she sat on the opposite corner of the blanket from Ollie and Miss Digby.

I could hardly blame her. But then she did something I did not expect: she spoke directly to Miss Digby.

"Do you enjoy reading?" Hannah asked her.

"No." Miss Digby shook her head. "I am far too busy with my art and dance lessons for leisure."

"Hannah lacks the patience to master such fine arts," Ollie said, but he was wrong. Had he seen how hard she'd practiced her mother's piece on the piano-forte this morning, I daresay he would not think her impatient at all.

"You know each other so well," Miss Digby said. "I didn't know. Why have you not mentioned Miss Kent before, Mr. Jennings?"

"There wasn't much to mention." He shrugged. "Miss Kent and I haven't seen each other for a *very* long time."

While that was true, why did Ollie have to say it so rudely? It was almost as though he were trying to make Hannah feel poorly. Did he realize?

"It is true that we haven't seen each other for a long while," Hannah said, "but Summerhaven was my home every summer of my youth. We all practi-cally grew up together."

"Quite so," I said. "Those were the best days of my life."

Miss Digby looked at Ollie, waiting for further explanation.

"It's true." Ollie smiled at Miss Digby. "We were like siblings."

Hannah frowned. "That is not at all how I remember things, Ollie. In fact," she continued, "it was under this tree that we—"

"Played," Ollie cut her off, and I would have given anything to hear how that sentence ended. "Hannah used to tie her skirt between her legs so she could better climb."

Miss Digby giggled. "You *are* like siblings."

Hannah's cheeks reddened with embarrassment. No, anger.

"That is not even the half of it," Ollie continued, seeming to gather energy from Miss Digby's excitement.

"Ollie," I warned with a shake of my head. I did not know precisely where he was heading, but I knew the general direction, and it led nowhere good.

But he continued anyway. "Hannah was always trying to compete with Damon and me. I think she wished she'd been born a boy."

Hannah sucked in a breath, Ollie's setdown seeming to inflict physical pain.

I did not think Ollie meant to be malicious. He'd likely only gotten caught up in courting Miss Digby again and forgotten about Hannah's feelings. Still, his behavior was inexcusable. "I believe we all sometimes wish we could be someone we are not," I said, hoping to both reassure Hannah and speak sense into Ollie.

"Yes," Miss Atherton hurried to agree with me. "My brother, for instance, wishes he'd not been born a gentleman but rather a common man so he could be a Bow Street Runner."

"It is true." Fred laughed. "Or at least, it *was* true until I discovered the profession would require a wardrobe completely devoid of any color."

Miss Atherton continued speaking, and Ollie glanced at Hannah. He gave her a sorrowful expression, but she shook her head and quietly excused herself. She walked toward the riverbank, and I waited a moment to see if Ollie would follow—she deserved an apology from him—but when he returned his attention to Miss Digby, I went after Hannah instead.

I found her at the river's edge, skipping stones—or at least attempting to.

"If you're planning to tell me what I'm doing wrong—"

"No," I said. "If I recall correctly, *you* were always better at skipping rocks than both Ollie and me combined." I silently searched for a flat stone, then skipped it across the river's surface.

Hannah sighed. "What is wrong with me, Damon? I know I'm not as lovely as Miss Digby, but what special trait does she possess that I lack?"

"Two thousand pounds," I said without a second thought.

Hannah's head jerked back in surprise. "You mean to say that Ollie is interested in Miss Digby because she is . . ."

"Wealthy? Yes. That is precisely what I'm saying."

"You're wrong." She shook her head. "Ollie doesn't care about things like that. He would never pursue someone based on their income."

"He does, and he is. I thought you knew." She shook her head and sat on a boulder. "Unfortunately, he has little choice in the matter."

"There is *always* a choice."

"Not if you are the second son of an earl. He is expected to maintain his position in Society but is given no means to do so."

"I understand well that his position in Society is precarious."

"You understand that his position is precarious, but do you understand why?"

"Of course I do. He is a second son and, therefore, will not inherit Summerhaven, nor the title that comes with it. But that hardly matters. He will inherit Winterset Grange from your mother."

"Yes, but the grange will only give Ollie a toehold with which to stand in the world and nothing more."

"What of his allowance? Your father doesn't intend to cut him off, does he?"

"No. But the entailment on Summerhaven only ensures a modest allowance for second sons. It is enough to run the grange and provide a humble living, but in order to enjoy the abundant life he has become accustomed to, he will have to marry someone of means, such as Miss Digby, or he will have to earn his keep through employ." He needed her money, and she needed his good surname.

Hannah frowned her disapproval, and her face sparked a fond memory of the last time we'd been in this place together. I laughed to myself.

"Is something funny?" she said, unimpressed.

"Not at all. I was just remembering how you made that same face the last time we stood here."

"You have no need to remind me of that awful day. I remember it well."

"Do you? I am not a mind reader, Miss Kent, but I do believe we remember a few things differently." Actually, I was certain of it. If she remembered half of what I did, she would not dislike me as much as she seemed to.

She glanced at me. "I will tell you what I remember, but you should know that my memory does not paint you in the best light."

"As I am well aware."

"We were skipping rocks just over there." She pointed to a shady spot on the riverbank. "I thought I saw a school of fish, but then you corrected me, saying they were tadpoles, nearly frogs, and I was so disappointed."

I frowned. "No, you weren't. You were excited. Don't you remember? You could scarcely tie up your skirt fast enough. And even though you didn't know how to swim, you walked right into the river. The water came right up to your waist."

"Even then, I was headstrong."

"No," I said. "You were *fearless*."

"Actually . . ." Her face scrunched in the most endearing way. "I do remember that. But it doesn't make sense. I hate frogs."

"You didn't use to," I said. *And you didn't hate me either*, I thought. How could I make her remember? "What else do you remember about that day?"

"Ollie grew bored of skipping rocks, so I suggested we play hide-and-seek in the garden."

"And I agreed."

"Yes, but only if we played in the east wing. Ollie said no because your father had forbidden us from entering that wing, but you goaded him until he acquiesced."

"I was trying to impress you with my bravery," I said.

"You wished to impress me?" She looked at me askance.

"Is that so hard to believe?"

"It is, actually. You were always playing so many pranks on me."

"I assure you, none were intended as such. Please, go on."

She seemed unsure but continued. "We ran across the great lawn toward the house. You were in the lead, but Ollie was close behind. I ran as fast as I could, trying to keep up, but I'd untied my skirts, and my foot caught the hem. I tripped." She shook her head. "You see? Ollie can hardly blame my dislike of skirts. They've caused me ire since girlhood."

"Yes." I laughed. "I suppose they have."

She got a distant look on her face and grew quiet. "You ran back for me," she said. "Why did you do that? You hated me."

"Never," I said in a low voice. "Do you remember anything else of that day?"

"You locked me in a traveling trunk."

"To protect you from my father. He'd returned early from London, and I didn't want him to find you in the east wing." He would have been furious. He tolerated Hannah and her mother because it made Mother happy but for no other reason. If he had found her, I did not doubt he would have sent both her and her mother home.

"But you left me there all day."

"I would have come back if I could, but Father—" I shook my head, not wanting to tell her what he'd done to my back when he'd found me. "I sent Ollie," I said instead.

"He never came for me. I was locked in that trunk for hours; it was a housemaid who finally found me."

"I didn't know." I imagined her locked in that small space for what would have felt like forever to a little girl, waiting for me to save her. And her despair when I hadn't come. Her dislike of me was beginning to make more sense.

"What about my hair?" she asked. "You cut it so close to the scalp that I had to disguise my baldness with bonnets and bows for months."

I dropped my gaze to the ground. "I never meant to cause you pain."

"Why did you do it, then? Have you no further explanation?"

"I do," I said. "But first, you must promise to hear me out."

She nodded.

"There was a footman," I started slowly. "Thomas was his name, and he was desperately in love with a scullery maid. She was leaving, though I can't remember why now. Thomas didn't want to forget her, so she gave him a lock of her hair . . ." I hesitated to tell Hannah more, unsure if she was ready to hear how I felt for her even back then, or perhaps I was afraid she would guess my feelings for her now.

"Go on," she urged.

"Well, it was nearing the end of summer, and you, too, were leaving Summerhaven soon, and I would be leaving for Eton, and I thought that if I had a lock of *your* hair, I would never forget *you*."

Hannah's gaze turned wary, but it was too late to take it back now.

"The night before you were to return home to London, while we all slept in the nursery, I crept over to your bed with a pair of scissors, intending to cut a small lock of your hair. But instead of trimming the end like I should have, I cut near the scalp.

"I knew right away that I'd made a mistake. I ran back to my bed and prayed the whole night for a miracle, that your hair would grow back. I will never forget how you screamed the next morning, how you shouted your hatred for me." Then I met her gaze and said, "I'm sorry."

She stared at me for a long moment, her gaze soft, and she finally whispered, "I forgive you."

I immediately felt lighter, it was as if a weight had been lifted from my shoulders.

"What did you do with the lock of hair?" she asked.

"You can hardly expect me to remember. I was just a boy."

"You seem to remember everything else about that day," she said, but I would not be divulging that the talisman was currently in my pocket, as it always was. "Well, will you at least tell me if it worked?"

"Did *what* work?"

"Did my lock of hair help you to remember me?"

More than she would ever know.

CHAPTER ELEVEN

I ROSE EARLY THE NEXT day, hoping to finish my errands before midday so that I might claim more of Hannah's time. Yesterday, as we sat at the pianoforte, something had shifted between us, and then as we'd stood by the riverbank, it had settled—at least for me. Hannah had shown me a softer, more vulnerable side of herself, and I'd allowed her to see me.

Still, I knew her feelings for Ollie were probably still raw.

I dressed quickly and left my room. I needed to check on the Turners to see if they'd begun fixing their roof with the thatch I'd had delivered. I hoped to have something positive to report to Father. But even more, I hoped to be home by luncheon so I could spend the rest of the day with Hannah.

I was halfway down the stairs when Hannah walked out of the library. My mouth slid into a smile. "Miss Kent, up early two mornings in a row."

Her gaze met mine, and I knew right away that something had happened; her eyes were too wide, her breaths too shallow. I flew down the stairs to her. "What is wrong?" I searched her face.

"Hanny," Ollie called.

I glanced over her shoulder into the library and then again at Hannah, trying to make sense of the situation.

"Take me away from here," she whispered.

Immediately, I tucked her under my arm and led her toward the door.

Ollie blocked our way. "Hanny, *please*."

She leaned into me, hiding her face from him. Saints above, what had happened this morning?

"I could be wrong," I said to Ollie, "but I don't believe she wishes to speak with you."

"*You*." Ollie glared at me, hate simmering in his eyes.

But Hannah was my only concern. I carefully ushered her around him and out the front door.

My curricle was already waiting on the drive. I handed up Hannah, and as soon as I was seated next to her, I gathered the reins and headed for the gates. Beside me came her quiet sniffles.

What had Ollie said to her?

I shifted the reins into one hand and produced a handkerchief from my coat pocket. I gave her a moment, then said, "Will you tell me what happened?"

"I would not know where to start."

"The beginning is generally advisable," I said, offering her a soft smile.

"That is the problem. I don't know the beginning of my and Ollie's story, only the end. And to recount that would be much too humiliating."

The *end*? By her choice or his?

"Would you have me guess what's transpired?"

She shook her head. "It is best that we both forget the entire scene."

I maneuvered the curricle around a mud puddle. "I'm afraid you ask the impossible. You ran from the drawing room crying, with my brother in full pursuit. Seeing as he thinks *we* are in the prelude to a relationship, I have half a mind to call him out."

"You would not call out your own brother."

"As a gentleman, I don't rightly have a choice. Unless you tell me otherwise." I was only trying to tease a smile from her, to make her feel more at ease, but it did not work.

"I will tell you what happened. But from this day henceforth, we will never speak of this again." She folded and unfolded my handkerchief, delaying her confession.

"Yesterday, after what you said about Ollie's circumstance, I thought perhaps you might be wrong. I hoped that if he knew he had another choice in life, if he knew that I loved him, then he wouldn't wish to marry Miss Digby. I thought—" Her voice wavered.

She still loved him.

He did not deserve her, but he still held her heart.

"It doesn't matter what I thought," she continued. "This morning, I confessed my feelings to Ollie, and he informed me he does not feel the same. You were correct." She paused. "He is determined to marry Miss Digby, even though he's admitted he does not love her. I shouldn't have doubted you. I must apologize."

"Please don't." I glanced at her. "You must know that I take no delight in your pain." I wanted her to be happy. "Do you want to know what I think?" I asked, and she shook her head, but I continued anyway. "I think you are in love with the *idea* of love."

"That is absurd." She let out a humorless laugh.

"Is it?"

"Yes!"

"You love Ollie, to be sure, but you love him as a little girl loves a puppy—with naive innocence and far too much idealism. It is admirable that you wish to save my brother from a loveless marriage, but he is his own man and must make his own decisions."

She frowned. "Have you no words of comfort?"

"I promised to always tell you the truth."

"Yes. But must you put it so bluntly?"

"The truth is often painful but not without virtue. That is to say, now that the truth is out, you are free to move forward."

"I don't want to move forward. Not without Ollie."

"Forget Ollie," I said sharply. "If he cannot see the strong, opinionated, *beautiful* woman before him, then he does not deserve you."

She looked up at me, listening.

"And forgive me for saying this, but is Ollie truly the man you want to marry anyway?"

"You know he is."

"I know he *was*, but my younger brother is not the same person you knew as a girl. *You* are not that same girl. Life, and all that it requires, has changed all of us. I fear my brother would censure the things that make you *you*." Her fire, her opinions, her spirit.

"He would never."

"He already has, Hannah. First, at the ball, then in the stable with your choice of horse, and even yesterday at the picnic."

She bit her lip and was quiet for a long while before she said, "How much farther to our destination?"

"Are you feeling ill?"

"Only mildly. Riding in the open air is easier. Your boots are in no danger." She gave me a half smile.

"To be safe . . ." I produced a small linen bag from my coat pocket and gave her a ginger candy. "May I interest you in a confection?"

"Do you regularly carry sweets in your pocket?"

"Only recently, Miss Kent. And to answer your original question, I have no destination in mind."

"Ollie said—" Her voice caught on his name. "That is, your brother said you had business."

"I was going to visit my father's tenants to check on the harvest," I said. "But now we are merely enjoying a leisurely ride together. We can return to the manor whenever you wish."

"I have no wish to return anytime soon. I would much rather join you in seeing to your affairs."

I bounced the reins in my hand, my jaw tight. "You would not."

"On the contrary, I am intrigued to learn what it is you do all day, and I should like to see your father's holdings. In all the years I have been visiting Summerhaven, I have never been to the corner of your estate that houses your tenants."

"That was not an accident, and we won't be going there today."

She frowned. "Then, what do you propose we do? I refuse to go back to the house, and you refuse to go forward."

"I suppose we shall have to drive the curricle in circles."

"Without a chaperone?" Hannah said. "What will your mother think?"

"What she thinks is not my concern right now." I cared only about Hannah's opinion, and it would not be improved by showing her my shame. "Luckily, we are riding in an open-air curricle and have not ventured from my family's estate. While our situation may not be strictly appropriate, it is also not entirely *in*appropriate."

"Yes, but your mother requested that we have a chaperone, and I don't want to disobey her wishes. Perhaps if we were seeing to your errand and surrounded by people, our offense would be much less severe."

"Hannah," I shook my head, but that only served to strengthen her resolve. Her stubbornness was one of my favorite traits. I loved her determination. But now, in this moment, I wished she would be a tiny bit less headstrong.

"Damon." She raised her chin. "Whatever it is you are hiding, I can handle it. I am not some helpless child you need to protect."

But I did wish to protect her. It was my duty. I glanced at my handkerchief and the sack of ginger candy in her lap and raised my brow at her in challenge.

She quickly hid the evidence. "I know you probably think me nothing more than a proper young lady who will swoon at the sight of sadness, but I'm certain Summerhaven is incapable of producing anything to rival the atrocities I've encountered in London with my service with the church. I've seen injured men returning from war, widowed women struggling to survive, and hordes of hungry, dirty children. So your tenants—even if they are struggling during this uncommonly rainy season—at least have a roof over their heads, fertile land to farm, and a wise and generous landlord."

"I wish that were so," I said. "Please allow me to spare you from this."

"I am afraid I'm far too *headstrong* to let you turn us back now."

"I feared as much." I chewed my lip, debating. Every option, I lost. "I see that I can't win this, but I hope you will at least remember that I did try."

I drove toward the Turners' farm, and as we came around the last curve, the cottage came into view: the stagnant water, the crooked cottage, the barren field.

Then the Turners emerged.

I pulled back on the reins, halting the horse.

"M'lord," Mr. Turner greeted, bowing as best he could. "We weren't expecting you."

"Mr. Turner," I said. "My father has sent me to check on the harvest. But are *you* well?" I asked, wondering why he wasn't at work in the field.

"I am well enough," the man said.

I lifted my gaze to the roof and saw that it had not yet been replaced. "Have you received the supply of thatch?" I asked, and he nodded. "But I see you have not made use of it."

"I've spent day and night trying to save the crops, m'lord."

I nodded. It was likely a wise choice, however unfruitful. "You are a hard worker, Mr. Turner. And a smart one too. But I was told to remind you that Michaelmas is only a few weeks away, and your payment is due."

Hannah bristled beside me, and of course, I understood why. Reminding Mr. Turner that his payment was due when it was obvious he had no harvest to earn the money would likely appear as though I were kicking him when he was already down.

"Yes, m'lord," Mr. Turner said.

"I will not take any more of your time, then." I'd wanted to talk with him about the new farming practices I'd been studying, but I could not do that with Hannah here—at least not without causing her to ask questions.

Mr. Turner nodded for his wife to go back into the cottage, which she promptly did. Then he hobbled to the side of the house, where there was a large pile of thatch. He secured a bundle onto his back and moved toward a ladder leaning against the front of the house.

"Surely, he doesn't intend to climb that ladder." Hannah gasped. "Is there no one to assist him in repairing the roof?" she asked, and I shook my head. "Then *we* have to help him."

"If I could, you must believe I would." More than anything I wanted to climb up that ladder and secure the thatch myself, but if Father found out, he would not hesitate to evict them.

"You *can* help them. Send word to your father immediately. His steward has obviously not informed him of his tenants' living conditions."

If only it were so simple. "He knows," I said, unable to look her in the eyes.

"And . . . so did you," she realized with disgust. "This was the reason you didn't want me to join you today."

"Please do not look at me that way. I know how this must seem to you, but if I were to get down from this curricle and assist those poor souls—" I cut off my sentence, knowing I could not tell her that Father would retaliate, and I started again. "There are forces at work here that you don't understand. I am not in a position to help them."

The disappointment in her eyes seared my soul. "You *are* in a position to help, and I must insist you do so."

"I am sorry, but my hands are tied." I flicked the reins to encourage the horses forward.

"No!" She grabbed the reins and pulled back to stop the horses, then flung them back at me as she stood.

"What are you doing?" I steadied her.

"What *you* will not." And then she gathered her skirts, preparing to climb down without my help.

In that moment, I was so incredibly proud of her that my brain stopped working correctly, and I said, "But it is about to rain."

"As I am well aware. Please return to your grand home, where you will be warm and dry by the fire."

"*Lud*, Hannah. Is that what you think I want?"

"What else can I think, *my lord*?"

Her words stung more than if she'd slapped me, and I swore under my breath.

Hannah stood, but I caught her wrist before she could step down. "I am content to offer my back," I said, "but I will not risk yours. *I* will assist Mr. Turner with the roof, and you will wait here."

"I most certainly will not."

"Though quarreling with you is a most enjoyable pastime, I cannot allow you to win this argument." I tugged her hand, pulling her back into her seat. "I will work more quickly knowing you are safe. Please. Wait here."

I did not know how I would explain my actions to Father if he found out, but I would think of something. Hannah was right; the Turners needed more than my financial help.

I hurried around the house to find Mr. Turner to discuss how I might best help him. We decided he would stay on the roof to place the thatch that I would carry up to him.

When I returned, Hannah was climbing out of the carriage.

"I told you to wait in the curricle," I said sternly, but I could not help smiling. Hannah was without a doubt the best of women.

"You did, but I never agreed. How can I help?"

"Thatch," I said. "Carry it from that pile there and bring it to me here on the ladder."

With a nod, she hurried toward the pile, and I went to the ladder. Together, we worked quickly and effectively. But apparently not fast enough for her, because when I came back down the ladder, she'd tied her skirts up out of the way.

My gaze dropped to Hannah's exposed ankles. She shot me a fierce look, as if daring me to say something. I knew better, even if she did have lovely ankles, and simply reached for the armful of thatch she handed me.

"You should go inside now," I called to her from the roof.

"Not until you have enough thatch," she shouted back.

It took a long while, but finally, I had enough, and Hannah went inside. When I turned back to work, Mr. Turner was grinning at me.

"Is she your—"

"No," I said.

"But you want her to be."

When I said nothing, Mr. Turner smiled again. "All right, m'lord. Keep yer secrets from me if you must, but you should tell yer lass before you lose her."

"I'll bear that in mind, Mr. Turner. Thank you."

When we finally finished, we crawled back down the ladder and went inside the small cottage.

We shared a meal with the Turners, who offered us dry clothes and a seat by the fire while they put their children to bed and we waited for the rain to pass.

Hannah and I sat quietly for a moment, enjoying the sounds and movement of life around us.

"What are you thinking of?" I asked.

"Nothing of import," she said.

"*Nothing of import* would not crease your brow so deeply."

"I was pondering whether it was possible to miss something that never belonged to you."

"I know it is." I held her gaze for a long moment. "So, you were thinking of Ollie, then?"

"No. I was mostly thinking about my mother," she said. "And her choice to marry my father. Though they did not have much in terms of possessions, they were happy."

"Could *you* be happy as a poor man's wife?" I asked her.

"Yes."

"You don't even have to think about it, do you?"

"What's there to think about? My mother married for love, and she was happy. Why not I?"

"Not many are as brave as your mother. Financial burdens often turn the sweetest of couples bitter."

"For some, that may be true, but I have never been afraid of living a simple and quiet life."

"You are a wonder, Hannah. My brother does not deserve you."

"I do not wish to speak of Ollie just now."

"Nor I." I shifted in my seat and leaned forward, resting my elbows on my knees. "What do you wish to speak of?"

"Your tenants."

"Of course you do."

"This home is in utter disrepair, but the tenants do not despise you. Why?"

I felt a shadow fall over my face. I thought about teasing away the topic, but then I met her gaze and said, "Because I help them."

"That much is obvious. I would like to know *how* you help them."

"Money."

"How is that possible? Everything in your possession is your father's. And seeing as he is aware of the conditions yet refuses to send aid, I hardly think he'd approve of your charity. And if you were to simply take his money without permission, he would notice when his books reflected a deficit."

"You miss nothing, do you?" I shifted in my seat, the wood creaking beneath my weight. "The money I give them I have earned through gambling."

"Gambling?" She frowned. "That cannot be a wise or reliable method of securing funds."

"No, but I am up at the tables more than I am down. And most importantly, my profits and the way I spend those profits are not easily traceable."

"And you freely give your earnings to your tenants?"

I glanced at the children playing on the threadbare rug. "They have more need of it than I."

"What you're doing here is good."

"Perhaps, but it is not enough. What our tenants need is for my father to give them more help."

"Will he?"

"No. My father sees the Turners' situation not as a failure on his part but on theirs. He believes if they had been good stewards of all he has given them, they would not now be in this position."

"But Mr. Turner's injury was not his fault, and neither is the failed harvest."

"I agree with you," Damon said. "But my father argues that if they had only prepared more in years previous, they would be able to now save themselves."

"That is madness."

"It is. The Turners live only from one harvest to another. On a parcel of land this size, there is very little surplus to save."

"Your father must be made to see reason."

"I have tried. Even going so far as to draw up and present plans to him."

"What sort of plans?"

"You will think me foolish."

"I promise I will not."

"I have been studying agriculture and talking with other landowners about the most beneficial farming techniques, and with some wise investments, better education, and up-to-date practices, I believe we can give the Turners and our other tenants the means to succeed."

"You must do it, then," she said, and she had no idea how much her faith meant to me.

"It is a great deal more complicated than that." Meeting my tenants' needs and Father's demands was a delicate balance.

"Not so," Hannah said. "You have the means and the desire; you lack nothing to bring about change."

"Only the authority."

"But one day, you will have it. And think of all the good you will be able to do."

I wanted to do good, to *be* good, but . . . "As soon as I inherit, I fear I will become exactly like my father and his father and his father's father. I have been taught my whole life that the only way I can ensure my family's survival is by doing what has always been done."

"You will not be like your father or any of the previous earls of Winfield," Hannah said, smiling softly.

"How can you be so sure?" After everything she'd seen today, her belief in me was too remarkable.

"Because you alighted from the curricle today and because you have been helping your tenants for a long time previous."

I'd alighted from the curricle today only because she'd insisted. And what I did for the Turners, I did in secret, and by gambling, no less. "You have too much faith in me."

"How can I not? Must I remind you of how you asked me to dance at Rumfords' ball even though it was not in your interest to do so?"

"Ah. But it was," I countered.

"We both know you could have found other means of avoiding an unwanted marriage. Your motivations in coming to my aid were purely unselfish."

"My motivations for asking you to dance with me were anything but pure, Miss Kent. I am a man, and you should not forget it."

"And *you* must not forget that you are not your father. You are your own man, and you can choose a different path."

Her words stunned me. I did not know whether what she said was true, but I wanted it to be. I wanted to be the man she believed I could be: good and true and worthy.

I'd known my whole life that Summerhaven would one day be mine, and I'd feared for just as long that it would change me. That my position would make me like Father—hard and hated.

But here, in this moment, as I sat across from Hannah and stared into her faith-filled eyes, I believed that I could be something, some*one* different from the man and master my father was. And more than that, I wanted Hannah to do it with me. I wanted more days like today.

But did she want more days with me?

Needing a moment to collect myself, I stood and walked to the window. "The rains have ceased," I finally said. "We must return home with haste." I let the curtain fall closed and told Mr. Turner to prepare the curricle for our departure. I prevailed upon the elder Mrs. Turner to serve as our chaperone.

I took the ladies to the curricle waiting outside and assisted both up. We made a snug fit, but I didn't mind sitting so close to Hannah. I relished her nearness.

It wasn't long before the gentle motion made Hannah quiet with sleep.

I held the reins in one hand and wrapped the other around Hannah.

"Careful, young man," Mrs. Turner said. "I'm not as senile as I look."

"She was cold," I said, giving her my best grin.

Mrs. Turner shook her head, but I didn't remove my arm from Hannah's shoulders.

We reached home far too quickly, and as we came to a stop, I murmured, "Hannah, we are home." I brushed the hair from her cheek. It was the second time in our lives I'd touched her hair while she slept. She smelled like roses and fresh thatch.

When Hannah awakened, I assisted her inside the entry hall, where we parted ways with Mrs. Turner. Hannah and I should have also separated to our rooms, but I didn't want this perfect day to end.

"Wait." I caught her hand. "I want to show you something."

I led her down the darkened corridor into the east wing and pushed open the ballroom door.

Hannah sucked in a surprised breath, turning to take in every inch of opulence. This hall was one of Father's many expansions to Summerhaven. And while it was lovely, nothing was as beautiful to me as her. I could not take my eyes off her. Wanting to feel her in my arms again, I asked her to dance.

"We should probably go," she said. "If someone sees us . . ."

"I have never cared one whit for my reputation, and I do believe your quadrille could use some practice."

"You'll be pleased to know my maid acquired some dancing papers, and I am now quite proficient."

"And what of your waltz?" I whispered in her ear.

As I thought, she couldn't resist this dance. She stepped closer and rested her hands on my shoulders.

Her nearness nearly undid me. I wanted to pull her into my arms and lower my lips to hers, but instead, I rested my hands lightly on her waist and led her through the steps, her movements perfectly matched to mine. It was sweet torture.

"I think you were being modest," I said. "You dance beautifully."

"If that is true, it is only because I have found the right partner."

I tightened my hold and stared into her eyes. I wanted this for the rest of my life. To know that she was mine as surely as I was hers.

I slowed us to a stop, and bowing low, I kissed her hand and then her cheek, silently trying to tell her what I was not brave enough to say aloud: *I love you.*

"What the devil is going on here?" Father's voice filled the ballroom.

Hannah stepped away, putting proper distance between us, but no amount of space would hide the fact that we were alone and dancing in a darkened ballroom.

"Miss Kent," Father said sternly, "you will return to your bedchamber forthwith. And, Damon, my study. Now."

I wanted to reassure Hannah, to tell her how I felt, that I wanted to marry her. Instead, I guided her to the entry hall and thanked her for the dance before bidding her good night.

As soon as I entered Father's study, he flew into his lecture. "Why, pray tell, are you dressed in peasant clothes?"

"I am wearing Mr. Turner's clothing because he kindly loaned them to me when Hannah and I were caught in the rain," I explained.

"I sent you there this morning. You should have returned hours before the weather turned. Where have you been tonight?"

"At the Turner farm," I repeated, and I gathered my courage and told him the truth. "Our tenants needed assistance fixing their roof."

Father's eyes bulged. "You *labored* with them? Of all the absurd, vulgar things you have done, this outdoes them all."

"They needed help. Urgently."

"I do not deny it, but a gentleman cannot work his own land. It is simply not done." He sighed, sounding exhausted. "Damon, you cannot be both lord and friend. I have tried to teach you this principle time and again. Had some-one seen you, you would have been shunned by the *ton*."

"I could not care less about the *ton*!"

"Oh, you could not? What about your sway in the House of Lords when the time comes? You have a desire to see reform in a number of laws, do you not? What about making an advantageous match? You must want for a beau-tiful and well-bred wife. And if you do not care about yourself, which, given your behavior tonight, it seems you do not, then you must at least consider your mother and how she will be treated in her social circles. And what about your brother's standing? Are you content to ruin him as well? You have led with your heart, not your head, again, and you cannot afford it, not if you wish to have any standing in Society."

"Hang Society," I spat back. "I refuse to turn my back on our tenants as you have."

"Is *that* what you think of me? That I have turned my back on them?" Father laughed humorlessly.

"I could hardly think otherwise. The Turners have been good, hardworking tenants; yet you will not fix their roof, invest in better farming equipment, or extend their payment."

"What has happened to Mr. Turner is regrettable," Father admitted in a rare show of compassion, "but I did not deal him the blow. War did. And while I wish I could house and feed every hungry man, woman, and child, I am running an estate, not a charity. I must see to the needs of my *own* family, and so must you. Soon, you will be lord and master of this estate, Damon. You must learn to act like it."

"Must act like *you*, you mean."

"Indeed."

"I am not you, Father. And I do not want to run Summerhaven in the manner you have. I want—"

"It does not matter what *you* want," Father interrupted. "In order for the estate to survive, you must do what has always been done," he said passionately. But he was wrong.

"I do not want it to merely survive. I want the estate to thrive. My education has taught me there is a better way."

"Then, perhaps it is time for a *re*education," Father said.

"Perhaps it is," I agreed, "but not for me—for *you*. Times are changing, Father, and you must change too."

Father raised one brow, surprised by my boldness, then gave me a stern look of warning.

My stomach clenched, but I would not back down. "I recently borrowed a book from the lending library and have been studying agriculture," I said. "I believe if we were to teach our tenants new farming techniques and invest in better machinery, we *all* could benefit."

He shook his head. "The only sure way for this estate to survive is by doing what has always been done."

"I disagree. Our tenants are suffering, Father. Doing the same thing will only bring about death. For the estate to prosper, we must evolve. We must try something new."

"Trying something new might work, but it might not. I am not willing to risk ruin."

I looked Father directly in the eyes and said, "Risk nothing, gain nothing."

Father stilled and silently appraised me for a long moment. "This is Miss Kent's doing," he finally said. "She has a bleeding heart like her mother had, and her beliefs are unduly influencing you."

"Hannah has nothing to do with this," I said, although it wasn't true. She had *everything* to do with this. Her courage to climb down from the carriage and help the Turners today had unleashed in me a desire to do what I knew was right, a desire to make myself into a better man, a man who was worthy of becoming an earl, of becoming her husband.

"*Hannah?*" Father repeated, and I recognized my mistake immediately. "Oh, Damon. A *clergyman's* daughter? You cannot be serious. She is so far beneath you it is laughable. A summer tryst before you finally take up your familial obligations is one thing, but you should be grateful I was the one who discovered you tonight. If it had been anyone else, you would have been forced into an undesirable marriage with the chit."

"I would be lucky to marry Hannah."

"Out of the question." Father laughed, and he sat as though that were the end of our conversation.

But this was my life we were talking about. My future. My family. "Respectfully, *my lord*, the decision of whom I will marry is mine to make."

"In that *respect*, you are sadly mistaken. I gave you until the end of the year to find a suitable wife. You have failed, so I will choose for you. Have your valet pack your bags. We will leave for London at first light."

"You are mad if you think I will go anywhere with you."

"There are things you don't know, Damon, but that you need to know before you make any unalterable decisions. You will come with me to London, and there, you will learn the truth. After that, you can make your decision."

Was he in earnest? "If I come with you, you will allow me to marry whomever I choose?"

Father pulled in a rattling breath. "As you said, I can hardly stop you. But know this: I cannot save you from the consequences."

His words hung in the air like a threat, but I heard only a promise. So long as I submitted to his will in this, I would finally be free.

CHAPTER TWELVE

FATHER SLEPT MOST OF THE journey to our London house. I had no idea what was on his reeducation agenda, but it didn't matter. He could throw anything at me, and my feelings for Hannah would not be swayed.

I loved her. And if she would have me, I would marry her.

As we entered London, I looked out the carriage window. The city was cold and gray, and I remembered how Hannah had mentioned she did not fancy it here. When the time came and I took my seat in Parliament, would she wish to accompany me here during the Season? Or would she prefer to stay at Summerhaven, as Mother usually did? I hoped she would come with me. I wanted her opinion on all matters, and of course, I would miss her desperately if she didn't.

But I was getting ahead of myself. There were so many steps between today and what I *hoped* would be my future. For one, I would need to wait until her feelings caught up to mine. Then, I needed to ask her father's permission to court her properly, and *then*, I could declare my suit to her.

It was early afternoon when we entered the city. As we navigated toward our home in Mayfair, I studied Father's sleeping form, wondering what he had in store for me. I was sure his plan was well thought out—Father was nothing if not a ruthless strategist—but sleeping, he did not seem so scary. In fact, for the first time, I noticed his age. His skin was soft with wrinkles, his hair more gray than brown, and heavy bags carved shadows under his closed eyes.

The carriage came to an abrupt halt, and Father blinked awake.

As we waited for the footman to let down the stair and open our door, Father said, "We have been invited to dine with the Duke and Duchess of Maybeck and their daughter Lady Margaret this evening."

This was not at all surprising, but I made my displeasure known with a frown.

"Be dressed in your finest formalwear, and be ready to leave by five, not a minute later."

I nodded that I'd heard him, and not wanting to give him any reason to break his promise, I resolved to be exactly obedient.

Once inside, Father went right upstairs. I'd expected him to disappear into his study—tireless in his efforts to train me—but he walked wordlessly to his bedchamber, closed the door, and did not come out until it was time to leave again.

It was common knowledge that the Duke of Maybeck was richer than royalty, but *knowing* it and *experiencing* it was something else entirely. From its neoclassical design—complete with Corinthian columns and a prominent portico—to its prime location overlooking Hyde Park and proximity to Tattersall's, Alsworth Hall exuded elegance and sophistication.

"Stand straighter, Damon, and square your shoulders. A gentleman does not slouch."

I suppressed the urge to roll my eyes and rolled my shoulders instead, forcing myself to stand even stiffer than I had been before.

Father inspected my bearing and nodded his approval.

No sooner than Father had dropped his gaze, a butler opened the door. "Welcome to Alsworth, my lords. If you will follow me, His Grace is waiting for you in the blue drawing room."

The opulent entrance hall was lavishly decorated and was an immediate testament to the Duke's impeccable taste and unsurpassed wealth. It *was* impressive, but as I climbed the grand staircase to the first floor, where our hosts waited, all I could think about was sitting in the Turners' cramped cottage with Hannah.

Hannah, who spent her days serving the poor with her father; Hannah, who said she could be happy being a poor man's wife; Hannah, who would be content to live a quiet and simple life.

We were announced at the drawing room door, and the duke and duchess stood to greet us. Their daughter Lady Margaret also stood but much more slowly and, whether by design or desire, did not meet my gaze.

"Lord Winfield, Lord Jennings," the Duke of Maybeck greeted. "Welcome to our home."

We bowed respectfully.

"We are honored to accept your kind invitation to dine with you, Duke," Father said. "I do not believe my son has had the pleasure of making your family's introduction. If I may?"

The Duke nodded on his daughter's behalf.

"Duke, Duchess, Lady Margaret, I present Lord Damon Jennings, heir to the esteemed earldom of Winfield, a gentleman of impeccable standing, renowned for his integrity and honor."

Finally, Lady Margaret looked at me, and I was struck by the contrast between her ivory complexion, dark hair, and blue eyes. She held herself with poise and was everything I would expect the daughter of a duke would be. If only she didn't look quite so . . . disgruntled.

I extended her a respectful bow and said, "It is an honor to make your acquaintance, Lady Margaret."

"A pleasure, Lord Jennings." She delivered me the expected pleasantry with grace but no feeling. She seemed about as happy to have me in her home as I was to be here.

The duke and duchess exchanged an inscrutable glance, seeming disappointed by their daughters' cool demeanor but not surprised. Perhaps she was as keen on our fathers' marriage machinations as I was.

Thankfully, the butler reappeared at the door and announced dinner.

"Shall we?" the duke gestured to the dining hall.

And as expected, I extended my hand to Lady Margaret. She set her hand atop mine, or rather, *hovered* her hand above mine, and we followed our fathers into the dining hall.

Once seated and served, our fathers began conversing, and Lady Margaret said, "I daresay our fathers have been devising our introduction for some time. I have heard nothing but your name for more than a month now. Tell me, Lord Jennings, do *you* dislike hearing your name as much as I do?"

I laughed into my spoon. Thankfully, it was not yet full of soup. "I believe I do, Lady Margaret. Likely more so, considering my father only sees fit to use my name when irritated." I glanced briefly at Father and found him frowning. I leaned conspiratorially closer to her, but not improperly so, and said, "Judging by the look on his face, I'd wager I will have the *dis*pleasure of hearing my name again tonight."

"Whose Father do you think is more proficient in delivering a lecture, mine or yours?" she asked.

"Well, no disrespect to your father, the duke, but *my* father is quite skilled at delivering lectures," I teased. "Indeed, he has been nominated for several prestigious awards in this area."

"Alas," Lady Margaret played along, sucking in a breath through her teeth, "*my* father indubitably has more practice." She sighed. "Had he known of these awards, he would have proven a top competitor."

I laughed lightly.

"Jesting aside, may I be candid, Lord Jennings?" I nodded that she could, and she continued. "My parents would like me to marry, but I see no benefit. As the daughter of a duke, I have already been bestowed all the blessings of that title. No man can offer me anything more than I already have. And that is to say nothing of the fact that most of my suitors have been more enamored with my father's title and wealth than they are of me. What say you to that?"

"May I also be candid?"

"I demand it, my lord."

I glanced at the head of the table to ensure our parents would not overhear me. "In truth, Lady Margaret, I know something about how you feel on the subject."

"Do you?"

"When women look at me, they tend not to see *me* but rather my eventual earldom. For that reason alone, I've had no interest in marriage. Until very recently, I thought I might remain a bachelor."

"You love your bachelorhood so much?"

"Not at all. I find bachelorhood quite dull and depressing."

"You said, *until recently*. What has changed your mind about marriage? Not the chance to marry a duke's daughter, I hope." She gave me a pointed look that made me smile.

"I should be so lucky, Lady Margaret, but no."

She eyed me. "Lord Jennings, are you in *love*?"

Hannah would be the first person I confessed my feelings to, so I answered Lady Margaret's question with a smile.

"What is her name?" Lady Margaret said.

"Hannah Kent."

"I don't believe I've had the pleasure of making her acquaintance. Is she of any relation to Duke Kent?"

"No, she is the daughter of a clergyman."

"She must be exceptionally beautiful."

"She is," I said. "But her beauty is not why I am attracted to her."

"You are attracted to her dowry?" Lady Margaret guessed.

"Hannah does not have a dowry of which to speak."

Lady Margaret's nose scrunched. "A true love match, then? I did not take you for a romantic, Lord Jennings."

"Nor did I, but alas . . ."

Lady Margaret smiled fully. "Will you tell me about her?"

"I should be happy to. Hannah is . . . well, she is outspoken and stubborn and headstrong, and until very, *very* recently, she thought I was the devil."

"And you like these qualities?"

"I *love* them. She is brave and beautiful and kind. Truly, she is my better in every way."

Lady Margaret's expression turned contemplative. "Why, then, are you dining with me?"

"My father does not approve of her," I answered honestly, and Lady Margaret nodded in understanding. "I meant you no disrespect."

"None was taken. To be honest, I am relieved I will not have to spend the entire evening thwarting your attempts at flirting. Tell me, how did you meet Miss Kent?" Lady Margaret asked, and my answer supplied us with an entire evening of conversation. And somehow, I found in Lady Margaret an unlikely friend.

When the dinner was almost over, I asked, "What will you tell your father about tonight?" As relieved as I was to be on good terms with her, I had no desire to make an enemy of the duke.

"The truth," she said. "That I found in you a friend but not a husband."

"Will he hold that against me?"

She shook her head. "If I consider you my friend, my father will too. I daresay the two of you would get along quite well. In fact . . . do you enjoy the theater, Lord Jennings?"

"As much as any man."

"And what about horses? Do you enjoy the subject?"

"*More* than most men."

"Wonderful. Father and I attend the theater together every week. Normally, we sit alone in our box, and he talks to me unceasingly about his horses. If you are willing, I would like to suggest that he invite you and your father to join us next week so that he might talk *your* ear off instead of mine."

"I would enjoy that immensely."

"So would I."

"It was a pleasure to make your acquaintance, Lady Margaret."

"And you, Lord Jennings."

As promised, one week later, Father sat with the Duke of Maybeck and Lady Margaret in their private box. And just as she'd said, the duke did indeed talk to me unceasingly about his horses.

Father seemed as pleased with me as he had ever been, until I told him the truth—that there was nothing between Lady Margaret and me—and he was furious.

The following day, when I came downstairs to breakfast, I found Father in his study with a man named Mr. Rowley.

Frederick's father, Lord Rumford, had employed Mr. Rowley last year. From Fred, I'd learned that Mr. Rowley was a gentleman's matchmaker. His methods of securing gentlemen advantageous marriages were peculiar but effective. Well, for everyone but Fred, apparently.

For more than a fortnight, Mr. Rowley had done his level best to indoctrinate me. Day after day, he'd dragged me about the city, but for all his efforts, my feelings for Hannah never strayed.

And then, one day, I returned to our London home an hour earlier than expected. As I entered, a doctor was exiting. He gave me a sympathetic look, then slipped past me out the door before I could question him.

Fearing the worst, I hurried into the drawing room and found Father buttoning his waistcoat. He looked . . . fine.

"Why was the doctor here?" I asked.

Father didn't answer my question; he only pointed to a chair. "Sit down, Damon." I did so, and without preamble, he said, "I am dying." Father always spoke without emotion, getting right to the business at hand, but his words still stunned me, and I struggled to take in his meaning.

I glanced over his person, searching for signs of sickness, but saw nothing to indicate disease or infection. He looked old and a bit tired but not as though he were dying. Perhaps this was another ploy to get me to take up my duties and marry. "Surely I misheard you."

Father shook his head. "No, it's true. My condition has been worsening for some time. I held out hope that this specialist might have a cure, but—" He lifted his shoulders in a shrug and began to say something else, but his breath caught, and instead, his bellowing cough filled the room.

As the coughing fit racked his body, I felt dread. He sounded awful. He'd had a cough for ages, but this was not a harmless cough. This was . . .

"Consumption of the lungs," Father said, confirming my fears.

I shook my head, not wanting to believe it but knowing it was true. "How long do you have left?"

"No one rightly knows, but it is getting harder to breathe each day."

A lump filled my throat, and my voice was hoarse as I tried to speak around it. "Does Mother know?"

"Not yet. I was hoping this doctor would have a cure, and I would not have to tell her." He pulled in a shallow, rattling breath.

How had I not noticed how bad his breathing sounded before now?

"There's more," Father said. "And . . . it's worse."

"What more could there possibly be?"

He retrieved a thick stack of papers from his desk drawer and handed them to me.

"What's this?" I asked.

"Your inheritance," he said and turned his back to me.

Confused, I thumbed through the papers. Bills, I realized. From his endless improvements to Summerhaven. And also debt from gambling. Page after page after page of debt. The figures were staggering.

"How much is owed altogether?" I said.

"More than we have."

"How *much* more?"

"It's gone, Damon. All of it."

It took several seconds for his meaning to sink in. And then, with a shaking voice, I said, "Summerhaven is *ruined*?"

"Very nearly."

I pushed away the papers and dragged my hands through my hair. "How did this happen?" I asked.

"Failed business ventures. Failed crops."

"Gambling?"

"That too," he admitted. "But that started only after I tried everything else to save the estate. I've cut expenses wherever possible. I invested with several shipping companies but never saw a return of a profit. The tenants haven't had a decent crop in years. I made some money at cards and horses, but"—he looked at his hands in shame—"I lost it all and more besides. Which is why you must marry Lady Margaret. Her dowry will secure the earldom."

"No." I shook my head. "Absolutely not. I won't do it."

"There is nothing else to be done. To ensure Summerhaven's survival, you must marry for money."

"I won't do it," I said again.

"Yes, you will. Because from this day forward, Summerhaven is under your stewardship." Father looked at me for a long moment, and then with tears welling in his eyes, he removed his signet ring from his finger and set it on the table in front of me. "Summerhaven is on the brink of ruin, Damon, and only you can save us."

I stared at the signet ring but made no move to retrieve it. "I don't want it," I said, meaning so much more than the ring.

"What you want is irrelevant," Father said. "A gentleman, nay, an *earl*, must set his desires aside and do his duty. *Conservabo ad mortem*," he recited the words of our family crest, words I'd heard my whole life: *I will preserve it until death*. "The earldom is now yours to do with it what you will. But your decision will break or bind generations. Do not be the weak link."

CHAPTER THIRTEEN

FATHER AND I ARRIVED HOME to Summerhaven just before dinner. I went straight to the portrait gallery and stood before the first Earl of Winfield's portrait.

William Jennings.

The earldom had been bestowed on him by King Henry VIII after the siege at Boulogne for his bravery and valor.

I'd heard this story so many times that I'd lost count, but it held new meaning for me now.

I wondered how he must have felt being thrust into the role of earl. Did he desire it? Or did he take up the role out of a sense of duty? Father had always said that an earl was not made—he was born. But William had not been born an earl; he'd become one.

The making of an earl depended on so much more than a man's blood and birth order, I decided; it depended on his dedication, his desire, his sense of duty.

Did I possess those qualities?

I'd thought I did, once, but now, I didn't know. If I could, I would give up all my earldom to be with Hannah. I didn't want the title or the estate. I'd only ever wanted to be Damon, to be free to make my own decisions.

But I could no more give up the earldom than I could change the color of my eyes. When Father died, I would be earl, and people would depend on me for their survival. No matter my feelings, Father was right: I needed to do my duty, regardless of my desires.

I dropped my gaze to the black-and-white marble floor and, in my mind, repeated what was quickly becoming my mantra: *I must set aside my desires in order to ensure Summerhaven's survival. I must set aside my desires in order to ensure Summerhaven's survival. I must set aside my desires in order to ensure*

Summerhaven's survival. But no matter how many times I repeated the words, I did not feel them in my soul.

"Damon," Hannah said softly, and I closed my eyes, savoring the sound.

"Miss Kent," I said as she stood at my side, and I bowed my head so I would not have to meet her gaze. How could I do this?

"I see Mr. Rowley was able to educate you in gentlemanly behavior." I heard the smile in her voice.

"Indeed. I found my lost manners in London." I smiled, but it was as weak as my resolve. Turning back to the first earl's portrait, I rubbed my neck.

"What is this?" Hannah asked.

I followed her gaze to Father's signet ring on my smallest finger. Tears filled my eyes, and I started to tremble. "My trip to London with Father was not an educational endeavor, as he led everyone to believe."

"Is everything all right?" she asked.

I shook my head.

"You're scaring me," Hannah's voice shook. "Why did your father take you to London?"

I told her of Father's failing health and how he didn't have much longer to live and that I now wore this ring because he'd had to pass the daily duties of the earldom on to me.

She reached for my hand, and I pulled her into a hug. I clutched her dress as I cried into her shoulder.

"How long does he have?" she asked quietly.

"No one rightly knows. His symptoms are worsening, but the man is stubborn. He will probably live forever—or at least until I have found a suitable wife."

Hannah stiffened. "A *suitable* wife?"

"Hannah." I clutched her arms, wanting to keep her close. "I didn't mean—"

"I thought—After all that has transpired between us this summer, I thought we were very near to an understanding."

"We were. I want desperately make you a proposal of marriage, but Hannah, my father is dying and—" I pressed my eyes closed because I did not have the courage to look at her when I said, "You will never know how sorry I am, but I cannot marry you."

And then, with a lump in my throat, I told her *why* I could not marry her. I told her of Father's failed finances, his bad decisions, and his debilitating debt.

"Summerhaven is . . . ruined?"

"Very nearly."

"What will you do?"

"What else *can* I do?" I paced the floor, pushing my hands through my hair. "In order to save Summerhaven, I must set aside my own desires and do as my father did and his father and his father's father and so on in order that I might ensure the estate's future."

"Even if saving it comes at the expense of others?" Hannah's eyes narrowed, and I knew she was thinking of the Turners.

"Not at their expense," I explained, "but for their *survival*. Hannah, I am all that stands between my family, my servants, and my tenants and certain ruin. I *must* marry for money."

It was the first time I'd spoken the words out loud. Had I not condemned Ollie for courting Miss Digby for the very same reason? He was right; I was a hypocrite, and I hated myself for it.

Hannah stared at me in disbelief. "After all that has passed between us, how can you say that?"

"Because I must. People are depending on me, Hannah. All I have ever wanted is to be loved by you." I could tell she did not believe me, and I understood why, so I produced proof from my pocket. "You once asked what I did with your lock of hair, and I told you I didn't know where it had gone. But I lied." I opened my palm so she could see the little lock of hair. The fine strands were lighter than her hair was now, but just as curly. "I have loved you my whole life. I will *always* love you."

Hannah looked away, hiding her heartbreak.

"Please try to understand," I whispered, "I don't want this separation, but I have no choice."

"There is *always* a choice," she said, her eyes welling with tears.

"You have no idea how much I wish that were true." But I had been over every possibility a thousand times, and there was nothing for it. I reached out to Hannah, wanting to hold her one last time.

She shook her head. "Goodbye, my lord," she said softly, then fled the room.

The ensuing days were agonizing and passed in a depressing blur of endless meetings and paperwork. With every moment that passed, my cravat seemed to cinch tighter around my neck until it felt like a noose and I thought I might suffocate.

After a particularly laborious meeting, I stalked to the stableyard and took Ares out for a ride, needing an escape. A moment to breathe, to clear my head, and to remember my reasons for sacrificing so much of myself.

But no matter how fast or far I rode, my misery followed.

Finding no reprieve, I finally surrendered and rode back the way I'd come. As I neared the house, I slowed Ares to a walk and directed him down a footpath to the river to drink.

"So you *did* hear a horse."

Ollie's voice caught me by surprise, and I immediately reined Ares to a halt. I'd been so deep in thought that I had not noticed anyone sitting by the riverbank. My gaze slid from Ollie to Hannah. They appeared to be having a private picnic.

My hands tightened into fists around the reins. It took every ounce of strength I possessed not to jump off my horse, scoop Hannah onto my saddle, and ride off with her to Gretna Green. In Scotland, I might be free of obligation and marry Hannah without obstacle. But of course, I could not do that. "Pardon me," I said. "I did not mean to interrupt." And I tugged Ares's reins, steering him in the opposite direction of the water.

Ares snorted unhappily but complied. And as soon as we reached the footpath, I kicked his flanks and galloped away.

I did not look back.

That night at dinner, Ollie assisted Hannah with her chair.

"The meal you've had prepared smells delicious." Father smiled approvingly at Mother.

"Roasted duck with fennel and mint," Mother said. "Your favorite in celebration of your return. Thank you for coming home early. The Garretts will appreciate your attendance at their ball."

"You were right to request it of us," Father said. "No matter how glum Damon was about it."

I gritted my teeth.

"Oh?" Mother looked at me.

I felt Hannah look at me, too, but I held my gaze on Father.

"I daresay our son met his future wife while we were in London," Father continued. "The Duke of Maybeck's daughter, Lady Margaret. Damon was quite taken with her. They spoke the entirety of the duke's dinner party and nearly all the way through a performance at the theater."

"I would thank you to keep my private affairs *private*," I said to Father.

"Marriage is not a private matter," Father replied. "It affects the whole family."

"As you have made me painfully aware," I said.

"So long as you *are* aware, I am satisfied."

I dropped my fork and pushed away from the table.

"Please don't go." Mother laid a gentle hand on my arm. "I have had Cook prepare your favorite dessert."

I softened at Mother's touch, feeling compassion. When would Father tell her? *Would* he tell her, or would he simply die and leave me to deal with his degradation? Either way, she would be devastated. As much as I wanted to walk away, I wanted to give her as many moments of happiness as I could, so I scooted my chair back to the table.

After dinner in the drawing room, Mother played the pianoforte. Father stood behind her, turning the pages of her music sheets when necessary. Hannah stood near the hearth with Ollie. I sat alone on the sofa and read my book on agriculture.

"Would you care to play chess?" I heard Ollie ask Hannah, and she readily agreed.

I should have been glad that he was trying to make amends with Hannah. I *was* glad, for her sake, but hearing her enthusiasm hurt.

I shifted on the sofa, trying to make myself comfortable, but there was nothing for it.

"I've been strategizing how I might steal both your first set *and* your supper set," Ollie said.

"Is that a question, Mr. Jennings?"

"It is if you will have me, Miss Kent," he said, sounding far too flirtatious for my liking.

And when she responded, "I will," I was gutted.

I could not endure this.

I slammed my book closed and stood, then crossed the room to the cellaret and poured myself some brandy. I drank it, then poured another and drank that too.

When I finally turned back, my gaze landed on the chessboard between Hannah and Ollie, remembering the game we'd shared at the beginning of the summer.

Hannah shook her head, and I wondered whether that meant she was disappointed in me or only disgusted.

I liked neither.

So I quit the room so I would not have to see it.

The night of the Garretts' ball, I stood alone in the entry hall. Wondering where everyone was, I glanced at my pocket watch for the time, and of course, that was when I heard someone starting down the stairs.

Glancing up, my gaze landed on Hannah.

My heart jumped into my throat at the sight of her. She wore her new red dress and was utterly breathtaking.

"Hannah." My gaze slid down her form. "You look . . ." I swallowed hard. I did not even have words to describe how lovely she looked.

She continued to the bottom of the stairs, to where I stood. "Your silence is uncharacteristic. Disconcertingly so. You must tell me as a gentleman, does this shade not suit me?"

"You know it does," I said and stepped nearer than was proper, then brought my mouth to her ear. "As I once said, every man in the ballroom will be yours for the taking."

Her breath caught at my compliment, but she set a hand on my chest and stepped back. "Not *every* man, my lord."

I winced at her use of my title. "Please don't call me that."

"We have had this conversation before," she said. "This time, I must insist on propriety."

My resolve to stay away from her was slipping. How could I endure the duties of an earldom without her? Hannah made me see reason and rise to my duties. With her, I would be a better earl. "Dance with me tonight."

"You know we cannot."

"I have been in agony these last days," I whispered. "*Please*. Dance the first set with me."

"Damon, I—"

"She has already promised that set to me," Ollie said, descending the stairs. "Perhaps if Lady Margaret is in attendance, you might ask her instead."

I glared at Ollie, and he held my gaze. Our silent standoff didn't cease until Mother and Father entered the entry hall.

Father took in Hannah's dress and frowned, but Mother more than made up for his negativity with praise.

The carriage ride to the dance was torture but not nearly as bad as watching Hannah dance with other men. Unable to bear it, I disappeared to the card room but not to play, only to hide. I'd promised myself that I would not become Father, and no matter how I might feel in this moment or how tempted I was by its false salvation, I would not gamble ever again.

I stood there for several sets, and then they announced the set that I would make *ours*: a quadrille and then a waltz. I quit the card room to find Hannah and claim my set.

I found her standing with my friends by the far wall. As I grew nearer, I heard Ollie say to Hannah, "Might I convince you to stand up with me for another set?"

"Actually, little brother, this set belongs to me," I said. "Perhaps you might convince Miss Atherton to stand up with you."

Ollie looked irate, but thankfully, he was gentlemanly enough to oblige and Miss Atherton ladylike enough to accept.

Hannah hesitantly allowed me to lead her to the dance floor. "You should not have asked me to dance," she whispered.

"One set is not a sin, Miss Kent."

"Then, why does it feel like it?" she asked as I led her to the dance floor.

We danced the quadrille without issue, but then it came time for the waltz.

I circled one arm around her waist, and together, we raised our arms above our heads to form an arch. I stared deeply into her eyes, wishing we were dancing alone at Summerhaven, wishing I could tell her how I felt, wishing I could kiss her.

"I can't—I can't do this," she said, dropping her hold. "Excuse me." She pushed through the crush, and I followed her to the balcony and then down the garden path to a private gazebo.

She stood in the center with her back to me.

"Please don't hide from me." I touched her elbow, turning her to face me.

When I saw her tearstained face, I pinched off my gloves and brushed my fingers across her cheeks to dry them.

Hannah leaned into my touch.

"Hannah," I whispered. "I'm sorry. I'm *so* sorry."

"Me too." She lifted her hand to my chest.

Too soon, she tried to drop her hand, but I held it in place. "Stay with me. Please. Just one more moment."

"We shouldn't. You have an obligation to your family, to Summerhaven."

"I know," I said. "But I don't think I can carry this burden without you."

"You can. You *must*."

I hung my head. "I am in love with you, Hannah."

"And I love you, Damon."

I froze. "You . . . *love* me?" I searched her face.

"More than I have ever loved anyone," she whispered.

I closed my eyes, knowing this would be the first and last time I would ever hear her speak these words to me and wanting to savor them. When I reopened my eyes, my gaze landed on Hannah's lips.

I lowered my mouth to hers, wanting to kiss her so badly it hurt, but paused a breath away, knowing I shouldn't.

But then Hannah raised onto the tips of her toes and pressed her lips to mine.

My resolve broke. I gathered her face in my hands and kissed her deeply. Hannah circled her arms around my neck, and her touch sent ripples of pleasure through my entire body.

I'd dreamed of kissing Hannah my whole life, but it was sweeter, softer, more *sensual* than I ever could have imagined.

I needed more.

I kissed her lips, her cheeks, her jaw, but still, it was not enough. I'd thought kissing her might make parting easier, a chance for us both to say goodbye, but I'd been a fool. Kissing Hannah had only unlocked an unquenchable thirst that could never be satisfied.

I deepened our kiss, stealing my name from her lips. "*Damon.*"

A plea.

Something inside me came undone.

I felt untethered, like I might float away from this feeling. I backed her up against a gazebo post, needing something solid to brace us against, and our kiss became desperate.

And then someone gasped. I instinctively shielded Hannah from view, but it was too late. Whoever was there had already seen us.

"Hannah?" Miss Atherton said.

"You need not worry, Miss Atherton." Ollie glared at me. "What you see is only a charade. One with which my brother has taken far too many liberties."

"It is not a charade," Hannah whispered. "Not anymore. Our feelings for each other are real."

She felt it too.

Miss Atherton seemed hurt, though I did not understand why, and she quickly excused herself.

Hannah watched her go, then turned back to Ollie.

"After all that he has done to tease and torture you," he said to her, "you must know that a daring dress and quick kiss will only entertain him for so long. How could you let yourself fall for his act?"

"It is *not* an act," I said sternly.

"Oh?" Ollie held my gaze in challenge. "Do you intend to marry her, then?"

More than anything, I wanted to say yes. I *wanted* to marry Hannah. I would give up everything I owned to be her husband, but so many people depended on me. "No."

Ollie's eyes lit with fire, and he lunged forward, grabbing me by the lapels and pushing me against the same post I had just braced Hannah against to kiss her. "You are a blackguard, Damon. A self-serving scoundrel and a cad. Just because you are a lord does not mean you can treat her like this. She is not beneath you."

"You're right," I said and pushed Ollie out of my way to stand in front of Hannah. "I should not have dishonored you. I'm truly sorry, Hannah."

"I know," she said.

"Your apology counts for naught if you refuse to do the honorable thing and marry her, brother." Ollie pushed past me, knocking my shoulder. "Come, Hannah. We must return if your reputation is to remain intact. I will tell Mother you have swooned and need to return home. I'll have the carriage brought around straightaway."

"No." I stepped forward, blocking her path. "I cannot endure this. We will find another way to save Summerhaven. *Together.*"

"You know there is no other way," Hannah said. "Please do not make this any harder than it already is. I will leave Summerhaven tomorrow morning at first light."

She moved to one side, and so did I, blocking her exit. There had to be another way. I could not let her go.

"Damon, if you care for me as much as I care for you, then you will let me go."

I cared for her more deeply than I could put into words. More deeply than I'd ever dreamed possible. And because I cared for her, I would do what she asked of me, no matter how much it might hurt.

So when she moved again to walk away, I let her pass.

But I would never let her go.

CHAPTER FOURTEEN

THE MORNING HANNAH LEFT SUMMERHAVEN, I watched from my bedchamber window. Perhaps I was a coward, but I could not bring myself to tell her goodbye.

The last time she left Summerhaven, I'd stolen a lock of her hair to remember her, but I didn't need a talisman now to remember the taste of her soft lips or the sweet scent of her hair. After what we'd shared, trinkets and talismans would never be enough. I needed Hannah in my life. And to have her, I needed to solve the situation Father had saddled me with.

I meant what I'd said to her last night in the gazebo. I would find another way to save Summerhaven so that we could be together. And so I'd spent a restless night devising and discarding plans that would set it all in motion.

As soon as Hannah disappeared down the drive, I searched for Father to present the plan I had finally devised in the early hours before dawn. I found him in the morning room, eating breakfast, and sat beside him on the settee.

"Miss Kent is gone," he said between bites and did not even have the decency to look at me as he said it.

"Not for long," I said.

Now he looked up. "She left for her home in London," Father clarified.

"I am aware."

Father's eyes narrowed. "I trust this means you've accepted your duty and will stop fawning after the chit. There are more important matters at hand."

"Yes, there are." I pinned Father with a stare and cleared my throat. "First, you will stop calling Hannah a chit. She will be part of our family someday, and I won't have her disrespected."

Father opened his mouth as if to object, but I held up a hand to silence him. "I'm not finished. Second, you will tell Mother about your health. She deserves to know the truth while there is still time to spend with you."

Father's eyes softened at the mention of Mother. I knew he loved her; perhaps the promise of time with her would make it easier to tell her the truth.

"Third, you have placed the burden of the earldom on my shoulders. I accept this responsibility. I will not rest until the estate is secure," I said, and he seemed relieved. "But in order for me to do so, you must relinquish every bit of your control over the estate to me."

"And how do you plan to secure the estate if you insist on marrying that *ch*—Miss Kent?"

I hadn't had time to think through the details, the first step was obvious to me, and I spoke with conviction. "I will sell every piece of furniture, every unentailed property, every candlestick and carpet and tapestry so that I might attempt to fix what you have bankrupt. I will do my duty, but I will not give up my heart's desire."

Father looked at me like I'd gone mad, shaking his head slowly from side to side. "Your sentimentality will bring the roof down around us all."

"Let it fall."

Mother stepped into the morning room. "I'm sad to see Hannah go," she said and wiped a tear from her cheek.

"Tell her," I said to Father.

His gaze hardened, but I would not allow him to bully me into silence. He held no power over me. I was not afraid of him anymore.

"Tell me what?" Mother said.

"Go ahead," I said and stood. "I will be here to pick up the pieces when you are done."

Mother watched me leave the room, and I closed the door behind me to give my parents privacy.

The days after Father disclosed his failing health to Mother were dark and depressing. Having unburdened himself, Father grew weaker by the day. He now spent most of his time in bed. And although she was distraught, Mother sat at his side, silent and strong. I did not know how she handled herself with such dignity.

I sold our possessions as quietly as possible, not wanting to add to Mother's woes and worries. The London house was the first to be sold, then my curricle, and finally the furniture. I even let go servants until all that remained was the barest number of staff.

But it was not enough.

"What if we sold a portion of Summerhaven?" I asked Mr. Bancroft during what was fast becoming our regular morning meeting. I'd decided to keep him on because he knew and loved Summerhaven, but the transition had not been easy on either of us. I demanded that business be done differently than Father, and Mr. Bancroft often disagreed.

"You cannot sell a portion. The property is entailed, my lord."

"Of course I know that." I was not addled. "I could petition Parliament to remove the entailment."

"You could," Mr. Bancroft agreed, "but I do not believe you will be successful."

I *did* try, but Mr. Bancroft was correct. I was *not* successful.

Still, I was determined.

I sold nearly everything not nailed down, until all that was left of value was Mother's carriage, which I would not deprive her of, and Ares. But deliverance from debt still felt forever far away.

I was sick with grief.

How had it come to this?

Standing in the stable, I ran my hand down Ares's neck. He was such a beautiful horse. He'd brought me so much happiness and peace these past months. I could not imagine my life without him, though I must, as he was scheduled to be auctioned off tomorrow at Tattersall's.

I hated myself for it. But I had no choice if I wanted to save Summerhaven and spend my life with Hannah.

So why, then, at that exact moment, did Hannah's voice sound in my mind? *There is always a choice,* she'd said as we'd said our last goodbye in the portrait gallery.

Ares nudged my shoulder, ready to run, and I swung myself up into the saddle, then led him out of the stableyard to take one last ride.

As we made our way across the property, I thought about riding these very same hills with Hannah and how wild and free we'd felt. It was the first time I'd felt her truly see me. She'd said I had a passion for horses, and she'd been right.

An idea came to my mind: what if I turned my passion into a way to provide? The Duke of Maybeck bred horses as a hobby, and he said it was quite lucrative. While an earl could not work, he could have hobbies. And if they were profitable, all the better for Summerhaven.

It was a mad idea, perhaps, but after going over the numbers, I was convinced that with a little help and a lot of time, it might work.

I decided not to auction Ares and wrote to the Duke of Maybeck instead, asking for his investment. His response, expressing his excitement and pledge to help, arrived only a day later. His investment was enough to build new stables and purchase horses to fill them. With luck, between the horse breeding and the improvements I was making to my tenants' agricultural education, Summerhaven would be saved.

Two weeks later, on the day we broke ground on the new stables, I sequestered myself in my study and wrote to Hannah.

My dearest love,

It has been four weeks since you left Summerhaven and four weeks that I have been in agony. You told me that if I cared for you at all, that I must let you go, but my heart demands otherwise. First, you must understand one thing. I am in love with you, Hannah. I will not marry Lady Margaret nor any other young woman who is not you. Every beat of my heart, every breath of my lungs—they are yours. I am yours, however unworthy.

From the day you bettered me at skipping stones across the river as a girl to the night you ate frog legs at Lord Rumford's table, my admiration for you exceeds all others. You see the world not as it is but as it should be, and you work fearlessly toward that end. You make me want to work fearlessly toward that end. And your brave example, your encouragement to serve my tenants openly, gave me the courage to be the man I always wished to be, regardless of my title.

My whole life, I have been loved not for who I am but for what I am and what I will one day possess. To my great shame, even I am guilty of reducing my identity and worth to my title and possessions. Would God give me the opportunity, I would go back to that day in the portrait gallery when I told you about Father's failing health and my responsibility to Summerhaven, and I would beg you to be mine, no matter the sacrifice.

But seeing as I cannot, I have worked in your absence to do all I can to secure Summerhaven's future and win you back. I have sold almost every rug, candlestick, and piece of furniture. My curricle is also gone, as is my pocket watch. I daresay the only thing that remains of any value are my ancestors' portraits that hang on the walls.

I have limited the number of staff to only the most essential. I have written family, friends, and foes, begging for their assistance.

But it was not enough to pay Father's debts.

I petitioned the government and pled to have the entail on the estate removed so that I might sell a portion of the land to secure the remainder's future. My request was denied.

You have never known a man more desperate.

And then one day, as I was riding Ares one last time before he was to be auctioned at Tattersall's, an idea came to me. It was something you said actually. About me having a passion for horses. Not two weeks earlier, I'd met the Duke of Maybeck in London. Father had arranged the visit in hopes that I might marry his daughter Lady Margaret, but it was her father I spent the majority of my time with, discussing his habit of breeding horses. It was a pastime for him, of course, as he is more wealthy than the Prince Regent himself, but also a lucrative one. One that I might undertake in an effort to save Summerhaven.

I raced back to the manor and wrote to the duke, explaining the dire situation and my plan. By the grace of God, he took mercy on me and supplied a loan. Work has already begun on the new stables, and horses are being acquired even as I write. For the first time in weeks, I have hope. I do not know what will become of my efforts, but it is my most fervent prayer that my endeavor will succeed.

As a betting man, I know the odds of this venture are not favorable. But I will never give up trying to do what I can for Summerhaven, for my family, for you.

You may think me a coward for confessing my feelings in a letter, and perhaps I am, but I cannot endure another day without you, my love.

Ever Yours,
x Damon Jennings

I sealed the letter and set it on the salver tray for Caldwell to send. Hopefully, Hannah's response would be as swift as the Duke of Maybeck's; I did not wish to live another day without her.

CHAPTER FIFTEEN

I SAT SILENTLY IN THE carriage across from Ollie the entire drive from his set of rented rooms in London to Captain Bromley's estate in the country. The invitation to attend his house party had arrived shortly after Hannah had left Summerhaven, and initially, I'd had no inclination to attend. However, the need to converse with the Duke of Maybeck regarding our joint venture and Ollie's eagerness to accompany me compelled me to go. Ollie had left Summerhaven a month ago, and we hadn't spoken since then. I'd hoped the forced proximity of our two-day journey would provide us ample opportunity to begin bridging the divide between us.

But despite my earnest attempts to engage him in conversation, Ollie remained resolute, and we shared the confinement of the carriage, enveloped in an oppressive silence. Ever since that fateful night in the gazebo, where he'd discovered Hannah and me in an intimate embrace, Ollie had not uttered a single word to me. I understood his decision to maintain his distance—he thought me a self-serving scoundrel and a cad—but I missed my brother, and now more than ever, I wanted us to be reconciled.

With nothing to do but twiddle my thumbs and nurse my aching heart, I inevitably turned my thoughts to Hannah. It had been a month since I'd penned my missive, outlining my plan to rescue Summerhaven and declaring my suit. But she'd not written me back. Her message was clear: she was not interested in a future with me. How could I blame her? Still, I felt like half a man without her. If I was ever given another opportunity, I would not hesitate to ask her to be mine.

When we finally arrived at Captain Bromley's, Ollie alighted first, and I followed. We wordlessly made our way across the great lawn to our host. He was greeting a group of guests, though I could not see who, as their backs were to me.

"Lord Jennings, Mr. Jennings," Captain Bromley greeted Ollie and me as we approached. "Welcome!"

"Captain Bromley," we returned, offering polite bows.

"Your timing is impeccable, gentlemen. We were just discussing the merits of old friends. I believe you both know Mr. Kent and his sister, Miss Kent." Captain Bromley indicated to the group of guests he had been greeting—Hannah and her brother, Henry—and my heart jumped into my throat.

"Hannah?" I blinked, barely believing my eyes. Hannah was here? *My* Hannah.

Only she was not *my* Hannah. She was Miss Kent.

I cleared my throat, struggling to regain composure. "We are not friends, Captain Bromley. That is to say, you were correct in your original assertion; Miss Kent and my brother hold the association, not I." And then addressing Hannah, I said, "Forgive me for speaking so informally, Miss Kent. It will not happen again."

Hannah nodded, and I was crushed. She truly wanted this separation. I'd held out hope that perhaps something had happened to my letter or even her return response, but no.

A woman cleared her throat, drawing attention to herself.

"Forgive me, Mrs. Kent," Captain Bromley said. "Please allow me to introduce to you Lord Jennings, the future Earl of Winfield, and Mr. Oliver Jennings, the current Earl of Winfield's second son."

Mrs. Kent—Henry's wife and Hannah's sister-in-law—curtsied to us, and I noticed how her gaze lingered on Ollie and then how she smiled meaningfully at Hannah. What did it mean? Had Hannah talked about Ollie to her? Had something developed between them in her absence? Perhaps he'd written to her, or she'd written to him, and they'd rekindled their former relationship.

I couldn't do this. I could not stand so near Hannah. I would go mad trying to make meaning of Hannah's every word and action. "A pleasure, Mr. and Mrs. Kent. If you will please excuse me, I see someone I must greet." I strode away from the circle, looking for Fred but finding the Duke of Maybeck and Lady Margaret.

Lady Margaret smiled and moved to make room for me beside her, and I was relieved to have someone to stand with.

"Lord Jennings," the Duke of Maybeck greeted. "How is work on the stable-yard coming along?"

"Splendid," I said. "I could not be more pleased with the progress made."

"I'm happy to hear it. I look forward to seeing it soon," the duke said.

Baron Whitmore and his new bride joined our company and pulled the duke into conversation.

Lady Margaret leaned close and said, "Rumor has it that we are only a breath away from announcing our engagement, Lord Jennings."

"Truly?" I asked, and she nodded. I supposed it should not surprise me that people were gossiping. I was rarely seen with young ladies in public, but this was the second time I would be seen with Lady Margaret. What would Hannah think?

Lady Margaret was quiet for a long moment. "Last we talked, Lord Jennings, I believed you were about to declare your suit to Miss Kent."

"I was. I *did*."

Her head tilted to one side in confusion. "Have your intentions changed?"

"They have not." Heavens, I would prostrate myself in front of Hannah this very moment if I thought it would change her mind about marrying me.

"Why, then, is she walking with your brother?" I followed Lady Margaret's gaze to Hannah, who was walking with Ollie toward the rose garden. My heart squeezed with envy. "Did she reject you?"

"In a manner of speaking," I said. "Although to actually reject someone, I believe a response is required."

Lady Margaret winced. "I'm so sorry, Lord Jennings. You deserve so much more. So . . . she didn't love you, then, only your fortune?"

"On the contrary." I shook my head. "I believe Hannah stepped aside so I might marry another and save Summerhaven."

Lady Margaret's mouth crowded to one side in thought. "Self-sacrifice is noble, I suppose, but I struggle to make sense of hers."

As did I.

"And now she has formed a *tendre* with your brother?" she asked.

A *tendre*? I followed her gaze to the rose garden and saw Ollie kiss Hannah's hand. I sucked in a quick breath, the sight as sharp as a farrier's hoof knife straight to my soul. "So it seems," I said, averting my gaze so that should he kiss her cheek, I would not have to witness it.

When had this developed? After Hannah's leaving Summerhaven, perhaps Ollie had visited her in London. Had Ollie known Hannah would be here? Was that why he'd agreed so readily to come with me? To see her? Did they have an understanding?

I felt sick, as though my stomach were seconds away from spasming and sullying my boots.

"I am sorry, Lord Jennings," Lady Margaret said, setting her hand on my arm and steadying me. "Truly. If it would help your cause with her, I would not be opposed to entering into a charade with you to turn her eye."

"That is kind of you, Lady Margaret, but I won't be entangling myself in any more charades."

She nodded and tactfully turned the conversation to a new subject. "I am also sorry to hear about your father's failing health."

"Thank you. I am still having trouble accepting it, but every day, he slips away a little more."

She offered me a sympathetic smile.

Not long later, Captain Bromley led everyone inside, and we were shown to our bedchambers. I was relieved to learn Ollie and I would be staying in a different wing from the Kents—the potential for having to pass Hannah in the corridor would have been too painful.

The next day, we were to ride to the ruins on horseback, and I could not wait. I wished I'd brought Ares, but I was glad he would be there for me when I returned home.

While waiting in the stableyard for the rest of the company, the Duke of Maybeck turned to me. "Have you given any thought to what types of horses you wish to breed at Summerhaven?"

"I have given it a great deal of thought," I admitted. "I have even purchased a few horses already, but as my principal investor, I want your input before acquiring any more."

"I'm sure my opinion is unnecessary, but I am happy to provide it: of course you must breed Thoroughbreds; they will lend credibility to your stable. And what about breeding that fine Friesian you won at Royal Ascot? What was his name?"

"Ares." I smiled.

"That's right. Have you considered breeding him?"

"I have actually. The breed is still quite rare in England, and I daresay it would get the *ton* talking and fetch us a nice profit."

"I agree. I think you should make Friesians your focus."

"It is decided, then."

Lady Margaret nudged my side, and I wondered if we'd bored her to tears, but she nodded to Hannah, who was walking toward the stables. Hannah's half-boots sank into the soft soil with every step. I wished I could offer her my arm to help her. Instead, Ollie trotted over to her.

"Miss Kent," I heard him say. "I was beginning to worry that you had abandoned me."

"Forgive my lateness," she said. "As much as I would like to say that I have never been tardy before, I must confess to having been told that Napoleon could have prepared an entire regiment for war in the amount of time it takes me to get ready."

My gaze met Hannah's. *I'd* told her that the morning of our ride together. But why was she repeating it now? Was she trying to tell me something, or had the words just slipped out?

"Miss Kent," Ollie said, reclaiming her attention. "I do not believe any of your party has had the pleasure of meeting Lady Margaret. Allow me to make your introduction."

Ollie led Hannah and her brother and sister-in-law to where I stood with Lady Margaret and made the introduction.

"It is a pleasure to finally meet you, Miss Kent," Lady Margaret said.

Hannah returned the sentiment and took Lady Margaret's measure. What did she see, I wondered. What was she thinking and feeling?

Lady Margaret continued. "I have heard so many wonderful things about you that I was beginning to wonder whether you were fact or fiction."

Hannah gave Ollie a reproving look. "Mr. Jennings has a habit of embellishing things, I'm afraid."

"*Mr.* Jennings?" Lady Margaret's brow furrowed. "Don't you mean—"

"Lady Margaret," I cut in, "it looks as though the horses will be ready soon. Might I assist you in choosing your mount?" I held out my arm to her.

She glanced at it, unimpressed. "You should like to help *me* choose a mount?" She raised an eyebrow in challenge. Besides her father, she was, without a doubt, the most experienced and accomplished rider in this company, and that included me.

"Please," I said, my voice low.

She glanced in Hannah's direction, then reluctantly took my arm and let me lead her away. We slowly walked down the length of the stable, peeking inside each pen. Unfortunately, there were few horses left inside to see, so we shortly returned to the group.

"And, Miss Kent," Captain Bromley was saying as we rejoined the group, "what of you?"

"I should like to ride a stallion," she said, doubling my confusion. Was she trying to tell me something? But what? And *why*, if she'd already declined me? Though I did not understand her meaning, I felt a spark of hope.

"You are a woman after my own heart, Miss Kent," Captain Bromley said. "There is no better way to explore the countryside than on the back of a Thoroughbred."

"Is it safe?" Mrs. Kent asked. "Hannah is a Londoner and not so accomplished on horseback."

"I believe Miss Kent is capable, madam," I said before I could think better of it. Coming to Hannah's rescue was so deeply drilled into the bedrock of my body that I was not sure it could ever be driven out.

Hannah glanced at me, and her expression was inscrutable. I quickly averted my gaze.

"I am glad you think so, Lord Jennings," Mrs. Kent said. "But as her chaperone, I am not so sure." Ultimately, Mrs. Kent allowed Hannah to ride a filly so long as Ollie acted as her guide.

He readily agreed, and after all the riders had mounted their selected horses, Captain Bromley led our party out of the stableyard. He pointed out the abbey ruins in the distance and allowed anyone who wanted to ride ahead.

Hannah urged her horse into a gallop, a clear message that she could not wait to get away from the party, from me. Ollie followed, and I was powerless to do anything but watch them go.

As we continued toward the ruins, Captain Bromley told the company about its history. I was sure his story was diverting, but I was distracted with looking for Hannah and Ollie.

I did not see them within the walls of the ruins and worried about where they were.

And then, in the distance, at the top of a nearby hill, I saw them.

They stood close together, Hannah's skirts billowing in the breeze. Ollie removed his hat and dropped to one knee before her.

The sight gutted me.

I wanted to kick my horse's flanks and gallop up the hill to rescue her like she was some damsel in distress. Only she was *not* in distress; she was decided.

I had no doubt she loved me, but she'd chosen Ollie.

I had to let her go.

During dinner, I kept my gaze down. I did not wish to see Ollie and Hannah's happiness, nor did I want them to witness my depression. I would do my best to reconcile myself to their marriage, but having to watch it would drive me mad—so I decided to leave the house party early.

The primary reason I'd accepted the invitation was to talk with the duke regarding our joint venture, and having done that, I no longer had any reason to stay. It was better I returned to Summerhaven to look after its affairs and sit by Father's side.

I whispered my decision to Lady Margaret over dessert, and although she wished I would stay, she understood and bid me goodbye.

After dinner, as soon as the women moved to the drawing room, I beckoned a footman and instructed him to have my carriage brought to the drive. I did not even go upstairs to have my valet pack my belongings. I just wanted to go.

It did not take long until I was safely seated inside the carriage and on my way home. I would send the carriage back for Ollie before he even noticed I was gone. I was sure he would be pleased not to have to navigate around me in our shared bedchamber anymore.

Closing my eyes, I rested my head against the back of the carriage cushion. Before arriving at Captain Bromley's, I'd held out hope that Hannah would see all I was doing to secure Summerhaven and eventually come to accept my suit. But now . . . what would life look like without her? I could not imagine it, nor did I wish to.

I tried to quiet my thoughts and let sleep claim me but to no avail.

We were not an hour into the journey when the carriage suddenly stopped. What had happened?

I opened the carriage door and leaned out. "Have we thrown a whe—" I started to say to the coachman but stopped when I saw her.

"Hannah." I blinked, barely believing that she was here. The flame of hope tried to reignite in my chest, but I tamped down the spark. I quickly stepped down and walked to where she sat on a horse. A *stallion*, I realized. But what did it mean? Was she hurt? Was Ollie hurt? "Is something wrong?" I searched her for injury. "Has something happened?"

"No, nothing. All is well. Help me down?"

A footman took the reins from her, and I helped her down. She quickly stooped to untie her skirts.

"If you are looking for Ollie—"

"No," she said. "Not Ollie."

She was engaged to him, though, and no matter how it hurt me, I would not begrudge them happiness.

But then Hannah pulled a paper out of her pelisse pocket—a letter, I realized—*my* letter.

"I did not receive your letter until this evening after dinner," she said, "and I did not think my response should be any more delayed."

Hannah had not received my letter until *today*? Why had it been delayed? Or perhaps a better question was, Why had it finally been delivered? If she had only just received and read it, that meant she had not known everything I'd done to save Summerhaven and to secure our future. She had not known how I felt for her.

But now she did, and she was standing before me. I tried—but failed fantastically—to make meaning of it. "What is it you want from me, Hannah?"

"Everything," she said, stepping close. "I want your ginger candies and to race you on horseback. I want to skip rocks with you across the river and best you at chess. I want to worry you will make me eat frog legs, and I want to dance every quadrille and waltz with you at every ball." Her chin quivered, and her voice caught when she said, "I want *you*, Damon."

The flame of hope tried to reignite in my chest, but I contained the spark, afraid. "You have no idea how much I wish I could believe you. To the limits of reason, I assure you. But you have been at Ollie's side constantly—walking in the garden, sitting next to him at dinner, riding alone with him to the ruins." I dragged both hands through my hair, then gripped the back of my neck. "At every turn, I have had to watch you love him. And I cannot do it anymore." I looked at the ground, feeling utterly defeated.

"I do love him," she admitted. "But *only* as a friend, which is why I have refused him."

"But today at the ruins. I thought . . . You refused him?"

Hannah nodded, and my mind hurried to hope. But I had to be sure. "Do you regret it?" I asked.

"No."

I stepped tentatively closer. "Are you sure?"

She laughed a little. "Are you trying to talk me into it?"

"No! But a man can never be too certain of a lady's mind."

"As you have told me before," she said, "with Ollie, I mistook friendship for love. But because of you, I now know the true meaning. I love *you*, Damon."

Her profession of love fueled the flickering flame in my chest, and it became a blazing inferno. "And I love you, Hannah."

I pulled her into my embrace, and she pressed her cheek to my chest. I was sure she could hear my racing heart. Heavens, it was beating so hard she probably felt it.

Hannah looked up at me, her beautiful eyes sparkling in the moonlight. Her hair had escaped its coiffure, and I brushed it back to cradle her face. I caressed her velvety-soft cheeks with my thumbs, and she shivered with pleasure.

Clutching the lapels of my coat, she rose onto her tiptoes, bringing our mouths so close I could feel her warm breath on my lips. But I didn't close the space between us. Not yet. She needed to know exactly what she was choosing first.

"Hannah," I whispered. "As I wrote in my letter, I do not know what will become of Summerhaven. Of me. But I promised myself that if I was ever given another opportunity, I would not hesitate to ask you to be mine. You once said you could be happy being a poor man's wife. Is that still true?"

She was quiet for a long moment, and I was glad she took time to consider her choice. I wanted her to be sure of her decision, whatever it may be. "As long as that man is *you*, Damon Jennings, nothing could make me happier."

"Then, marry me, Hannah. Promise me that I will not have to endure another day without you by my side."

"Yes, I promise. For richer or poorer, I am yours."

Hannah's words momentarily stunned me. I had loved her my whole life, had hungered to hear her speak those words, to hold her, to kiss her, to call her mine. For so long, I'd waited. And now, finally, I held her in my arms.

I drew her closer—one hand gripping her waist, the other threading through her hair—and lowered my mouth to hers. Unlike our feverish first kiss, I took my time, wanting to convey the depth of my feelings for her. I kissed her slowly, savoring the silky smoothness of her lips. I kissed her deeply, indulging in her intoxicating taste.

Hannah's hands glided up my chest and wrapped around my shoulders. Her cool fingertips traced the neckline of my cravat, and somehow, I managed to maintain composure. But then she tunneled her fingers through my hair, tugged, and I came undone.

Desire flowed through my veins like an untamable wildfire.

She must have felt the same because she matched me motion for motion, losing herself in the moment, in our kiss, in *me*.

A low noise escaped my throat, and I didn't try to hide it. I wanted her to know how fervently I loved her and how fully I belonged to her. But no matter how passionately I tried, I couldn't hold her close enough, couldn't kiss her deeply enough. No, that would take me an entire lifetime.

Breathless, I ended our kiss and rested my forehead against hers. She sighed contently, and as the sweet sound settled in my soul, I whispered the words I had wanted to tell her since I was a boy, "And I am yours, Hannah. I have *always* been yours."

EPILOGUE

THREE WEEKS LATER, HANNAH AND I were married in the quaint parish church near Summerhaven. Dressed in an ivory gown, with ringlets framing her face, she'd never looked more beautiful. Tears filled my eyes as she walked down the aisle to me.

We exchanged our vows in a small ceremony, surrounded by loved ones. Mother and Father sat in the first row, and Ollie stood at my side as my best man. Mr. Kent solemnized mine and Hannah's union, and we sealed our marriage with a kiss.

I'd dreamed of marrying Hannah for as long as I could remember but had never believed I would be so blessed. Heaven knew I did not deserve her, but I would do anything to make her happy. She was my whole heart. My love. And from that day forward, my wife forevermore.

Yet even on that joyous day, Father's frailty could not be ignored. He was overwhelmed by weakness and retired to his bed immediately following the ceremony. For all his faults and failings, he was still my father, and one day, far too soon, I would miss him.

After the ceremony, we returned home to Summerhaven and enjoyed a delicious wedding breakfast. It was then that I noticed Ollie slip outside.

I followed after him, hoping to have a private moment to finally talk with him. He'd been silently supportive of my marriage to Hannah, and I was grateful, but I wanted more. I wanted my brother back.

Ollie was nearly down the front stairs when I stepped outside. "Ollie," I called after him. He stopped and spun to face me. "Where are you going?" I asked.

"Away," he said simply.

I frowned. "Weren't you going to say goodbye?"

He shrugged. "Honestly, I didn't think anyone would notice."

"Of course we would notice if you just disappeared." I laughed lightly.

"I really don't think so," he said, sounding sad. "Ask me how I found out about Father's failing health."

I wasn't sure what that had to do with anything, but . . . "How did you—"

"Your letter to Hannah," he said. "I found out that Father was dying and that Summerhaven was on the brink of ruin when I read your letter to Hannah. No one thought to tell me."

It took me a moment to take in his meaning. But when I did, I hung my head with guilt. I had *not* thought to tell Ollie. Not because I didn't love him but because everything that was not Summerhaven or Hannah *had* come second. To my shame, that had included Ollie. "Ollie, I—"

He held up his hand, cutting off my apology. "All I have *ever* wanted," he said, voice anguished, "is to be an equal member of this family. But I am not, and I never will be. I am a second thought. A spare."

"That's not true," I said. "You cannot know how sorry I am that you found out about Father's health and debt the way you did, but the oversight did not happen because you are unequal. You are *not* a spare, Ollie."

He held my gaze. "In your letter to Hannah, you wrote that to save Summerhaven, you begged help from family, friend, and foe. But you did not come to *me*. Why not?"

"Because . . . I am supposed to be your protector."

"I do not need you to be my protector," Ollie said. "First and forever, I need you to be my *brother*."

Hearing my own words spoken back to me hurt because I knew I had not acted toward him as a brother should. He'd confided in me his greatest fear: being forgotten, and I'd promised him it was not possible. And then I *had* forgotten him.

"I wish you would have confided in me," Ollie continued. "I could have helped you."

I shook my head. "Father's debt was too great. You could not have helped."

"I *could* have," Ollie insisted. "Winterset is not entailed. It could have been sold to decrease the debt."

"I would *never* steal your inheritance to save Summerhaven."

Ollie's disappointment was palpable. "You would not have had to. Summerhaven is—*was*—my home too."

"Summerhaven will *always* be your home too."

"It's not," he said. "Not anymore. Which is why I must go."

"Ollie—" I reached out to him, a desperate plea for forgiveness, but he stepped back, unreachable. I searched for the right words to bridge the divide between us, but they eluded me. Silence hung heavy between us, punctuated only by the distant sounds of celebration. "Is there anything I can say to get you to stay?" I asked, and Ollie shook his head. "You are decided, then?"

"I am."

"But where will you go? Back to London?"

"There is nothing for me in London anymore," he said.

I was relieved to hear he thought so. London had not brought out the best in Ollie, and he was better off without it. At least for a time. "You will go to Winterset, then?"

But again, Ollie shook his head. "I am not yet ready to take up my duties there. I need to discover who I am beyond the shadow of Summerhaven and the confines of London Society. I am going to tour the continent for a time."

"You are leaving England?" I said, surprised.

He nodded. "I board a boat for France tomorrow at first light."

It did not take long for the realization of his departure to sink in, nor the pang of loss that accompanied it. "When will you return? To Summerhaven, I mean."

"I'm not sure I will," he said quietly.

My heart sank, understanding the depth of his pain. "I wish you would."

"I think it might be better for everyone if I don't. I don't belong here, Damon. I never have."

"You *do* belong, Ollie. Of course you do. All I have wanted since your return is to have my brother back. I have tried to repair our relationship, but you keep pushing me away. I have given you distance only because that has been what you have required of me. But I've been trying for all these months to show you that you matter to me. I haven't been perfect, but it's difficult to navigate the arm's length relationship you've demanded. My greatest desire is for us to be reconciled. You are my brother, Ollie. We are family."

"Hannah is your family now."

Ollie turned and descended the remaining stairs to the hired hackney waiting in the drive. The footman let down the stair. Before climbing inside, Ollie looked back at me. "Goodbye, Damon," he said and stood there as though waiting for me to return the sentiment.

But I refused to tell him goodbye. I wanted no part in Ollie's leaving. I wanted him to stay and help me fight for Summerhaven, for our family.

After a long moment, Ollie ducked inside the carriage.

I stood there watching his carriage travel down the long drive, my heart
two. I'd been unable to bridge the gap that ran deep between us, and
might never be reconciled. I wanted to run after him. To talk with
try. But I could do nothing but watch his carriage disappear into the

n't know how long I stood there on the steps before Hannah joined
de.

d Ollie leave?" she asked, wrapping her arms around my waist.

s," I said, my voice rough with emotion.

here is he going?"

He is leaving England for a time," I said. "He's seeking his own path and
in the world."

"I wish he would have told me goodbye," she said, sounding hurt. "When
ll he return?"

"I don't know that he ever will," I confessed.

Hannah tightened her hold and was silent for a long moment. Finally, she
said, "He will."

"I wish I had your faith," I said. "But his wounds run deep; I really don't
know that he will." The future felt uncertain and the path to reconciliation
treacherous.

Hannah cupped my face, drawing my gaze down to hers. "*I* know," she
said. "*Our* path was not easy, but here we are standing together as husband and
wife. Ollie may need to travel a different path for a time, but I believe he will
find his way home."

I felt so much love for Hannah in this moment, for her faith.

Despite the many doubts and regrets that weighed down my mind, I decided to rely on her faith and believe that somehow, someday we would find a
way to mend what we had broken.

"What did I ever do to deserve you?" I said to Hannah.

She smiled at me. "I daresay you orchestrated a charade and won me over
with your charm."

I laughed lightly. "However did I manage that?"

"I have no idea, seeing as I am quite stubborn. But I will be forever grateful
that you did."

"Me more," I murmured.

And as I gazed into Hannah's eyes, I found the strength to believe that our
love would serve as a beacon that would one day bring Ollie back home.

ACKNOWLEDGMENTS

As with any book, I have a multitude of people to thank for its existence. a single word of this story would have been written without the assistance the amazing people named below.

First, thank you to my readers and reviewers. I would not be able to publish my stories without you. Every review, email of encouragement, bookstagram, and post "like" or "share" has given me the confidence to continue writing. Thank you for making storytelling so much fun!

Next, I thank Ellisa Barr, who is, and will forever be, my first and last and everything-in-between reader. I could not write books without you. Thank you for seeing me through all the ups and downs of life and writing.

Also, thank you to my critique partners: Teri Christopherson, Natalee Cooper, Leah Garriott, Aubrey Hartman, Melanie Jacobson, Brittany Larsen, Lindsay Sanchez, Deb Stevens, Sabrina Watts, and Jen White. I am grateful to have such wise women on my team. Thank you for lending me your ears and your expertise.

Thank you to my beta readers: Karen Thornell, Anneka Walker, Chalon Linton, Joanna Barker, and Esther Hatch. This book is so much better because of your feedback!

Amber Pollei, Melissa Roth, and Jessica Wells, thank you for watching my littles so I could write this year—it would not have happened otherwise.

A huge thank-you to my first publishing team at Covenant, especially my editor, Ashley Gebert, who I was blessed to work with on the first edition of *Summerhaven*. Thank you for loving Damon and Hannah's story as much as I do and for making this book the best it can be!

And thank you to my second publishing team at Shadow Mountain for giving me the incredible opportunity to revisit *Summerhaven* and tell Damon's the story in this beautiful collector's edition. Heidi Taylor Gordon, ou for making this dream of mine come true! Samantha Millburn, your n to detail and knowledge of the writing craft is incredible. Thank you ing my manuscript shine. Callie Hansen, thank you for directing the on of my book, and thank you, Heather Ward, for creating such a cover. Thank you also to Bre Anderl for your incredible typesetting y Parker, I owe so much of *Summerhaven*'s success to you! Thank you thing you have done to get both editions into readers' hands. Also, ou to Ashley Olson, Haley Haskins, Troy Butcher, Lehi Quiroz, Bri , and Mckenzie Bliss for helping me reach new readers.

ould also be remiss if I did not thank my family. Mom, thank you for g the part of my counselor once again and for introducing me to dark dimly lit movies. Kiddos, thank you for being patient with me every time aid, "I'm almost done," on repeat. And, Kevin, thank you for giving me my ery own happily ever after. Without you, I wouldn't know a thing about love.

And most important of all, I must express my gratitude to my Father in Heaven. Thank you for giving me stories to tell and people to share them with, and for sending me Revelation 21:5 when I needed it the most.

ABOUT THE AUTHOR

TIFFANY ODEKIRK believes cooking s̶ take less than thirty minutes, frosting is be̶ than ice cream, and all books should end w̶ happily ever after. After earning her bachelor degree, she worked in the nonprofit sector to help homeless women and children. Tiffany is the author of four romance novels and has received a five-star Reader's Favorite medallion and a Benjamin Franklin Gold Medal Award (IBPA) for her regency romance *Summerhaven*.

These days, you can find her reading or writing a book in her Southern California home, where she lives with her handsome husband and four adorable children. You can also find her on Facebook, Instagram, and Bookbub @AuthorTiffanyOdekirk.